THE WORST KIND

DEAR CELESTE

J.R. ERICKSON

Copyright @ 2024 J.R. Erickson
All rights reserved.
This is a work of fiction. Names, characters, places and incidents are the product's of the author's imagination or are used fictitiously. Any resemblance to actual persons, living or dead, businesses, companies, events, or locales is entirely coincidental.

For Willow Renee Mulder.

PROLOGUE

Dear Celeste,

A year ago, I stumbled upon a letter you wrote in response to a plea from Orphan Alex, who sought help in locating his birth family. Today, I reach out to you with a similar request, except, unlike Alex, I possess no birth certificate, no orphanage records, nor adoptive parents who could offer guidance.

I once believed I could live my whole life without roots—without familiar soil—but recently, an old ache, long suppressed, has stirred within me, a rumble deep in the earth of my being. There's something inside of me that niggles, an unscratchable itch that jolts me awake in the dead of night. Sometimes I imagine it like phantom limb pain, a sensation of loss for a part of oneself that no longer exists. Yet, unlike amputees who keep memories of their missing limbs, I lack even the faintest recollection of the piece of me that is gone.

Let me tell you what I remember with the disclaimer that, as I'm sure you know, memories are fluid—subject to evolution with the passage of time and the changing of ourselves.

Ted, who introduced me as his daughter though I don't

remember calling him Dad, was a tall man with a scraggly black beard who wore faded jeans and big, gaudy belt buckles. Ted and I lived in an old apartment building, a friendly kind of place where the residents held Sunday potlucks in the open-air courtyard and shared bits of gossip in the stairwell. There were few intact families. It was mostly single mothers and grandparents raising grandchildren.

I was five when Ted dropped me at Dottie Smith's door to play with her grandchildren before he left for the last time. He'd left before, sometimes for a couple of days, but usually he told Dottie how long he'd be gone and he'd always returned. This time he never came back. After he left, Dottie's daughter, Lynn, decided to keep me—maybe even adopt me. Until I started to draw the pictures.

I've never seen them and, in my child's hand, I doubt they were extraordinary except for their subject matter. One memory that stands out to me, even after all these years, is overhearing Dottie and Lynn discussing the images in the kitchen. Dottie called them murder pictures.

After that, my life became a blur of foster homes. Ted never returned to claim me and the truth is I have no desire to claim him. It emerged during therapy that Ted had assaulted me. I'll spare you the details.

I have no doubt my dad, Ted, was a predator of the worst kind. It is my mother I yearn to identify.

Who is she? Did she willingly release me into the clutches of such a vile man? Or did he abduct me, leaving her, like me, to spend a lifetime in search of answers?

These questions first plagued me in adolescence but took on greater significance after the birth of my daughter, Hope. It is through motherhood I came to believe my mother might search for me still. I would scour the ends of the earth if my child disappeared.

In the past year, I've developed insomnia and panic attacks.

I check on my sleeping daughter half a dozen times each night. My marriage is buckling beneath the weight of my fear. My therapist has told me that trauma, even that which we don't remember, lives in the body. It will not go away until we release it. There is only one way to purge myself of this trauma. I have to know the truth.

It is time to go home, as they say, but first I need to know where that is. Home is not a place for me—it is my parentage. I want to know my mother's name. I must know the story of my beginning. I am sure it is the only chance my little family has of escaping the dark shadow that has descended over our lives.

Celeste, can you help me find my mother?

Sincerely yours,

River Adair

1

Celeste's hands grew clammy as she read. She wiped them on her flannel pajama pants. The letter caused a visceral reaction in her body, a stress response, and she pushed away from her computer and stood.

In the kitchen she poured a glass of Scotch and drank it fast, gasping when it blazed down her throat.

"Celeste."

She jumped. Jonathan stood in the doorway. He must have just arrived home from work. She'd not changed out of her pajamas all day. She'd gotten lost in the column—answering questions, doing research to answer questions, answering more.

"Oh, hi." Her hand shook as she brushed a clump of unwashed hair off her forehead. She needed to shower. The letter so disturbed her, she'd begun to fear-sweat—the kind that smelled animal-like, pungent.

"I told the group at work we'd have dinner tonight. You said this morning you were up for it."

Shit.

She'd forgotten all about the dinner—loathed the thought

of an evening with their colleagues from Dynamic Laboratories.

Still, their therapist, Joyce, had made it clear that Celeste needed to make space for their former life—compromise.

"Let me take a quick shower," she told him.

Jonathan glanced at his watch, pressed his lips together, and nodded. "The reservation is in forty-five minutes."

THE DRIVE TO LUCIA'S—THE Italian restaurant they'd been to dozens of times with co-workers from Dynamic Laboratories—was too quiet, the conversation forced. Celeste asked about his day. Jonathan launched into an explanation of a new anti-epileptic drug they were testing against mood disorders and, when Celeste didn't immediately start talking shop with him, grew irritated and stopped talking. They sat in awkward silence.

Celeste needed to try harder, but the letter from River had taken up residence in her brain. She might have written it herself as a younger woman. That emptiness—that deep throb of longing to know her mother—lived with her still despite many years of burying it. Except Celeste had been much more fortunate than River. She'd had a dad who'd raised her, and she'd had her brother, Adam. Their mother had left. Celeste hadn't been abused, but she had been abandoned and, like River, she'd fled from that pain a long time ago, but since her accident it had grown from a pulse to a drumbeat. Someday soon, she'd have to trace it all back. And if she answered River's letter and embarked on that twisted path of discovery, she feared her own past would demand its due.

Celeste wouldn't, couldn't respond, and that was okay. New emails came in daily. Dozens of people needed help.

As she confirmed the thought in her mind, a large dark

van splashed through a puddle, sending a wave of water into the murky air. For an instant the water cascaded over a shape, a woman with dark, haunted eyes glaring at her from the curb.

Celeste's mouth fell open. She was enraged on the woman's behalf for her having been soaked by the passing vehicle, but before the thought could reach completion, the woman was gone, the residual water running along the storm sewer toward the drain, puddles iridescent in the headlights. Celeste twisted in her seat, watched the empty space where the woman had been fade from view.

"Celeste? Are you even listening to me?"

Warmth flooded her face. Jonathan turned into the lot and parked the car.

"Sorry. Mind wandering," she admitted.

"I *said*, Kirk got passed up for that promotion and he's quite sour about it, so best if you avoid that topic."

"Sure. I can do that." She opened her door and climbed out, grabbing her cane.

"Why don't you leave the cane?" Jonathan suggested. "I can hold your arm."

Jonathan hated her Victorian cane topped with a brass raven. Weeks before he said it looked like a prop from *Game of Thrones*, which had bothered her more than she cared to admit. The cane had literally saved her and Joanna's lives when Randy Mills had tried to murder them both, but Jonathan preferred not to talk about 'the incident,' as he referred to it. He preferred not to talk about a lot of things—her accident, the person who'd tried to kill her, the strange abilities she'd come back with.

"I feel better with it," Celeste said, gripped the cane and hurried away.

The restaurant was warm and loud and so crowded, she and Jonathan had to weave between chairs and wait for groups near the bar to part before they could make their way to a large table at the back where five of their co-workers sat.

Two of them—Kirk and Dean—stood, offering Celeste half hugs and squeezing her shoulder.

"Celeste," Dean said. "We've missed you. Haven't we?"

The rest of the group nodded and Celeste's face flushed as she maneuvered into her seat, resting her cane against the wall.

"That's an interesting-looking cane," murmured Liz, a woman Celeste had largely disliked due to her tendency to undermine anyone who challenged her. "Good to see you haven't lost your sense of humor."

Celeste blinked at her, wanted to offer a sharp response, but the heat and the loudness of the restaurant, the buzz of her own body had rendered her mind mostly useless. She searched for the waiter, but saw only throngs of people.

"I'm going to use the bathroom," Celeste blurted, standing too quickly. Her left hip cried out, but she gritted her teeth and lurched away.

Her cane clicked loudly against the wood floor. The thrum of voices and clinking glasses likely drowned the sound for everyone else in the restaurant, but it boomed to her. She bypassed the alcove to the bathrooms and walked to the bar.

"Scotch," she said when the bartender leaned toward her. "A double, please."

Glass clutched tightly in her hand, wishing she'd made some excuse to avoid dinner, she started back through the crowded restaurant. The door opened and a blast of wind blew Celeste's hair off her face. For an instant the woman from the curb filled the doorway. As before, she stared directly at Celeste, her eyes dark with anger.

Celeste faltered, watching as the door swung closed and the woman dissolved. What remained of the entity rushed into the restaurant and through Celeste. Something akin to despair shook her and she nearly doubled over.

"Ma'am? Are you all right?" an older man perched on a barstool asked her, face a groove of worry lines.

"I'm fine. Thank you."

As Celeste hurried toward the table, she collided with Darlene. Her Scotch spilled over both of them. Darlene gripped Celeste's arm just as she lost her balance and fell backwards.

"Oh, gosh, Celeste. I'm sorry. Did I hurt you?" Darlene asked, righting Celeste before she landed on the table behind her.

"You saved me, but I've doused us both with my drink."

"Here, let me help you back to the table. I'll get some paper towels."

"I can manage. Really. Thank you," Celeste told her.

Despite Celeste's insistence, Darlene didn't release her arm until she was firmly back in her chair. Darlene had smelled the spilled Scotch on her clothes and seen the dark stain marring her white blouse. Jonathan stared at her, incredulous, then looked away without a word.

THE FIRST FIFTEEN minutes after her collision with Darlene was met with nervous laughter and awkward conversations. Eventually, the group of researchers, as they'd done so many times before, lapsed into talk about the latest drug they were testing.

"What do you think, Celeste?" Liz asked.

Celeste looked up, hadn't heard the question as she'd drifted back to thoughts of the letter from River. "Oh, umm... sorry. What did you say?"

"Do the benefits outweigh the risk? PX962 is having a major impact on pain and neurodegenerative disorders, but in some case studies, we've seen a pretty powerful sedative effect."

"Extremely minor," Dean cut in. "In some instances, ten to twenty seconds."

"And in others the sedation lasts for hours, even days," Liz argued.

"Huh. Umm…" Celeste scratched at her thigh beneath her slacks. They were wool, too warm for the weather and the hot restaurant, and they belonged to former Celeste who got dressed up business casual for dinners with friends from the lab. They didn't fit right and her hip itched and complained. "I honestly couldn't say without reviewing the results."

"You're really not coming back?" Kirk asked, mopping the last of his spaghetti with a slice of garlic bread.

Celeste shook her head. "I don't think so. No."

"It won't be the same without you," Dean added. "It hasn't been the same without you."

"What will you do instead?" Darlene asked softly. She'd barely taken a bite of her lasagna. The thick reddish slab made Celeste's stomach churn.

Celeste brushed a lock of hair behind her ear and shook her head. "I still don't know. We have savings, so…"

Jonathan pulled in a sharp breath and she looked at him.

"What?" Celeste asked.

"Nothing." He didn't look her in the eye, but busied himself placing his silverware on his mostly empty plate. The leftover marinara pooled in the center and for a moment the red sauce looked darker, congealed.

Celeste blinked and forced her eyes up to Jonathan. "It's not nothing. Are you concerned about me not going back to work because of money?" It was such an insane question to ask at a dinner surrounded by their colleagues that everyone fell immediately silent.

Never, in the years Celeste had worked at Dynamic Laboratories, had she or Jonathan aired their so-called dirty laundry in front of co-workers. Part of it was the environment. In a competitive workplace, it was best not to show weakness, but Celeste struggled to adhere to the former rules of appropriate social interaction. She wanted it all on the table.

"I can imagine it's been difficult adjusting after the accident," Liz broke in, reaching to pat Celeste's hand.

Celeste pulled her hand away. Color rose into Liz's face.

"It wasn't an accident. Didn't Jonathan tell you? The police believe it was attempted murder," Celeste told them.

The silence that had already fallen over the group somehow grew thicker. Celeste stared around at the once-familiar faces of her co-workers. She didn't know them anymore. Their eyes were wide. Some of them had grown so uncomfortable they stared at their plates or locked their gazes on some other place in the restaurant.

Finally, Jonathan spoke. "It's a theory," he said. "Obviously it's hard to confirm, but—"

"But another woman in the neighborhood witnessed everything. She told me herself someone swerved to hit me. I stepped out of the way and they swerved right at me."

"Jesus," Dean whispered.

"Why would someone do that?" Kirk asked. "You're not in some kind of dispute with a neighbor, are you? I watched one of those investigation shows a couple of years ago about a neighbor who killed half the family next door because they were fighting over the property lines or some nonsense."

"Of course not," Jonathan said, not bothering to hide his irritation at the suggestion.

"No," Celeste added. "At least not that I'm aware of, but who knows, right? People can get fixated on weird things and the focus of their rage might not even know they exist."

"Like a stalker situation?" Liz asked.

"Can we talk about something else, please?" Jonathan drained the last of his wine.

"We probably should get going," Darlene said, looking at

Liz. "We rode together and I hate to leave my dog for too long. He gets antsy."

"Me too," Dean agreed. "Not my dog, obviously." He released an uncomfortable laugh. "I'm beat and we all have an early morning. I mean... most of us do."

THE DRIVE HOME was somehow more miserable than the drive to the restaurant. Jonathan barely spoke. He gripped the wheel so tight his knuckles turned white.

As they came toward the intersection they'd turn on to go home, Celeste spotted something lying in the road—a baby. A truck barreled toward them from the opposite direction.

Celeste screamed, her eyes bulged, and she jammed both feet into the floorboards though she sat on the passenger side of the car.

Jonathan gasped, hit the brakes and they both shot forward, caught by their seat belts. As the car screeched to a stop in the middle of the busy intersection, the truck ran over the little form. Celeste stared at the doll, her heart hammering in her chest.

2

When they arrived home, Jonathan, additionally furious now about her reaction in the car, went to bed with little more than a goodnight. Celeste returned to her office and logged onto her computer.

She'd received an email from Harris about the upcoming near-death experiences conference along with a link to purchase tickets. Celeste bought a ticket and then sent him confirmation she'd be there.

More emails had come into the Dear Celeste column. They'd pushed River's message down the page. She spent two hours drafting responses to the latest messages and posting several of them on her Dear Celeste column website.

She sent a message to a man whose dog had died and who found himself unable to get out of bed in the morning. As Celeste typed, she saw a large gray wolfhound in her mind's eye. Dougie, she thought was his name. She assured the man Dougie had gone to his true home and for a moment she saw a vision of Dougie with a man wearing a pilot's uniform. She added that to her message, explaining she believed someone close to the writer had been a pilot and that person had welcomed Dougie into the afterlife.

Even as she dove into the letters of others, her mind constantly shifted back to River Adair. She opened the email and read it again and, like before, her hands grew wet and shaky.

She didn't have to respond at all. Emails fell through the cracks. Most people who wrote her didn't expect an answer, were shocked when they received one.

"I'm sorry, River," she murmured, beginning to type.

Dear River—

I am deeply sorry that I am unavailable to assist you at this time. I've added a few resources that might help you in locating your birth mother.

Sincerely,

Before she could type her name, the screen went black.

"No." She frowned and hit the power button. The computer didn't restart. "Please, no."

The laptop was not old. She'd had it for less than two years. Celeste checked the power cord. It was plugged in.

"Please start, please start..." she murmured, hitting the power again.

It powered on and she clicked back to her inbox.

The email she'd started to River was gone. She sighed and typed the message a second time.

Before she could hit send, the lights flickered and the power went out. Celeste opened the flashlight on her phone and left the room. The usual soft drone of electricity was gone. The power in the whole house had apparently shut off. As she made her way downstairs to the fuse box in the laundry room, the lights shuddered back to life. The soft hum of the refrigerator drifted from the kitchen.

Uneasy at the prospect of returning to her office, Celeste made her way into the living room and sat on the couch. Cash appeared and rubbed against her legs. She bent and picked up the cat, who cuddled into her lap.

Celeste turned on the TV and found a baking show. She wasn't a baker and had never been a fan of reality TV, but found something soothing about the baking competitions, where the stakes were low and the worst that could go wrong was a burned pan of cupcakes.

Pillows propped behind her, she leaned back and closed her eyes.

CELESTE STOOD *in a yard beneath the scorching sun. The grass scratched brittle against her bare legs as she walked forward toward the gathering of ravens. They stood nearly as high as her, their black eyes shining, the feathers as slick as oil. They surrounded something, something she desperately wanted to see, and she faltered, sensing they didn't want her to see it, were somehow shielding her from what lay before them. Still, her legs plunged forward, child's legs. She was a little girl and, as she walked, she dropped the small heart-shaped pillow she'd been clinging to the previous two nights in the grass.*

A voice boomed behind her.

"Celeste! Stop!"

And the ravens took flight. For an instant she saw only their wings as she hovered in the center of their vortex and then she was in her near-death experience, skyrocketing up and away from her broken body.

She drifted in black space and thousands of images flashed by— her own life, and then another life, a little girl asleep on a dirty sleeping bag in the corner of a barely furnished apartment. A broken doll lay on the floor. A tall man, faceless, mostly in shadow, stood in the corner of the room watching the girl sleep. He started towards her.

Celeste startled awake on the couch, her hands flinging out.

Cash jumped up and raced from the room. Her heart thumped in her chest, the remnants of the dream solid in her mind. It was as if she'd only just been there, back in that extraordinary place, and the other place, the opposite of paradise—a hell on earth for the little girl on the mattress. The man who'd been walking towards her had done terrible things, intended to do more.

And though it seemed impossible, Celeste knew the little girl was River Adair. Somehow Celeste had glimpsed the girl's past, a snapshot of a moment in time when River had been a vulnerable, terrified child and the worst things imaginable had been done to her by a person meant to protect her.

Celeste rubbed her eyes, willed her breath to slow, her heart to steady.

"Okay," she said to no one at all. "I'll help her."

Cash reappeared in the doorway, his eyes accusatory.

"Sorry, Cash," she told him, leaning over and wiggling her fingers. "Did I spook you?"

The cat returned and jumped onto the couch beside her, opting not to return to her lap. Celeste stroked his neck.

The baking show no longer played on the television. Somehow the streaming channel had switched to a horror movie she remembered seeing as a child. The movie, *Dolls*, depicted a young girl stranded with her parents at the home of a dollmaker. Celeste and Adam had been subjected to the movie by a babysitter and both had been plagued with nightmares for weeks after. As Celeste watched, the little girl came upon a blood-soaked young woman seconds before she was dragged away by murderous dolls.

Celeste grabbed the remote and turned off the TV, ending the woman's screams.

CELESTE OPENED her email and drafted a letter to River offering to help her, with the caveat, as she'd given Joanna, that she had no technical training in identifying birth families, had never before done it and, though she was soon taking a genetic genealogy class, was still largely in the dark about the process.

If you're up for it, I'll come to Wisconsin and we can talk through some things in person, she wrote.

Celeste wanted to meet the girl from her dream.

3

River read the email from Dear Celeste and chewed the edge of her thumb. Not only had the woman offered to help, she was coming to Wisconsin.

Light-headed, a tumult of joy and grief warring in her body, River left the library and hurried to her truck, desperate to be alone. As she drove, tears slid down her cheeks and soon morphed into huge racking sobs. When the tears became too thick to see the road, she pulled into the ditch and wailed.

Garth Brooks' *Thunder Rolls* played low on the radio. Beyond the confines of the cab, the midday sun baked the field beside her. Sunflowers this year as it had been corn the last.. Breath robbed by her weeping, River focused her attention on the dull stones in the dry soil and dandelions forcing their way through the cracked edges of the road. River cranked the song loud and sang along, channeled her despair, more screaming than singing.

Kenny Bishop, who owned the farm she'd parked beside, passed in his red pickup, slowed and rolled down his window.

River swiped a hand across her face, a futile attempt to hide the tears, lowered the music, and cranked down the window.

"You all right, River? Saw you through the back window and thought you were having a seizure."

She forced a smile. "I'm fine, Kenny. Thanks for checking. Got the sunflowers planted?"

He stared at her, forehead creased, but didn't push. "Yes, ma'am. We spent all last week in the field because we knew rain was comin'. You and Owen got all your crops in? Sandy says your cucumbers last year were the best she's ever had."

River smiled, bobbed her head in thanks. "You tell her we'll bring some by."

"Owen was braggin' on you the other day at the feed shop, sayin' you're heading on some big tour. We hate to see anyone else discover our songbird."

River smiled. "Don't worry, it's not taking me too far."

"Is Owen goin' too? Playing the banjo?"

"He'll miss this one. We can't both leave the property for that long. Too much tending to do, and we like to keep Hope at home where she has her routine."

"You bring Hope over next week, huh? We got five little lambs born last week. She'll be tickled pink."

"I'll do that. Thanks, Kenny."

Kenny tipped his baseball cap and went down the road.

River tilted the mirror down and grimaced at her puffy, blotched face. She hated to imagine what Kenny had been thinking when he'd caught sight of her.

In her rearview mirror, she spotted a dark truck. It was pointed toward her, but didn't seem to be moving, as if whoever sat inside had pulled off the road as River had. She stared at it and thought of the truck she'd noticed the night before, dark and big, obscured behind its headlights, brights on as if to blind her. It had most likely been a careless driver who'd forgotten to switch to his low beams, but the truck had followed her out of town for several miles and, in her paranoia, she'd taken weird turns, intent on not leading him back to her house.

Eventually he'd gone a different direction and she'd continued home, shaken.

As River pulled back onto the road, she thought of the email she'd received from Dear Celeste. It had taken months to will herself to write the letter, to ask for help in finding her mother. River had been singing from that dark place for years, but she'd never imagined walking into the shadowy world, shovel in hand, ready to dig up her past. For the longest time, she'd told herself it didn't matter. It didn't matter she'd been abused and abandoned, that she had no birth date, no name, no history. She'd reinvented herself—life had begun when she'd been adopted by Clay and Cordelia.

But it did matter. Even as she told the lie to herself year after year, another voice disagreed with her, whispered there'd come a time when she'd have to know.

4

"You're going to Wisconsin?" Jonathan stared at Celeste across the kitchen table, incredulous.

"Yes." Celeste nearly laid out her reasons, but could already tell from Jonathan's expression her reasons would be met with little more than annoyance.

"To meet someone who wrote to you?" He stood and paced away, shook his head. "You're playing with fire here, but you know that, don't you? Some part of you is intentionally dousing yourself in gasoline."

She studied him—stiff shoulders, clenched teeth, his whole body as rigid as a bear trap, steel jaws set, the spring waiting for something to trip it. "I'll be back in time to meet with Joyce."

"Maybe I should call Joyce right now and see if we can squeeze in an emergency session."

"I hardly think my traveling for a day or two constitutes an emergency."

"That might be true if you weren't running off to meet some stranger who might hack you to bits and throw you in a river."

Celeste bit back the gurgle of laughter that welled in her belly. "I'm helping a woman find her birth mother, Jonathan."

He spun to face her. He'd heard the laughter in her voice and was clearly incensed. "How do you know that? You're liable to show up there and discover it was all a ruse to lure you to some middle-of-nowhere town in Wisconsin."

Celeste had never known Jonathan to be a paranoid person, but as he stood glaring at her, she understood that beneath his anger was fear. She stood and walked to him, wrapped her arms awkwardly around his unyielding body, rested her head against his arm. "I'll be careful. I promise."

He uncrossed his arms and pulled her closer, his body trembling. "If you're helping find her birth mother, why do you even need to go to Wisconsin?"

The truth was she didn't, not really, and yet she did. It was another of those strange new realities. There was more to River's story. Celeste felt the mystery rumbling somewhere far off, a bigger truth waiting to be exposed. "Because it helps me feel more connected to the person I'm working with."

"Working with? Is this a job now?" Jonathan couldn't hide his contempt. He was frustrated she hadn't yet found a proper job to replace her position at the lab. Daily, he mentioned they'd happily take her back if she wanted to return.

Celeste had savings. Since childhood, she'd been a frugal person. Though she and her brother Adam had rarely wanted for anything, Celeste always sensed some tenuous thread holding their lives together, as if they might wake up one morning and their dad would be gone and it would be on Celeste to pay their bills, buy their food. The misfortune had never come to pass, but by the time Celeste was eighteen, she'd saved over ten thousand dollars. Now she had nearly a hundred thousand in the bank, plus her 401k. She couldn't live forever on the money, but she could manage for a while. Despite having left work, she continued to add money to their joint account for bills. Before her accident, watching her savings account balance would have sent her into a panic. Now she felt largely indifferent. It was only money. She'd make more, she'd spend more. It came and went.

"It might be a job at some point. Who knows?"

He frowned. "Don't you need a license to charge people for advice?"

She laughed, but he pulled away from her, walked to the sink, and filled up a glass of water. "I'm not providing therapy. I could go sit in a chair at the end of the driveway right now with a sign. 'Five dollars for advice. Ask me questions.' I promise you it'd be perfectly legal."

He scowled as if the suggestion revolted him. "That'd be just great. I can already see what the primary discussion will be at the next homeowners' association meeting."

"I was using it as an example. Don't worry, I wouldn't dare offend the association with something as tacky as a card table at the end of the driveway."

"Good," he muttered. "They still haven't gotten over the Paulsons putting that hideous stone fountain in their yard."

Celeste lifted a hand to her face to hide her smile. Gerard Paulson had spent a pretty penny the previous summer on the enormous stone fountain complete with naked cherubs pouring water from pitchers. Half the neighborhood had taken up walking so they could pass by the house and gawk at the new water feature plunked in front of the Paulsons' house.

"Are you laughing?"

"No. Not about... I was thinking about the fountain. I'm sorry."

"I really do not think you should go."

"I'll be fine. I promise."

CELESTE HAD TAKEN a ferry boat years before from Muskegon to Wisconsin with a group of college friends to attend a Green Bay

Packers game. She'd never been a sports fan, but the enthusiasm of her college roommate, who had been born and raised in Green Bay and insisted her blood ran green and gold, had inspired the group to make the trip.

Now, as Celeste rode the ferry across Lake Michigan, she wondered what had become of those friends. For their initial two years at college, when they'd all been tossed into the deep end of higher education, they'd clung to each other, but little by little they'd diverged. Celeste had moved to Grand Rapids for graduate school and last she'd known, her roommate Lacy had gotten a teaching internship in Chicago.

As she thought of her old friend, an odd sensation tickled the base of her skull. Suddenly, a piercing pain lit from the back of her head into the center. She gripped the rail of the ferry as nausea rolled through her. The boat had not even moved, but she thought she might throw up. As the pain abated, an image of Lacy appeared in her mind's eye. She was lying on the hot sticky asphalt of a parking lot, people rushing to her aid.

"She's dead," Celeste murmured, squeezing the rail tighter as the boat pulled away from the dock and the deck beneath her heaved.

"What was that, dear?" an elderly woman who stood near Celeste asked.

Celeste shook her head. "Nothing. Sorry."

Clutching her cane, Celeste made her way to the interior of the ferry and sat down near a window. The nausea had mostly gone, but the shock of seeing her friend dead—of an aneurism, she thought—unnerved her.

No one had called her. When had it happened? Did any of her old friends even know or had they, like Celeste, moved on with their lives, closing the door on those once-fierce friendships? Perhaps it had only been her out of the loop. She hadn't stayed in touch, hadn't called to check in on her friends, but that didn't mean they'd not stayed connected.

She sighed and leaned her head against the window, imagining all the people who'd slipped in and out of her life.

AFTER THE FERRY DOCKED, it took just under two hours for Celeste to drive to Baraboo, Wisconsin.

As she drove down the country road toward the address River had given her, she slowed. A tiny deer, a spotted fawn, watched her from the high weeds on the roadside. Celeste searched beyond the baby deer for its mother, but saw no other deer nearby.

"Be careful, little fawn," she murmured.

She turned onto the dirt driveway marked by the hand-painted wood sign of a guitar with wings.

5

The driveway ended at a small stick-built house painted a pale yellow.

A young woman with wavy cocoa hair, a wriggling baby goat in her arms, waved and walked toward the truck. She wore jeans, a zip-up sweatshirt and rubber boots to her knees.

"Celeste?" the woman asked, her expression hopeful.

Celeste smiled. "You must be River."

She nodded. Celeste stared at her eyes, two different colors —one blue, the other brown. It was a startling feature. Celeste had never met anyone with eyes of two different colors.

"And this is Simon," River said, hoisting the goat a bit higher in her arms. "Garfunkel's in the pasture over there stuffing himself on grass."

Celeste patted the coarse fur on the goat's head.

River set him down. "He's a wanderer and has a tendency to run right in front of any car that pulls into the driveway. Go find your brother," she told the little goat, patting its backside. She straightened up and wiped her hands on her jeans.

"Thank you for answering my letter." River fixed Celeste

with cautious eyes. "Is it unusual for you to meet the people who write to you?"

"Yes. But sometimes it feels like the right thing to do."

"And it did with me?"

"It did," Celeste said, remembering the little girl from her dream.

River nodded, looked as if she'd like to ask more, but music began to drift from behind the house. "I'll introduce you to Owen and Hope and we can talk."

Celeste followed River to where a young man sat on the open tailgate of a blue pickup truck, strumming a guitar and crooning an interesting rendition of *Cats in the Cradle*.

A little girl, wobbly on pudgy legs, wearing a checkered dress that looked handmade, twirled on the grass. Two dogs flanked her, one howling with the music, the other jumping up and down.

"There's Owen and his barnyard band." River laughed.

Chickens pecked at the ground beneath the truck and a large rooster stalked about, occasionally adding his own wail to the music.

Celeste grinned. "He's putting on quite a show."

The man saw them and smiled. He stopped playing and hopped off the tailgate. The little girl followed and, upon seeing River, ran full speed toward her. River bent and lifted her up.

"Celeste?" the man asked, looking from Celeste to River.

"Yes. Hi." Celeste extended her hand. Owen took it and, rather than shake it, pulled her into a hug. He smelled of grass and cut wood.

"River practically rammed the truck right through the front door, she was so excited you responded to her email. What a pleasure to meet you. And to come all this way, that's really something."

Celeste smiled as he released her, face flushed. She wasn't

much of a hugger and was never entirely sure how to complete the maneuver without a bit of awkwardness, though Owen didn't seem to notice.

"This is Owen," River said, exasperated.

"Oh. Jeez." He smacked the side of his head. "Owen Adair. It's a pleasure, ma'am."

"Good to meet you, Owen."

"And this little spark plug is Hope."

Hope watched Celeste curiously.

"Hi, Hope. Nice to meet you."

Hope blurted something that sounded like 'hello' and pointed excitedly at the baby goat Celeste had seen earlier, who trotted toward them with his brother following. "Sime Garf!" Hope exclaimed.

"Yep. Simon and Garfunkel," Owen agreed. "The two naughtiest goats in Sauk County."

"I was going to take Celeste to the back porch to talk," River told him.

"Gotcha. Me and Hope will take the dogs out to the pasture and let 'em chase rabbits. Does that sound fun, Hope?"

Hope nodded and held out her arms for Owen.

Celeste followed River into the rustic house. The floors were wood. Exposed beams crisscrossed the ceiling. One wall had an array of instruments: guitars, banjos, and two drums on the floor beneath them. A wooden rocking chair sat nearby and a toddler-sized guitar. Plants lined the windowsills and a breeze through the open window rustled their leaves.

"I made sun tea this morning, or I can brew some coffee?" River offered.

"Tea sounds perfect. Thank you."

River poured them each a glass of iced tea and they walked to the back porch, covered by an aluminum shingle. Several rocking chairs looked out over the sprawling back property where a large garden was surrounded by chicken wire.

"Owen's dad builds these," River explained, touching the back of a rocking chair.

"They're beautiful. This whole place is beautiful."

River settled into a chair and stared out. "It is." She had a melancholy in her tone, and worry lines drew away from her mouth. "Where should we start?"

"Wherever feels relevant. Do you mind if I record our conversation?"

"Not at all."

"Great." Celeste took out her phone and turned on the voice recorder.

"I don't have any living memories of my mother. None that I can point to and say, 'Yes, that happened.' There are slices of memories. A scent, like talcum powder and lilacs. One memory that I want to trust, but sometimes I fear I picked up in a movie or saw someone else's mother doing it, is a woman singing me to sleep in a rocking chair. Every now and then I wake up with this song in my head, *She Talks to Angels*. Ever heard that one?"

"I'm not sure," Celeste admitted. "Is it a lullaby?"

"No, it's not. It's actually a song by the Black Crowes. Who knows, I probably heard it sometime and it got embedded as a memory or..." River shook her head. "In this memory, she's singing, my hands are tangled up in her long dark hair, and she has one foot on the window ledge, pushing us real slow in a rocking chair. Rain is pouring down the window pane. The trim around the window is painted with little clouds and rainbows. Is it real? Nothing feels real to me lately."

"That's a difficult space to be. And you said in your letter you're talking to a therapist, right? Because the truth is finding your birth family might not make those feelings go away."

"I am. I've been in therapy off and on for years."

"That's good. I started therapy myself this year—marriage counseling." Celeste wasn't sure why she shared the detail.

"Has it helped?" River asked.

Celeste chewed her bottom lip. "I don't know. It feels like a place where we can talk about things that are hard to talk about at home, so in that regard, yes. Let's discuss what you do know about your childhood. You said in your letter you were abandoned by your dad at an apartment building. Where was that?"

"In Madison. About an hour from here."

"Okay. And what do you recall from that time?"

River fiddled with the zipper on her sweatshirt. "Uh, let's see." She pulled her long hair over one shoulder and finger-brushed it. "Ted and I lived in a one-bedroom apartment on the first floor. I know it was the first floor because I'd crawl out the window sometimes when... when I heard him come home. I was five, or that's what he told people. There was no birth certificate found after he left."

"Why would you climb out the window? Do you remember?"

"No. I assume it was because he was molesting me, but I don't have any solid memories of that. I remember feeling"—River hunched forward and hugged herself—"afraid of him."

6

"In the daytime," River continued, "he was nice, big and loud and funny. He'd give me quarters and me and the other kids in the apartment building would run to the little grocery store that had a gumball machine. I spent a lot of time at Dottie's—our neighbor across the hall. Her apartment always smelled like tuna fish because she watched her grandkids every day and that's what they ate for lunch. Tuna fish on Ritz crackers with little pickles cut up in it."

River released a humorless laugh. "Weird what sticks with you, but that's one of the things. I played over there a lot and then one day Ted left and never came back. One of Dottie's daughters, Lynn, hadn't been able to have children, so she wanted to adopt me. She packed up my stuff—I didn't have much; a sleeping bag, a Barbie doll, a few pairs of clothes—and she took me to live with her and her husband. I'd already started drawing the pictures by then. That started at Dottie's, but then I guess..." River's cheeks grew pink. "I guess I started to touch Lynn's husband inappropriately and say weird things. Don't remember any of that, but it was in my file from the social worker. Anyway, Dottie took me back and called social services and that was that."

"Was there an investigation? Did the police try to find Ted?"

"As far as I know social services contacted the police, but I don't remember ever being interviewed by a detective or anything."

"And Ted never resurfaced?"

"I'm assuming he didn't. I was with Dottie and Lynn for about a month before they called the social worker. The landlord of the building had thrown all his stuff out. Apparently, he'd already been behind a few months in rent, so they re-rented his apartment and I never saw him again."

"Do you know if Dottie looked for mail? Paperwork? Anything that could identify him?"

"I think she did. I remember her and Lynn having a lot of hushed conversations and many of them seemed to point to not even being able to figure out his last name. He'd put a false social security number and name on the lease. That was in my social work file. They couldn't find him."

"After that you entered foster care?"

"Yes. I was in the system for about seven years. When I was thirteen, I was adopted by Clay and Cordelia, who live in a commune called Be Free. In some ways that was the beginning of my life, the beginning of River's life. Before that I was called Agnes, a name that never fit right, and when I moved to the commune, I told Cordelia that and she said I could change it, but I had to sit with it for a few days. There's a river at Be Free and that was my place to… just be. One morning I knew that should be my name—River. So we changed it, legally, and that's always felt right."

"That must have been quite the transition moving into a commune."

"You'd think so, but foster care is a lot like communal living, only far less kind and intentional. Be Free is named after the

Loggins and Messina song by the same name. Both Clay and Cordelia are musicians. Most everyone at the community is in some way or another. That was such a huge part of our life. Every night after dinner we played music and sang. I took to it immediately. The moment I picked up a guitar, I never wanted to put it down.

"I had the choice to do public school or commune school and I did commune school because public school was a nightmare for me. I never had friends. I went to five different schools and I was a foster kid so I never looked nice, never fit in. One of my fosters rarely had a functioning shower. My foster mom would pile all her clothes in the bathtub. I stank for months. Not to mention my eyes. Kids came up with a lot of creative, and pretty mean, things to say about those."

River rubbed her temples. "I was scared when Clay and Cordelia adopted me. I'd heard stories of kids ending up on farms, basically indentured servants. It was nothing like that. They adopted kids to give them a chance, to get them out of the system. I was the fourth, plus they had two biological children, Autumn and Henry. Six other families lived on the commune. It really is a kind of utopia. I didn't know places like it existed. Most people don't, I guess.

"That's not to say it was perfect. It's life, after all. Eventually Cordelia started to nudge me towards some of my own healing. She encouraged me to write songs as a way to get it out and then there was open mic night in town. I went and played guitar and sang, ended up meeting Arnie, one of my bandmates, who saw something in me that I sure didn't. He put together our band and we all just clicked. Then I met Owen about four years ago and I left Be Free and moved to Baraboo."

"Why Baraboo?"

"Owen's grandfather gave him this property and after he and I got married we moved here. Owen's family all live within a ten-minute drive, so that played a part in the decision. We visit Be Free pretty often, but life is busy." She gestured at several chickens picking along the perimeter of the garden.

"I bet. This must be a lot of work."

River shrugged. "Some days. Harvest time, spring planting, but nature does her thing. The buckets collect the rain, the animals graze the land. It's not as complicated as people think and it's good to have hands in the dirt, feet in the stream. That's what Clay always says, and he's right. During the times when I've not had that, I've felt... not okay."

"What do you think is causing you to search for your mother now?"

"I've always had an almost superstitious need not to look for her, not to examine my past. When I first moved to Be Free, Cordelia offered to help me track down my birth parents. She believed healing could only happen when we exposed the fear. She'd say, 'The monster is far more terrifying in shadow than in the light.' But I wouldn't do it.

"By then my life was finally going well. First Clay and Cordelia, then the music, then Owen and Hope, and every now and then it would come up—maybe it's time to look into it. I'd say no because in the back of my mind I felt if I dared go there all of this would be taken away from me. Like I'd made a deal and my end of the bargain was to let those secrets stay secret and in return I could have this beautiful life. Except... except then something started to shift inside of me. I started to feel this pain and this loneliness. Even surrounded by people I cherish, I felt utterly alone—rootless. And I started to think, *I've built this beautiful house, but I'm living on sand. There's no foundation.*"

Celeste listened to River's story that so closely mirrored her own. She too had spent so long outrunning her past that it had grown into something nightmarish, impossible to turn around and look in the face.

"I understand how you feel," Celeste admitted. "My mother

abandoned my brother and I when we were small children. My dad wouldn't speak of her and so I learned to never go there. In order to not long for her, wonder about her, I imagined her as something horrible. The heartless woman, the mother who went against her most vital nature and walked away." Celeste gripped the arms of the rocking chair. In years past, she'd researched why mothers abandoned their young and discovered it wasn't uncommon in nature. Mothers abandoned their young most often if the baby was defective or weak in some way.

"I'm starting to believe all the scary stories I told myself about my mom were a coping mechanism. I'm a grown woman now and I don't need those stories, and neither do you, River. Look at the world you've created here. I've only known you for a half hour and I'm astounded by your strength. You're ready to face this. Whatever it is."

River leaned her head back against the chair and closed her eyes. "I think I have to," she murmured. "I think the monster has finally caught up with me."

7

"Mama!" Hope yelled from across the yard.

Owen hurried behind the little girl, who ran surprisingly fast on her tiny legs. She waved two very dirty hands.

"Oh, my," River said. "What did you get yourself into?"

Owen laughed. "The compost pile. In her defense, Luna started it."

The large white, now brown-streaked, husky, trotted into view.

"Luna!" River scolded. "You both need a bath."

"Mama bath!" Hope said.

"You want me to give you your bath?" River examined Hope's dress—also splattered with dirt. "Okay. Do you mind, Celeste? It won't take more than five minutes."

"Take your time," Celeste told her. "I'll talk with Owen."

River and Hope walked into the house.

"Mind if I hose Luna down while we talk?" he asked.

"Not at all." Celeste walked to the edge of the porch and watched Owen unspool a hose and turn it on. Luna leapt in and out of the spray. The second dog, a black and white spotted hunting dog, snapped at the stream of water.

"Here you go, Garth. Have a drink, buddy," Owen said, shifting the hose.

"Is the farm your primary work, Owen?" River asked.

"Oh, no. We're mostly a hobby farm at this point. I'm a field service technician. Basically, I work for a company that sells tractors and other farm equipment. I go out and service the tractors, fix stuff, that kind of thing. I grew up on a farm and also had a mechanic father, so I learned to repair tractors. River and I sell some of our produce—honey, maple syrup, firewood. My parents have the big livestock, so I help over there throughout the year as well. We're not getting rich, but we do well enough. River makes money as a folk musician. The band has really taken off this year—she has a tour comin' up—so that's exciting."

"How did you and River meet?"

"I saw her at Andy's Roadhouse playing up on the stage and I..." He smiled, shook his head, sent the spray of water flying towards a group of chickens, who squawked and marched away. "I knew right then and there. Like God reached down, clamped a hand on top of my head and swiveled it in her direction. She was playing *Adrift*, still one of my favorite songs of hers, and dancing around. She does that when she really gets goin'—starts singing and dancing and playing guitar with her eyes closed, so into her music she forgets the crowd—and that night she fell right off the stage." He tilted his head back and laughed. "Good Lord. I went runnin' up there to save her like I thought I was Indiana Jones. Jumped right over a table and about landed on my face. By the time I reached her, she was up, crawling back onto the stage, not even fazed, and boy..." He blew out a breath. "I mighta been whacked in the head with a frying pan for how dumbstruck I was. I couldn't take my eyes off her."

Owen's words landed heavy in her mind. Celeste thought of Jonathan, of the ever-widening gap between them. Had they ever come close to a love like Owen described?

"And that was it then? Together ever since?" she asked.

"Mostly, yeah." He dropped the hose and pulled a pocket knife from his jeans, flicked it open and cleaned beneath his thumbnail. He smiled at her. "Sorry. Got some compost lodged under here. We didn't go straight to happily ever after. River tortured me for about a year. We'd go out then she'd not answer my calls for a couple weeks, refused to say we're boyfriend and girlfriend 'til we were practically living together.

"River needs a lot of space and a lot of intimacy at the same time. It's not always easy to know, but I keep tryin'. I'll never stop tryin'. I know she's worried about that, that this sadness, confusion she's been dealing with will somehow be our end, that I'll leave, but I never will. I'm telling you, Celeste, I knew the moment I laid eyes on River she was meant for me. When I said ''til death do us part,' I meant it. I still mean it. I'll never leave unless she makes me, which sometimes scares me. If River wanted me gone, she could make it happen. There's nothing she can't do."

"Why would she want you gone?"

He closed the knife, returned it to his pocket. "I don't know. To be alone, maybe. Trust isn't easy for River. This life, me and her, and then add Hope... you have to have a lot of faith to love like this. It's scary. It's vulnerable. And I feel that too." He rested his hand on his chest then lifted the hose and rinsed his fingers. "The thought of losing her brings me to my knees. Sometimes I'm afraid she's just like her name, River—water running through my hands."

"What is your sense of how River's doing right now?" Celeste asked.

"Oh, God, she's magic, truly. But I think that magic sometimes only comes outta people who've survived horrible things.

Maybe it's a gift from God making up for all that pain. She's playing here in Baraboo tonight. You should come. She'll make you bawl your eyes out one minute and dance on a table the next. She's special, everyone sees it, but this... this thing with her birth parents, it's been eating at her. Cordelia says it's like a dragon, that kind of trauma. You find a way when you're young to chase it into the closet and barricade the door, but it's been scratchin' all these years, diggin' a hole. Eventually it gets out and you have to face it down, slay it once and for all."

Luna walked between them and paused, then shook her whole body hard, splattering them both with water.

"Luna! Go on!" He shoed the dog away. "Sorry about that."

"No big deal," Celeste told him, wiping water from her face. "River mentioned your family lives nearby. Are you close with them?"

"Oh, yeah. My parents, grandparents, brothers—we all still talk every week. They all live here in Baraboo. My ma calls me every day." He smiled. "Sometimes that's a bit much. But I can't imagine who I'd have become without them. River never had any of that. No mother, no father, no siblings. Just a couple decent social workers and a bunch of foster families until Cordelia and Clay finally took her, but she was thirteen by then, so I think the seeds had been planted or, in her case, no seeds had been planted. One of her songs is like that. She talks about herself as a barren field, too rocky for anyone to bother tilling."

Celeste swallowed, massaged her hip, and wished his words didn't resonate so deeply within her. What would it have been like to grow up as Owen had, with two parents, an extended family, a mom who still called him every day?

When River emerged from the house she held a freshly washed Hope on her hip, wet curls resting on the collar of her little pink robe.

"Clean as a whistle," River announced. "No more playing in the compost pile. Got it?"

"Ya, Mama."

River handed Hope to Owen. "Want to get started on dinner? I'm going to get some paperwork around for Celeste."

"You betcha." He kissed River's cheek then leaned into Hope and smelled her wet hair. "Ooh, Mama used the tea tree shampoo. Smells good."

River turned to Celeste. "Will you stay for dinner? We'd love to have you."

Celeste thought of the evening she'd imagined—takeout and a bottle of Scotch at a motel somewhere in town. "Oh, well..."

"You've got to," Owen insisted. "I'm making braised beef short ribs. River whipped up a strawberry cream cheese pie this morning. Plus, Arnie's coming over. He's a hoot."

Celeste considered saying no, but knew spending large amounts of time alone with her computer and a bottle of liquor was what her and Jonathan's therapist called 'dysregulated behavior.'

"Okay. Sure," Celeste agreed.

"The paperwork I have is in the cabin," River said. "It helps keep clutter out of the house and... well, I don't like to look at it. That's weird, right? It's just a folder with a few sheets of paper."

Celeste followed River across the property to a small log cabin. A little concrete patio covered by a wood arch held two rocking chairs that flanked the front door. For a moment, a man sat in one of the rocking chairs, a pipe balanced on his lip. By the time Celeste and River reached the patio he had dissolved into the air.

"It's rustic, much like the house. Owen's grandparents lived here when they were first married and Owen and I lived here when we built the main house. I say we built it, but it was mostly him and his dad and brothers."

"Is Owen's grandfather dead?" Celeste asked, gazing at the empty chair, still rocking slightly.

"Yes. He passed a couple years ago," River said. "Sometimes I still get a whiff of his pipe when I'm over here. It's strange."

River opened the door and Celeste stepped into the cabin. A stone fireplace stood against one wall; a small sofa and a rocking chair faced it.

"Bathroom in here," River explained, opening a door.

A claw-foot tub sat on the wood floor beneath a window, a porcelain pedestal sink on the opposite side.

"What a beautiful bathtub."

River shuddered. "I actually hate taking baths. I've never set foot in that thing. Owen put it in after we moved into the main house."

Celeste looked from River to the bathtub.

"I know, I know. My name is River and I hate taking baths. I've heard it before. I love water, flowing water, moving water, but still water..." She rubbed her arms. "I don't like it. You know what one of my foster moms said when I told her? That an aversion to baths had come from the Devil to ensure I'd never be baptized and I'd rot in hell like the rest of the sinners."

Celeste's stomach tightened. "A foster mother told you that?"

"Yeah." River's jaw hardened. "She's not a foster parent anymore. I made it my mission after I moved to Be Free. I wrote the social services office, the local prosecutor, the governor, and the police about every family who abused me or other kids in their care. I put every detail in those letters. Some of them were darn long."

"Were there ever criminal charges against any of the parents?"

River sighed, rubbed beneath her eyes. "One. A man who used to... do stuff to us girls. He and his wife only fostered girls. He got six months, is already out."

"You're kidding."

"Nope. 'Trust the system,' that's what the social worker told me when they wanted me to testify. So I did and then I spent a year getting terrible phone calls from his wife. When he got out, he showed up at Be Free. I was sixteen. Nothing happened. Clay and several other Be Free guys chased him off. That was years ago, but I still have nightmares about him sometimes. Still, I'm happy I testified. They lost their right to foster kids and he has a record, so it wasn't a total waste."

A bookshelf made from sturdy-looking oak planks stood along one wall. River pulled a folder from between two books. She laid the folder open on a little kitchen table.

"I don't have much," River admitted. "I printed a few things from the ancestry website, but I think the research has to be done there. We don't have a computer or internet here. We go into town to the library when we need to get online. No cell service even, but we have a landline."

"I think I'd go crazy," Celeste said, sifting through the papers.

River gazed out the window where Hope was chasing one of the goats in a circle. "It's not as hard as you'd think. I have enough noise up here without adding to it." River tapped her temple. "And honestly, neither Owen nor I miss it. The worst thing is when I'm trying to cook something and can't look up an ingredient replacement." She laughed. "But I can live with that."

"What about scheduling shows and stuff for your music?"

"Arnie does all that. He's our de facto manager. He schedules the shows, updates the website, even has several social media accounts. I just show up when and where he tells me to."

"I like the sound of that."

"Yeah." She nodded. "I try to keep my energy here on the farm. It's either here or it's with my music. I don't have much left after that. And I don't want to give what I do have to a bunch of strangers on the internet." She looked quickly at Celeste and shook her head. "I can't believe I just said that. Here you are literally a boat ride from home to help a stranger on the internet. Jesus. I swear sometimes I don't source my words before I spill 'em out. What you do is extraordinary, Celeste, and I can't thank you enough."

Celeste shook her head. "It's okay, River. We all have to find our own way. I think what you've created here is beautiful. I could use a little more of this. Maybe someday I'll unplug a bit. God knows I could use it." She turned her attention back to the paperwork. "I'll need the login information for your ancestry account, if you're okay sharing it."

"Absolutely. Yeah." River flipped over one of the pieces of paper and groped through a drawer until she came out with a dull pencil. She wrote a username and password.

Outside a vehicle bumped down the driveway and stopped. Someone honked their horn.

"That's Arnie."

Through the window, Celeste saw Hope hobble toward the Jeep where a young man with long black hair tied in a ponytail and ripped jeans stepped out. He picked her up and opened the back door of his Jeep.

Celeste followed River from the cabin.

Arnie saw her and waved. "Wait 'til you see what I brought the little bean."

He held up a scrawny white kitten, its fur gray with dirt. A single black spot covered one eye.

"Kippy! Kippy!" Hope shouted, wiggling to get closer to the cat.

"Good grief, Arnie. Did you really think we needed another animal around here?" River asked.

"River, this sweet little thing was a quarter mile up the road. Looked like a little hitchhiker trying to get home, and where else could home be but right here in paradise?"

Owen walked out, a dishrag in his hands. "What have you got there, Arnie?"

"He's brought us a kitten," River announced flatly.

"I'm allergic to cats," Owen said, mouth turned down. "I'll itch my skin right off if I touch that thing. He sure is cute though, isn't he?"

River petted the kitten's head.

Arnie frowned. "Maybe my mom can take him. She used to have a cat."

"I'll take him," Celeste blurted.

8

Arnie stared at Celeste as if noticing her for the first time.

"Oh. Sorry. Arnie, this is Celeste," River said.

Arnie extended a hand. "Good to meet you. Are you serious about taking him?"

"You don't have to," River insisted. "You already came all this way and—"

"No. It's not a burden. I want to." And Celeste realized as she looked at the kitten with his patch over one eye and his exhausted little body that it was true.

"Do you have any animal formula?" Celeste asked. "Puppy or something for the goats? I had to bottle-feed my cat Cash as a baby. His mother had been hit and he was abandoned. This little guy looks too young for solid food."

"We do," Owen said. "Puppy formula, and you could use one of Hope's bottles."

"I wonder if there are any motels in town that'd allow cats," Celeste said.

"You don't need to get a motel," River insisted. "Stay in the cabin. That's what it's there for. It'd be perfect and if you're up for it, we could drive to Be Free tomorrow and get the social work file Cordelia has."

Celeste glanced at the cabin. She'd only been at River and Owen's place for a couple hours, but something about it tugged at a tendon of nostalgia within her. The smell of the fresh earth and grass and a creek somewhere not far off took her back to a place she barely remembered—her childhood home in West Virginia, those distant years when she'd had a mother and a father and brother all together under one roof. "Okay. Yeah. I'd love to."

After Celeste bathed and fed the kitten, Hope assisting with gently toweling him off, she put him in a box lined with a blanket and left him in the cabin.

Hope followed Celeste from the cabin and tugged on the leg of her jeans. "Pick," she said. "Pick."

Celeste looked down where Hope's arms were extended up. She knelt and lifted the little girl. Hope wrapped her arms tight around Celeste's neck. The little girl smelled like shampoo and the slightly musky odor of the kitten.

"We'll eat on the back porch," River called. "Do you want me to take her?"

"No. I've got her," Celeste said. Hope's weight in her arms, her heartbeat against Celeste's own, caused a flutter of longing deep in her belly. She'd never given much thought to having children, couldn't imagine having them now as her and Jonathan's life had begun to careen out of control, but she inhaled Hope's scent and felt grateful for the moment.

Celeste carried her around the back of the house to where Owen and River had arranged platters of food on a wooden table on the porch. A bouquet of wild flowers stuck from a wine bottle in the center.

"How's the cat doing?" Arnie asked.

"Asleep, and he sucked his bottle down in about two minutes, so that's a good sign."

"It sure is," he agreed. "Thought of a name yet for him?"

Celeste smiled. "Romeo." The name had popped into her head while she and Hope bathed him.

"Hmm... the star-crossed lover, huh? I like it. It suits him. River and Owen said you're here to help find River's birth mother. Is that what you do for a living? I'm so curious how it all works."

Celeste sat Hope in a chair and took a seat, accepting the glass of wine River handed her. "It's not what I do. I resigned from my job as a scientist a couple months ago. I worked in a pharmaceutical lab for the previous eight years, but last year I was hit by a car and nearly died. Or I guess I did die and the doctors brought me back. That changed me, changed my focus, my purpose."

"You were hit by a car?" River murmured. "How scary."

"Did they catch the person who hit you?" Owen asked.

Celeste shook her head. "No. But... I try not to dwell too much on that. I know it sounds strange, but in retrospect it feels like something I needed to happen. Like my life was off course."

"Wow," Arnie said, heaping food onto his plate. "It's pretty cool you see it that way."

Celeste thought of her near-death experience. No part of her wished it hadn't happened. It was an odd way to feel, but it was true. "I was really fortunate. Other than some lingering hip and leg pain, I've almost fully recovered."

"Well, I've always told Owen and River an hour in one of their rocking chairs staring at the trees adds a year to your life, so I think you've come to the right place."

"And the band is playing at Revival tonight," Owen said. "You can hear River sing. Ain't nothing more healing than that."

After dinner, Celeste and River followed Arnie, Owen and Hope to River's gig.

"Is this a church?" Celeste asked, pulling into the parking lot next to Arnie.

"Used to be, but that's been decades ago," River said. "It's called Revival. It's a bar and restaurant. We play here quite a bit. Grady Monroe—the owner—is really supportive of local musicians. His is the only place in town you can find live music almost every night of the week."

When they walked in, Owen, Hope on his hip, and Arnie headed toward the bar, where a Goliath of a man in a Revival t-shirt stood.

Chandeliers crafted from old wine barrels hung from the high vaulted ceilings. A massive oak slab bar ran nearly the length of one side of the room. The altar had been converted into a stage. The arched windows held stained glass, likely the same stained glass from its time as a church. Celeste stared at the depictions of religious figures, doves exploding into colored light, holy crosses.

Faded and scuffed wood planks comprised the floor. For a moment Celeste saw hundreds of feet shuffling along in polished black shoes. The hems of dresses brushed the worn wood. Voices murmured and cried out and a stream of images coursed through her mind—the whispered prayers of former congregants set free in that space, some filled with hope and others with desperation. She heard the sounds of knees hitting the floor, hands slapping the planks.

"Celeste?"

Celeste jumped when River touched her elbow. "Sorry. I was..."—she gestured at the space—"just taking it all in."

"It's something, isn't it? At night after shows, sometimes I like to sit here and just... breathe. Feel it. This place." River led

Celeste to the stage where a group of men, including Arnie, had assembled.

"Here they are," River said. "I'd like you to meet the band Grace not Grit. You already met Arnie, our banjo man. Morgan plays the bass and violin. Wayne is our drummer. And we have a few others who come and go depending on the gig. Guys, this is Celeste."

Celeste shook the hands of the men. They were a patchwork group of old and young. Arnie, the youngest of the trio, was likely mid-twenties, around River's age. Morgan looked to be late thirties with a thick blond beard and fluffy blond hair. He wore a deerskin vest over a long-sleeved black shirt and black pants. Wayne was the oldest, mid-fifties, Celeste guessed, clean-shaven, with striking blue eyes and a deep weathered tan as if he'd spent decades in the sun—a farmer, perhaps.

"All right, River," a woman who approached them from behind said. "Your groupies are here. What can we help you with?"

River gave the woman a half hug. "Celeste, this is Shay."

The woman, middle-aged with kinky black and silver hair, extended her hand to Celeste. "Aka River's number one fan," she said. "I never miss a show if she's in Baraboo, and we're even going on the road with her for her tour next week. There's quite a little posse of us at this point." She gestured to the bar where a group of other men and women stood. They wore t-shirts with winged guitars and beneath the name of the band, 'Grace not Grit,' in chunky black letters.

"They help with setup and teardown, get us drinks. Basically, they spoil us rotten," River explained.

"Are you here to be inducted into the groupie fan club? We have t-shirts," Shay said.

River smiled. "Celeste is helping me find my birth mother."

Shay grinned and squeezed River's arm. "That's wonderful

news. I hope you're successful, Celeste. No doubt she's a crooner like our River here."

"Sorry to interrupt," a large man in a black cowboy hat said. "The group wants to know if we should start unloading equipment?"

Shay grinned at the man. "This is Tex," she told Celeste. "Another of our groupies."

"Like Texas?" Celeste asked.

Tex put a hand over his heart. "Born and raised in the Lone Star State."

"And how'd you end up in Wisconsin?"

"Oldest story in the book, followed a pretty girl." He grinned. "Course, she ended up deciding she was more into bankers than cowboys." His eyes sparkled as they shifted toward Shay. "But that's fine with me. Plenty of fish in the sea."

Hope, who'd been twirling around on the stage, suddenly veered sideways and toppled off the side. Tex leapt forward and caught her, swung her high in the air. She squealed with delight and he set her on the ground. "Be careful, little lady," he said, patting her head.

River bent and gathered Hope into her arms. "Thank you, Tex. That was a close one."

"Hey, Tex, here are my keys," Arnie called, tossing his keys to Tex. "Amps, cords and my and River's instruments are in the back."

"Gotcha." Tex nodded his head at Celeste. "Good to meet you."

Celeste sat at a table to the right of the stage. A candle flickered in a mason jar. She sipped the Scotch and water she'd ordered.

River sat on a stool, guitar balanced on her thighs, eyes closed as she sang about an old oak tree. "Oh, the wind it wails through the hollow bark, like a heart that's been broken and torn apart."

As Celeste listened, her heart grew heavy behind her ribs. The song was achingly beautiful, River's voice, the melody, but something more transcendent and enchanting. At the table beside her, a woman was crying, dabbing her eyes with a napkin and rocking from side to side.

Though River started the set crooning songs that had all of Revival hushed and tearful, just when Celeste thought she too might begin to cry, the band shifted to a series of more upbeat tunes. River stood and sang about dancing beneath the full moon and getting married in a hay barn. She stomped her feet and spun.

Hope and Owen danced in a growing swarm of people crowded in front of the stage. Celeste watched their feet thump to the sound of the music and felt the reverberations up her leg, longed for the days when her body moved that way. She wondered if she'd ever dance again or if it would always be a chore, a painful, jerky exercise in acceptance.

Her hip ached as she shifted in her chair. She'd left her pain pills in her truck and now stood, wincing at the stiffness in her leg. If she didn't take them now, the pain might reach a tipping point that would make sleep that night impossible.

The parking lot was dark and quiet. Celeste shook a couple of pills into her palm and swallowed them dry.

As she moved back toward Revival, a sound started her. The scrape of a match. A flame lit the black to her right, and she turned, blinked at the large figure. As the match reached his face, she saw a cigarette poking between his lips.

"Howdy," the man said. The flame had briefly lit his pockmarked face, dark beady eyes.

She blinked at him. "Hi. You spooked me."

He smiled and shook the flame out, returning to darkness save the orange ember at his mouth. "Sorry about that."

It was after midnight when Celeste and River drove back to River's farm. Owen had left Revival with Hope hours earlier, hitching a ride with a nearby farmer whose family had gone to see River play.

After telling River goodnight, Celeste slipped into the little cabin. She hurried to the bedroom and peered into the box to find Romeo curled on his side asleep. When she brushed her fingers down his knobby spine, he woke with a mewl and stood up on shaky legs. Celeste took him out, fed him a bottle and then returned him to the box. River's voice still hummed in her mind when she climbed into bed.

For a while she stared at the ceiling, the usual hamster wheel of thought taking over. She had letters piling up in her Dear Celeste inbox to respond to, the ongoing issues with Jonathan to figure out, the fact that someone had tried to kill her. Instead of facing any of it, she'd run off to Baraboo to wade into someone else's problems.

Eventually her eyelids grew heavy and, despite her brain's best efforts to lecture her, Celeste drifted to sleep.

Celeste walked *through an eerie orchard at dusk. A pale mist drifted above the ground. The leafy earth was littered with rotted apples, their sickly sweet scent filling the air.*

In front of her, she spotted a little blue bungalow with red shutters. It was dark, but candlelight flickered in the windows. Somewhere music played—a mechanical song, an eerie lullaby—and water dripped as if from a faucet.

From a branch of a tall warped apple tree, something swayed in the breeze.

A doll hung by its neck.

Celeste's eyes snapped open.

She couldn't move, couldn't speak. Her legs were paralyzed, her arms, her body. The dream fled and was replaced by the dark shapes of the bedroom inside River and Owen's cabin. Dread clogged her throat.

From the corner of the room, the sound of watery, choked breath found her. Celeste blinked into the darkness and discovered the spirit she'd seen during her drive to the restaurant with Jonathan. She was little more than a silhouette, ragged, almost as black as the surrounding darkness. Stringy pale hair hung from her mottled scalp. Her mouth opened and, in place of a voice, a haunting mechanical song, like that from Celeste's dream, drifted out.

Celeste tried to speak. No sound emerged. She could not even move her lips. Save blinking, she had no control of her body. Suddenly the woman darted forward, eyes fixed on Celeste's. She lifted a withered finger to her rotted lips and flicked her eyes to the window, and Celeste saw the shape of a large man as he passed by the window.

It could have been Owen, but Celeste knew better. She suddenly didn't want to move or make a sound. The man had turned and she feared he stared into the room. She clenched her eyes shut, praying he couldn't see her.

After several minutes passed, the kitten shifted and meowed in his box. Celeste opened her eyes. The man at the window had gone and the spirit too no longer hovered in the room. The pressure on her body released and Celeste sat up so quickly her head swam.

The kitten released another mewl and Celeste leaned over the side of the bed and scooped the little creature up, cradling him against her chest, feeling the rapid flutter of his heartbeat against her own.

9

The following morning, River carried a mug of coffee to the little cabin.

Celeste pulled open the door. Her red hair, which River thought must be dyed based on the hue, stuck at funny angles from her head. River suspected based on Celeste's face she'd also not slept great the night before.

"How'd you and Romeo sleep?" River asked, handing Celeste the cup.

Celeste yawned and took the coffee. "Decent, but I'm ready for this. Thank you." She lifted the mug to her nose and inhaled.

"Come over when you're ready. I'm making blueberry pancakes. Owen and Hope already left to go to his parents'. They're preparing for calving season over there."

"Okay. I'll feed Romeo and get changed and be over in a few."

River drove her and Celeste in the farm truck to Be Free. She and Owen often shared the blue pickup, but the farm truck allowed them a second vehicle, though it always smelled of mildewed hay and motor oil.

They arrived at Be Free, marked by a large hand-painted sign decorated by the handprints of all the children who'd passed through the commune. River's own print, a mixture of red and yellow, occupied the lower left corner.

"How big is this place?" Celeste asked as they followed the curving gravel driveway.

"Forty acres, with six houses, three large pole barns, a communal kitchen and a massive vegetable garden. They use solar panels for a lot of their power. It's a very self-sufficient homestead."

"River!" a little boy squealed, running up to River after they parked the truck. She knelt and scooped him up.

"Goodness, Lennon. You've grown a foot since I last saw you." She mussed his hair and kissed him on the cheek.

"I've got a baby possum. Mama found it on the road coming back from town and Daddy said we couldn't keep it, but Cordelia and Mama built it a tiny house and I've been feeding it with a bottle. I named it Dodo. Want to come see it?"

"I do," she assured him, returning him to the ground. "Give me a few minutes first, okay?"

"Okay. I'll go get it ready." Lennon darted toward a large tan-colored barn.

Cordelia, wearing the same style of handmade grain sack dresses she'd worn all of River's life, hurried from the house, Clay behind her.

"Clay, Cordelia, this is Celeste, the woman I told you about." River had called her adopted parents days before when she'd received the email back from Celeste. She hadn't wanted to blindside them with her intention to search for her birth mother.

"Lovely to meet you," Cordelia told Celeste, taking her hands and squeezing them.

Clay held up his palms, streaked with dirt. "I've been digging in the garden, so I'll refrain from soiling you." He put his two hands together as if in prayer and bowed his head. "Good to meet you, Celeste. And River, where is our little Hope?"

"She's with Owen, but we're going to plan a visit in a couple weeks after the tour. I promise."

"That's what I like to hear. And of course we'll be coming to your show at the Velvet Theater. Half the commune will be there."

River swallowed the lump in her throat and smiled. "Thanks, Clay."

"We can't wait," he said. "And I just finished building Hope's tricycle. All it needs now is a coat of paint, or no paint? What do you think?" He led River toward a woodshed.

"Cordelia, could you grab those papers for Celeste?" River asked over her shoulder.

"You bet I can. And Clay is making homemade pizzas for dinner. Will the two of you stay?"

River looked at Celeste. "It's up to you, Celeste."

"Sounds delicious," Celeste said.

"Perfect. Come with me." Cordelia looped her arm through Celeste's and led her into the house.

River watched them disappear into the first true home she'd ever known. She'd shared a room in the house with Autumn, Clay and Cordelia's biological daughter, who was three years older than her and who now lived in Montana, where she worked as a park ranger. Autumn, like River, had loved music and they'd often fallen asleep to the Sarah McLachlan album *Mirrorball*.

"Paint or no paint?" Clay asked. "I was thinking yellow with some little flowers." He held up the tricycle.

"It's adorable," River said, spinning a wheel. "Let's go with paint. Hope loves flowers."

"River! Are you coming?" Lennon popped his head out of the barn.

"I better go visit this infamous new possum who's joined the commune," she told Clay.

He nodded, returning the tricycle to his workbench. "Watch out. That bugger's got sharp little teeth."

River started toward the barn.

"River," Clay said.

She turned back to see him watching her. "Maybe go visit the God Box after you're done."

"Yeah. I think I will."

AFTER RIVER SPENT twenty minutes visiting with Lennon and Dodo, the little possum that hissed each time she petted it, she made her way to the flower garden that grew wild behind the barn. When she'd first come to Be Free, she'd thought of the garden as a place of magic filled with fragrant prairie phlox and bluebells. Clay, more than anyone else in the commune, tended to the garden and she'd taken to accompanying him to pull weeds or to sit among the flowers and write poetry that later became songs.

Clay had been her touchstone, the person at Be Free who didn't push her to open up, to make small talk, to tell him the details of her day. A few months after she'd moved to the commune, she'd started to join him in daily tasks. She'd take a fishing pole and follow him to the river. She'd go out and muck the pig pens, feed the chickens. If he was diggin' a hole, River would grab a shovel and they'd go on all day practically in silence.

In the center of the garden stood the God Box. It sat in a

hollow in a large weathered oak tree stump. Over the years the bark of the trunk had fallen away and the intricate whorls and spirals left by the crumbling wood remained etched in the pale surface of the long-dead tree.

The box held the prayers of those who lived at and visited Be Free. Anytime she'd struggled, Clay or Cordelia said, 'Put it in the God Box,' and River wrote her woes or her dreams on little slips of paper that each Sunday during an evening intention circle were taken out and tossed into a bonfire—sent to the heavens to be answered, according to Cordelia, by the angels.

River's faith in the God Box had often wavered. Her life had made the concept of God and angels feel alien and unlikely. How could there be a God who allowed small children to suffer? Still, she'd found solace in the box, hope, and now as she wiggled the plastic bag that held slips of paper and pencils free, she'd already begun to craft her prayer—that the apathy that had invaded her life, that had crept slow and poisonous into her veins, be stripped away.

THAT EVENING, River and Celeste joined the other Be Free members at a long wood table beneath a canopy of trees. Fairy lights hung from the branches overhead and the children of Be Free had filled vases with bouquets of wildflowers that ran the length. Twenty-two people in all sat at the table, talking, eating pizza, drinking water from mason jars or cups of homemade blackberry wine.

River fielded questions from the men and women she thought of as her aunts and uncles, the children she considered her nieces and nephews.

As River took a drink of wine, a truck ambled onto the property and Clay's brother Torrence stepped out.

"Torrence is here?" River asked, eyes narrowing.

The man walked toward them, a baseball cap pulled low on his forehead, his jeans and long-sleeved shirt wrinkled.

Cordelia looked pained, but forced a smile at River and Celeste. "For a couple of days. Apparently his girlfriend kicked him out again and he had nowhere else to go."

"If it isn't my favorite niece," Torrence said, staring at River.

River shuddered and focused on her pizza..

"I thought you were eating in town?" Clay said stiffly as he passed Torrence a slice of pizza.

"Would have, except Janie's Diner is charging fifteen bucks for a burger these days. Guess nobody told 'em they're still serving Shitsville, Wisconsin, not Manhattan's Upper East Side."

River, her appetite gone, stood abruptly. "We better get going, Celeste."

Celeste pushed back her chair and stood.

Cordelia stood as well, grabbing River's hand. "Already? You're not done eating, and—"

River, sensing Torrence's eyes on her, nodded. "Yeah. I need to get home to Hope."

10

River barely spoke during the drive. She stared through the windshield, her face impassive.

"Are you okay?" Celeste asked.

River nodded, but seemed unwilling or unable to speak. The emotion hung heavy in the truck.

"I saw him at Revival last night. Your Uncle Torrence."

River looked at her sharply, face pale. "You saw him? Where?"

"In the parking lot smoking a cigarette."

River returned her eyes to the road, but when she brushed a lock of hair behind her ear, her fingers trembled. "He's not my uncle," she said.

When they returned to River's property, it was full dark. A coolness had settled in the air. The stars shone brightly in the dark sky.

"Looks like Owen and Hope are still at his parents'," River murmured. "If you'd like, I can make some tea or…?"

"Nothing for me. Thanks," Celeste said. "I'm pretty exhausted and I'm sure Romeo needs to eat."

"Okay. Good night, Celeste."

Celeste walked into the cabin and lifted the kitten from the box. She'd left a little dish of formula in his box and he seemed to have drunk it all.

"Hey, there, Romeo," she murmured as he purred and pushed his face into her chin. She fed him and left him asleep on her bed.

Her hip ached and, as she brushed her teeth in the bathroom, her eyes lingered on the claw-foot tub. She ran a hot bath and climbed in, resting her head against the lip of the tub.

The dream took her.

Celeste stood on the sidewalk and stared at the neat little blue house with red shutters. Flowers bloomed in window boxes and from one window a white curtain fluttered in the wind. A sound, the beginning of a scream, rose in the air and then abruptly ended, as if cut by a hand clapped over a mouth or fingertips crushing someone's throat.

The sun shone. The grass grew green and luscious. The road behind Celeste stood eerily quiet. Other than the silenced scream, nothing about the house should have unnerved Celeste, and yet her whole body had begun to shake. Her knees clacked together, her elbows racked against her sides, her teeth chattered. Without meaning to, she started forward, moving effortlessly, almost floating, and she realized there was no pain in her leg or hip. She wasn't limping.

It was that realization that tugged Celeste from the dream, from that picturesque yet disturbing little yard. If her hip and leg didn't hurt, she must be dreaming. She gasped and flailed her arms, splashing water out of the tub as she sat up.

The little blue house receded, but didn't vanish. She blinked at the tiled wall of the tub, arms coated in gooseflesh despite the heat of the bathwater.

Overhead, the lights flickered. The bathroom door creaked and swung open. Celeste stared at it, frozen, expecting someone to walk in. The hall beyond stood empty.

Celeste woke early to the rooster's cry outside. Strange dreams had ruptured her sleep. She fed the kitten and returned him to his box before walking onto the porch. Dew clung to the tall grass and a morning mist hovered over the farm.

"Damn it, damn it!" River's voice came from the direction of the chicken coop.

Celeste walked over to see River, wearing a nightgown and knee-high rubber boots, hunched over two dead chickens, feathers splayed across the dirt. Her face was tear-streaked.

"River?"

She looked up and quickly wiped her cheeks. "You're awake."

"The rooster is an effective alarm."

River nodded. "I'm surprised we didn't hear him last night. Usually if an animal attacks the chickens, he goes wild. Ugh. Poor girls."

"An animal did that?"

"We've had a coyote a few times. I don't know. These look" —she shook her head, her face troubled—"different."

"What else could have hurt them?"

River sighed. "I don't know. I should get Owen." As she started toward the house, she paused and turned back to Celeste, her expression grim. "Torrence tried to rape me when I was fifteen."

"Clay's brother?" Celeste stared at her, shocked.

"I never told anyone, and he wasn't successful. Clay had given me a folding knife that day as a gift and I had it in my pocket. I got it out and stabbed Torrence in the leg. He took off, went to the hospital and told everyone a lie about cutting himself by accident. He left Be Free that day and didn't come back for months."

"You didn't tell Clay?"

"I should have, but..." River shook her head. "I finally had a home, a place I belonged. I thought if I told, they'd want me to leave."

Celeste imagined Cordelia and Clay, two people who'd devoted their lives to helping children like River escape abuse. She suspected they'd have been devastated.

"I know it's not true," River went on. "I know that now, but... I didn't then, and after a while it seemed easier not to say anything."

"And Torrence never tried anything again?" Celeste asked. The man she'd met the night before had had a menacing presence. She was surprised he hadn't sought revenge against River.

"I made sure to never be alone with him again. If he came to the commune to stay, I'd glue myself to Clay and not leave his side. Given the opportunity, I think Torrence would have. I never gave him one."

Celeste returned to the cabin and changed into a pair of jeans and a t-shirt. As she made her way to River's house, she saw Owen picking up the dead chickens.

"Sleep well?" he asked.

"Decent." She thought of the man she'd seen outside the window two nights before. It was possible he, like the woman, had been an entity, a spirit passing by, but Celeste didn't think so, and she wondered if he'd returned and killed the chickens. "Just out of curiosity, does anyone check your property at night?"

"Check it?" Owen asked.

"Yeah. I thought I saw someone the night before last outside my window."

"Huh. Really? I guess someone could have stopped by. Maybe Arnie, if he had something to drop off for River. Maybe she forgot something at the gig."

Celeste knew it wasn't Arnie with his thin frame. This man

had been large, well over six feet, and foreboding even without features. "He looked bigger than Arnie. A lot bigger."

Worry lines appeared on Owen's face as he stared at the road. He glanced down at the chickens before stuffing them into a canvas sack.

"What is it?" she asked.

"River had a stalker last year."

"A stalker?"

"We never caught him, but he left notes, over twenty. Notes and love poems ripped out of a book. He'd leave them on her truck outside of gigs."

"What did the notes say?"

"Nothing threatening. She was beautiful, he was her biggest fan, she sings like an angel. The poems were equally harmless—stuff by Shakespeare, Edgar Allan Poe. They might not even have bothered her except he started to leave them on her truck at other places—outside the grocery store when she was inside with Hope, once at her therapist's office—and they got... a little stranger. The last few mentioned how he knew she couldn't sleep at night, how he'd sing her to bed if she'd let him, how Hope looked pretty in this little bunny romper she'd worn to a dinner at my parents' house. He was clearly following her."

"Did you report it to the police?"

"We did, yeah. I started putting a big cardboard sign on her windshield that said 'We're watching you.' Me and my brothers and some of the groupies patrolled the parking lot at her gigs. I made it plain if I caught him, jail would be the least of his problems. And after that, it stopped."

"And she hasn't had any issues with him since?"

"Nothing for six months at least, maybe longer."

"Are you worried it might have been him?"

Owen frowned. "I prefer not to consider that, but I don't want to be naïve. Did you get a look at him at all? Any facial features? Anything specific?"

Celeste remembered the dead woman lifting her skeletal finger to her lips, silencing Celeste, as if warning her not to alert the man to her presence. "No. He was in shadow and... really, I just saw his silhouette."

Owen scratched his head and cinched the bag. "I'll walk around today. See if there are any strange tire tracks."

"I didn't mention it to River. I didn't want to scare her."

Owen stared at the ground. "Yeah. Maybe that's for the best right now. She goes on tour next week and I don't want to add any more pressure."

CELESTE LEFT WISCONSIN AFTER BREAKFAST, driving to the ferry with the kitten in the box on her passenger seat. Romeo did surprisingly well on the trip home, emerging only periodically to stare at the movement beyond the window with suspicious curiosity.

Back in Michigan, she stopped into her vet. His checkup confirmed he was likely around eight weeks old.

At home, Celeste quarantined the kitten in the spare bedroom. Afterwards she took a long hot shower and changed into sweatpants and a loose-fitting t-shirt. She poured a glass of Scotch and carried it to her office. She spent an hour answering letters in the Dear Celeste column then switched to focusing on River.

Cordelia had given her a manila envelope with about ten papers stapled together. There were write-ups on the various foster families River had lived with and medical records. No birth certificate or any evidence that might point towards her birth family. The envelope also contained a letter from River's original intake social worker, who'd picked her up from Dottie Smith. In the letter, the social worker outlined Dottie's story about River's alleged abuser, her disturbing drawings and their inability to trace the father who'd abandoned her—Ted. The letter was old and faded and it was difficult to read the worker's name. It looked like Mona with a last name that started with a W.

Celeste set the folder aside and logged in to River's ancestry account online.

The matches connected to River were distant and, when she searched the names of the connections, she found little online that offered more detail about each person's family tree. In several days, she had her genealogy course, but in the meantime, she scrolled articles that described how to use online public databases to track distant familial connections to closer relatives.

After an hour with little progress, Celeste gave up. She clicked out of the browser window. It instantly reopened, filling her screen with River's name and basic heritage information. Celeste closed the window again and clicked to turn off the desktop.

When she opened the door to leave the office it slammed shut before she could step out. Celeste took a breath, twisted the knob and pulled it open hard. Again it jerked closed.

"What?" she demanded, spinning, scanning the room though no one stood inside it. "What do you want?"

Behind her the computer came to life. It returned again to the ancestry website.

"Leave me alone," she hissed, snatched the door open and rushed through it. She paused in the hallway, but the door didn't slam behind her and nothing stirred in the house.

11

Jonathan arrived home from work just after six o'clock. Celeste, intent on distracting herself from the strange events in the office, had cleaned the kitchen and made a chicken stir fry.

"Smells good," Jonathan said, kissing her cheek stiffly. "How was Wisconsin?"

"Nice. The woman I'm helping lives on a farm, so I got to spend a couple days there. It was really peaceful."

"A farm?" He wrinkled his nose. "With cows and chickens?"

"Chickens. No cows. Complete with a rooster who woke everybody up at dawn."

"You stayed on their farm? With complete strangers?"

"They're not strangers anymore."

"Because you spent a day with them?"

Celeste sensed his growing agitation, his desire to argue. "I brought a friend home with me," she announced, smiling.

"A friend?" He scowled.

"One sec." Celeste trotted up the stairs and returned with the kitten. "Meet Romeo."

He sighed and closed his eyes. "Please tell me you're not serious."

"Clearly I am," she said.

"We already have a cat."

"I'm aware of that, but this one showed up and he needed a home, so here he is."

"He showed up where? At the farm full of animals, and he couldn't stay there?"

He was meant for me. She didn't say it, but she knew it was true. "Owen is allergic."

"Owen?" His eyes narrowed at her.

"River's husband. The woman I'm helping."

"Fine. It looks sick though. Probably won't live a week."

She held the kitten closer, wanted to tell Jonathan he could eat alone, she was no longer hungry, but she knew that would only make things worse.

The door to the laundry room creaked open. Jonathan, who stood in front of it, spun around. He pulled the door the rest of the way open. Celeste expected to see Cash behind it, but the laundry room stood empty.

"Weird," he muttered.

Celeste returned Romeo to the spare bedroom and forced herself through dinner, making small talk with Jonathan over happenings in the lab.

"*Jeopardy's* on," he said after dinner, walking to the living room and sitting on the couch.

"I'm going to have a bath. My hip's a little achy tonight."

He looked annoyed, but nodded. "Whatever you want."

CELESTE SANK LOWER in the tub, the oil from the bath salts swirling iridescent on the surface of the water. She massaged her hip and closed her eyes, let her whole body settle.

The near-death experiences conference was the following day. She looked forward to seeing Harris and Eliza and getting their thoughts on the situation with River.

The faucet dripped. *Drip, drip, drip.* The warmth of water lulled her, carried her away.

Minutes ticked by and then a cool breeze flitted across her face. Celeste opened her eyes and froze. The bath water had turned a deep crimson color. The odor came then, an abrasive metallic smell. Blood.

For a moment Celeste thought the old stitches, long healed, had opened back up. She reached a trembling hand into the dark water, felt along her hip and thigh.

The door opened, and she screamed.

Jonathan jumped. "Jesus," he snapped. "I brought you a glass of wine. I nearly spilled it all down my shirt."

Celeste lifted a handful of the water, trembling, but Jonathan only stared at her.

"What's wrong?" He demanded. He scanned her face, then down to her body.

Celeste forced her eyes back to the bath—clear, the surface marred only by a spiral of bath oil.

"Nothing," she stammered. "I dozed off and you scared me."

He looked at the glass of wine. "You dozed off? Maybe you'd better skip the wine."

"No. I'll take it. Thank you." She held out a hand and he reluctantly walked it to her.

THE FOLLOWING MORNING, Celeste found Jonathan in the kitchen opening and closing drawers so hard the contents rattled.

"What's wrong? What are you looking for?"

"Did you move my keys?" he demanded.

"No. Aren't they on the hook?" She pointed at the little metal hooks where they both hung their keys. Hers were there. His were not.

"Obviously not," he said, "but I hung them there last night. They didn't get up and walk off on their own."

"I didn't touch your keys, Jonathan."

He ignored her and continued his search, marching from the room. Celeste wandered the kitchen, opening many of the same drawers Jonathan had with no luck.

"What the hell?" His voice carried from the front hall.

Celeste walked out to find him leaning over his slippers, the same slippers he'd worn the morning of her hit-and-run. For a moment she saw that discarded slipper again, watched it shrink as she rushed into the sky.

"They were in my goddamned slipper," he muttered, holding up his keys.

CELESTE PARKED on the street near the Amway Hotel where the near-death experiences conference would start in fifteen minutes. She sat in her truck, watching the hotel as two women, arms linked, disappeared through the double doors.

She'd stayed at the hotel years before with Jonathan. They'd been there for a wedding, had dined and danced in the large ballroom. The same ballroom now likely packed with others who'd died and returned to tell their stories.

From the corner of her eye, she caught movement as someone stepped up and knocked on her window. Harris and Eliza stood outside.

"Oh, good," Celeste told them, pushing the door open. "I was dreading walking in there alone."

Eliza gave her arm a squeeze. "You're never alone."

Harris hugged her. "How have you been? Any news on the Randy trial?"

"No news. I spoke with Joanna a couple weeks ago and there have been a few delays, so no date is set. Apparently, there's some talk of him representing himself."

"Typical psychopath," Harris said. "I hope he does. Gary Wilson is a solid prosecutor. He'll eat him alive."

Celeste looked at their shirts. They each read 'Memento mori—Memento vivere' on either side of an hourglass topped by a skull. "Matching?"

Eliza grinned. "We are. Lena made these. You'll meet her soon. We better head inside."

THE LARGE CONFERENCE room held rows of chairs, most of them filled. Harris and Eliza led Celeste to a row near the front where they'd saved several seats.

The keynote was offered by a woman named Dorothy who described the near-death experience she'd had decades before. She'd died during a boating accident and passed into the afterlife, where she'd experienced a stream of images about future events, many of which had come to pass. She'd interacted with her father, who'd died years before, and her daughter, who'd lived for only weeks after her birth.

Harris spoke third. He stood at the podium, his blue eyes scanning the crowd. They landed briefly on Celeste, and he smiled.

"Some of you have heard my story before, many of you perhaps, but for some reason Dorothy asked me to share it again this year and, as we all know, if we're given the choice to come back, the story of the other side is an important one to tell. It's the story of our truth, that we are not merely these meat suits."

The crowd laughed.

"I used to roll my eyes at those wooden inspirational signs you'd see for sale at craft stores, 'You are made from stardust' and the like. Imagine my surprise when I died and discovered we actually are made from stardust." He chuckled. "That was the least of the shocks I was in store for.

"Most of us like a little background when we hear a near-death story, so let me take you back to the months before I died. I was living in Traverse City, happily married to Nell, my wife of eleven years. My daughter, Bonnie, had just turned five. She was starting kindergarten in the fall. My wife, a nurse, had planned a summer trip for us to the Upper Peninsula, to Pictured Rocks. A couple days of camping, swimming, the usual northern Michigan adventures. I was a detective with a busy caseload and sort of dreading the trip. Looking back now, I believe I understood what was coming, but of course we can only understand that once we're shown how we design our lives on the other side.

"The week was great. Beautiful weather. Bonnie swam like a fish. Nell got some reading in and I spent way too much time thinking about a couple of cases back in Traverse City. On our way home, we stopped for lunch at a little pancake house. It had been sprinkling all morning, the first crummy weather of the trip, and as we left the diner it started to downpour. I contemplated pulling over, and sometimes I think about that now. Was it a nudge from my higher self? The part of me that knew I was minutes away from an exit for myself, my wife and Bonnie and I was being given the chance to not take this one, to choose an alternate death? I still don't have an answer for that.

"Not five miles down the road from the diner, a pickup truck driven by a young man on his way back to start his fall semester at Northern pulled out in front of a woman driving a large SUV coming toward us. The driver swerved into my lane and hit us head-on."

12

Harris paused, looked toward the ceiling. Celeste felt the grief rising up, the memory stark in his eyes when he returned them to the crowd.

"The next seconds, minutes, are a blur. I remember my wife's scream and then the crunch of metal and the sensation of rain on my face. The next instant I was out of my body and staring down at the wreckage and... paramedics arrived and they were working on Nell and they needed the jaws of life to get Bonnie..." His voice broke. He took a breath.

Celeste, heart trapped behind her ribs that seemed to be shrinking, closed her eyes and willed the unshed tears to stay buried.

"To get Bonnie from the car," he continued. "They also needed those for me. I understood that Bonnie and my wife were already gone, that I too was dead. I remember moving upwards and then all of these beings surrounded me. It was the most incredible love, and I knew these beings. They had no form. I think of them now as my soul family and we've been traveling together for a very long time. We'd witnessed many of each other's lives and they were there to welcome me back to the true life, the eternal life of infinite love. This went on for some time and I saw other lives they'd lived and I'd lived, but I can no longer recall specific details about those lives. Then I began to watch a review of this life as if on a giant screen. And as I watched I felt the emotions of every person in every interaction. How I'd made people feel loved and seen, how I'd hurt people, either intentionally or not. And I felt it, I felt their emotion.

"What happened on the other side was timeless—endless. That's how much personal transformation it brought, how much information I absorbed. But as many of you know, it wasn't long at all, not by our human clocks. I didn't have a choice to come back." He stared at the floor for a moment. "When I first started listening to people's near-death stories and heard some people had been given a choice to return, that bothered me. If I could have, I would have stayed. I didn't want to come back to this life.

"My wife and daughter were dead. I've had some time now and I understand that before I came into this life, I'd already chosen that death and to return, and they, my wife and daughter, their souls, their eternal selves, offered to do this for me—to die in this life for my growth, the growth of my soul. We agree before we come in how we will assist each other during this lifetime." He smiled and brushed his hands through his hair. It had gotten a bit longer since Celeste had last seen him. "That's never an easy point to explain to grumpy Uncle Ed at Christmas dinner. This idea that we signed up for all the suffering and then chose to forget it."

The audience laughed.

"So anyway, I came back, through no choice of my own, with the awareness that, no matter how uncomfortable it might be, I'm meant to share this story." He gestured at the crowd. "This is my real work now. I'm still a detective and that matters, but the truth is that it all matters. Smiling at the barista who made my coffee this morning is as important as putting a murderer in prison. Most people can't understand that, but I know all of you can. That's the impact we each have every day. We all have a purpose here and it's not about some grand accomplishment, it's bringing kindness and love into the world in every interaction. So that's ultimately my message to you. Stop defining your life by the big goals. It's the small stuff that counts."

AFTER SEVERAL MORE NEAR-DEATH STORIES, the assembly broke for lunch.

Celeste followed Harris and Eliza to where a trio of people stood outside the hotel.

"Celeste, meet Lena, Taylor and Jack," Eliza told her.

"Instead of the Witches of Eastwick, we're the witches of East Bay." Lena laughed, offering a hand covered in silver rings. Metal bracelets clinked on her wrist and, in Lena, Celeste saw the persona she'd expected when meeting Eliza. Like Eliza and Harris, Lena wore a 'memento mori' t-shirt, but hers was paired with a long black lace skirt cinched at the waist by a belt with a crescent moon buckle. Smoky eye makeup, black lipstick that matched her black fingernails and long flowing dark hair completed her look.

"I prefer warlock," Jack said wryly, shaking Celeste's hand, "and I live outside of Detroit."

"Oh, come on," Lena said, bumping Jack with her hip. "Warlocks of Detroit isn't nearly as mysterious."

"It sounds downright scary to me," Harris said.

"Nice to meet you, Celeste," Taylor interrupted, extending her hand. "Don't let Lena's look put you off."

"Really," Lena agreed. "Believe it or not, I was actually like this before my near-death experience. Drove my parents wonky. Wicked cane, by the way." Lena gestured at Celeste's cane.

"Thank you," Celeste murmured.

"Anyway," Eliza broke in. "This is our group. Me, Harris, Lena, Taylor and Jack started meeting, what, two years ago?"

"Yep. Two years and two months," Jack said. "I was only three months out from my NDE." He shifted his attention to Celeste. "I walked into the wrong hotel. I was in Grand Rapids for a conference and got turned around, ended up here and who should I ask for directions but Taylor, who knew right away I'd had an NDE."

Taylor smiled, tucked a strand of light hair behind her ear. "I'd dreamed of him the night before. Knew to expect him."

"She even knew my name."

"Really?" Celeste considered the woman, who looked slightly embarrassed by the attention.

"It's not always that clear," Taylor said.

"Thai? Ooh, or Indian food?" Lena asked, staring at her phone.

"I was leaning towards a burger," Jack admitted.

"Jack. Do you know how often I get to eat at restaurants that serve something other than burgers? Twice a year. You will not take this from me," Lena said.

"I vote Indian," Harris said. "I've had a hankering for butter chicken."

"Seconded," Taylor added. "That place we went last time had the best rice pudding."

"I'll throw my hat in the Indian basket. Celeste, have a preference?" Eliza asked.

Celeste wasn't hungry. She was overwhelmed, her brain buzzing with the stories shared that morning. More than anything she wanted a drink. "I'm open to whatever."

"That means she's with us," Lena said. "Jack, you're outnumbered."

The Indian restaurant was three blocks from the hotel and the group walked. They were seated in a long table in a back room. Celeste ordered the butter chicken and, feeling Scotch might be a bit too extreme for lunch, opted for a beer.

Lena reached across the table and pinched Jack. She grinned and pointed at the ceiling. "There's your answer."

Celeste looked up, unsure what Lena could see that she could not.

"What?" Jack asked, also staring at the ceiling.

"Listen," Lena said. "The song. *It Never Rains in Southern California.*"

Jack nodded his head slowly. "Ha. Good call. I wasn't even paying attention."

"What was the question?" Harris asked.

"I've been on the fence about visiting an old college friend in San Diego," Jack explained. "I was just telling Lena about it on the walk here."

"The universe always answers," Lena said. "You just have to listen."

The waiter delivered their drinks and Celeste squeezed lemon into her tea and took a sip.

Taylor leaned toward her. "You have an angry ghost."

Celeste blinked at the woman. "Excuse me?"

"You're already aware of her, right? I sense she's made herself known to you."

Celeste nodded slowly. "I don't know who she is. Can you see her?"

"Not right now. I saw her the first time when you were getting coffee this morning at the hotel and again on our walk here. She's giving off some very hostile energy."

"I can feel her too," Jack added.

Celeste shifted her attention to Jack.

"What are you guys talking about?" Lena asked, leaning forward in her seat.

"Celeste's ghost. Can you feel her?" Taylor asked.

Lena pursed her lips, eyes sweeping over Celeste. "I'm not getting her. Wait, I'm seeing apples. Does that mean anything?"

"I might be picking up something," Eliza admitted. "A name that starts with B. Brenda? Bethany?"

Celeste shook her head. "I don't know who she is. I've seen someone, a woman. I think she's connected to a young woman who's asked for my help, but I don't understand why she's angry. I'm helping River."

"She's probably not angry with you," Lena said. "I've encountered spirits who are angry about their death, about the abrupt way they passed. That anger is part of their tether to the world, the reason they struggle to transition completely."

"Do you work as a medium as well? Professionally?" Celeste asked.

Lena nodded. "Among other things. My best friend and I opened a metaphysical shop last year. I do mediumship readings and tarot."

"Do you like it?"

"More like love it." Lena stuck a piece of naan in her mouth. "Though it's not without its risks. I've encountered a few unstable people who seem to take it personally if the loved one they wanted to talk to doesn't come through. I can't always get them. That's just the way it is. Not to mention the non-believers who think I'm doing the Devil's work. They're fun." She rolled her eyes.

"People really don't understand the sacrifice you make to live that kind of life openly," Eliza added. "I've talked to so many clairvoyants or mediums who couldn't take it. They have special abilities after their near-death and they understand part of their purpose now involves sharing that gift and enlightening people who don't realize it exists. So they share and then nine out of ten people turn on them. I worked for a while with a psychic who kept telling her uncle to get his heart checked. He laughed it off, even called her out at a big family dinner and said she was seeking attention. He died of a massive heart attack a few weeks later. Instead of recognizing that she knew what was coming, her family believed the stress she'd put on him by even mentioning a potential heart issue caused his death."

"That's ridiculous," Celeste murmured.

Eliza nodded. "Don't think for a minute we don't still live in some very medieval times. The world might look modern, but human beings don't evolve as fast as technology. The witch-burning mentality is alive and well and, more often than not, it finds an easy target in people who have psychic abilities. That's the crucible of coming back from the other side with these gifts. You know the truth, you feel compelled to share it because you understand it will ultimately liberate humans from suffering, but when you share it, you're ostracized and hated and labeled a charlatan and a liar."

"Hear, hear." Lena held up her glass and the others in the group clinked their own against hers.

"Let's not scare her," Taylor said.

"Do you work as a medium?" Celeste asked Taylor.

"Oh, God, no." She shook her head. "I don't have a thick enough skin for that kind of abuse."

As they walked back toward the hotel, Celeste noticed ravens filling a maple tree on the sidewalk in front of them.

"Guardian angels," Lena said, gesturing at the dark birds.

Celeste stared at them. "Are they? I've been… seeing them ever since my accident."

"They're talking," Lena said, smiling. "Anyone getting anything?"

Celeste looked at the group, who'd all shifted their focus to the branches filled with birds.

"Nothing specific, but I agree. They have a protective energy. I think they're watching over you," Jack told Celeste.

When they reached the hotel, a pretty woman wearing a long peach-colored skirt and white sleeveless blouse hurried over. Harris waved, stepped toward her and his lips brushed her cheek. Celeste's stomach tightened, and she looked to the ground, unsure of the sudden discomfort she felt witnessing the moment of intimacy.

Harris guided the woman toward Celeste. "Robin, this is Celeste. You know Eliza. And this is Lena, Taylor and Jack."

"Lovely to meet you all," Robin said, shaking their hands. "I've been so looking forward to the conference today. I had hoped to make it this morning, but I'm in town for a patient advocacy seminar and couldn't get away."

Celeste studied the woman, the easy way she leaned into Harris as they returned to the conference room. They were clearly dating. Had it been going on for a while? Harris hadn't mentioned her, but then she hadn't seen him in more than a month.

They filed together into a long row and took their seats. Occasionally Celeste heard Robin whisper something to Harris, and she strained to pick up on their conversation, then, embarrassed at her interest, forced her focus back to the stage.

13

After the conference ended, Robin returned to the hospital for the second part of her training and the rest of the group split up for their hotels.

"Take a walk?" Harris asked Celeste. "You can catch me up on this woman you're helping."

"That'd be great. There's a park up the block here."

"I saw a pie place on the corner. Mind if we grab a piece? I've had a craving for key lime."

"Sure, but what if they don't serve key lime?"

"They do."

"How do you know?"

He winked at her. "I just do."

Celeste walked beside Harris through the park. Lilac trees released their heady perfume, clumps of purple flowers bobbing in the breeze. Celeste explained the letter she'd received from River and her subsequent visit to Baraboo.

"Sounds like an interesting puzzle to put together," he said. "With the added caveat of an angry ghost? What's that all about?"

"She first showed up the night I received the letter from

River. I saw her on the street, didn't realize she wasn't real until... until she was gone, just not there anymore."

"Do you think it's River's mother?"

"I'm not sure. I'm not getting a clear connection, but I sense she's connected to River. The social worker who did River's intake suspected her father killed her mother. She mentioned River might have witnessed a violent act against her mother based on some drawings River did."

Harris stuffed his hands in his pockets. "You may be searching for a murder victim then, not simply a birth mother."

"It's possible."

"Not so long ago, you told me the situation with Joanna and Katie was a one-time deal."

"It was. River's mother might not even be dead."

"Your tone lacks conviction. You think she's dead."

"I'm trying to keep an open mind until evidence points me elsewhere."

"Evidence, huh? Already got your corkboard set up?"

Celeste frowned. She had assembled her board the night before, but hadn't yet tacked any information on it. "Maybe."

He chuckled. "What else is going on? Have you heard from Joanna?"

"We chatted a couple weeks ago. She's good, liking Arizona, mentally preparing herself for the scorching summer ahead. There is something else I wanted to talk to you about, though."

"What's that?"

"The police suspect the person who hit me did it on purpose."

Harris slowed and looked at her. "They do?"

"Yes. A woman who lives not far from the site of the accident said the SUV swerved to hit me."

"Do they have a make and model of the vehicle?"

"Yes. A Jeep Cherokee. The color is called winter chill pearl, which is basically silver."

"And do you know anyone who drives one of those?"

"No. I looked up the car to see if I'd ever seen it in the neighborhood. I didn't recognize it."

Harris frowned, rubbed the back of his neck. "Were you having any trouble with anyone before it happened?"

Celeste shook her head. "Not really. I've gone over it in my mind. There was some tension at work. That's not unusual in a lab. Everyone is scrambling to get their drug into clinical trials."

"And how about things with Jonathan before you were hit?"

Celeste frowned. "Everything was fine. And Jonathan is not that kind of person. He'd never do something like that."

"Have the detectives working the case questioned him?"

"I'm sure they did right after it happened."

"Have you tried to get a sense of the driver? Psychically?"

Celeste stared at the park bench where a woman sat alone reading a paperback copy of Ann Rule's *Dead Before Sunset*. "I did try once to open myself to that information. What came up was my near-death experience. I didn't get any impression of the person in the vehicle. Honestly, I'm still not sure I believe it. My neighbor said the driver looked like they swerved to hit me, but..." Celeste shook her head. "What if they dropped their cigarette and leaned over to pick it up, or a bee flew through their window and stung them?"

Harris raised an eyebrow.

"What? It's feasible."

"Sure. But you're ignoring a critical point. The driver should have seen you well before the split-second moment of impact, right? You said it's a stretch of quiet neighborhood road."

"Right."

"So long before the killer bee lobbed its attack, that driver was aware you were walking down the road."

"Maybe it was some junkie tripping on acid and they feared I was a zombie."

He smiled. "I see you're willing to accept any wild theory except the one that's most likely."

"Is it most likely, though? That someone tried to murder me during my morning walk?"

"It's a time when you're alone and the walk was part of your routine. A person would take those things into account when plotting such an act. Smart criminals do their research."

Celeste brushed a hand through her hair, wanted to swipe the scenario from her head. She'd been relegating it to the back of her mind because contemplating it made her insomnia worse, made her brain feel as if she'd tossed it on a treadmill and left it to run and run, no stop button, no exit point. "Would you want to believe someone tried to kill you?"

"No one wants to believe that, Celeste. But ignoring it puts you in danger."

"I'm not afraid to die anymore."

He nodded. "That aside, you're here. You returned to this life for a reason. Finding out who tried to do this to you might be part of that reason. Consider the person who did this is just some unhinged nut having a breakdown. What if next time they swerve into a group of little kids walking to school?"

Celeste's stomach plunged. She hadn't considered the possibility of the driver killing someone else. "That changes things then."

"Remember, it's all connected. Nothing happens by chance. Examining the moment that took our life is very important. In your case, it may make all the difference in someone else's life. You had the life review. Every moment, every action or non-action matters, can change everything."

"Jesus," she muttered. "I thought we were going to get a piece of pie, Harris."

He grinned. "Humble pie."

A BLAST of warmth and sugar-scented air enveloped them when they walked into the little bakery. Bistro tables crowded the sidewalk outside the large windows. A dozen or more pies covered the counter beneath a large chalkboard sign that listed the menu. In the cold case sat a key lime pie, thick with fluffy meringue, next to a little placard that read 'Today's Special.'

They each ordered a piece and carried it to an outdoor table.

"I understand you're not keen to talk about the hit-and-run, but bear with me. Let's make a list, a few people who could potentially want to hurt you." He forked a bite of pie in his mouth, then took out his phone.

Celeste picked at her pie and watched the crosswalk change to green. A group of people dressed for work—suits and ties and pleated skirts—hurried across the road. "The only person who comes to mind is Randy Mills or the Boyd family, but obviously I didn't meet them until after the accident."

"How about at work? You said it's a competitive environment."

Celeste bit her lip, nodded. "A couple of people might have been unhappy with me before I was hit. A guy named Hugh seemed to think I'd advised our group leader not to promote him, which absolutely isn't true. Now would it have been a terrible mistake to promote him? Yes. He's a typical scientist—good with chemistry, terrible with people—and he'd have been managing five scientists."

"Could he have sensed you felt that way?"

Celeste considered her demeanor around the lab in the weeks before the accident. She nodded. "I'd been pretty consumed by a drug I was modifying and might not have been concealing my true feelings about him."

"What's his full name?"

Celeste frowned. "I feel weird giving you his name."

Harris stared at her, gaze steady, unwilling to drop it.

"Fine. Hugh Thatcher."

Harris typed it into his phone. "Anyone else at work?"

Celeste pictured Liz, who'd she seen at dinner days before. She'd been her usual unpleasant self. "Liz Ratcliffe. She'd been working on an antidepressant she was pretty excited about, but when I tested it, I couldn't replicate her results. I advised the group leader we needed way more in vivo testing before they could apply for clinical trials. She was pissed, didn't speak to me for weeks, and I suspect intentionally squished my sandwich a few times in the breakroom refrigerator."

"Really?"

"Yeah. We scientists are not a confrontational bunch. Passive-aggressive attacks are preferable—thus the squished sandwich. Which is why I'm pretty confident if any of my colleagues wanted to get rid of me, they'd have used what we know best—drugs."

"Hmm... On that note, did you get ill at all in the weeks or months before you were hit?"

"No."

"Anything else unusual happen? Anything go missing from your desk, your car?"

"No. Jonathan and I usually drove together."

"How were things really with Jonathan? You said everything was fine, which is basically a non-answer."

"He was home that morning. I saw him during my near-death experience running down the road, frantic. It wasn't him."

"Humor me."

She sighed. "I was busy. We both were. Work consumed our lives, and we were both content with that. We never fought."

"Do you fight now?"

Celeste took a bite of pie and imagined Jonathan's near-constant irritation with her. "Things have not been great since the accident."

"Do you have life insurance?"

"Sure. Dynamic Laboratories has a policy on each of us for one hundred thousand and we both have a personal policy of... I don't know, a couple hundred thousand dollars."

"Any financial troubles?"

"Before the accident, we were two workaholics who both made good money and rarely spent it." She laughed. "No money troubles."

"What are Jonathan's vices? Gambling, girls, anything like that?"

Celeste snorted. "God, no. If anything, his vice is his lack of vices."

"No one is that clean."

"Spoken like a true detective who spends his days brushing up against people who are drug addicts and criminals. Neither of us have vices. I guess mine was the Dear Celeste column, if I had to choose something."

"Which you kept secret from him?"

"Yes."

"Why not tell him about it?"

Celeste shrugged. "He would have considered it odd."

"And if he discovered it? And found out you'd lied to him?"

"I didn't lie about it," she said, annoyed. "I didn't tell him. It never came up."

"Have either of you ever had an affair?"

"Of course not."

"Okay." Harris continued eating, eyes fixed on his plate as if deep in thought.

"Are you sensing something about Jonathan, about his involvement?" Celeste asked, a sudden tingling rippling down her spine.

Harris massaged his chin, squinted at the ground. "I don't know. Sometimes my detective brain and my psychic brain get muddled. Statistically, the husband makes sense, but maybe there's something more."

"It wasn't him. No way. Seriously, he's not that kind of person."

"Good to see you," Celeste told him when they returned to her truck.

"And you." He hugged her. "Oh, one more thing." He jogged over to his car and returned a moment later with a 'memento mori' t-shirt.

"Does this mean I've been invited into the club?"

"It's official."

"Before you go, do you get any sense about River? The woman I'm helping in Wisconsin? Jonathan is all over me for staying with strangers. He's acting like I'm the most reckless person on the planet."

Harris laughed. "I wouldn't go that far, but I'd be wary of staying with people I don't know. Honestly, I think you should help her. I can see your face light up when you talk about it. Clearly, what you're doing feels right. Still, I'd keep your guard up. Okay?"

"I will. Thanks, Harris."

14

River pressed her toes into the floor and sent the chair rocking gently. Hope slept in her lap. Her hand-sewn bear dropped to the floor. Rain pattered the metal roof and streaked down the windows. It was a beautiful moment, the soft bubble on her daughter's flower bud mouth, the wisp of red-blonde hair that fluttered with her breath. Luna dozed on the rug in front of the wood burner—a rarity for the energetic husky, her paws occasionally spasming, a disjointed bark as she chased rabbits in her dreams.

There'd been a time not long ago when River would have grasped the magnitude of such a moment, the perfection of her simple, sweet life, but today, like so many days lately, her stomach roiled as if she'd swallowed a belly full of snakes. Her nerves were on edge, her heart beating a little too fast. There was no urgency in the moment and yet...

She shifted and adjusted Hope's head into the crook of her tingling arm. Soon she'd move her to her bed, but just then River needed the heaviness of her daughter's slumbering body, the steady rhythm of her breath.

Outside, the wind picked up and suddenly the door

slammed open and crashed into the wall. River jumped and Hope startled awake, blinking up at her mother, her lower lip trembling as she started a half-asleep cry.

"Sshh... it's okay." River stood and hurried to the door, Hope snuggled in her arms, and closed it with her foot. Luna had woken and sat staring at the door, ears perked. She looked at River as if to ask who'd opened it.

"Beats me," River told her, carrying Hope to the crib in their bedroom. She laid her inside and pulled a quilt, made by the aunts at Be Free, up to Hope's chest.

Her little girl drifted back off to sleep.

River had a hundred things to do. Work on the set list for the upcoming tour, get baby food made for Hope, wash laundry and tend to the animals. But she'd slept poorly the night before —couldn't honestly remember the last night she'd slept well.

River climbed into bed and closed her eyes.

"RIVER... RIVER!"

River woke to a woman screaming and to Owen shouting her name, his hands on her shoulders, his face inches from her own. He looked afraid. His eyes were big in the lamplight. Hope began to wail.

The scream stopped when River closed her mouth and, though she'd hardly begun to form a coherent thought, she realized the shrieking had emerged from her own lips.

"Hope," she whispered, her voice raspy.

Owen blinked. "I'll get her. Are you okay?"

"I'm okay," she said, waving him off. "Get Hope." River sat up, swallowed. Her throat felt raw.

For the next ten minutes, they hardly spoke. River got up and took Hope, carried her to the rocking chair, and lulled her back to sleep. River's own eyes were sticky, her head full of cotton, but something kept her awake, a terror that had followed her from the void. She'd been having a nightmare, could not grasp even a tendril of it. Nothing save the fear remained.

When Hope began to snore softly, Owen took her and carried her back to her crib. He emerged a moment later and sat on the chair across from River.

"You had a nightmare?"

River nodded. "I don't remember it." And she didn't, not really. Although something remained—a mechanical song, a haunting lullaby.

"You just started screaming." He rubbed his hands across his face, through his hair. "I think my soul jumped out of my body for a minute."

"I'm sorry," she murmured, eyelids so heavy, but her brain refusing to let them fall.

"Don't be sorry, River. Never be sorry for that. I just... I want to help. It's my job to protect you, and I feel like I'm failing."

"You're not. You're so good. More than I deserve."

He shook his head, stood and walked to her. He crouched and took her hands in his, kissed her fingers. "What can I do? What do you need?"

She searched for an answer, found the belief that always rose up. *You can't help me. I'm broken.*

Sometimes River feared Owen would figure her out. When they'd met, he'd worked so hard to get close to her, but she'd been terrified of him—knew instantly he was a boy who'd grown up in a house with his own bedroom and a mother who cooked big Sunday morning breakfasts and a dad who taught him to play ball. He'd likely been popular in high school, gotten a car at sixteen, always had health insurance to see a doctor if he developed a sinus infection or sprained his ankle. He'd lived an entirely different life from River, who'd been shuffled between foster homes, had more cases of head lice than she could count, lived in houses that were boiling in the summer and freezing in the winter. Until she'd gone to live at Be Free, she'd never once owned a pair of tennis shoes or a coat that hadn't been a hand-me-down.

And there'd been more, worse things, darker things, but she'd managed to force those things into the back rooms of her mind. She'd locked them away, but a part of her still feared she'd somehow brought it all on herself. Her own father had abused her in that way. It was as if he knew at her birth that she was merely meant to be used and discarded, and so when other foster dads and foster brothers did it as well, she'd almost expected it. Parts of her had beaten those beliefs. She'd written the letters, told the truth, stood up to Torrence, but the little damaged girl never went away. She was sitting there now, looking out at Owen, terrified he'd see her, see the girl no one wanted.

"I need to take a walk," she said, throat full of tears she knew wouldn't come.

He stood, touched her gently on the arm. He was holding back, wanted to wrap his arms around her, but he didn't.

"Okay," he said, then his face darkened and he shook his head. "Actually, no. It's dark out and..."

"I've taken lots of walks at night. I'm not going to the road. Just out to the chicken coop."

"Do you mind if I watch you? Just to be safe."

She stared at him. "Okay."

River slid on her rubber boots and walked out the door. The night was chilly and damp from the earlier rain. She wrapped her sweater tighter around her body and tried to ignore Owen's eyes following her. It was unusual for him to caution her about walking on their own property, and she feared he wasn't worried about what she might encounter so much as what she might do.

15

Celeste had spent most of the day organizing the corkboards on her office wall with names. A yellow Post-it with River's name occupied the center. Above her, she placed two additional sticky notes, one for Ted, River's dad, and a blank one for River's mom. Celeste had three other names on the boards, but she hadn't connected them to River. They were listed as distant relatives on her ancestry account and none of them had family trees, so Celeste wasn't sure how they were related.

She left the room, closed the door behind her, and walked into the spare room. Romeo lay stretched on the bed in a slant of sun.

"Look at you, pretty boy." She ran her fingers down his back and he purred.

After a moment, Cash appeared in the doorway. He stared at the bed, giving it a wide berth and pressing his ears back when Romeo sat up.

"Ready to meet your new brother?" Celeste murmured. She moved to the floor and scratched Cash's neck as he continued staring at the kitten.

Romeo jumped off the bed and approached Cash, rubbed against him, and flopped on his side. Cash smelled him and stalked from the room.

"Aww, don't worry, Romeo. He'll warm up in no time."

Celeste picked up the kitten and walked down to the kitchen. She'd skipped lunch—too busy searching online for links to River's potential family. She took out a box of crackers and ate a handful from the box.

Through the sliding glass doors, she saw Jonathan red-faced as he trudged up the back porch and yanked open the door. He froze when he saw her, his face pale. She hadn't heard him come home.

"What?" she asked.

His eyes narrowed, and he turned and looked back toward the tree line. "How did you get back here? You doubled back? Tried to trick me?"

"What are you talking about? I just came down. I was in my office."

"I followed you into the woods not five minutes ago. I yelled your name."

"It wasn't me."

He frowned, expression unbelieving. "Who was it then? It looked like you. It was you. What is this?" He blinked at her. "You're screwing with me for some reason?"

"Jonathan, I was not in the woods. Why would I lie to you?" The kitten wriggled in her arms.

"That thing looks like it has fleas."

"It does not have fleas," she said, holding Romeo closer.

"Fine. We have therapy this evening. Or did you forget?"

"I remembered. Just let me change quick. Oh, and Adam is coming to town for a continued ed thing and he's going to crash here."

"Crash? Are we a frat house now?"

"You know what I mean."

"Well, hopefully I'll see him. I'll probably be late at the lab late most of the nights this week and since Adam likes to sleep in, I might have to catch him next time."

"That's fine."

"Tell her about Wisconsin," Jonathan blurted the moment Celeste sat down on the therapist's couch.

Joyce smiled and crossed her legs. "That's fine if you're ready, Celeste."

Celeste bent and set her purse on the floor next to the couch. "Sure. I went to Wisconsin a few days ago."

"And why is that?" Joyce asked.

"A writer to the column asked for help to locate her birth mother."

"And were you successful?"

Celeste noticed Jonathan's knee. He'd inched it away from hers. "Ugh. No. Not yet. It's going to take some time and some digging."

"Which means what?" Jonathan demanded. "That you're planning to go back?"

"Probably at some point," Celeste said.

Joyce smiled, though Celeste saw the strain in her expression. "Okay. And clearly this intention bothers you, Jonathan. Tell us about that."

"Of course it bothers me. She's running all over the damn country meeting total strangers. The last time she did this, she nearly got killed."

"I'm not looking for a missing teenager this time. I'm helping trace this woman's birth family. It's completely different." Even as Celeste uttered the words, she knew they weren't entirely true. Something dark drifted in the shadows of River's past. Celeste feared she'd begun to court it.

"Is it necessary for you to travel to Wisconsin to help this person?"

"Necessary?" Celeste massaged her leg. "Ummm... I think it is. Yes."

Jonathan snorted.

Joyce pressed her lips together. "Why is it necessary?"

"Most of her documents are there and... well... her history is complicated. If I'm there, I can track people down."

Joyce frowned. "That does sound a little risky, Celeste. You're still healing, still walking with a cane. Visiting people you don't know—"

"I'm careful," Celeste interrupted.

"I see. What's the compromise here?" Joyce asked. "Remember how we talked about meeting in the middle?"

"Didn't I compromise enough the last time you did this and nearly got murdered?" Jonathan demanded.

Celeste stared at him, the hard set of his jaw. "No. You didn't compromise. You brought me home and left me stranded so I couldn't go back up north."

His eyes went wide and, when they locked on hers, Celeste struggled to hold his gaze. "If you'd been honest with me from the beginning instead of feeding me some drivel about fresh air and nature, I might have been more supportive."

"If you hadn't been looking at me like I was insane since the accident—" Celeste retorted, but Joyce held up a hand.

"Okay. Let's not get sucked into the past here. We've talked at length about that and we want to come into the present now. Am I right?"

Jonathan said nothing. He crossed his legs and stared out the window.

"Yes," Celeste murmured. She released a long breath and tried to calm her jittery body.

It wasn't fair to be angry with Jonathan, but she continually bucked against the sense that he'd shifted from her husband to some authority figure, intent on control and open hostility when she didn't accede to his demands. In truth, they'd built their life together and only Celeste had diverted and begun to speed down the road less travelled, giving little thought to Jonathan plodding along on the course they'd both set out on years before. It wasn't fair for her to simply expect him to catch up, to change course, and yet she did.

"I'll try to do more of the work from home or check in more or whatever. What do you need me to do, Jonathan?" Celeste asked.

He didn't speak for a moment. When he finally turned back, his eyes were stormy. "The truth? I want it all to stop. The advice column. The running off to meet strangers. But I don't get to ask that, right? You've resigned from the lab. This is what you do now... even if you don't get paid for it."

"I still have a lot of savings."

"Even so. Is this what you intend to do with your life? Answer questions on an advice column all hours of the night? Sleep until noon?"

"I rarely do that."

He shrugged, brushed invisible lint from his pants. "I don't want you to do this. You asked me what I want. That's what I want."

Behind Jonathan, high on a bookshelf, a pendulum that hung above a sand tray began to move slightly. Celeste stared at the little silver pendulum, its sharp point carving unseen designs in the sand beneath it.

"Celeste?" Joyce's voice pulled her back.

"Sorry, yes. I mean, I'm sorry you feel that way, Jonathan, but—"

"But you're going to do what you want to do."

16

The previous day with Jonathan had been strained and, when Celeste woke, she was relieved he'd already left for work.

After making her coffee, she visited her physical therapist, who said she could start walking without her cane. At home, she practiced moving through the house and up and down the stairs, her cane tucked in the coat closet.

In the afternoon, Celeste closed herself in her office and turned on her computer, navigating to an online newspaper archive. She continued tracking family members connected to River.

After a while, with little progress, she pulled out the envelope from Cordelia and examined the letter from the social worker who'd originally worked with River. The organization was called Faith Lutheran Services, with an address in Madison, Wisconsin.

Celeste found their phone number online and called the office. A woman answered.

"Hi. I'm searching for a social worker who worked at Faith Lutheran Services twenty years ago. I know that's a long time ago, but I'm hoping you might have her information somewhere. Her first name was Mona? I don't have a last name, but I believe it started with a W."

"Mona Wilkens? Sure, I know Mona. She's not in foster care anymore, but she runs the food bank. Hold on." Celeste listened as the woman she'd been speaking to called out. "Deirdre, is Mona in the pantry today?"

Celeste couldn't hear the response, but a moment later, the woman returned. "Still there?"

"I am."

"Mona's in the pantry. I'm going to transfer you there."

"Thank you."

The phone rang several times before a woman answered.

"Faith Lutheran Services Food Pantry. This is Mona."

"Mona, hi. My name is Celeste Cleary. I'm actually calling about a child I believe you placed almost twenty years ago."

"Twenty years ago? Huh. Go on then. I can spare a few minutes, but I can't guarantee I'll remember. Was it a boy or a girl?"

"A girl. She was called Agnes, and she was abandoned at an apartment complex in Madison by her father, who might have been abusing her."

"Oh, golly. Sure. I remember her. Poor thing. Her father just left her there at that apartment building and never came back. Course, given what he'd been up to, it was probably a blessing."

"Do you happen to remember the woman who turned her over to the state? The woman who lived at the complex? I'm helping the girl—she goes by River now—locate her birth family and I thought the lady who cared for her might have some information. I know her name is Dottie Smith, but that's it."

"Hmm... that's where this'll get sticky. Even if I did know Dottie moved to Cottage Grove, which is just outside of Madison, because

I went to high school with her daughter and we're friends on Facebook, I couldn't give that information out." She sucked in a breath. "There I go again. This brain has no control over my mouth."

Celeste quickly wrote down the name of the city. "Any chance you have Dottie's number?"

"Now that I can't help you with, honey."

"I understand. Thank you. And there was never any luck locating the father who abandoned Agnes?"

Mona sighed. "It's fuzzy now, but I remember we spent some time trying to track him down once the girl got turned over to the state. She was interviewed by a child psychologist who was convinced she'd been molested and likely witnessed violence against her mother. We had a detective on the case at one point, but the father had left no discernible trace. We all hit a dead end and sadly, in my line of work, we're understaffed and overwhelmed. Once the girl was placed, searching for her father became less urgent and... eventually it faded. Best of luck on your search and thank you for calling. Warms my heart to know that girl made a life for herself despite those nasty beginnings."

"Thanks, Mona. I appreciate it."

Celeste returned to her computer and searched for Dottie Smith in Cottage Grove, Wisconsin. A phone number popped up on a people search database, but when she called it, the number was disconnected.

As Celeste ended the call, a text came through her phone.

Adam: *Just pulled into your driveway!*

Celeste logged off her computer and walked downstairs, greeting Adam at the door.

"I stopped for donuts!" He held up a bakery bag.

"Donuts for dinner?" she asked. "You better have a blueberry glazed in there."

"I did, but I ate it on the drive."

She snatched the bag from his hand and carried it to the kitchen. "How was your trip?"

"You mean my two-hour highway drive with the gorgeous views of billboards and semi-trucks? Uneventful, unless you count the minivan I passed where two teen girls flipped me off through the back window."

Celeste laughed. "There's no ruder creature than a teenage girl."

"They terrified me as a teenager, and still do today."

"Coffee with these?" she asked. "Or is it too late for coffee?"

"It's never too late. But I need something stronger. Margaritas?"

Celeste grimaced. "Donuts and margaritas? That sounds terrible."

"Poppycock. Come on, what do you have?" He opened a cupboard. "Please tell me we have a choice other than Scotch."

"There's vodka in the freezer and I think we have some orange juice."

"Screwdriver it is," he said, taking down a glass. "One for you?"

"I'll go for the Scotch," she said, pouring a glass.

Adam pulled a face. "I can barely smell that stuff without getting queasy."

"I always have had a stronger stomach than you. Want to have these on the porch?"

"As long as the mosquitos won't eat us alive."

"They haven't gotten bad yet. Not enough rain." Celeste carried her glass and the bag of donuts to the back deck.

Adam took out a glazed donut and plopped into a chair, propping his feet on the seat beside him. "Dad is coming to Michigan. I thought we could all go out to dinner."

"He is? Why?"

Adam stared at her, exasperated. "To see us, I suppose."

Celeste gazed back at him. "Don't give me that look. Since

when does he schedule visits to Michigan for the sole purpose of seeing his kids?"

"Celeste, Dad did the best he could. I've talked with my therapist a lot about our childhood and the truth is you and I don't have a clue what it'd be like to be a single parent. Can you even imagine? Your spouse walking out on you when you have a toddler and a baby?"

Celeste frowned, thought of their dad. He hadn't been a bad parent. He'd been an absent parent, always working and busy. They hadn't sat around a table and eaten dinners, played board games, gone to the park. But then again, who did that? Maybe no one except the families in sitcoms. "All right. Let's do dinner."

Adam clapped his hands together. "Perfect. I already made reservations for the Chop House."

"Oh, great. We can listen to him complain the whole time about how overpriced the steak is."

"The steak *is* overpriced, but the fried Brussels sprouts are to die for."

Celeste laughed. "I wouldn't go that far. Are you on a new anti-anxiety medicine?"

He made a face at her. "If I didn't know you better, I'd take offense to that. The answer is no."

"You seem so... easy-going."

"And normally I'm high-strung?"

"No. That's not what I'm saying at all. Truly. You just seem lighter."

"I am lighter. I met someone."

"You did?" Celeste grinned. "That's so exciting. What's her name?"

"Top secret. We've only gone out twice and it's a bit of a long-distance thing. I'm keeping her under wraps so I don't jinx myself. On that note, let's change the subject. How's the hip? It seems like you're moving better."

Celeste nodded. "Improving. I should tell you something though."

In the aftermath of what had occurred in Graves, Celeste's life had been momentarily consumed by that story. She'd told Adam about going to help Joanna and ultimately discovering a man Joanna trusted, her half-sister's uncle, had murdered her half-sister and multiple other young women. It had been more than enough fodder for their previous visit and, frankly, Celeste had been reluctant to examine the possibility that someone had intentionally swerved to hit her less than a mile from her home.

"The police believe the hit-and-run wasn't an accident."

Adam gaped at her. "Wait. What? Not an accident. So, they think...?"

"Someone hit me on purpose."

"No freaking way. Right? No way. Why would someone do that? *Would* someone do that? Who?"

"That's the mystery. Someone driving a silver SUV."

"How long have you known? Why am I just hearing about this?"

"I've been in a bit of denial."

"What does Jonathan think?"

"I don't know. I mean, obviously he doesn't know who did it."

"But he must be freaking out, right? Someone tried to kill you!"

Celeste took a bite, closed her eyes. She hadn't had a blueberry donut in years and the taste was instantly nostalgic. She remembered the little bakery she and Adam had walked to as children. It had been on their way to elementary school at their first house in Michigan and her father, never a breakfast maker, always gave them a dollar each so they could get a donut on their way to school. "I wouldn't say he's freaking out, no. We don't really talk about it."

Adam stared at her. "You don't talk about it? What else could you possibly talk about? Isn't he worried?"

Celeste imagined Jonathan the day before. Worried wasn't the term to describe him—angry, frustrated, fed up. "I think he's more worried—"

The door slammed behind them.

"He must be home," Celeste murmured.

Jonathan appeared a moment later, the top of his shirt unbuttoned, glass of red wine in hand. "What a day!" he said, eyes lit up. "We had a breakthrough on the PX962. Finally. You should have been there, Celeste. One tweak and the effects changed dramatically. It's early days, but—sorry. Hi, Adam. How are you?"

"Good, until Celeste told me the person who hit her did it intentionally."

Jonathan blinked at him, took a sip of his wine and then nodded. "That's what the police say anyway."

"But you don't believe them?" Adam asked, shooting a questioning gaze at Celeste.

"It just seems implausible. Who intentionally runs someone down in a neighborhood in broad daylight?"

"A psychopath," Adam said.

Jonathan shook his head. "I doubt it. If it was intentional I'd say it was a drug addict."

"A drug addict driving a newer-model SUV," Celeste said, playing devil's advocate with a theory she herself had considered.

"I'm not talking about a gibbering crackhead on the street, I'm talking about these new druggies, suburban wives who sit home pill-popping all day and drinking hard liquor." His eyes flickered to Celeste's glass.

Adam's face paled and Celeste, embarrassed, shifted her eyes to the woods, focusing on the trees and trying not to spit the acid words suddenly filling her mouth.

As if sensing how his comment had landed, Jonathan held up his hands in surrender. "It's only a thought. There are women who do. I wasn't trying to imply you do that. Not at all. I obviously wasn't referring to you. You're the one who got hit, for Christ's sake. I'm merely pointing out that not all drug dealers fit the stereotype."

Neither Adam or Celeste said anything and after a moment Jonathan cleared his throat. "Well... did you guys eat or... I can order pizza?"

"Pizza would be great. Thanks," Celeste said.

Jonathan hurried back into the house.

"Well, that was weird," Adam murmured.

"Yeah." In many ways, Celeste had lost touch with normalcy in her marriage. She no longer quite remembered a time when her and Jonathan's conversations hadn't been tense and loaded with unspoken hurt.

"What's going on with you two? Has it been this bad for a while?"

"For a few months. He's mad over everything." Celeste thought of him stomping onto the back porch, the fury in Jonathan's face. Despite her insistence she'd not taken him on a wild goose chase through the woods, he'd clearly not believed it wasn't her, and why should he? She couldn't tell him it was an angry spirit who'd attached herself to Celeste. He'd already tried to get her hospitalized once. If she started claiming a poltergeist had moved in, he might actually have her committed.

"But why is he mad at you? Shouldn't he be mad *with* you? At whoever tried to kill you?"

Celeste finished her drink. "I'm going to get a refill. Want another?"

Adam watched her, clearly didn't want to drop the subject. "No. I'm good for now."

Celeste and Adam stayed up talking until after midnight. When she climbed into bed, Jonathan was already asleep and snoring softly.

The dream took Celeste nearly as soon as she drifted into sleep.

She stood on the sidewalk gazing at the blue bungalow with the red shutters. It was dark. The windows glowed with lamplight. The front door stood ajar and music poured from the interior of the house.

Celeste knew she'd been here before and, despite the sweet exterior, sensed something terrible lay inside, something she didn't want to see, but her feet had begun to move, one foot after another. They made no sound as they struck the sidewalk and she looked down to see she was barefoot and leaving a trail of red footprints.

As she walked forward, something plummeted from the front door and rolled down the sidewalk, landing at her feet. Celeste stared down at a cracked doll's head, two glassy blue eyes staring up at her.

The cold tugged Celeste from the dream. She opened her eyes into the dark room and, when she released a breath, she saw the halo of white. The room was bitterly cold, as if she'd woken in the dead of winter with all the windows in the house thrown open. The temperature disoriented her and she groped beside her, finding Jonathan beneath the comforter, the heat of his back startling against her icy fingers.

Her heart pounded and, though she was sure they were alone in the bedroom, she felt as if the woman stood in the corner of the room watching them—watching her sleep.

Suddenly something crashed to the floor. Jonathan shot up. Celeste found the light switch on her bedside lamp and turned it on.

"What was that?" he asked, eyes wide.

Across the room, a large framed photograph of their wedding lay on the floor, splinters of glass speckling the carpet.

17

River sat on the stump near the stream. She propped her guitar on her legs and flicked the strings. She'd written a lot of songs in this place, allowing her thoughts to roam, her mouth to sing whatever came up. Sometimes it stuck, but today no words rolled off her tongue. She strummed the guitar and watched the sun-dappled water trickle over blue and gray stones.

Heavy as a river stone, washed clean. Heavy but empty. How could one be heavy, but empty?

The lyrics didn't make sense and yet... they did. That was how she felt. Heavy, but empty.

She sighed, flipped open her notebook and searched for the song she'd been working on days before. It wasn't yet a song, merely a string of words, no rhythm, no structure. Clay always said all songs begin as poetry and this song was little more than that.

The lean years shaped me
the hollow where love should have been
ribs wrapped tight, tighter searching for a substance to cradle, protect

but there was nothing there
And now my days are bursting with love
but my spindly ribs are too tight, my cage
they won't open to let you in, make space
the river is rushing but I am thirsty
the harvest was plentiful but I am starving

She sang the lyrics, but struggled to feel them, to form them into something more than scratches of ink on a sheet of lined paper.

A gust of wind shook the trees and blew River's hair off her face, fluttered the pages of her notebook. The sound of the stream disappeared for a moment and then, as quickly as it had arrived, the wind receded and quiet returned.

In the forest behind her, a twig snapped. River's head shot up. She twisted in the direction of the sound and studied the forest—the shapes of the trees, the bushes that had already begun to fill out. In deep summer, the forest would be a jungle; she'd have to stay on her footpath to prevent her hair getting caught by briars, her ankles scratched with thorns, but now in spring, it had not yet thickened. Still, she couldn't discern what had made the noise—a squirrel as likely as anything else, but her spine tingled and the hairs on her arms stood as if her body sensed something unseen.

River started back toward the house, cautious, alert for sound. Another branch crunched and she spun, ready to defend herself. Instead of a man lumbering toward her, she gazed at a small deer. A fawn, golden with white spots, watched her from the shade of a young maple tree.

River's heart had jumped into her throat at the sound, but now she smiled and stepped toward it.

"Hi, baby," she murmured. "Where's your mama, honey?"

The baby deer didn't move.

From the property she heard the sound of Owen's truck

returning home. The little deer's ears twitched and it turned and disappeared into the forest.

Owen waved as he climbed out of the truck. He unbuckled Hope from her seat and set her on the ground. She ran toward River, something extended in her hands. As she drew closer, River's eyes locked on the porcelain doll.

Without thinking, River snatched the doll from Hope's hand. She turned and flung it into the forest, scooping up Hope, who'd begun to scream. She sprinted toward the house, but Owen intercepted her, wrapping his arms around River and their hysterical daughter.

"Jesus, River. What'd you do that for? It was a gift."

Hope wriggled and cried out, reaching toward the dark place in the woods where River had flung the doll.

"No!" River shook her head, her whole body trembling. "She can't have it. I won't have it in the house. I won't."

"Okay. Calm down. Here, let me have her." He peeled Hope out of her arms, face lined with worry. "Hope, honey, listen to Daddy, okay? That dolly had a big ole bumble on it and Mama didn't want it to sting you. Okay? That's why she did that. Let's go inside and I'll make you an ice cream with fresh strawberries on top. Hmm? Does that sound good?"

Hope, tear-streaked, continued to stare at the forest. When she looked at River, her expression was wounded, fearful, and River tried to reach for her, but Hope buried her face in Owen's shoulder.

It was a half hour before Owen calmed Hope down enough to eat her ice cream and allow him to read her a book. When she fell asleep in his arms, he moved her to her crib. River sat in the living room, knees pulled against her chest, her body shaking.

"What happened out there? Why did you throw her doll?"

River stared at him, tried to put into words the horror she'd felt upon seeing that doll, but found no explanation that seemed worthy of her reaction. "Where did it come from?" River asked.

"It was in the mailbox. It was a birthday gift for Hope. There was a card with an apology they'd missed the day. Probably one of my brothers dropped it off. Why?"

"I don't know why, but..." She rubbed her arms, still prickled with gooseflesh. "When I saw it... I..." She shook her head. "You have to get rid of it. It can't come in the house."

"Okay," he said. "All right. I don't get it, but... obviously it bothers you."

"It does."

"It's gone then. I'll go put it in the trash right now. We'll tell Hope it had a bees' nest inside it. Problem solved."

OWEN AND HOPE had gone to bed hours before and River sat in the living room, thumbing through her notebook and thinking about the upcoming tour. Arnie had set everything up and he'd gotten them a coveted show at the Velvet Theater in Baraboo, a venue River had been dreaming about playing at ever since Clay took her to see Joanna Newsom in concert there years before.

She needed to go to bed. The days ahead were busy and she couldn't risk another day walking zombie-like around the property attempting to remember all the tasks she had to accomplish before the tour. She stood and walked into the bedroom, peered into Hope's crib. Her little girl slept on her belly, one arm flung above her head, her blanket bunched near her feet. River lifted the blanket, smoothed it out and draped it across her daughter's body. She studied the soft curve of Hope's face, her pudgy cheeks, her perfect pink mouth.

The ache came again then, longing and fear and guilt for her reaction to the doll. Underneath it all lived the sense that River was both there and not there, missing some critical piece of herself that Hope needed.

She moved to her bed and crawled beneath the comforter and listened to Owen's deep, steady breaths.

RIVER OPENED her eyes and stared at Owen's shirtless back. He slept on his side, facing away from her. Something had woken her, though she couldn't place it. She listened for Hope, but heard no sound from the crib.

Beyond the window on River's side of the bed, something crunched. She sat up and stared at the glass, dark on the moonless night. She hadn't shut the hand-sewn curtains, rarely did, and felt her skin prickle as she gazed at the darkness.

Someone watched her.

The thought sent an immediate jolt of fear through her body. For several minutes, she didn't move, waited to see if anything shifted outside the window. Nothing moved and finally she forced herself to lie back down and close her eyes.

18

Celeste and Adam had coffee and the last of the donuts for breakfast the following morning. They hugged goodbye in the driveway with plans to meet their dad for dinner the following week.

Celeste arrived to the Grand Rapids Public Library just before ten a.m. and made her way to the conference room where the genealogy course was being held.

Two women stood at the front of the room setting up a projector. Only three people occupied seats at the several long tables that filled the room.

"This is the genealogy course?" Celeste asked.

"It surely is," a petite woman in a long blue and white striped dress said. "You must be Celeste. Everyone else is checked in."

"Yes. I am. Should I sit anywhere?"

"Go right ahead. I'm Catherine and this is Tia. We're part of a volunteer group who use genetic genealogy to help people locate their birth families."

"Oh. Wow. I didn't even know such a group existed."

Catherine smiled. "Most people don't. We don't advertise, but we're there when people start looking."

The class lasted two hours and covered multiple ancestry websites including GED Match, an open-source DNA database that police used to track violent offenders using DNA samples taken from crime scenes. It was a cursory overview, but offered Celeste some helpful tips on how to better identify members of River's family.

After the class ended, Celeste approached Tia. "Do you have a minute?"

"Certainly."

"I'm trying to help a young woman who submitted her DNA to an ancestry site a few months ago. She got the results back, but there are only a couple of matches and they're pretty distant. I'm trying to figure out how to narrow down her parentage from there. I understand what you went over today, but wondered if you could point me toward some resources in the meantime, since the next course isn't for a few weeks."

"Do you have access to her results? If you do, we can log in and get started. Catherine, come on over. We'll tackle this as a trio."

Celeste pulled up River's login information on her phone and typed it into the computer. Her account popped up and Tia navigated around the site.

"Okay, so we have a couple jumping off points here. This person Trent is our closest match." She tapped the name 'Trent Miller.' "Two hundred and twelve centimorgans is about a three percent DNA match. He's likely a third cousin, which means he shares a great-great-grandparent with River. He doesn't have a family tree listed on here, unfortunately. That would have made your job a little easier."

"So I need to try and figure out who his great-great-grandparents are?"

"Yep, and once you've built his tree back to his great-great-grandparents, then you have to build the tree forward to find what branch River is on. First off, reach out to Trent and ask him. Depending on how close the family is, he might even know about River. One issue is sometimes people set up these accounts and never look at them again, so he may not receive your message. Fortunately, public records offer us a way to bypass direct contact with the family. While you wait on his response, newspaper archives and social media will likely be your richest sources of data. You can order birth and marriage records from most city governments, but you often can't search them online."

For the next half hour, Tia and Catherine showed Celeste the many online databases they used to trace birth lines. They managed to find several death notices that listed Trent as a surviving member of the family as well as an article in a newspaper that listed his high school graduation years before.

When Celeste left the library, she felt hopeful. Research had always been one of her strengths and somewhere in the public records Trent would lead Celeste to River's birth parents.

As she drove home, she turned on a podcast where the host interviewed near-death survivors. The radio suddenly switched from the podcast streaming from her phone to a station playing Paul Simon's *50 Ways to Leave Your Lover*.

Celeste glanced at her cell phone and hit play on the podcast. The interviewer asked the woman who'd died and crossed over to describe the last day of her life. Before the story began, another song hijacked the speakers, *Brandy* by the band Looking Glass.

She again switched to her podcast, but the radio immediately returned to *Brandy*.

Celeste stared through the windshield and listened to the song about the sailor who opted for the sea over the girl who worked the bar and waited for him. Celeste remembered Lena during their lunch break from the near-death experiences conference pointing out a song as an answer to a question Jack had been struggling with.

'The universe always answers,' she'd said. 'You just have to listen.'

CELESTE WORKED LATE in her office, scouring public records using several of the tips offered by Tia and Catherine. She added the family names they'd already found to her corkboard plus several more.

Celeste created the family tree for Trent Miller, adding string attached to pushpins to point toward his parents, who'd gotten divorced at some point, which sidetracked her when she accidentally followed his stepmother's birth line instead of his biological mother's. Eventually she realized her mistake, removed the stepmother from the tree and started again. She eventually discovered one set of grandparents thanks to a death notice that listed the deceased grandmother, her surviving husband, and her children and grandchildren. Still, she had a long way to go.

Jonathan didn't return from the lab until after eight p.m. They ate leftover pizza from the night before, and Celeste returned to her study. For two hours, she answered questions in the Dear Celeste column before returning to her search for River's parentage.

The knob twisted behind her and the door cracked open.

"Are you coming to bed? It's nearly midnight." Jonathan's face was sleepy as if he'd woken, realized she was still up and come to fetch her.

She spun her chair to face him. "Soon," she said. "A few more minutes."

After they'd eaten, she'd changed into a t-shirt and wore

only that with a pair of underwear. Jonathan's eyes were locked on her tattoo—the raven and the word 'evolve.'

"Evolve from what?" he asked, eyes flicking up to hers.

Celeste shifted, pulled her t-shirt lower. "Just... from the person I was."

He sighed and closed the door.

When the tiredness got to her, she arranged all the papers in a careful pile and set them on the corner of her desk. Before she could ease the door fully closed behind her, a dry whisper emerged from the dark room.

Celeste pushed the door back open and flipped on the light. The papers, stacked seconds before, lay fanned across the carpeting. She looked at the window, closed. The ceiling fan was still.

The papers had drifted across the floor nearly to the walls. The one at her feet was the letter from River's first social worker —Mona.

"Ouch. Jesus, Celeste."

She blinked, saw the hazy form of her husband sitting up in bed. He stood and turned. It was too dark to see his face, but she sensed he glared at her.

"What?" she asked, groggy, struggling to understand what had upset him. Lamplight filled the room and she cringed and closed her eyes, pulling the blanket up to shield her face.

"I'm bleeding," he shrilled.

She shifted the comforter down and stared at his chest, where long red welts cut across the skin. "I didn't do that," she said. "You think I did that?"

He stared at her, unbelieving, then held up his hands as if he couldn't even muster a response. He turned and stormed into the hall.

Celeste stared at the open doorway. She lifted her hands slowly to her face, feared she'd find blood and skin beneath her fingernails. They were clean.

The bedside lamp flickered.

She found him in the kitchen, the welts on his chest angry and red. He stood near the table, drinking a glass of water, a box of Band-Aids open but unused on the counter.

"Do you want me to help put some of those on?"

His eyes narrowed at her. "Don't you think you've done enough?"

Celeste brushed her hands through her hair. Her leg throbbed dully and the bottle of Scotch on the counter gleamed. She wanted a drink. "It wasn't me."

He laughed, rolled his eyes up and looked at the ceiling. "You are incapable of taking personal responsibility for any of the havoc you've wreaked in our lives. Look at this!" He pointed a finger at his chest and, as had happened once before, his hands appeared as if he'd dipped them in blood.

When she blinked, they were bare once more, the only color the single gold band on his ring finger and the freckles on his knuckles.

'You have an angry ghost,' Taylor had told her.

From the corner of her eye, Celeste watched the motion-activated porch light turn on. Ravens, dozens of them, crowded the back porch. They stood on the rails and the patio furniture, intently watching her and Jonathan.

As Jonathan turned, sensing she stared at something over his shoulder, the light went dark, obscuring the birds.

"What?" he demanded. "What are you staring at? Are you even going to say anything?"

She started to defend herself, to repeat it wasn't her, but to do that would be to reveal what it was and the truth was that would only make Jonathan angrier, more convinced she was unstable. "I'm sorry. I must have been having a nightmare and... I genuinely don't remember doing it. It wasn't on purpose."

He sighed and pressed his lips together. "I miss you, Celeste. I miss our old life."

She went to him and wrapped her arms around his waist, rested her head against his chest, careful not to touch the broken skin.

"I'm sorry I overreacted," he murmured into her hair. "I shouldn't have snapped at you."

"It's okay."

"Back to bed?"

She stared at the dark glass, imagined the ravens gathered beyond. She wanted to pour a Scotch, flip on the porch light and get a better look at them, try to make sense of why they were there. She was wide awake now, but the hopeful expression on Jonathan's face made her turn away from the door. She followed him back to bed.

19

River washed a bowl of strawberries and set them on Hope's play table. She returned to the kitchen chair where she'd piled clothes from the dryer that needed folding.

Hope, who'd been scribbling in a coloring book with a red crayon, set the crayon aside. She picked up a strawberry and walked across the room. She paused near the corner and extended one pudgy little arm. "Suffa-berry."

"I don't think the wall wants a strawberry, little bean," River told her, watching Hope shake the berry.

"Nana. Suffa-berry," Hope said, taking another step, head tilted up as if staring into the eyes of a much taller person.

River stared at the empty corner, a chill prickling her spine.

"There's no Nana here," River told her. Nana was the name they used for all the aunts and grandmas at Be Free, including Cordelia and several of the other senior women.

The song on the record player, *Where Have All the Flowers Gone* by Peter, Paul and Mary, began to skip. River moved toward it, eye still trained on the corner and Hope. As she lifted the record off, the doorknob on the front door began to turn.

River froze and, when the door pushed open, she screamed.

Owen stared at her, surprised. "Whoa." He laughed. "I guess you didn't hear me pull in?" Garth crowded into the room behind him, sniffing around River's feet.

The record continued to skip, the words 'girls gone' on a disturbing loop.

"Dada!" Hope exclaimed, dropping the strawberry to the floor and toddling across the room.

He swept her up and kissed her on the mouth. "Is that my beautiful girl?"

Luna, who'd been staring at the corner as well, stood, crossed the room and ate the strawberry.

River lifted off the record and returned it to its envelope. "No. I didn't hear the truck," she murmured.

Owen sat Hope on the floor and sidled up to River. He kissed her and then leaned his face into her hair. "Mmm... you smell good."

"Like I haven't taken a shower in two days?"

"Like you." He reached past her and pulled out an Emmy Lou Harris record and put it on the turn table.

River sat down at the table and returned to the clothes, shaking out a pair of Owen's jeans and folding them.

"Dance with me," Owen said, pulling River back to her feet.

She swiped a hair from her face. "I need to get these folded."

"No, you don't. Those are mine. Wrinkled is my style."

She sighed as he slipped a hand to her back and pulled her close. *Love Hurts* poured from the speakers, a song she'd had a momentary obsession with in her teen years, had even sung frequently at Be Free while sorting out her voice.

Owen rested his chin on the top of her head and they swayed slowly through the kitchen, her bare feet picking up the bits of dust carried in throughout the day. Her skirt swirled up Luna's stiff white hair in little tornadoes of fur.

It was the most beautiful moment and yet even from within it, River felt removed, as if she were staring through the window of a dollhouse at this perfect snapshot of a life with the music and the dancing and the golden light in Owen's hair. She felt his hand in hers, the pressure of his body, but the emotion within her remained stiff, inaccessible. She wanted to cry, but her eyes were dry and gritty.

"Up, up!" Hope said, pulling on River's and Owen's legs.

"You want to dance too, little bean?" Owen picked her up, cradled her between him and River, and they danced.

IN THE EARLY EVENING, they tended the garden. Hope was asleep in her crib, the window cracked so they could hear her.

"I could make chicken breast for dinner," River said. "Sweet potatoes, green beans."

"Shoot." Owen straightened up from the section of crabgrass he'd been pulling. "I have all that smoked pork my dad dropped off, but forgot to stop for barbecue sauce."

"I'll go to the store," River said. "Hope's napping. It's a good time for me to go."

"Are you sure? I don't mind running up there."

"No, you stay. I have a few other things to pick up."

RIVER HADN'T BEEN to the grocery store in nearly a week and, though she didn't want to do a full shopping trip, she'd had a list running in her mind of things to get before her tour.

She grabbed a cart, dropped her purse inside and made her way to the deli to order sandwich meat and cheese. Owen would appreciate having some convenient snacks for Hope, so she grabbed yogurt, squeeze pouches and peanut butter pretzels.

At the wall of local foods, much of it sold to the grocery store by the farms neighboring River and Owen's, she scanned the jams and jellies. Hope had a particular fondness for strawberry rhubarb from the Dillards' farm, but she didn't see any on the shelf. River pushed other jars aside and hunched down to look deeper.

"River Adair?"

She stood up to see Tawny Louis holding a basket over one tanned arm. Tawny had dated Owen in high school. They'd even been crowned homecoming king and queen. In Owen's old yearbook, River had once found Tawny's inscription, 'We're going to make beautiful babies,' followed by a heart and a string of x's and o's.

"Hey, Tawny. How are you?" River pushed a lock of unruly dark hair behind her ear and wished she'd changed out of her dirt-streaked garden clothes. Tawny, as she'd been every other time River encountered her around Baraboo, appeared perfectly put together. She wore high-waisted white shorts and a tight-fitting black and white t-shirt. Her long blonde hair shone in the grocery store fluorescents.

"I'm great! Just picking up a few things for a dinner party this weekend. I ran into Arnie and he said you're heading on tour. How exciting."

"Yeah. Grabbing a few last-minute groceries for Owen and Hope while I'm gone."

"Poor things. I'm sure they'll be just lost without you. Maybe I'll stop by and drop off some of Mama's sourdough bread. It's the best and Owen absolutely loved it. He told her to enter it in the county fair, and she won the blue ribbon."

"That's really wonderful. I've tried sourdough a few times without much luck."

"I'll do that then. You let Owen know. Bye, River. Best of

luck on your tour." Tawny turned and walked away. She stopped at a rack of specialty pickles and bent over.

River stared at her shapely legs then, face flushing, quickly looked away. As she pushed her cart toward the checkout, she tried not to think of her own body, wide hips that had thickened during her pregnancy with Hope and never entirely shrunk back down. She looked a mess, clothes dirty, hair tangled, and the swell of emotion rumbled deep in her belly, but didn't rise up. Like everything lately, it was trapped down there, held hostage by some monster she couldn't name.

She paid quickly, noticing Tawny sliding into an adjacent lane, and hurried toward the door.

"Ma'am. Did you forget something?" a man asked, blocking her path.

River stared at him, confused, the two paper bags heavy in her arms. "Did I?" She glanced back at the checkout lane, but the woman who'd rung her up watched her oddly.

"Did you forget to pay for something?" he asked.

River frowned, glanced into her bags. "No. I don't think so."

He stepped toward her and she flinched. He plucked something from her purse and held out a bottle of sunshine drops—a locally made tincture meant to alleviate depression.

"That's not mine," she said. "I didn't put that in there."

"I'm going to need you to come into the manager's office for a moment."

She took a quick step back. "No. Absolutely not. My husband and daughter are home waiting for me and I didn't—"

The man grabbed her arm roughly and started to pull her toward the office. His fingers dug into her biceps and a sudden fury roiled through her body.

"No!" she screamed and flung both her bags to the ground. The glass bottle of barbecue sauce struck the floor and shattered. River jerked her arm from the man's grip and raced toward the door. She didn't make it. The man grabbed her around her waist. She reached her hands down and raked her fingernails across his wrists.

"Call the police," he shouted.

As he dragged her toward the office, River caught sight of Tawny watching her.

OWEN HELD Hope in his lap. He sat beside River on a hard plastic chair in the Baraboo police station.

"I didn't put that tincture in my purse," River repeated. "Someone else put it there."

"You heard her," Owen snapped at the officer before them. "Some little asshole, excuse my language, must have snuck it in there as a sick joke. What I want to know is what you're going to do about the security guard who left those marks on her arm."

"Your wife is the one who drew blood, Mr. Adair."

"As well she should," he barked. "This is ludicrous. Why don't you just tell the store owner to look at the security cameras and find out who put it in her purse?"

"Unfortunately, the cameras they have aren't working."

Owen snorted. "That's convenient. What, do we need a lawyer? If that grocery store charges her, we're going to court."

The officer held up his hands. "Calm down, please. Think of the example you're setting for your daughter."

"Oh, you mean standing up for my wife, demanding the truth? Believe me, I'm very clear about the example I want her to see."

"The grocery store has chosen not to press charges. I think we can all be grateful for that."

Owen scoffed and stood. He shifted Hope and offered his hand to River. She swallowed, avoided the eyes of the officer and followed Owen from the police station.

As they drove home, River, hands shaking, clutched the grocery items the store had haphazardly thrown in plastic sacks. The glass bottle of barbecue sauce had broken and splattered across the floor. The red of it still seared in River's mind.

"You have bought those before, right? The sunshine drops."

River bristled. "Yeah. So?"

"I'm not implying anything. I just wonder… could you have picked them up and accidentally dropped them into your purse instead of the cart?"

River squeezed the bag of groceries in her lap, the shame acid in her stomach. Shame despite having done nothing, but Owen's puzzled eyes took her back to one of the foster houses. Paulette, who had hated her, had snuck the foster mother's jewelry into River's bedroom. River had been eleven, didn't even like jewelry, but the mother had snatched the gold necklace from beneath her mattress and marched River outside to sit on the curb wearing a cardboard sign that stated 'I Am a Thief' in red marker. For hours she'd sat there as neighborhood kids rode by on their bikes laughing, as adults gawked at her through windshields.

"No. Owen. No. I didn't put it in my purse. I didn't even go into the section of the store that has medicine." She held her breath, waited for his reaction, wasn't sure what she'd do if he didn't believe her.

"Okay. I'm sorry. Forget it." He reached for her hand. "Squeeze my hand before you murder the buns."

River looked down, realized she'd squeezed the burger buns so tight she'd smooshed several of them into warped balls.

"Did you notice anyone hanging around your cart? Or watching you?"

She turned and stared out the window, watched corn and wheat fields zooming by. "No. Well… I saw Tawny."

"Tawny Louis?"

River nodded.

"Huh. Okay. I mean, you're not saying you think Tawny did it, right? She wouldn't do that."

"No. I'm not saying that. She's the only person I talked to, so…"

"It must have been someone else, probably some dumb kid playing a prank."

"Yeah," River agreed, but a pit had formed in her stomach.

How could some teenager who didn't know her happen to pick up a tincture she herself had bought multiple times, an item she'd stopped buying because it was expensive? Tawny wouldn't have known River previously used the tincture either. No one short of her and Owen would have been aware of it.

From the backseat, Hope yelled, "Baba!"

River turned to see a herd of sheep standing at a fence watching them pass by.

20

For a couple of days after the clawing incident, Celeste and Jonathan settled into a mild contentment. They drank coffee together in the morning and had dinner together in the evening. They talked about developments in the lab, local news, and carefully avoided anything to do with Celeste's hit-and-run, near-death experience, or Dear Celeste column.

"Oatmeal?" Jonathan asked, spooning a glob of oatmeal into a bowl and sprinkling it with a few raisins.

Celeste eyed the food, gooey and glistening. She hadn't enjoyed oatmeal since the accident. It had been her daily breakfast for years and now the sight of it made her stomach churn. "No. Thank you. I'm going to make some toast."

As she busied herself getting out the bread, butter, and jam, she thought of Dottie Smith in Wisconsin. The woman still hadn't called her back. She was the only person who had met River's father, and she might be the key to finding him. Which meant returning to Wisconsin, an intention Celeste knew would shatter the careful peace she and Jonathan had cultivated in the previous days.

"A lot of sugar in that jam," Jonathan said when she sat at the table with her plate of toast.

"Memento mori," she said.

He raised an eyebrow.

"It means 'remember you will die.' It's how I justify my sugar habit these days."

Jonathan smiled, but didn't laugh. "I thought we could grab dinner tonight at that German restaurant on Fuller Avenue. We haven't been there in ages."

Celeste chewed her toast slowly, dreaded the words at the back of her tongue. "I actually need to go back to Wisconsin. I thought I might go today."

He stared at her, then turned to gaze out the sliding glass door. "Huh. I knew it was only a matter of time."

"I told you I'd be going back."

"You did, didn't you?" He stood and walked his oatmeal, barely eaten, to the sink and dumped it in. He flicked on the garbage disposal and the room filled with the harsh mechanical grinding.

When he turned it off, Celeste spoke. "It will only be for a day or two. I don't understand why it's such a big deal."

"It's fine, Celeste. Do what you *need* to do." He left and, several minutes later, she heard him pull out of the driveway.

CELESTE OPENED her computer and logged into River's ancestry account.

'You have a new DNA match!' a pop-up screen announced.

The match's name was Dillon Culver and the ancestry website estimated he was a first cousin to River Adair.

"Yes..." she murmured.

She sent a message to Dillon. She still hadn't received a response from Trent Miller and hoped that since Dillon had only recently added his profile, he might be more active on the site.

Hi Dillon,

I'm assisting a friend in tracking down her birth family and she's related to you. She's twenty-four years old (she thinks) and spent most of her childhood in foster care. I've only recently started this search and I'm not sure if you're related on her mother or father's side. Do you know of a cousin who fits this description? Would you be open to sharing some details about your relatives?

Thank you,

Celeste

IT WAS JUST after noon when Celeste's cell phone rang. She'd spent the whole morning in her office. Jonathan's name appeared on the screen. She stood, gasped at the pins and needles that shot through her leg, and answered his call. "Hello."

"I need you to come to the lab." Jonathan's voice was tight.

"Why? What's wrong?"

"Someone slashed my tires."

"What?"

"Just come, please. I'll be waiting outside."

AS CELESTE PULLED into the parking lot at Dynamic Laboratories, she spotted Jonathan huddled near the sidewalk talking with Liz and Darlene. When he saw her truck, he waved and hurried over.

She parked and climbed out, grimacing at the pain that vibrated up her leg. She'd been sitting too much in the previous days, not doing her exercises often enough, and her hip and leg were making it known. Her cane sat in the back, resting against the center console, but she left it behind.

"What happened?" she asked.

Jonathan gestured to his car where two uniformed police stood, one talking on a radio, the other bent down, examining the tire. "I came out and found all four of my tires sitting on their rims. Someone cut them."

"Did you talk to Wally? The security cameras must have captured whoever did it."

Jonathan shook his head. "Cameras are down this week for maintenance."

"Then whoever did it works at Dynamic Laboratories," she said, eyes drifting to the mirrored windows reflecting the glaring sun.

"We don't know that," he said.

"You think it's a coincidence someone slashed your tires during the one week when the cameras are down? No way."

Jonathan frowned and shoved his hands into his coat, eyeing the several people who'd walked through the front doors.

A black car drove into the lot and parked beside the police cruiser. A man, vaguely familiar, stepped out. He was tall, dark-skinned, wearing a white button-down shirt and black slacks.

"Who is that?" she murmured.

Jonathan stared at him. "It's the detective who worked your hit-and-run. I don't understand why he's here."

The detective spoke for several minutes with the two officers, then made his way across the parking lot.

"Mrs. Cleary, Mr. Cleary." He offered his hand. "You might not remember me. I'm Detective Bowman."

Celeste shook his hand. "Call me Celeste, please, and I'm sure my husband is happy with Jonathan."

Jonathan's face looked pinched as he shook the man's hand,

as if he would have preferred Mr. Cleary. "Is it usual to send a detective for something like this?" Jonathan asked.

"It is when we're also working a potential attempted murder," Bowman said, shielding his eyes as he studied the building.

"You think this is connected to the person who hit me?" Celeste asked.

"It's too early to say, but you two don't strike me as the types who regularly attract this kind of hostility and violence, so it doesn't feel like a reach to connect the two."

Jonathan cleared his throat loudly.

"Am I wrong about that?" Bowman asked.

"Well." Jonathan cast a narrow look at Celeste. "Celeste was recently involved in a murder case in Northern Michigan and she is likely to be called as a witness in the man's homicide trial, so..."

Celeste stared at him. "You think Randy Mills escaped from prison and drove down here to slash your tires? How would he even know where to find your car?"

Jonathan threw his hands up, exasperated. "I'm just saying we've suddenly become exposed to some very disturbed people."

"You were involved in a murder case?" Bowman asked.

Celeste nodded. "I went up to Graves, a little town east of Traverse City, to help a woman locate her missing sister, Katie. It turned out Katie's uncle had killed her and..." Celeste shifted uncomfortably. "It was a pretty intense couple of weeks."

She thought then of her original belief that the Boyds had been behind Katie's disappearance. According to Joanna, Declan had been released. Could he be now seeking revenge for his family?

Bowman took a notebook from his coat pocket and flipped it open. "What was the name you said? Randy Mills?"

"Yes. And... well, there was another family I originally

thought was involved because the son had been dating Katie and there'd been a burglary. It's a long story, but the woman I helped, Joanna, she and I ended up getting several of those men arrested. Warren, Todd and Declan Boyd, though I believe Declan is out on bond."

Jonathan sputtered. "Great. You might have told me that, Celeste."

Celeste stared past him at his car and shook her head. "I never thought he'd do anything like this. Honestly, I still don't, but—"

"But it's worth following up on," Bowman said. "We probably should also consider the possibility that whoever hit you, Celeste, is involved in this."

"And do you have any leads on who that might be?" Jonathan asked. His eyes drifted to the group gathering outside the building. "This is making a spectacle. Maybe we should..." He gestured to a little patch of trees beside the building.

"Go stand behind a tree?" Celeste asked. "I think your car sitting there with the tires slashed and the police surrounding it is more of a spectacle than us right now."

He frowned, but said nothing. Celeste knew Jonathan hated the type of attention they were now getting, loathed the thought of his colleagues speculating about him at their dinner tables that evening.

"We don't have any persons of interest in the hit-and-run. Still doing the legwork on that one, but I did have a couple of follow-up questions I intended to ask, so we might as well cover those now. Another angle we haven't really discussed is family inheritance. Do either of you stand to gain an inheritance from a parent? Money that would be split among siblings?"

Celeste shook her head. "Unlikely. My dad lives in Florida. He does fine, but I doubt he'll he be leaving the world with a bunch of money stashed somewhere."

"And do you have siblings?"

"A brother, Adam."

"And how's that relationship?"

"It's great. We're very close. He just spent the night at our house this week."

"And he's not involved in any kinds of illegal activity? Drugs, theft?"

"No. Not at all. He's an elementary school teacher."

"And how about you, Jonathan? Stand to inherit any family money?"

Jonathan shook his head. "My parents are solidly middle class. They're both retired. My dad has a pension from GM. They own their house, but no other assets."

"Siblings?"

"One sister. She lives out west. We see her once every couple of years. That's it."

"Okay." The detective closed his notebook. "Celeste, if you could email some names and details about what occurred in Graves, that would be helpful."

"Sure. And I'll reach out to Joanna. She's the person I helped, though she lives in Arizona now. I'm sure she can tell me if there have been any updates on what's happening with Randy."

As Celeste drove Jonathan home, he stared gloomily out the window.

"Maybe it was a mistake," Celeste murmured. "They confused your car with someone else's. Or maybe... maybe it was some kid having a bad day."

"I don't think you should go to Wisconsin," he said.

"Well, obviously I won't until your car gets fixed, but—"

"But what? How much worse does it have to get for you to make us a priority?"

"Jonathan, me helping River find her birth family doesn't have to detract from us. You're gone at the lab all day. It's not as if we were ever together twenty-four seven."

"Except that's where you're wrong. We literally were. We drove to work together. We had dinner together. We went to bed together."

Celeste stared through the windshield. He wasn't wrong—they had done all those things together—but there'd still been a distance, a lack of intimacy. Except before her accident, it hadn't seemed to bother either of them. "I can't return to the way it was. I'm different. We're different."

"I'm not," he snapped. "Pull in there." He gestured angrily at a rental car agency.

"You don't need to rent a car. I can drive you to work tomorrow."

"No. It's better if we both have a vehicle. I remember how you reacted the last time you felt stranded at home."

AFTER JONATHAN RETURNED to the lab, Celeste dialed Joanna Ellis.

"Celeste, wow. I was just thinking about you. How are you?" Joanna said.

"I'm pretty good. How's Arizona?"

"Hot!" Joanna laughed. "But seriously, it's beautiful, and I started a new job at a coffee shop and I'm actually dating the owner, which is probably not the wisest move, but he is such a wonderful man. You'd love him."

"And Floyd and Camile are good?"

"They are. Floyd isn't quite back to himself and the heat has him grumbling about Northern Michigan, but honestly, it's been a relief to be in such a foreign place. There I go showing how little I've travelled, thinking Arizona is foreign, but it sure is to me. Cacti and red rock as far as the eye can see. This time up north the forests would be filling out, the mosquitoes making an appearance."

"Do you miss it?"

"Oh, well..." Joanna's voice grew quiet. "I guess the key I've found is not thinking about that. I've been taking a class on mindfulness. Just being here in this moment, not letting myself spend much time thinking on the past or the future. It's hard. My mind wanders, but... it's really helped. Sometimes I feel guilty about that, like I'm forcing myself to forget Katie, like I'm not honoring her memory enough, but I try to remember Katie is gone. She's gone, and this is what she'd want for me. She'd hate for me to spend my life closed in somewhere, burning candles in her memory and crying all day. I've had a few of those days too, though."

"As you should. But you're right. Katie would want you to have a life. The very best way to honor her is by living your life, not taking a day for granted."

"Yeah. I'm working on it. What's been happening with you? I read all your columns. Makes me feel a little more connected to you and to home."

"Thanks. I'm grateful for that. Joanna, something weird happened today and it may be totally unrelated to Randy and the Boyds, but someone slashed Jonathan's tires at Dynamic Laboratories."

"What? No. They slashed his tires? And you think that it might be connected to Randy?"

"I honestly don't know, but I don't want to ignore the obvious. If the police hadn't shown up, Randy would have killed us both that night."

"He's in jail. The prosecutor's been checking in regularly. There's no way he's out."

"Do you think there's any chance he paid someone in there who's on the outside?"

"Oh, gosh. Ugh. I hate to even consider that."

"I know, and I'm sorry for planting that seed in your head. It may be totally unrelated."

"I'll talk to the prosecutor, okay? Maybe he can have some of the guards ask around at the jail, see if anyone has heard anything."

"That'd be good. And how about the Boyds? Any news on them?"

"Camile's best friend in Graves calls every day. Declan's mom is in the hospital and he's apparently staying with his uncle. Warren and Todd are still in jail. But... I could see Warren setting up something like that, but how would he know where Jonathan worked? What car he drove? He is absolutely a person who'd seek revenge, but I don't know if he has the brains or the resources to get to your husband, and why would he, right? If he were paying someone, I think they'd go after you."

"Yeah." Celeste sighed. "That's the part that doesn't make sense. Why target Jonathan? And they didn't leave a message, so it's not as if the warning was clear."

"Maybe it's not connected to anything. What if it was just some jerk who got fired and decided to slash someone's tires? Maybe they had an issue with Jonathan."

"Yeah. The detective is talking to the staff at the lab. We'll see if anything shakes out. Jonathan is the one who brought up Randy, and I figured it'd be naïve of me not to consider it. Have you gotten any more phone calls? The ones where no one talks?"

"No. Just that one. I'm sure it wasn't him. Probably a wrong number or one of those robot calls."

"Yeah."

21

As River walked back toward the house, she saw Cordelia's car parked near the chicken coop. Cordelia's trunk was open and she leaned inside.

"Hi," River called, waving.

Cordelia straightened up. "There she is," she said. "I brought the tricycle Clay made and some pickles and stewed tomatoes."

"Oh, gosh. I love it," River said, when Cordelia lifted out the little wooden tricycle painted yellow with pink flowers.

"It's cute, isn't it?" Cordelia agreed.

"Hope and Owen went to his parents for dinner."

"But not you?"

River shook her head. "I have rehearsal with the guys tonight and honestly, I just wasn't feeling up for the big family dinner. It's pretty loud in that house when everyone is there."

Cordelia frowned and put a hand to River's head. "Not feeling well, honey?"

The touch was such a Cordelia gesture, the natural caretaker who'd hugged River the first time they met, an exchange that had felt both startling and soothing.

"Not sick, just…"

"Heartsick?"

"A little. Yeah."

"Now I know why I got the bug to bake these last night," Cordelia said, moving to the passenger door and reaching through the open window. She held up a tin. "Carrot cake cookies."

"Those are my favorite."

"I know. Come on. Let's go inside. I'll brew us a cup of chai tea to go with these."

River followed Cordelia inside, grateful to be led, to be taken care of. It was a foreign experience, one that had taken ages for her to adjust to at Be Free, and she still struggled with it.

"Do you want to talk about it?" Cordelia asked, filling the kettle with water and setting it on the stove.

River ate a cookie, savored the spices, the sweetness of the cream cheese frosting. "I don't know. I'm not even sure what I'm feeling. How do you talk about something when you don't know what's bothering you?"

"You start with the mundane. That's what my grandma always said. Start with a story about shucking peas and next thing you know, you'll be crying over the mean thing your teacher said in first grade."

River smiled. "Hmm… well, today I washed some of Hope's baby clothes and I weeded the garden and fed the chickens. And even though I used to love all those little daily tasks, I can't seem to find that love anymore. It's been… months. Months of feeling off. Like I'm not here, I can't feel my life. I have no past, no roots, no foundation."

Cordelia poured the tea and set a mug painted with guitars in front of River. "You know part of the reason Clay was so devoted to building Be Free is because he grew up in a difficult home."

"He never talks about it."

"I know. And I'm sure you can relate to wanting to bury the past, forget it. But the truth is early in our marriage Clay went through a really dark period. He was drinking heavily, was even arrested twice."

"He was?"

"Yes. Once for drunk and disorderly and the second time for assaulting his father. His father was quite cruel. He beat all the boys, pitted them against each other, started giving them alcohol before they were even teenagers."

"What about Clay's mom?"

"She died when Clay was nine—a drowning accident—and his father, who'd already been abusive, became intolerable. Clay moved out when he was fifteen. Lived on friends' couches, slept in tents, in old buildings."

"But he went to college? How did he manage that?"

"In high school a teacher took him under her wing. Mrs. Galbraith. She taught band and got him into music. She had an apartment her mother had lived in connected to her house and her mother had died, so she let Clay move in. She helped him get into college. He was still living there when we met. We started daydreaming about a different kind of life, a life with more community, more support. I didn't know anything about communes, about intentional communities, but we spent a year traveling around the country, staying in communities and gathering what we loved, discarding what didn't work.

"For a lot of years, Clay didn't look back. He was forward-focused and frankly we were too busy to be bogged down by the past, but it catches up. No one outruns it forever and Clay became very depressed about two years after we got Be Free off the ground. That's when he had those arrests. He started drinking. First he got the drunk and disorderly, then about a month later he attacked his father. He spent a month in jail for that one. I was at my wits' end. We'd worked so hard to build Be Free and he was throwing it all away.

"Then Torrence was involved in an armed robbery. He ended up turning state's evidence on the other guys involved and that's how he managed to stay out of prison, but it was a wake-up call for Clay. He realized if he didn't get better, he'd squander everything we'd built. As they say, you either get better or you get bitter. Clay started journaling and talking. He'd never shared stories about his childhood, not in any detail. He'd suddenly tell me a story about the muskrat casseroles his mother used to cook for dinner or the time his father jerked him out of the car so hard he dislocated his shoulder. These were memories he'd all but forgotten. This was what his healing looked like. Him finally letting himself go there, remember, share it. The good and the bad."

"And you think that's what I need to do?"

"I think it's a good place to start. Working with Celeste is also a good place to start. We have to bring what has remained in shadow into the light. Are you writing music about the way you're feeling?"

"I'm trying, but... it all feels too thin."

"Keep going. That's my best advice for you. Keep excavating, dig into those feelings and then get underneath them."

"Sure. Thanks, Cordelia."

River walked Cordelia to her car and they hugged goodbye. Cordelia held her for a long time.

As Cordelia climbed into her car, River remembered the porcelain doll. "Cordelia, you didn't drop off a doll for Hope, did you? In the mailbox?"

"A doll? No. Did someone leave one for her?"

River nodded, gooseflesh prickling her neck. "Yeah. Owen thought it was one of his brothers. I guess it was."

River hadn't cleaned the cabin after Celeste stayed there. She went in now and stripped off the bedding. As she gathered it up and put it in the hamper, her eye caught on the corner of something white under the bed. She knelt and pulled it out. It was a Polaroid photograph.

The photograph was of a little girl, no older than two or three. The child's back was turned to the camera, her dark hair sticking out at funny angles as if she'd only just gotten out of bed. She wore a frilly purple nightgown and stood in front of a Christmas tree, her arm outstretched as if to pluck off a popcorn strand decorating the glittering tree. Despite the girl's turned back, there was something about her, familiar and unsettling.

River sat on the edge of the bed and stared at the picture for a long time. Had Celeste left it? She didn't think Celeste had children, but realized with embarrassment she hadn't asked her. She tucked the photograph into the large pocket of her sweater and carried the hamper back to the house.

22

"I stopped for takeout," Jonathan said, unpacking boxes of Chinese food. "I don't want to fight."

Celeste paused beside him, rested her head on his shoulder. "I don't either."

"Good." He kissed the top of her head. "Red wine? Might not be the ideal pairing with beef and broccoli, but how bad can it be?"

"Sure. That sounds good." While Jonathan poured the wine, Celeste took out plates and silverware. She filled them each a plate. "Do we want to sit on the back porch?"

"Yep. I'll meet you out there."

Celeste carried their plates out and sat down. He handed her the wine, and she took a sip and wrinkled her nose. "It's a tad bitter. Was this bottle already open?"

Jonathan sipped his and shook his head. "No. Tastes fine to me."

As they ate, they carefully avoided the day's events. She wanted to ask him if anything strange had been happening at the lab, if any part of him believed the person who'd hit her was now targeting him, but something about that line of conversation felt like a minefield. They couldn't seem to go there without getting into a fight.

She leaned her head back against the chair and looked up at the darkening sky. Her vision had grown fuzzy, her eyelids heavy.

"Tired?" he asked.

"Yeah, all of a sudden."

"Go to bed. I'll clean up out here."

"Are you sure?"

"Yep. I'll be up soon."

"WHAT WAS THAT?" Jonathan hissed.

Celeste, dragged from sleep, opened her eyes to see Jonathan sitting up in bed. His hair stuck up at angles. She hadn't noticed how long it had grown—so unlike him to not keep it meticulously short. He stared toward the door, his body stiff.

"Did you see it?" he demanded.

Celeste sat up, leaned to the side and flipped on her lamp. Yellow light flooded the room and she blinked against the sudden brightness.

Jonathan's pupils shrank, but his eyes remained alert, still fixed on the open bedroom doorway. "Someone walked in here," he said. "I saw them."

A chill rippled down Celeste's spine. "Was it a woman?" she asked. She didn't even remember falling asleep, but the exhaustion chased her now. She struggled to keep her eyes open.

Jonathan whipped his head toward her, fear morphing into suspicion. "What does that mean? Was it you? Snuck in here and climbed into bed? Spooked me on purpose?"

Jonathan sounded borderline hysterical. She'd never heard

the tone before and it scared her. "Jonathan, I was sound asleep. You woke me up."

For several moments he stared at her, eyes boring into her own as if she might buckle under the intensity of his glare and come clean. He lifted a hand to his eye. The skin twitched. His hand was red, the fingers wet and glossy, the red dark, almost brown.

Celeste released a little gasp and he recoiled, pulled his hand away and looked at it, then brushed it across his face.

"What is it? Is there something crawling on me?" His fingers skittered over his forehead and into his hair. They were bare, the red gone.

"Nothing... I..." She swallowed, searched for a response. "It was my hip. I got a little jolt of pain. I'm going to get a drink of water."

She shuffled from the bed, bit her teeth together at the fire that lit down her leg. Hiding her limp, she lumbered from the room, feeling Jonathan's eyes following her. Her body felt clunky and uncoordinated and the dreams she'd been having before Jonathan woke her floated in the periphery of her mind, though their details did not emerge.

In the kitchen, she bypassed the water and poured a glass of Scotch, picked up her cell phone. On her screen she saw a text that had come in just minutes before from Taylor, the woman she'd met at the near-death experiences conference.

Taylor: *Are you awake? Call me.*

Celeste thought of ignoring the message. It was nearly two in the morning. Instead, she pushed the button to call her and Taylor answered on the first ring.

"Celeste. Is everything okay?"

Celeste stared through the sliding glass doors at the darkness beyond the back porch. "Yeb." Celeste heard the thickness in her mouth and cleared her throat. "Sorry. Yes. I'm fine. What is it?"

"Are you sure? You sound strange."

"I just woke from a dead sleep. I'm a little out of it."

"Okay. You're positive? Is anyone there with you?"

"My husband Jonathan is upstairs. Taylor, what's going on?"

Taylor sighed. "I don't want to freak you out, and normally I wouldn't reach out in the middle of the night, but I was sitting here working on a crossword puzzle and had a sudden vision of you standing in this bedroom and there was blood on the walls and all over the floor."

"And you thought it was happening now?"

"It's hard to gauge if it's now, the past, the future, if it's never going to happen at all. But it was a powerful enough vision to warrant me calling you."

"I'm in my house. Ten minutes ago, when you texted, I was sound asleep in my bed."

"Well, that's good news."

"Except my husband woke me up and said he saw someone sneak into our bedroom."

"Who was it?" Taylor's voice sounded uneasy.

"No one. I think it's her. The—"

"The woman? The angry ghost?"

"Yes. But would he sense her? I mean, he's never had any experiences like that. He thinks I'm crazy."

"Who are you talking to?" Jonathan stood in the doorway, robe cinched tight at his waist, eyes narrowed on her glass of Scotch.

Warmth flooded Celeste's face. "It's a friend, Jonathan. I'm coming to bed now. Can I call you tomorrow, Taylor?"

"Yes, please do. I'm not far from you. Fruitport. You could come over. We could talk."

"That'd be great." Celeste ended the call.

"Who was that?" he demanded.

"Taylor. I met her at the near-death experiences conference."

"Her?"

"Yes. Her."

"Hmm... and why did you call her?"

"I came down and saw she'd just texted me a few minutes ago."

"At two in the morning?"

Celeste nodded.

"I think you should come back to bed," he told her.

As Celeste followed him from the kitchen, Jonathan veered to the front door. He unlocked and relocked the dead bolt. He pulled on the windows on either side of the front door—locked.

"You're worried someone broke in?" Celeste asked.

"No," he said gruffly. "I must have dreamed it, but... just in case."

THE FOLLOWING morning after Jonathan left for work, Celeste struggled to shrug off her grogginess. She'd consumed an entire pot of coffee and done her physical therapy exercises to no avail. A cold shower slightly revved up her sluggish brain, but as she left the house to drive to Taylor's the sun pierced her eyes and gave her an immediate headache. She walked back inside, found a ball cap and a pair of sunglasses.

Celeste drove to Taylor's house in Fruitport. Though she'd intended to go to Wisconsin, fatigue compelled her to wait another day. She parked in the driveway of the ranch-style red brick house and knocked on the door.

Taylor pulled it open. She wore a Detroit Red Wings t-shirt and a pair of black yoga pants.

"Come on in. I brewed coffee," Taylor told her.

"Thank God," Celeste murmured. "I've already consumed my daily quota, but I cannot seem to wake up."

Taylor handed her a mug. "Didn't sleep well last night?"

Celeste took off her sunglasses and propped them on her ball cap. "I did actually. I slept hard other than when Jonathan woke me up, but gosh, I feel like I've been hit by a freight train."

Celeste followed Taylor to a screened porch that looked out over a backyard with several hammocks hanging in the trees. On a small child-sized chair next to a potted flower, sat a small primitive looking doll made from colored wool with twigs for arms and legs.

Taylor, as if having noticed where Celeste's eyes landed, smiled. "That's my spirit doll."

"Did you make it?"

"No. It was a gift from a woman I met during a nature retreat. She said the doll would be my guardian. I did a bit of research after I received her and found several ancient cultures who considered certain dolls sacred. Hopi Native Americans created dolls that they believed were messengers between humans and the world of spirits."

Celeste thought of the disturbing dreams she'd had lately, several of which had included dolls. "You don't find it creepy?"

"I've grown quite fond of her actually, but let's talk about you. Any other strange things happen last night?" Taylor asked.

"No. Thankfully. We went back to bed. Did you... see anything else?"

Taylor shook her head. "No. I tried to get some insight into the vision, but nothing else came up. I even texted Eliza and Lena, asked them to tune in and try to get a sense of what it meant, but neither of them had anything to offer."

"Can you tell me anything about the bedroom I was in?" The idea it might have been her and Jonathan's bedroom disturbed her.

"Yeah..." Taylor closed her eyes. "The bedspread is white, or it was." Her face was glum. "White with little colorful butterflies. A lamp on the table. It has tassels, a purple shade with silver tassels. Umm... I think the carpet is grayish. And I'm seeing a little glass ball, a souvenir with beach sand and seashells inside."

"Okay," Celeste said, relieved. "That's not our bedroom. Mine and Jonathan's."

"Good," Taylor said. "And as I'm sure you realize, sometimes the visions are symbolic. What's happening might be about a feeling of shock or a situation of danger. I wish I could offer something more specific."

"No. It's okay. I am wondering though about the ghost you saw at the conference. Is she here now?"

Taylor scanned the space around Celeste and shook her head. "I don't see her, don't feel her in this moment. Has she been bothering you?"

"I think it was her last night. She seems to be tormenting my husband. I don't know what she wants, if she's connected to River—the woman I'm trying to help. I'm also having a consistent dream about this little blue house. Something bad has happened inside it. I know that. I keep getting closer, but then I wake up. I can't make heads nor tails of all this stuff that I'm experiencing."

"What else has she done?"

Celeste blew out a breath. "I don't know if it's all her, but my computer has shut down, the power's gone out, doors have slammed, a picture fell and broke in our room, something clawed Jonathan. There's so much coming in. I don't know how to filter out what's relevant and this... this new spirit is... scary."

"I can understand that. I will say I've never been hurt by a spirit, even an angry one. That's not to say they have no power in the physical world. I've seen with my own eyes how they move things, but... I've never had the sense their purpose was to inflict pain or harm. I have run across a few dark entities, but spirits, the departed souls of recent humans are different than that. I didn't get a sense from the ghost I saw near you that she was demonic."

"She feels powerful to me in a way that no other spirit I've seen has felt."

"Power doesn't mean evil. I would imagine there is unresolved pain with this spirit—anger, injustice. I didn't feel evil when I encountered—more like desperation, desperation with a core of fury."

"How do you know what's connected?" Celeste asked. "I'm getting so much data lately. Is it all about River? Is none of it about River?"

"Are you meditating? Getting quiet and then waiting to see what answer comes up to those questions?"

Celeste chewed her lip. She wasn't meditating. Sitting in silence was not her preferred state. When she had a moment not contemplating River's situation, she logged into her Dear Celeste column and answered questions. During the rare slow moments, she'd find herself thinking about the accident and who might have caused it—a thought line she preferred to avoid. "No. I used to be so focused. At the lab I had blinders on, saw only what was in front of me. Now it's like I'm one of those dogs who's obsessed with squirrels. Every time something moves, I'm darting after it."

"I remember some of that overwhelm in the beginning. Now, I think of what comes through as tuning into different radio stations. After my NDE, it was as if I'd grown new antennae that pick up a lot more frequencies. What comes through isn't always clear. Sometimes it's staticky or completely garbled. Often it's scattered, arrives in bits, and it's my job to interpret what I receive. If I get quiet, I can usually get a pretty good sense of what's coming through and why, but again, I have to take Taylor's lens off, Taylor's noise-muffling headphones. I have to listen without my usual biases. Does that mean everything will suddenly click into place with crystal clarity? Nope.

But I think you know this spirit is connected to the girl you're helping. Right?"

"I think so, yes. I guess what's odd is I'm looking for this girl's mother and my natural instinct is to think this is her mother coming through, but... I'm just not getting that loud and clear. And if it's not her mother then who is she?"

"She's probably trying to tell you. Remember, a spirit often communicates in unremarkable ways by drawing your attention to a song, a billboard, a name. The hardest part is taking notice and piecing together what those little nudges mean."

"Do you think it's possible she could... slash someone's tires?"

Taylor raised an eyebrow. "Did someone slash your tires, Celeste?"

"No. My husband's—Jonathan."

She shook her head. "No. I don't think so. Now are there stories of very extreme poltergeist activity? There are. But that feels like a leap. It sounds like someone is trying to scare you or scare your husband."

Celeste sighed. "That's my sense as well. I just started to wonder..."

"It makes sense you'd connect it when you have that type of energy in your home, but..." Taylor frowned. "I find it very difficult to believe any spirit could do that."

"That's a relief. Dealing with a shitty person seems a lot easier than getting rid of an angry ghost who has the power to slash someone's tires."

Taylor nodded. "Although people are a lot more dangerous than ghosts. I think you need to be careful, Celeste."

"How did you integrate this into your life? Your near death? Seeing spirits? I feel like my life before was a dream. It's gone."

"It's been hard," Taylor admitted. "And it's definitely not something I asked for. I was raised Catholic, went to a Catholic school, attended Mass every Sunday. I believed in heaven and hell, in good and evil. Four years ago, I was twenty-five and on my path. I didn't see it coming. Not even for a second.

"I'd gotten my degree in advertising and got hired right out of school. I was dating a Catholic man my brother had set me up with and I thought we'd get married, start having children. The usual track. And I wanted that. I was doing my parents proud. And then that morning we had a bad storm—thunder and lightning. I'd let my cat out and she was under the patio table meowing, desperate to come inside, but scared, so I ran out to get her and then..." She shook her head. "I don't even remember getting struck by lightning. I didn't feel a thing. One second I was running through the rain and the next I was floating in darkness."

23

Taylor sighed and smiled. "I'd come home. I recognized it instantly. Yes. I remembered this place." Taylor stared into the backyard—her eyes had gone dreamy. "In human terms, I was unconscious for about forty-five minutes, but as you know, there is no time on the other side. It was the most beautiful forty-five minutes of my life and I wasn't even in my body. Now coming back, that's when things got hard and I knew it'd be hard. I understood when I crossed over that we come to earth for the experience of contrast, of duality and friction. Immense growth happens through managing that dark and light interplay.

"I didn't tell anyone what I'd experienced when I woke up. I had a memory of this sermon from when I was a child and the priest had talked about false prophets and how the Devil disguises himself as mystical experiences to lure us from the truth. That's not what had happened, but I also understood if I told my priest that's what he'd say to me and so I"—she shook her head—"chose silence. I tried to compartmentalize it, set it aside, return to my life, but... as you're aware, we're not the same when we come back. You can't unknow it, you can't pull the veil back over your eyes once it has been lifted. Throw in the ghosts and the premonitions and... I experienced a pretty dark night of the soul. I wanted it to go away. I wanted my old self back. I could fulfill that role for a handful of days and then something would happen. A spirit would come through, or a premonition.

"I saw my sister-in-law with this terrible wound in her chest and I sensed it was breast cancer and it was early and if she visited the doctor right away, she could treat it and be okay, so I called her and told her to get a mammogram, and at first she argued about it, and I completely lost it on the phone and I scared her. I'd been holding it all back since my near death. I'd been denying it and repressing it and I completely spewed it all over my very sweet, very gentle sister-in-law who happened to be pregnant at the time. I didn't know that yet. Her and my brother hadn't announced it because she'd only found out the week before.

"Anyway, she got the mammogram, and they found cancer and she ended up having surgery. It was a big deal and my family sort of acted like it was a Catholic miracle and I'd been given this vision from Mother Mary, which wasn't true. I figured why not let them believe what they wanted? But then I'd bump up against how many people were excluded from that religion, how many people had been murdered and tortured under the tenets of that religion, how it excluded and judged and shamed, and so I refused to play along with the narrative and that caused a lot of tension. They stopped inviting me to Christmas and Easter, stopped calling to check in. My family had been the foundation of my life and just like that, they were gone.

"That's when I moved here to Fruitport. I needed to be out of the city. Too much noise, not only literal noise, but energy noise. The noise of people's thoughts and emotions, the noise of their fear and hatred. They're not wrong for having those feelings, it's part of living a human life, but it all became too much for me. I needed more space, more quiet."

Celeste watched a large fuzzy bumblebee land on a purple peony, bending the fragile stem. She understood Taylor's desire for solitude, for nature and peace. "Do you ever get lonely?"

"Sometimes. It's been hard to let people in. I'm so grateful for the group—Lena, Jack, Harris, Eliza. They're the reminder that I'm not alone in all this. Each of them had their own losses, their own suffering as a result of this change. Not everyone loses their entire extended family. That's been hard, but a couple of weeks ago I got a postcard from my mom—a few lines about how she missed me. That's the first anyone from the family has reached out to me in months, so…" She shrugged. "It's a start. The truth is, I don't blame them for how they feel. To accept what I'm saying is to deny the religion they've believed their entire lives. I wish they could understand the truth is so much larger than any religion can contain. Men wrote the rules of religion and when you come back from the other side, you realize humans don't even have language for how extraordinary life is, and I don't mean human life, I mean all life."

Celeste considered how difficult her life with Jonathan had become. Even as she imagined the constant tension in her house, she struggled to imagine a life other than the one they'd created. "What happened with your fiancé?"

"He ended the engagement. Honestly, I went about it all wrong. I pulled away from him and eventually he got fed up and ended things. I should have been honest and told him I'd changed and we didn't fit anymore. I took the coward's way out."

"What do you think I should do, Taylor? About this spirit? About what's happening?"

Taylor smiled. "For starters, let's go lie in the yard."

Celeste followed Taylor into the house, where she grabbed two yoga mats and followed her into the backyard. They stretched out their mats and lay side by side in the grass. Above them, the leaves on the tree shimmered.

"Now just breathe," Taylor said. "One hand on your heart, one hand on your belly. Inhale to a count of four into the heart and exhale to a count of six from the belly."

Celeste's mind ran, stumbled over Jonathan's reaction the night before, his slashed tires, the engine of the vehicle behind her moments before impact. She took herself back to her breath, counted the seconds of her inhale, exhale, softened her body. A breeze blew the scent of flowers and grass, the smell of Lake Michigan only miles away.

When the alarm on Taylor's phone sounded, a gentle sound of tinkling bells, Celeste's eyes popped open. She'd drifted away, not fallen asleep, but gone... somewhere. A memory of someone nearby, a woman, Celeste's mother leaning down, whispering in her ear, 'Feed the ravens.'

24

River stared at her notebook, flipped through pages of song starts and stops. Owen and Hope had gone to visit Kenny Bishop's farm so Hope could see the lambs. River had begged off, not up for catching up, pretending to feel fine, feigning excitement for the upcoming tour.

Her phone rang and she saw Celeste's name on the screen. Her stomach tightened. Celeste couldn't possibly have already discovered her birth mother and yet what if she had? What if River picked up the phone and heard a name and a story and her life changed forever?

"Hello?"

"Hi, River. It's Celeste. How are you?"

River scratched a frowning face in her notebook. "I'm okay. How are you?"

"Pretty good. I'm calling because I'm going to come back to Wisconsin tomorrow. I'd like to speak with Dottie Smith and haven't been able to get in touch with her."

"I hate for you to travel all the way back here. I could go. Do you know where she lives?" River did not want to find Dottie

Smith. She wasn't sure how meeting the woman who'd first contacted foster care all those years ago would affect her two days before the tour.

"You have a lot going on right now and this works for me. I like the travel, the time away. I can stop by the farm if you want or not. No pressure either way."

"Yes, please. I'd like to hear what she says."

"It's a plan then. I'll see you tomorrow afternoon."

After River hung up the phone, she returned her eyes to her notebook. She read a song she had started writing the week before.

Sun's risin' now, but I still hear your voice
It's faded down that long dark hall of the mind
That passage we walk from dreaming back to here
I'm lying in my bed, sun pushin' up the curtains, rilin' up that rooster, stirring the birds from their nest
And I just close my eyes tight and try to hold onto the sound
Don't know if it's real
But it's the most real there's ever been
Night's coming soon
I run toward it, desperate, reaching
But the dream doesn't come
Only the creak of the floor, rain pressin' down on the roof, wind slippin' through every crack, coming in from the walls, up from the floor
And my eyes are gritty and my head filled with thoughts of you that have no roots, no anchor. You're a dream, steam rising from the morning pond, clouds drifting by
And the sun's risin' now and I don't hear your voice.

River had been daydreaming in her chair, half-dozing, the stream of her song not yet formed, humming in her mind. The sound startled her, brought her out of the ether back into the room. She blinked at the floor, saw Luna's head perked, the hair on her nape erect. The dog's ears twitched as she stood and moved cautiously toward the door. Beyond the window, night had fallen.

For a moment, silence resumed—Luna stiff, staring hard at the door, the whisper of River's breath and the ceaseless hum of the ancient refrigerator in the kitchen. Outside something fell over, the aluminum trash bin near the chicken coop, she thought, which meant coyotes or raccoons might be trying to get in.

"Come on, Luna," she muttered. "Let's go see."

As she rounded the chicken coop, she froze. The porcelain doll Owen said he'd thrown away sat in a rocking chair in front of the smaller cabin. It had two braided pigtails, bright blue bows in each that matched its frilly dress. It watched River through shiny black eyes.

River's heart thundered behind her ribs and she let out a whimper that caused several chickens to flutter out of the coop and stare at her from behind their wire fence. Luna, also staring at the doll, barked and then started toward it.

"No!" River yelled. "Come." She turned and ran back to the house, nearly tripping over her own feet. She scrambled inside, Luna behind her, and locked the door.

River led Luna to the back bedroom, where she closed the door. The fear and loathing at the sight of the doll was so intense she wanted to scream, but it had no roots. It was a doll. But someone had put it there. She crept to the closet. The shotgun was on the top shelf beneath a stack of quilts. She eased it free, willed her shaking hands to steady.

As she stepped back, she caught her reflection in the mirror above the dresser. A man stood behind her in the open doorway that she'd shut seconds before. She swung the gun around, aimed, nearly pulled the trigger. No man rushed forward. The door remained closed, the lock engaged. Luna watched her expectantly—alert, ready.

River turned back to the mirror. No open door. No man. Just her face, washed of color, her eyes big and scared.

A half hour passed, an hour. River sat on the edge of the bed. Luna had fallen asleep at her feet. The landline phone was in the kitchen. She'd considered going out there, calling Owen, but felt safe closed in the room. Night had fallen. The darkness beyond the window could hide anything, anyone.

There were lights scattered around the property and several had turned on when darkness fell. The bulb near the chicken coop suddenly went dark. River imagined the man beneath it, unscrewing the bulb, setting it on the dirt.

Luna released a shrill bark and a moment later something rattled in the kitchen, the coffee mugs clinking together, a distinct sound when someone closed the front door, but she hadn't heard it open. Had someone done it quietly? Were they standing in her kitchen now, still, waiting to see if she'd heard them enter?

River trained the gun on the bedroom door, steadied her hand on the trigger.

More sounds, movement in the kitchen. River tensed ready to fire.

When the knob twisted and the door swung open, she nearly shot out of reflex, out of terror, but at the same moment the light flipped on and Owen, Hope asleep on his shoulder, came into view.

His eyes went big when he saw her and he instinctively turned away as if to shield Hope, take a shot in the back rather than put his baby daughter at risk.

"River," he said, slowly turning around. "What are you doing?"

River eased the gun to the floor. The fear in Owen's voice made her blood hot with shame. She wanted to lie down, curl into the fetal position, disappear.

Owen didn't ask again. He walked Hope to the crib and

gently laid her inside. He picked up the gun and returned it to the closet. Then he moved to River and helped her from the chair. "Let's go out to the living room. Okay?"

She nodded, couldn't look him in the eyes. She sat on the couch beside him, stuffed her hands between her knees.

"What happened?"

"The doll..." She pointed a shaky hand in the direction of the second cabin. "Did you put it there? Did you put that porcelain doll on the rocking chair?"

He stared at her. "River, I threw the doll away. No. I didn't put it there."

"It was there. Tonight. I walked out because I heard something by the chicken coop and it was there."

He frowned. "Okay. I'm going to go look."

"No." She stood and clutched his shirt. "Please. I don't think you should go out there."

"Honey, I was just outside. There's no one out there. Give me two minutes."

River paced around the kitchen waiting for him, straining to hear a sound. When he returned, his expression was concerned.

"River, the doll isn't there."

"It is. I saw it. Luna saw it." At the mention of her name, Luna's ears perked up.

"What do we need to do, River? I know you're hurting. I know something is happening that I don't understand, but hiding it from me, pulling away from me, is not the way through this."

"You can't help me."

"You don't know that."

"Yes, I do," she said. "Okay? I don't even know what's wrong. I can't tell you how to help because I don't even know what's wrong."

He slid closer to the front of the couch, wrapped an arm

behind her back and pulled her against him. "Okay," he murmured. "Then this is what we'll do. We'll sit here together and just be."

River leaned her head on his shoulder, closed her eyes and wished she could cry.

25

Celeste arrived in Wisconsin just after noon. The morning had been unpleasant, with Jonathan barely speaking to her as she packed her bag. When she'd attempted to hug him goodbye, he'd pulled away abruptly.

She drove to the address she'd found listed for Dottie Smith. The house was on a dead-end street of other small, older houses. Sagging fences, peeling paint and yards scattered with toys punctuated the street. Dottie's house appeared unkempt, the yard overgrown. Unruly bushes crowded the dirt driveway.

Celeste parked behind an old Buick, the muffler hanging dangerously low to the ground. Two faded lawn chairs sat on the weathered front porch. The screen door, slightly open, creaked in the breeze.

Celeste rapped her knuckles on the aluminum door. After a moment, a woman appeared from the dim interior.

"Hi, are you Dottie?" Celeste asked through the screen door.

The woman, likely in her seventies, squinted at Celeste. She lifted a pair of spectacles dangling from a chain around her neck and slid them on. "I'm Dottie," she said. "And who might you be?"

"I'm Celeste Cleary. I've been trying to get in touch, but the number I found for you online was disconnected."

"I'm not interested in donating to whatever it is. Hard enough to keep my own lights on some months."

"I'm not here for money," Celeste assured her. "Twenty years ago, you temporarily had custody of a little girl named Agnes. She'd been abandoned at an apartment building in Madison."

The woman's lips parted slightly. "He got her, didn't he? Came back and killed her?"

Celeste stared at the woman, surprised. "Who got her?"

"Ted."

Celeste shook her head. "No. She's alive and well and goes by the name River now." The 'well' part was not entirely true, but she didn't want to tell the woman that while standing on her front porch. "Do you have a few minutes to talk?"

Dottie nodded and opened the screen door, hinges screeching.

Celeste followed Dottie into the dark little house. The curtains had been drawn and the interior smelled like a mixture of floral perfume and musty carpet.

Dottie sat on a worn pink sofa and Celeste sat opposite her on a matching chair. "Can I ask why you suspected Ted had killed her?"

"Because he was a bad man. I think I knew it even before he split. A couple times, he offered to let the kids play in his apartment and I was adamant that they should stay in mine. I never let them out of my sight. It wasn't until later, after he'd left and Agnes started drawing the pictures, that we knew he'd done terrible things to her and to whoever was in those images. I still have the drawings," Dottie said.

"You do?"

Dottie nodded. "I saved them. I moved a few times over the years and almost threw 'em out, but some part of me knew there'd come a day when I'd need them. That probably sounds batty, but it's true. Give me a few minutes."

Dottie left the room and Celeste considered the room. The scarred coffee table held a scattering of magazines—*Better Home and Garden*, *O*, and *People*. The walls held framed photographs—Dottie's children and grandchildren, most likely.

Dottie returned and handed Celeste a coffee-stained folder. Celeste flipped open the cover and stared at the first picture.

They were crude—to be expected from a five-year-old—and yet Celeste understood why Dottie had been concerned by the pictures. The crude, shaky lines of the drawing depicted a stick woman sprawled on the ground, her form colored in with a jagged black crayon. Surrounding her, red scribbles bled outwards, a grotesque representation of blood pooling beneath her lifeless body. On the floor sloppy stars had been drawn.

Above the woman stood another figure, tall and menacing, drawn with harsh, almost violent strokes. The figure's face was a black void, empty except for two piercing, slitted eyes. In one hand, the man held something long and pointed, its tip dipped in the same crimson shade as the blood on the floor.

The smallest figure—a self-portrait of River, Celeste thought—stood off to the side, her eyes depicted by two large round circles and an O for a mouth. Little blue dots trailed from the child's eyes—tears.

There were ten drawings in total, all variations on the first, though at times an oblong shape had been drawn around the mother figure. In several drawings, additional stick figures, much smaller than even the child stick figure, had been drawn to the side as if watching the scene unfold.

"These are disturbing," Celeste said. "Did you ask her about the pictures?"

"Oh, yes. And she pointed out Mommy, herself and Ted. But when I tried to ask what happened, she'd get quite upset. Sometimes she'd curl into a ball, cover her ears and scream."

"That must have been scary."

"Very. It wasn't only the drawing. She was saying stuff, too. I wrote some of it down." Dottie took out a piece of paper. "I started jotting stuff on the back of an electric bill one day." She flipped it over, squinting at the faded words. "'Mama took a pink bath.' She said that quite a few times. 'Mama took a pink bath. Daddy's looking for the holes.'" Dottie read the words. "This part here is about him touching her." Dottie shuddered. "'Daddy said good girls don't wear underwear.' There were other things. He'd clearly been molesting her and I'm sure he killed her mother."

Dottie handed her the page and Celeste struggled to read the scrawled words. What she could decipher made her stomach clench. She thought of River. What a terrible life the little girl had lived. A terrible life that haunted her now, despite having built such a beautiful world for herself and her daughter.

"She also had a bit of a mean streak," Dottie said. "My granddaughter Erin had a beautiful porcelain doll she'd gotten for Christmas and one day, Agnes picked up a hammer and just smashed the face to bits. My goodness, how Erin cried. It was terrible."

"Did you ask River why she did it?"

"I'm sure I did, though I can't recall her answer now. But I remember she locked herself in the bathroom that day or the next and screamed like a wounded animal." Dottie rubbed her breastbone. "It hurts to think of it. That's when I called the foster care. I was in way over my head."

"Did you have any contact with the police after you found her?"

"Oh, sure. They sent someone out and took a statement.

Eventually, they had a detective on the case and they had a child psychologist talk with her, but the problem was they didn't have a clue where Ted and Agnes had come from. When the apartment complex handed over his paperwork, they found out he'd lied about everything. Fake name, social security number, and he always paid cash."

"She stayed with your daughter for a while. Do you think she'd have anything more to add?"

"Doubtful," Dottie said. "Lynn only had her a couple weeks and then Agnes came back to me because of the touchin' stuff. Sometimes she'd touch my daughter's husband down there. It was clear she'd been taught to do that, but it scared my daughter that they could get in trouble, so Agnes came back to me and eventually went into foster care."

"And you never had contact with her again?"

"Sadly, no. She was a sweet little girl, but we returned to the life we'd had before and... I didn't forget, that's not it, but I think a part of me didn't want to think about her too much. It made me sad. I have a few photos too from back then. Let me see. I know I saw one of Agnes. Lynn pointed it out a couple years ago when we were making scrapbooks."

Dottie left for several minutes and when she returned she held a large scrapbook with a family photo glued to the cover. "I organize them by years. This one should have the picture with Agnes. Let me see." She flipped the heavy plastic pages. About midway through the book, she paused. "There it is. See here."

Celeste leaned over the page and stared at the image. A child River sat on the couch, unsmiling, a red popsicle clutched in one hand. River wore a t-shirt with the words 'Wild Rose Grill' printed above a picture of a rose in a coffee cup.

"Wild Rose Grill," Celeste read. "Did you give her that shirt?"

"Nope. Never heard of the diner. I took this picture when

Ted was still around, so that was a piece of clothing that came with her to the apartment building. There is a town named Wild Rose though, here in Wisconsin. I've never been there. It's a couple hours up north."

"Is there any chance I could borrow this photo? I promise to mail it back to you."

"No reason for me to keep it," Dottie said, pulling it out. "It's the least I can do if it gets the girl some answers."

Celeste wasn't sure what to do about the drawings. She could show them to River, see if they jogged her memory, but she feared they might cause some kind of trauma response. Or perhaps they'd barely register. Maybe River would have no memory at all of the drawings.

When she arrived at River and Owen's house, River was in the garden with Hope. Hope followed Luna around waving a well-chewed toy bone at her.

River stood and made her way to Celeste's truck. Celeste looked at the dark flesh beneath River's eyes. The young mother wasn't sleeping, had taken on a haunted look since Celeste last saw her. Celeste stepped out.

"Hi. It's good to see you again." River wore a pair of shabby jean shorts and a t-shirt, both streaked with dirt. "I've been in the garden trying to get rid of these beetles before I leave for the tour."

"Good to see you too."

"Did you find Dottie?" River looked hopeful, but afraid as she asked the question.

"I did. She still had your drawings. The ones from when you were a little girl."

"Hope. No! Don't touch those." River hurried over to where Hope was straining to reach a pair of garden shears hanging from a fence post. River returned, her expression frazzled. "Sorry, she's into everything."

"It's okay," Celeste told her. She sensed River's agitation and knew it wasn't about Hope.

"I'd like to see the pictures," River said.

"Are you sure? We don't have to do this right now."

"I need to see them," River said.

"Let me grab them." Celeste opened the passenger door and took out the folder Dottie had given her.

River took the folder from Celeste and sat it on the hood of the truck. Hope toddled after Luna. "They're just pictures," River murmured. "Maybe they don't even mean anything, anything real."

"If you don't want to look at them—"

"No. I do. I need to." River took a breath and flipped open the folder. The picture on top showed the three stick figures.

"Are they familiar at all?"

River squinted hard at the drawings, shook her head slowly. "No. I hate them, they're horrible. But they're not familiar." Beneath the drawings lay the photograph. River picked it up and stared at it.

"Do you remember that?"

River shook her head.

"Your shirt says Wild Rose," Celeste noted. "Apparently, that's a town here in Wisconsin. Any memory of visiting there?"

River sighed and handed the folder back to Celeste. "I wish I could say yes, but it doesn't ring a bell. Did Dottie tell you anything else? Did she think I might have lived in Wild Rose?"

"She didn't know, but it's worth looking into. It's also possible Ted picked this shirt up from a thrift store or bought it when you guys were passing through some little town. But I've made some progress on the genealogy website. I really think it's only a matter of time."

"That's good then," River murmured though her voice

lacked conviction. "Would you like to stay again? Owen's at work, but I thawed some chicken breast for dinner. You're welcome to the cabin."

Celeste shook her head, thought of Jonathan and how hurt he'd been she was leaving again. "Better if I go back home, but I'll reach out again when I find out anything new."

"Thank you, Celeste."

She drove to a coffee shop, ordered a large coffee and settled at a table near a window. The ferry out of Milwaukee didn't leave for two more hours. She opened her laptop and checked her email. Dillon, who'd appeared on River's ancestry as a first cousin, had responded. He'd left her a phone number.

Celeste picked up her phone and dialed.

26

A man answered the phone. "Hello."
"Hi. Is this Dillon?" Celeste asked.
"You got him."
"This is Celeste. I emailed you about River, the woman searching for her birth family."

"Oh, yeah. Okay. Pretty bizarre. I tried to think of whose daughter she might be, but I'm honestly not sure. What might make this difficult is I come from a big family. Well, that's not totally true. On my dad's side, it's only him. He was an only child, so she didn't come from his side. My mother had four siblings. I'm only close with cousins from her sister. Her three brothers are spread out. I don't know them, don't know much about their children."

"It still helps enormously just getting a little background on them. Did any of your mother's siblings ever live in Wisconsin?"

"All of them. Born and raised."

Celeste knew she had to tread carefully here. She was either looking for River's father, a child molester and potential murderer, or her mother, who, based on River's childhood drawings, had possibly been murdered.

"I can say for certain this girl isn't connected to my aunt Sheila," Dillon said. "She has three kids—two boys, one girl—and I grew up with all of them. Her and her husband Darren have been married since high school."

"Can you give me their full names?"

"Sure." Dillon rattled off their names, and Celeste wrote them in her notebook.

"And what are the names of your uncles?"

"Three uncles: Mitch, Frank and Brian."

"And their last names?"

"They're all Fultons. That's my mother and aunt's maiden name too."

"Are any of your uncles married?"

"Yes, two of them."

"And what are their wives' names?"

"Umm... let's see, Brian is married to Heather and Mitch is married to... damn. I can't remember her name. My great-aunt Birdie told me at a family reunion last year she's an air traffic controller. That's all I remember. I've never met her. They live down south somewhere."

"Do you think your great-aunt would be willing to talk to me? Maybe she could fill in the family tree a bit more. Or perhaps one of your grandparents?"

"My grandpa's dead. He died a few years ago. My grandma has major dementia. She lives in a nursing home in Milwaukee. But my great-aunt would talk to you. She's the family gossip. My mom says if no one visits her for a couple days you'll find her in the kitchen boring her birds to death with family secrets."

"Does she have a cell phone number you could give me?"

"A landline. She'll talk your ear off, so be ready. Her name's Bernadette Fulton, but everyone calls her Birdie."

"Fulton? Did she never get married or—?"

"Nope. My mom says she's a spinster and proud of it. It's just her and her birds. She's got a whole bunch of them. Parrots and cockatiels and finches."

Dillon gave her the number and Celeste ended the call. She'd been getting annoyed looks from a few patrons in the coffee shop. She packed up her stuff and returned to her truck for the next phone call.

An elderly woman answered on the first ring. "Thank you for calling. This is Birdie," the woman said eagerly.

"Hi, Birdie. My name is Celeste Cleary and I just spoke with your great-nephew, Dillon."

"Dillon. Oh, yes, the boy with all the tattoos. If I were his mother, I'd have told him to put on a proper shirt and cover those up, but Jillian never listened to her own mother and she sure wasn't going to listen to me. Both of her children look like they got raised by a biker gang—the Hell's Angels. You heard of them? A nefarious bunch to be sure."

"Birdie, I'm actually wondering if you could talk me through your family tree?"

"My family tree? My gosh. You got all week to sit on the phone? How about this? You come on by and have a cup of cranberry juice. I buy the Ocean Spray. That's the good kind and my doctor says it helps my bladder. Once you get to be my age, you're prone to those pee infections."

"Where are you located, Birdie?"

"Well, in West Milwaukee, of course. Same as Dillon and Jillian and Sheila. Been here my whole life, in the same house my own ma was raised in. I did some updates ages ago. New carpet, upgraded the stove because that beast was costing me a fortune in utility bills."

"Great. I'm less than twenty minutes away. Can I have your address? I'll come over."

"Sure, sure." Birdie offered her address and started to launch into a story about the mayor wanting his rich buddies to buy up all the houses on her street to sell to an investor for a shopping mall in the nineties. After interrupting her several times, Celeste managed to end the call.

BIRDIE LIVED in a small gray house, the wood siding weathered, the white shutters faded. A fence, once white, surrounded the yard, a gap-toothed smile missing several boards.

Celeste parked behind a small red SUV with a license plate that read 'BEAKS.' Before Celeste could knock, the door opened and a small woman wearing a bright orange sweater paired with white stretch pants smiled up at her.

"I've been waiting impatiently for you!" she said. "Come with me. I've set the back patio table and brought the macaws out. Don't worry, their wings are clipped so they can't fly away."

As they walked through the house, clean and surprisingly sunny, Celeste heard a cacophony of chirps, whistles and titters. Cages containing birds sat on nearly every surface.

"Those are the finches." Birdie pointed at a small cage on the counter that held three little birds with orange beaks. "Tito, Millie and Francois." She gestured at a tall cage nestled beside a grandfather clock. "That's Arnie. He's the macaw who can't go outside because he'll get so worked up, he'll pluck all his feathers right out of his backside." She chortled. "Those on the table"—she gestured at a metal cage—"are the cockatiels. Zinny and Malory. Sisters. Just the sweetest things."

Birdie pushed open the screen door and led Celeste to a back porch. Antique-looking wrought-iron patio furniture, shaded by a large yellow umbrella, sat on the deck.

"My big boys, Gordon and Kiwi, are out there in the tree. See?" Birdie pointed at two large red parrots perched on the peeling white branches of a birch tree.

"They're beautiful," Celeste said, watching the birds.

"Aren't they? Macaws are the world's largest parrots and

some say the most colorful birds. Gordon is twenty-two and Kiwi is seventeen, but they're just babies. Did you know macaws can live to one hundred years old? Those two will probably outlive me!"

"I didn't know they lived that long." Celeste's eyes fell on a cage sitting in the grass near a bush. "Is that a raven?" she asked.

"Right you are," Birdie said. "I've been calling her Madam Mim after that old witch in *The Sword and the Stone*. She's bit me twice now, hard too." Birdie held up her hand to reveal a Band-Aid wrapped around her thumb. "I found her wounded last week. Something with her wing, it seems. I hope to let her loose once she heals up. Ravens, if you didn't know, are very smart birds."

Celeste watched the bird watching them. After a moment, she took her notebook from her bag and flipped it open. "Can you talk me through your family tree?"

"Oh, yes, yes. I forgot all about the family tree." Birdie chuckled and pushed herself out of her chair. "Best if I get the albums. Hmm...? What's a name without a face to go with it? Am I right?" She pointed at two glasses of cranberry juice and a plate of crackers. "Have a snack while you're waiting. That cranberry juice is good for your bladder."

For an hour, Celeste listened as Birdie detailed the family history, starting with her grandparents on her father's side, who'd come to America from Germany in the late 1800s. Her grandmother was as mean as a rattlesnake and her grandfather was as tight as a tick.

Celeste added their names to her notebook. "Dillon told me he has three uncles, but he doesn't know them well. Could you tell me about them?"

"Let's see," Birdie mused. "The oldest boy is Frank. He lives way up north in Michigan on some island. Drummer Island, I think."

"Drummond Island?"

"That's the one. He was Esther's first child and took the most abuse. Esther married Amos when she was just eighteen and that man was a terror. He truly was. He's the reason Esther's in that home, her mind mushier than the applesauce they feed her. I saw with my own eyes how he'd reach out and clobber her over the head for any little thing. Took too long to get his beer, she got smacked. Didn't clean the windows well enough before his ma came for a visit, Esther took a beating for it. I can tell you, watching Esther's life with Amos is the single reason I never had any interest whatsoever in getting involved with a man. No, thank you! Give me my birds and my books and I'm all set."

"Does Frank have any children?"

"No. Again, we can thank old Amos for that. He beat that boy silly. Frank was barely sixteen when he moved out. Lives alone as far as I know. No children. I doubt I'd know him if I passed him on the street, it's been at least ten years since I laid eyes on him."

"And you're sure he has no children?"

"As sure as I can be. He was only ever close to Esther and she claims he still calls when I visit her at the nursing home, but half the time she thinks we're fifteen getting ready to go roller-skating, so she's not exactly right in the head. Anyhow, even when Frank was young, he barely spoke a word. Now Brian is another story altogether. He'll chat your ear off. Course, he never has nothin' nice to say. Complains about his wife, his kids, his boss, his neighbors. It's exhausting."

"Have any of the brothers ever been in jail?"

"You betcha. Frank was into all kinds of trouble as a boy. Got arrested the first time for assault when he was seventeen or eighteen."

27

"Who did he assault?" Celeste asked, circling his name in her notebook.

Birdie twiddled her fingers. "Some boy he got in a tussle with at a bowling alley, if memory serves. He was into fightin', preferred to solve problems with his fists just like his dad."

"Birdie, did you ever hear rumors about one of Esther's sons having a child they gave up or didn't have contact with? A little girl?"

"Gosh, no. Amos would have skinned them alive if one of those boys had a kid they ran out on. He had real strong opinions about a man's duty to his wife and children. A total hypocrite, if you ask me. He didn't blink an eye about beating 'em to a pulp, but God forbid you give one up for adoption or have a child out of wedlock. If it happened, Esther kept it under wraps, assuming even she knew."

"Where did you say Esther lives?"

"The Ivy Senior Care Facility. Not ten miles away from here. Jillian wanted to put her in Blessed Meadows because it's closer to her place, but it's clear on the other side of town from me and I told her, 'Jillian, you and I both know I'll be the one going to see her the most.' Not to mention the traffic going through town takes my blood pressure right up to here." Birdie held up her hand above her head.

"Are there visiting hours or—"

"There may be, but I come and go as I please. Folks in there are probably thinkin' I'm gonna be checkin' myself in any day now." She released a high laugh and one of the macaws laughed in response. "You gonna go see Esther? Like I said, she's scrambled. You'll be lucky if she knows her own name."

"I think I will," Celeste said, standing. "Thanks, Birdie. I appreciate the help."

"You don't have to go just yet. I've got some cold cuts in the fridge. Stay and have a sandwich. I've got some stories to tell about my uncles. They were a wild bunch."

"I appreciate that, truly. But I do have to get going."

Birdie followed her through the house to the front door. "What do you want all that for anyhow?" Birdie asked if it had only just dawned on her that Celeste was a complete stranger probing into her sister's children and their children.

"I'm helping a young woman track down her birth parents and... Dillon came up as a possible first cousin."

"A first cousin? Well, that doesn't make a lick of sense. All the children are accounted for. You're tellin' me it's true? One of Esther's boys had a secret kid?"

"I think so. I'm going to dig a bit deeper."

"Well, you call me when you find out. Hear?"

"Sure. Thanks, Birdie."

CELESTE HAD MISSED the ferry back to Michigan during her talk with Birdie and another wouldn't run until the following morning. She texted Jonathan to let him know. He didn't respond.

The Ivy Senior Care Facility occupied a two-story brick building on a dead-end street. Celeste parked on the street. A vacant lot sat adjacent to the nursing home and a dog, skinny with suspicious eyes, watched her as she walked into the building.

The interior of the facility was old, but clean and smelled vaguely antiseptic. Faded floral wallpaper covered the walls. The wood floors gleamed. It was quiet, the hush thicker when the door swung closed behind her.

At the front desk, a young man in blue scrubs sat scrolling through his phone.

"Hi. I'm here to see Esther Fulton."

"Second floor, third door on the right. Room 204. Stairs and elevator are down that hall to the left." He hadn't even looked up as he spoke.

"Thanks," Celeste said as she moved off down the hall. She opted for the stairs, which were carpeted and wide.

Beneath the room number 204 hung a small chalkboard sign, which read 'Proverbs 3:33—The Lord's curse is on the house of the wicked, but he blesses the home of the righteous.'

Celeste knocked and waited, but no sound came from within the room. After a moment, she twisted the knob and pushed the door open. "Mrs. Fulton?"

Heavy curtains covered the windows and the room was dim and gloomy. It took a minute for her eyes to adjust, but as she scanned the space, she found Esther Fulton in a chair in the corner of the room, thin and frail-looking with wisps of white hair surrounding her sunken face. A blanket lay draped over her lap, a wooden cross sitting on top of it.

"Mrs. Fulton?" she repeated.

The woman didn't move and a pit formed in Celeste's stomach. Had she died? Celeste stared at her chest, searched for the rise and fall of her breath. She detected no movement.

Celeste tried to leave the door open as she crept into the

room, but it swung closed behind her. As she neared Esther's chair, the woman's eyes popped open and she thrust the cross out in front of her. "Get back!" she hissed.

Celeste froze and held up her hands. "Esther, my name is Celeste. I just visited with your sister, Birdie."

"He's comin' for me," Esther whispered.

"Who?"

"Satan, but he's wearin' my husband's skin." Esther's eyes darted around the room and she waved the cross. "I see you! I see you, Amos. You're not foolin' me this time."

Celeste turned on several lamps. The light washed the shadows from the room. "There's no one in here but us, Esther. See?"

Esther leaned forward in her chair, squinted into the corners of the room. Her eyes went wide and she pointed a shaky finger. "He's under the bed."

The hair on Celeste's neck prickled. She moved to the bed and knelt, peered into the dark crevice beneath. For an instant there was a man there, all shadow and slitted eyes, and then he was gone and nothing save a glob of dust and hair remained.

Celeste stood. "Nobody there."

Esther eyed Celeste mistrustfully, but after a moment, she lowered the cross back to her lap and her shoulders relaxed slightly.

"Esther, I'm trying to find out about your son, Frank. Have you spoken to him lately?"

"My boy is dead... dead, dead, dead."

"Wait. Frank is dead?"

Esther sputtered and smacked her cup off her table. Dark juice spilled down the wall and her straw skittered across the wood floor.

Celeste stood and picked up the cup. She grabbed a hand towel from the bathroom and wiped up the juice. It smelled like prunes.

"Not Frankie. Oh, no. Not Frankie, but he did it. Frankie did it."

"Did Frank hurt someone?"

Esther didn't speak. She rocked forward and backward in her chair, gnarled hands gripping the armrests. A line of drool swayed from her bottom lip.

Celeste returned the towel to the bathroom. As she moved back toward Esther, she spotted several pieces of mail sitting on a shelf. Pretending to read the titles of the few books, she flipped through, reading the return addresses. They appeared to be cards, birthday perhaps, unopened. The third card, a green envelope, had a return label that said 'Frank Fulton' with an address on Drummond Island. Celeste took out her phone and typed the address into her notes.

"Esther, does Frank have any children?" Celeste asked.

"He's gonna marry that whore, Frank!" Esther suddenly shouted. "Trapped him! She trapped him!" Esther had begun to rock harder.

Celeste hurried to the bed and hit the call button for an aide.

"Whore! She's a whore!" Esther shrieked.

When the orderly arrived, Celeste slipped from the room and hurried to the stairs.

AFTER CELESTE LEFT the senior facility, she found a motel near the dock for the ferry and rented a room. The neon vacancy sign buzzed and flickered as Celeste carried her bag up the concrete stairway to the row of second-floor rooms.

She ran a bath, steam rising from the faucet. Esther's parting screams of 'whore' still reverberated through her skull. It had been an unpleasant encounter, and though she'd gotten

Frank's address, she felt guilty for upsetting the woman, who'd clearly lost her mind.

As she stripped off her clothes, Celeste brushed her fingers over her tattoo, the dark raven and the message 'evolve.'

Evolve from what? Jonathan had asked.

And she'd given him no satisfactory answer, but as she stared into the yellowed fiberglass bathtub, rust stains marring the drain, she suspected, like Taylor, she was evolving from her old life completely, from her old self, from everything she'd once thought mattered.

Her hip throbbed dully. As she lowered into the hot water, muscles softening, she closed her eyes and drifted.

Celeste stood outside a weathered wood door. As she twisted the knob and pushed it open, she heard a melody, the far-off sound of a lullaby from somewhere in the house—played from a toy, she thought. The air was thick and dark, but faint light spilled down the stairs.

Into the house she went and up the stairs. They shrieked beneath her as if each step caused the soft boards intense pain. But as she reached the top, she understood it was not pain, but a warning they conveyed. Stay away. Go back!

The melody trickled from a room at the end of the hall and when Celeste reached it, she saw through the cracked door a woman sat inside. Celeste pushed the door open.

The woman's back was to Celeste. Her long silver-blonde hair hung down her back. In her hands, she clutched a porcelain doll, its face shattered. The woman's fingers moved delicately, clicking each piece of broken porcelain back into place.

Celeste stood transfixed by the woman as an icy breeze crept along the floor and rose vaporous into the room.

Suddenly, the woman stopped. Her hands went still and she slowly turned her head, just enough for Celeste to see her profile. Her face was delicate, doll-like, but there was a crack running down her cheek, jagged and dark. As the cool mist rose higher, the woman began to transform. Her perfect skin started to sag and turned gray. Her hair thinned and fell to the floor in clumps, revealing patches of mottled, decaying flesh. The crack in her face widened, splitting open like a wound, and from within, black ooze seeped out, dripping onto the doll in her hands.

She suddenly darted from the chair to where Celeste stood and pressed cold, slimy lips to Celeste's ear.

"Behind you!"

28

Celeste gasped and startled awake, sloshing water from the bathtub onto the cracked tile floor. The water had cooled and her blood thrummed in her ears. She grasped the side of the tub, hands slippery, and stepped out.

The nightmare had left her body coated in gooseflesh. She wrapped a towel around herself and staggered from the bathroom. She sat on the edge of the bed, teeth chattering. The room had grown icy as if the air conditioner had kicked on high, though she heard no sound from the vents.

The nightmare still held her, the woman's putrid lips brushing her ear—and worst of all the words, 'Behind you.'

Shaky, Celeste toweled off and put on sweatpants and a t-shirt. She double-checked the locked door, snatched her cell phone from the bathroom counter and returned to her bed.

She saw a missed call from Jonathan and nearly dialed him back, but her heart had not settled and she knew the conversation would only add to her distress. She scrolled through her contacts, paused on Harris, but thought of Robin, the woman at the near-death experiences conference. It felt odd calling him. What if they were together?

Taylor answered on the first ring. "Everything okay?" Taylor asked.

"Yeah. I think so. I just had a nightmare and wanted to talk to someone who gets it."

"Tell me about it."

Celeste described the disturbing scene in the room at the end of the hall finishing with the message, 'Behind you.'

"It's the woman who's been haunting me," Celeste said. "It's her."

"So she's elbowing her way into your dreams," Taylor said. "She clearly has something to tell you."

"Apparently," Celeste murmured, leaning back on the pillows. "But I can't imagine a more obscure message than a doll with a cracked face. How do I make sense of that?"

"You probably can't. My advice? Get out a notebook and write down every detail then give the objects a meaning. What did the doll feel like it meant? Could it be a symbol for a child? Or did it feel like a literal doll? That kind of thing. I did that a lot in the first year after my near death because I realized dreams carried a lot of messages if I could get clear about what certain things meant. For me an old house often symbolizes a longing for something that's gone, some kind of nostalgia. I've dreamed of my childhood home and then had friends from my old neighborhood suddenly send me an email."

"This wasn't a familiar house for me. I didn't like it. It felt... dark."

"Write it all down. And then free-write a little bit. Ask yourself the question: what's this dream trying to tell me? And see if anything comes up."

After Celeste ended the call, she opened her notebook and wrote the dream in detail. At the end, she posed the question: *What is this dream trying to tell me?*

Before she could write an answer, her cell phone rang. She saw Jonathan's name on the screen. She sighed and answered.

They talked for fifteen minutes, small talk and mostly forced, but Celeste listened as Jonathan aired his frustrations about goings-on at the lab. They didn't know who'd slashed his tires, but he and everyone else at the lab had decided it was some thug passing through the parking lot and Jonathan was the unlucky recipient of his ire.

When they ended the call, Celeste forgot all about the dream journal. She pulled the covers up and closed her eyes.

CELESTE SLEPT late and rushed around to leave for the ferry. As she grabbed her notebook from the table, she paused. Two words had been written beneath her question from the night before.

Behind you.

The writing appeared odd, not at all like her own, the letters long and skittering, one bleeding into the next. She hadn't written them, but there they were in black ink on the page—the same words the woman had spoken in her dream.

Unable to spend any more time contemplating the unnerving, Celeste stuffed the notebook in her bag and hurried to her truck.

CELESTE ARRIVED home to find the house in disarray. Jonathan's breakfast dishes were in the sink, the cats were both locked in the spare bedroom and a drawer from the coffee table had been dumped on the living room floor. Pens, an old remote and a scattering of batteries littered the carpet.

Celeste called him.

"Yeah?" he answered, sounding distracted and irritable.

"Hey. I just got home. Is everything okay? There's a drawer out of the coffee table."

"Thanks to my keys going missing again," he said. "Pretty sure it's that damn kitten. Don't know how he's doing it, but he is."

"Romeo?" she asked, doubtful. It seemed unlikely the kitten somehow had gotten to the key ring high on the kitchen wall. "Is that why the cats were shut in the room? Where did you find your keys?"

Jonathan huffed and she heard things crashing together in the background and a moment later glass shattering. "God damn it," he swore. "Jesus. Celeste, I can't talk right now. I'll call you later."

He hung up and she frowned. Obviously, he was having a bad day. Was he unraveling because of her? Because she'd gone to Wisconsin? Because she'd so dramatically abandoned their former life?

She cleaned up the living room and walked into her office. It felt different. She stared at the bulletin board with River's family tree. Nothing appeared out of place, but she suspected Jonathan had been in her study, had gone through all of her work and then taken pains to cover it up. She didn't understand the secrecy, if that was what it was. She didn't lock her office, didn't ultimately mind if Jonathan looked at what she'd uncovered. Still, it struck her as strange.

Celeste logged into her computer and started her search for Frank Fulton. She considered the Fulton family tree. Though Birdie had insisted she knew all there was to know about her nephews, the eldest one, Frank, had moved to the Upper Peninsula of Michigan and virtually cut off contact with most of his family. It was possible he was River's father and had concealed the child. Birdie had described extensive abuse; such abuse might have turned the man into a monster.

Celeste typed in his name, but her only hits were two obituaries that listed Frank Fulton as a surviving family member. The first was Amos Fulton, Frank's dad and the abusive husband of Esther whom Birdie had described. The other was a grandparent. Frank had no social media, no birth or wedding announcements connected to his name, nothing at all in the newspaper archives. The man was a ghost.

When she searched for him in Michigan, a single obscure article appeared beneath the headline *Local Painter Captures Eagle in Flight*. The article did not include a photo of the painter, Frank Fulton, but did contain a photograph of the painting, which depicted an eagle, wings stretched as it soared over a rocky shoreline. The article was dated nearly a decade before and was printed in the *Drummond Island News*.

Celeste had never been to Drummond Island, but knew it was isolated. As she read about the island, population less than one thousand, she imagined the man who'd fathered River. Had he murdered the mother and then, to escape his crime, fled to a remote island?

Her phone rang and Harris's name popped onto the screen.

"Hi," she said.

"Hey. How are you?"

"Good. Just tracing family trees. My new obsession."

"Any progress on the girl's parents?"

"Yes. Actually, I wonder if I've tracked down River's father."

"Really? Interesting. I'm on my way to Grand Rapids now for some meeting my partner was supposed to attend, but he came down with the flu. I could meet you for a lunch after?"

"That'd be great."

As Harris walked toward her, Celeste caught sight of a

young man, thin and gaunt. He moved just behind him, flowing, vanishing. There and then gone.

"This is off topic, but are you, uh... working a case about a younger guy, maybe nineteen or twenty, longish blond hair?" Celeste asked.

Harris' eyes went wide and he nodded then glanced behind him as if expecting to find the young man nearby. "Kris Monroe. He's been missing for two weeks."

Celeste felt a pinch in her arm, the sensation of heat flowing through her veins and then enormous pressure around her heart. She rubbed her arm, shook the sensation away. "I think he died. Maybe an overdose or... something that caused a heart issue."

Harris sighed. "Damn it. Did you see him or...?"

She nodded. "Yes, and felt." She traced the movement from her arm to her chest.

"Do you have any idea where he's at?"

Celeste bit her lip, pictured him and after a moment an image slid into her mind. "I'm seeing a symbol, a blue eight-pointed star. Does that mean anything?"

"Not really. No. I'll have to ask his mom. That's going to be a hard phone call. He was struggling, but I hoped... maybe he'd gone off to get high, would show back up."

"You never know," Celeste said. "I don't want to point you in the wrong direction."

"I've had no direction at all. It's helpful. Truly. Always feel free to share, okay? I get it. I know it's imprecise and I don't expect everything that comes through to be written in stone."

29

As they ate burgers and fries, Celeste filled Harris in on what she'd discovered about the Fulton family.

"It makes sense, right? This Frank guy? I found the other two brothers online. They both have families and have a trackable history. River was abandoned almost twenty years ago. Mitch, the youngest son, was in college then, so that pretty well crosses him out. I couldn't find much on Brian at that exact time frame, but he's on Facebook. He's been married for fifteen years, has twin sons, both seventeen, and he just looks... wholesome. The way River described Ted as this sort of hulking figure with a beard and gaudy belt buckles, this Brian person just does not look the part."

"And Frank does?"

"I haven't been able to find a picture of him. The only photos Birdie had were from when he was a little boy, so not exactly helpful."

"Age range? Did Dottie have any idea how old Ted was?"

"Twenty-five to forty," Celeste said, shaking her head. "Also not very helpful. But I think if I can track down Frank, maybe get a photo and send it to Dottie, see if she can confirm, that'd be a game changer."

"You need to be careful."

"He's in Drummond Island. I don't think I'm in danger. Not to mention he doesn't know I exist. I doubt he has any clue his long-lost daughter is looking for him."

"You don't know he's in the UP. Just because he was mentioned in a newspaper article years ago doesn't mean he's still there or that it's even the same Frank Fulton."

"He is. I found an envelope in Esther's Fulton's room at the senior facility with his name and address. If I give you that, can you get background information about the guy?"

"I can search for a criminal record, but that's about it. I might be able to pull driver's license information, but really, I'm not authorized to do that and the bottom line is if he is a criminal, especially a murderer, his defense attorney will dig up any wrongdoing that led to his identification. Want my thoughts on how to do this? Go back to the aunt or the nephew and see if you can find out who he knew during the time River was born. Who was he dating? Who were his friends? Where was he living? Someone knew him. You need to figure out who. If he was River's dad, someone in his life knew she existed."

Celeste slouched in her chair and rubbed her eyes. "You're probably right, though I have to tell you I'd rather get a root canal than call Birdie back."

Harris chuckled. "That bad, huh?"

"Oh, she was nice enough, just a talker like you wouldn't believe. Her great-nephew warned me, but I was hardly prepared."

"Not to change the subject, but I brought something for you to look over." He took a stack of papers out of a briefcase.

"What is this?"

"It's a list of car rentals in Michigan, Ohio and Indiana. They're Jeep Cherokees with the winter chill pearl color. The kind of car that hit you. These are rentals that happened around the time you were hit."

"How did you get this?"

"I called in some favors, I pushed a bit. You'd be amazed how many people will turn over documents if a detective is requesting them. They were obtained without warrants, which means they're not admissible in court, but they might point us in a certain direction. Recognize any of these names?" Harris asked.

Celeste scanned the names: Tom Vince, Stacy Kimball, Ross Highland. There were twelve total names. Celeste paused on Percy Stiles.

"Do you know one of them?"

Celeste bit her lip, thought of Darlene at Dynamic Laboratories. She shared a last name with this person, but it didn't seem like an entirely uncommon surname. They might have no connection whatsoever. "I worked with a woman at the lab. Darlene Stiles. Same last name as this guy."

"Could this be her husband? Percy?"

Celeste shook her head. "She's not married. I do think she has siblings—could be her dad, a brother. But honestly, this feels ridiculous. She has no reason to hurt me. We've never had any issues at all. Darlene is quiet, nice. She isn't competitive, a climber in the company. I don't think she's ever even published any research. She's probably the last person I'd suspect of trying to hurt a colleague."

"Sometimes the quiet ones have a lot of inner turmoil. I see it often. They might be suppressing their true feelings, on the outside, anyway. Maybe she was jealous of your success."

"And so she tried to kill me?" Celeste laughed, brushed both hands through her hair and shook her head. "No way. I'd sooner believe it was Jonathan. This is some random person who happens to share her last name."

"Maybe," Harris agreed. "But just in case, I'd like her full name and any other information you have on her. Phone number, address."

"Don't you think the Grand Rapids police are already doing this?" Celeste asked. "Shouldn't we leave the investigation to them?"

Harris raised an eyebrow. "I have faith they're doing their job, but I know how difficult hit-and-run cases are. Add to that a busy city with new, more urgent, more solvable cases coming in every day. Why not help them a bit? You saw how things went with Katie, right? Sometimes the detectives are on the ball, sometimes they're not. In the meantime, a truth you best not ignore is that you're in danger. If someone tried to kill you last year, you can bet they're disappointed to have failed and likely plotting how to succeed next time."

Celeste stared at Harris. It was common sense. If someone had tried to kill her—had put the effort into renting a car, learning her routine, risking prison by hitting her—it seemed likely they'd try again. "Maybe not. What if my surviving scared them? And they don't want to risk getting caught?"

"They already risked it once. They already considered what would happen to them if they got caught and went ahead with it anyway. Someone wanted you dead, Celeste. They wanted it enough to kill you. They weren't successful, but they already reached the point of no return and walked through that door. Don't be naive about this. Don't make it easy for them to do it again."

Celeste scowled at him. "And how do you suggest I prevent it? Hmm? Lock myself in my house and peek out the curtains every time someone drives by?"

He raised an eyebrow. "It's not absurd to take basic precautions even when someone hasn't tried to run you over. Keep an eye on your rearview mirror, notice if anyone follows you when you're out and about. Be more aware of your surroundings, make sure you lock your doors and windows at night. It's simple, but those little things are often the way bad people manage to get in. Vary your routine. Probably most importantly, pay attention to the signs, the messages. You're open in a whole new way now. Don't turn off that intuition."

"Where were you today?" Jonathan asked. He sat at the kitchen table, a glass of wine in front of him. Something in his expression made Celeste wary.

"I got home around eleven. Met a friend for lunch, went to physical therapy and ran into the pharmacy to get my pain pills." She held up the bag as proof.

"Who'd you meet for lunch?"

"Harris Mayne. He's a detective in Traverse City."

Jonathan took a sip of his wine. "Huh. Interesting. I've never heard about him before. You didn't think to mention to me you were having lunch with him?"

Celeste considered his words, the sharp tone. "He literally called me this morning on his way into town."

"You could have texted me."

"I called you when I got home and it seemed pretty apparent you were busy. And when have I ever given you a play-by-play of my day? When do you ever text to let me know who you're having lunch with?"

"I ate lunch at the lab today—alone."

"Okay. And?"

"And Dean came back from lunch to tell me he saw my wife eating lunch with another man."

"Jonathan, get to the point. Yes, I had lunch with another man. He had a near-death experience. Now he helps other people who've gone through similar experiences. That's how I met him at a meeting up north and, frankly, I didn't tell you about him because you've made it abundantly clear you don't want to hear about my experience. You want to forget it ever happened."

"Regardless of how you know him, it'd be nice to not get blindsided at work by the news you're out to lunch with another man."

"What are you trying to say? You don't trust me? You're upset because you think I'm having an affair? I assure you I'm not, and considering I've never given you a single reason not to trust me, I'd imagine your first response would not be to jump to that conclusion."

"And I wouldn't have with Old Celeste, but I think we both know New Celeste is rather unpredictable. I no longer know what you will and won't do."

The terms 'Old Celeste' and 'New Celeste' bugged her, the way he said them, as if she'd suffered a midlife crisis and gotten a boob job and taken up rollerblading. She thought again of Joyce and her encouragement for Celeste to put herself in Jonathan's shoes, to imagine the emotions he was experiencing. Yes, Celeste had gone through the near-death experience, but Jonathan too was adjusting to the altered life that resulted from it.

She swallowed her anger. "Okay. I apologize for not telling you."

He took another drink of his wine, watching her. "Fine. Thank you. And I'd appreciate it in the future if you would tell me when you're meeting someone. My tires were slashed last week. You were nearly killed in a hit-and-run. It's not absurd of me to worry about you."

30

River held up a hand to stifle her yawn. Grace not Grit had been practicing for nearly four hours in Arnie's studio and she was struggling to stay focused.

"Are we sure we want to open with *Old Oak Tree*?" Arnie asked. "It's a bit slow. We might do better to push some energy into the room then bring 'em down, take 'em back up. What do you think?"

"We've rehearsed the set list at least three times tonight. I don't think we should change it now," Wayne said. He looked at his watch and frowned. "It's going on midnight. We've gotta wrap this up or my ole lady's gonna lock me out of the house."

"Becky thinks you hung the moon. She'd sooner lock the dogs out," River said.

"I say we stick with *Old Oak Tree*," Morgan cut in. "It's an emotional one. We all feel it and it gives us deep River straight away, which is what they're lining up to see."

"Deep River, huh?" she said. "That implies there's a shallow River."

"Are we talkin' about waterways or the person? I'm getting confused," Wayne said.

"All right, fine," Arnie said. "*Old Oak Tree* it is."

"Morgan, what's the deal on the van?"

"The van's good to go, got her fit as a fiddle last weekend."

"Are you sure?" Arnie demanded. "We're not trying to have a repeat of Green Bay."

The group groaned. River thought back to that show two years before when the van had broken down at three in the morning on the side of a country road in January. None of them had cell service and they'd ended up sleeping in the van, half frozen, waiting for a passing motorist to stop and offer help.

"Not gonna happen," Morgan insisted. "She's ready to drive."

"All right." Arnie stared at him pointedly then stood and stretched. "Let's call it then. Enjoy your next fifteen hours because we're headin' on tour!"

RIVER LEFT ARNIE'S HOUSE. She'd parked her truck a block away at Paulie's Diner where she'd met the band earlier that night for dinner before walking to Arnie's.

It was dark and the warmth of the day had been replaced by a chill. A cool breeze blew back her hair and rustled the leaves in the trees that lined the sidewalk. She adjusted her guitar on her back and pushed her hands into the pockets of her knee-length cardigan.

As she walked, she spotted something lying in the center of the sidewalk. She bent down and picked up a Polaroid photograph. The picture was a little girl from the back with dark hair brushing the collar of her yellow dress. In the background a large rickety-looking farmhouse loomed. As she studied the photograph something stirred in her belly, an odd familiarity. Weirdly, the little girl in the photo looked like the same girl in the picture she'd found in the cabin.

River glanced around, wondered if someone from one of the surrounding houses had dropped the picture, but who? She could stick it in someone's mailbox. Instead, she slipped it into her purse. As she continued down the street, she heard an echo of footsteps behind her. She glanced back, expected to see one of her bandmates—Morgan or Wayne—but the sidewalk stood empty. The streetlamps cast long, strange shadows on the cement and, beyond their halos of light, the darkness was too thick to discern anyone within it.

Her pulse quickened, but she tried to reason herself out of the looming panic. She was in a neighborhood. Someone was likely taking out the trash, running to their car to grab something they'd forgotten.

Still, River faced forward and picked up her pace. Her shoes crunched over bits of stone. Again, she heard the sound of footsteps behind her. When she glanced back the footsteps stopped. No one occupied the street. She fumbled her keys from her pocket and gripped them tight, focusing on the distant silhouette of the truck. She wanted to run, but had the uncanny feeling if she took off, someone would give chase, much like Luna did when a rabbit fled from the bushes on their property.

When she reached the truck, her body sagged with relief until she noticed the paper fluttering beneath the windshield wiper. She didn't want to touch it, but the sense someone gained on her, would soon grab her from behind, overwhelmed her.

River snatched the papers and jumped into her truck, locking the doors. She twisted the key in the ignition and the engine didn't start. Nothing. Not even a whimper. The battery was dead.

"No," she murmured.

She fumbled through her bag in search of her cell phone. She couldn't find it and tried to remember when she'd last had it. In Arnie's basement, she thought, when they'd been going through the set list. Had she left it?

Beyond the windshield Paulie's Diner was dark. The restaurant had closed hours before. She leaned her head back on the seat and felt tears prick the backs of her eyes. Someone could be watching her at that moment, standing in a grove of trees waiting for her to step from the truck.

Minutes ticked by. If she waited much longer, Arnie would lock his door and go to bed. Then what? She'd have to stand on his front stoop pounding to get inside, praying whoever stalked her didn't get to her first. She had to make a run for it.

River searched through her glove box and found the pocket knife Clay had given her years before. She flipped it open and clutched it hard in her hand. She flung the door open and ran for Arnie's house.

She was halfway there, sandals slapping the pavement, her heart so loud no other sounds reached her, when the man grabbed her arm. River shrieked and dove forward, hit the pavement and rolled onto her back, knife ready if he attacked. She pushed hard against the grass with her feet, heels digging into the soft earth as she tried to slide away on her backside.

"River? Jesus. Are you okay? I'm sorry. I didn't mean to scare you." Morgan stood over her.

River stared at him, nervous system still locked in flight mode, unable to respond.

"Hey." He knelt beside her and then, seeing her knife, gently pulled it from her grip and closed it. "What happened?"

After a moment she took his offered hand and climbed to her feet. "My truck is dead. Can you give me a jump?"

He studied her, obviously unsatisfied with her answer, but nodded. "Yeah, of course. I'm parked behind the diner. Give me a couple minutes to drive back to you."

"I'll walk with you," she said, staying close as they started down the road.

"What is this?" Owen asked. He held up the papers from beneath her windshield wiper. River hadn't even read them. She'd balled them up, carried them in and discarded them on the kitchen table. Owen had flattened them and she saw now one was a poem.

River rubbed her eyes, looked away from the pages. "They were on the truck after rehearsal last night."

Owen blew out a frustrated breath. "We need to call the police, River."

"I'm leaving for the tour this afternoon. I really don't feel up for all that." The thought of dealing with the same cops who'd been ready to arrest her for shoplifting days before made her want to scream. "I'll be out of town, so…"

"So what? You'll be safe if you're out of town? I don't trust that. Maybe this tour isn't a good idea." Owen clasped River's hands, rubbed his thumbs across her palms.

"I'm not backing out now," she said. "Arnie has put so much work into this. The venues are expecting us. I wouldn't do that to the band." And she couldn't do it to herself.

Owen sighed, leaned close and pressed his forehead against River's. "Then what can I do? Do you want me to ask for the time off? Travel with you?"

"No. Definitely not. We need the money. Our summer taxes will be coming due."

"I'll find a way to make up the money. I'll work overtime after the tour."

"No. I'm okay, Owen. I promise."

Arnie arrived to pick her up just after four in the afternoon.

When River picked up Hope, the tears that never seemed to come flowed down her face.

"Mama cry?" Hope wiped one pudgy hand over River's wet cheek then leaned her forehead against River's.

"You're going to have so much fun with Daddy," River told her. "And before you know it, I'll be back home."

When River tried to hand Hope to Owen, their daughter squirmed and cried out, waving her hands at her mother to take her back. Finally, River allowed Arnie to lead her to the van and she climbed into the backseat. As she watched her little girl reaching for her, River's face crumpled and she put her hands up to shield her tears.

They pulled up to Wayne's house and he climbed into the backseat beside her. "Why so sad, River? Homesick already?" he asked.

She wiped her face and blinked back more tears, gathering herself to look at him. "I'm okay," she said, and she wished she meant it.

31

Though Celeste had spent much of the day attempting to track down more information about Frank Fulton, she'd mostly hit dead ends and, in truth, her mind had been on the upcoming dinner with her brother and dad that evening. She hadn't seen her dad in months, since just weeks after the accident when he'd visited her in the hospital with a bouquet of flowers and a few mumbled words about how he was praying for her.

The work on River's birth family had her thinking more and more about her own mother. Like River, she struggled to understand how her mother could have abandoned her two young children. Why had she left? Had she been overwhelmed, fed up? Had she intended to come back and then met with foul play?

WHEN CELESTE ARRIVED at the steakhouse, her dad and Adam were already seated. Her dad stood and gave her a stiff hug.

"Seem to be walking better," he said, glancing down at Celeste's cane.

"Better every day," she told him.

"How was the flight?" Adam asked their dad.

Their dad opened his napkin, set his silverware neatly aside and spread it in his lap. "Cramped and full of crying children."

"Sounds like my everyday life," Adam joked.

Their dad didn't respond, but signaled to their waiter. "Are we ready to order?" He looked from Celeste to Adam, neither of whom had even opened a menu.

"Ugh, sure. I can be," Adam said, scanning the dinner options.

"No," Celeste said. "We need a few minutes, but I'll take a Scotch and water on the rocks, please. Dad?"

He pursed his lips, picked up the little drink placard in the center of the table. "A Corona."

"Oh, jeez. Let's see," Adam said, bobbing his head. "How about... uh, do you have a full bar?"

"Yes," the waiter told him. "And a very talented bartender. If you can imagine it, she can create it."

Adam laughed. "Wow. Great. I'll take a strawberry daiquiri."

"Are you on spring break?" Celeste smiled and knocked her knee against his.

Adam blushed and stole a glance at their dad, who stared intently at his menu. "I can't help it. They're so good. They remind me of those strawberry slushies we used to get in Three Rivers. Remember those?"

Celeste grimaced. "How can I forget? I drank so many one time I puked red all over the couch in the basement."

Adam wrinkled his nose. "Ugh! I forgot about that. That couch smelled like rotten strawberries for months."

For the next half hour, they made small talk. Their dad spoke of the weather in Florida, the heat already ramping up.

Adam explained how his first-grade class had taken a field trip to a science center and the kids had gone wild for the dinosaur artifacts.

"What's happening with your work, Celeste?" their dad asked. "Have you returned to the lab?"

Celeste shook her head. "I resigned. I quit. I'm not going back."

Her dad flinched and rubbed the bridge of his nose. "That's unfortunate. You had a very good job there. What will you do instead? Or are you already working?"

"I'm still figuring all that out," Celeste said.

"I'm thinking of adopting a dog," Adam blurted. "Look at this one. I saw him at the shelter the other day. He's a beagle-dachshund mix named Boris." He opened his phone and scooted closer to their dad, scrolling through pictures. "This was a German shepherd-Lab mix named Rebel. So sweet, but maybe too big for me."

Celeste finished her Scotch and asked for another. Adam switched from strawberry daiquiris to a margarita. Their father continued to nurse his beer.

Adam managed to steer their conversation, for most of the evening keeping the mood light. Their dinners arrived, but halfway through eating, Celeste couldn't hold back any longer.

"I'd like to talk about Mom," she announced.

Their dad, who'd been cutting the last of his steak, stabbed a piece and shoved it into his mouth. He chewed for a long time. "There isn't anything to talk about."

"Of course there is. Where is she? Who was she? Why hasn't she contacted us all these years?"

"I don't have answers to those questions."

"Tell me about her," Celeste urged.

Adam looked uncomfortable. He seemed to be silently signaling the waiter with his eyes.

Their dad sighed, pulled his napkin off his lap and bunched

it on the table. "She looked like you, or you look like her. Except now with the red hair... well, that's different."

"What about me looks like her?"

He twiddled his fingers near his eyes. "Your eyes, smile."

"Did you ever talk to her after she left?"

"She called a couple times, sent a letter." Their dad, too, had fixed his gaze on the waiter, as if the man couldn't bring their bill soon enough.

"Saying what? Where she'd gone? Did she ask about us?"

Adam practically fell out of his chair when the waiter arrived. "We're ready for the bill," he said.

"I'll be right back with it," the waiter assured him, and Celeste saw the despair in Adam's face as the waiter headed not to the register, but to greet a group of women waiting to be seated.

"She didn't ask much. As I've told you in the past, she had a breakdown, a mental breakdown."

"And that's it? You let her walk out of our lives, out of your life, with the cop-out of a mental breakdown? What even is a mental breakdown?"

"Jesus, Celeste. I don't know." He flung his hands in the air, bumping the table and sending their glasses teetering. "I'd imagine... she wanted a different life, okay? Being a parent was hard. Until you have children, you won't understand what I'm talking about."

Celeste found his answers infuriating and his attitude even more frustrating, as if he was annoyed she even wanted to know.

He rested a hand on his chest, then pulled out his wallet and laid two fifty-dollar bills on the table. "I think I need to get back to the hotel to take my medicine. Good to see you both." He stood and hurried away without looking either of his children in the eye.

"Well, tonight was a shit show," Adam murmured, taking another sip from the mango seltzer he'd bought a six-pack of on the way to Celeste's house.

He and Celeste sat on the back porch. The evening was unusually warm for late spring.

"Yeah. Sorry. I couldn't help myself."

"I felt it coming," he admitted. "And..." He shrugged. "You're right. I have those questions too. I just don't want to push Dad even further away."

Celeste heard a car in the driveway. A minute later, Jonathan slid open the patio door. "How did dinner go?" he asked.

"It was fine," Celeste told him.

"So fine, we're out here getting sloshed," Adam said, holding up his seltzer.

"I don't think it's even possible to get sloshed on those." Celeste laughed.

"Au contraire," he said. "I'm walking the tightrope of inebriation as we speak."

"Why don't you grab a glass of wine and join us?" Celeste told Jonathan.

For a moment she thought he might, hoped he might. That for an evening, she and Jonathan could have a night like they used to, share a few drinks, laugh about old times. But his mouth turned down.

"Some of us have to work tomorrow," he said.

Celeste bristled, but didn't respond as Jonathan walked back inside.

"Damn," Adam murmured. "He's pissed. Do you think he's mad that I'm here again?"

"No. It's not about you. It's about me."

"But why? Because you left the lab?"

"When I had the accident, something happened."

He turned and watched her.

"I died. When the car hit me, I left my body and... well, I went to the other side, to heaven, though I don't love that word. I went home. That's what it felt like, home. Except there aren't really words to explain it."

"Are you serious?"

"Completely."

"Why didn't you tell me before now?"

Celeste sighed and leaned back, took a drink of her Scotch and watched a dark shadow swoop toward the grass. A raven. It landed and stood watching them. "I told Jonathan in the hospital and he didn't believe me. He acted like I was crazy, like I'd hallucinated because of the head injury."

Adam scoffed. "That's Jonathan for you. What was it like? What did you see?"

Celeste smiled, growing warm at the memory. "It was beautiful and... perfect. Nothing hurt, nothing was scary, and there was someone with me, a woman. Not in the body, but a presence. I think it was our mom."

He frowned. "Our mom."

"Yes."

"So, you think... she's dead?"

Celeste nodded. "I do."

Adam sagged back against his chair. "Did she talk to you?"

"Not with words, no."

"Did you ask her if she was our mother?"

Celeste shook her head. "It's not like here. The questions we have here aren't relevant there. It didn't even cross my mind to ask her because... I felt like I already knew."

Adam blinked several times.

"Do you feel that way, Adam? Like she's gone?"

He swiped at his eyes, tilted his face up as if that might quell the tears. "Um... when I... when I graduated from high school, for weeks before the day, I had this absurd idea she'd show up. What mother misses her son's high school graduation? And I know by then she'd already missed yours, so I shouldn't have been surprised, but honestly, I was. I walked across the stage and looked out and had this moment where, um..." He released a shaky breath. "This really beautiful woman, probably in her forties, had her eyes locked on me. I convinced myself it was her. I broke into this ridiculous grin."

Celeste closed her eyes. She remembered the grin, how his face had suddenly lit up.

"And then I realized she was looking at the kid in front of me. Drew Baxter. It was his mom."

"You said you had a stomach ache, weren't up for lunch afterwards," Celeste murmured.

"Yeah. Exactly. Once I realized who she was, I felt sick to my stomach and like I was going to cry, which is the last thing you want to do in front of your entire graduating class. I couldn't have made it through lunch. Anyway..." He took another drink. "That was the moment for me when I realized she could be dead. We assumed she left and started a new life somewhere else and maybe she did, but then... who knows? She got hit by a car, she killed herself. People die every day. If she'd covered her tracks so people didn't know it was her, they might have buried her thinking she was someone else."

"Don't you want to know?"

"Of course I want to know, but people disappear, Celeste, and we don't always get to know. She left."

"I need to know."

"How will you find out?"

"People leave a trace. Everyone does. I've been helping a woman in Wisconsin trace her birth parents. We started with an ancestry database and I might have found her dad, though I'm not positive about that yet. Anyway, it's easier than you'd think."

Adam sat forward, hands braced on his knees. "You want to use one of the ancestry things to find Mom?"

"It's a start. If I can track down her side of the family, they might know where she went. Who knows? Maybe she is still alive."

32

They were five nights into the tour, and River was already worn out.

She sat on the edge of the bed in a little motel outside of Detroit where they'd performed a standing-room-only show. Exhaustion surrounded her, made her shoulders slump, her eyelids heavy. But she'd not yet talked to Owen and Hope. She needed to hear their voices before she'd fall asleep.

She tried Owen's cell phone and got his voicemail. Next, she dialed their home phone again. It rang and rang. She ended the call.

She'd toured before, but this time seemed different, in much the same way everything in her life had felt different lately. The buzz of excitement had been replaced by a drone of foreboding. After the show, as the rest of the band reveled in the afterglow, the energy of the audience, River wanted nothing more than to return to her hotel room.

She was exhausted but couldn't sleep. Each night in a new motel, unfamiliar odors, strange noises. This one smelled of the previous occupant's perfume. The springs of the bed creaked when she moved. The carpet was stiff in spots, the walls an off-putting gray.

This tour was a big deal. The venues were paying them more. Arnie had set up merchandizing. Their social media had grown by more than ten thousand in the previous two weeks.

The dream was coming true. She'd prayed for this, literally—had put it in the God Box when she was seventeen years old. She'd longed to reach more people with her music. For validation that she was good enough.

Instead of euphoria, she felt exposed. Each night before she walked onto the stage in a new venue, a tremor of fear crawled up her spine with icy sharp fingers. She expected it to wrap its gnarled hands around her throat and cut off her voice, her breath. It was panic, Shay told her. Anxiety.

River had never suffered from such an affliction—stage fright. But now it tailed her, an unwavering shadow.

It lay beside her now in bed, pumping her head full of terrors. Her heart thundered and her stomach felt acidic.

Had Owen not answered because something terrible had happened at home? Had the person who'd been lurking outside stolen in and murdered Owen and Hope?

"Stop. Shut up," she hissed at the horrible voice with its dark lies.

She sat up and dialed Owen again. This time, the phone picked up and a rush of relief flooded her body. "Owen. Thank God. I've been trying to call you. Where have you been?"

Owen didn't reply.

"Owen?"

No one spoke.

"Who is this?" River demanded.

Someone had picked up the phone, and it wasn't Owen. It wasn't impossible for Hope to grab the phone and answer it, but there was nothing quiet about their two-year-old. She'd have babbled. Whoever was on the line said nothing, but after a moment another sound emerged, the tinny melody of a music box—an eerie lullaby.

River jerked the phone away from her ear as if someone had pierced her eardrum with a needle. Her body shook and the rush of her own blood filled her head. The room swam and River blinked and sank to her knees. There was something familiar about the lullaby, a haunting sound that took her back, back to some dark place she'd buried.

Trembling, she put the phone back to her ear. The song no longer played, but the breathing had returned.

"Who's in my house?" she screamed.

Another click. The line went dead. She called back. It rang and rang.

River called Owen's brothers—no answers. Then she dialed his parents—voicemail. She wanted to call home again, feared the breath, the music. She paced around her hotel room then moved into the hallway, stopped at Arnie's door and pounded.

Stay calm. Don't freak out.

But she was freaking out. Her heartbeat filled her head. She wanted to slam both fists on the door, scream his name.

He pulled the door open, sleepy-eyed. She'd woken him. "River?"

"Have you talked to Owen? I can't get ahold of him and the last time I called, someone picked up and they just breathed and—"

"Hey. Hold on. Owen is camping tonight at Devil's Lake State Park. Remember? His whole family was going for his brother's birthday. They probably don't have cell service."

"Devil's Lake..." she murmured. She'd completely forgotten Owen's mother had scheduled an overnight camping trip for Danny's thirtieth birthday.

"Do you want to come in, River? I have... uh..."—Arnie scratched his mussed head, glanced back in the room—"a couple of bottles of beer in the fridge."

"No... I'm okay." She started to turn away, then stopped. "But someone answered the phone," she told Arnie before he closed his door.

He frowned. "Maybe one of the dogs knocked it over."

"No..." She shook her head. "They would have been barking, making sounds. I heard someone breathing." She didn't tell him about the music, feared that detail would cast the story in some unbelievable light.

Arnie, clearly tired and unsure what to say, fidgeted, pressing a hand against the doorframe. "You could call a neighbor, have someone stop over, but..." He held up his wrist and squinted at his watch. "It's after two in the morning."

"You're right. Okay. I'm sorry I woke you. See you in the morning." She hurried back to her room, did not glance back at Arnie, who she imagined had an expression that would have made her uncomfortable.

She sat on the edge of her bed and imagined their little house. At that moment, someone stood inside of it, a stranger moving amongst their things, touching Hope's clothing, sifting through River's notebooks. It made her want to scream, to call the police and demand they go to the house and catch him. But she didn't because when they arrived, he would be gone, all trace vanished with him.

River lay on her bed and stared at the ceiling, knowing sleep would not come.

The band was on the road the following day when Owen finally called River back.

"Owen?" she said, trying to keep the alarm out of her voice.

"Hey, babe. Hope and I just got home. Everything okay? I saw your name on the caller ID a bunch of times."

"I called last night," she said. "And someone picked up and then hung up on me."

"Someone answered our home phone?"

"Yes. There was someone in the house." River listened to Hope's voice in the background.

"I'm walking through the house now. Everything looks just the way I left it. Doors are locked."

"Someone was there," she insisted. She wanted to tell him about the music, the mechanical lullaby, but she thought of that horrible porcelain doll that she'd seen in the rocking chair that had been gone when Owen went to find it and the expression on his face—the concern he had for River, that she was coming undone.

"Huh. Weird," he said. "I wonder if... I don't know, there was something going on with the phone lines or—"

"Pit stop," Morgan called from the driver's seat as he maneuvered the van into a rest area and parked.

"Is everything all right, River? You sound... upset."

She waited until the guys got out of the van to respond. "I am upset," she told him, her voice rising a pitch. "Someone was in our house last night."

"Okay. I'm going to look around, see if I can see tire tracks, or anywhere a window or door was messed with. Right now, everything looks okay, but—"

"You don't believe me."

"River, I believe you. I just wonder, could... I don't know, phone lines have gotten crossed or whatever?"

"Are you sure you threw the doll away?"

"The porcelain doll? Of course. I told you, I stuffed it in the trash can and they picked the trash up days ago. It's in the landfill by now."

No, it's not, she thought, but she didn't tell him that. "Did you ask your brothers if one of them dropped it off?"

"Hope, no—no, honey," Owen said. "Sorry. She's got the

refrigerator open and is trying to get the strawberries. Umm... I forgot to ask about the doll. I'm sorry. I'll call them, okay?"

"You need to be careful," River told him, gripping the phone so hard against her ear it ached. "Promise me you'll triple-check the locks tonight."

"I will. Don't worry, honey. Okay? Just enjoy the tour. We're fine."

33

Celeste woke to the sound of a text message coming through on her phone. She squinted at the message.

Owen: *Hi, Celeste. Is there any chance you could go see River at her show in Traverse City tonight? I'm not sure how far that is from you, but I think the shows have been hard on her and she could use the extra support. I'd go if I could get away, but there's a big auction I need to be at.*

Celeste stared at the ceiling. Jonathan would be angry if she went, and yet she knew Owen wouldn't ask if he didn't really feel like River needed some help. She responded: *I'd love to. Where's the show and what time? I'll be there.*

When she arrived in the kitchen, Jonathan was loading his bowl and coffee mug in the dishwasher. "I'm working late again tonight at the lab, so I'm afraid you'll be on your own for dinner," he told her.

"Actually..." Celeste lowered her gaze. "I'm going to head up to Traverse City for the night. River's on tour and she's playing up there."

Jonathan remained expressionless, but she felt the

unspoken outrage. "And you intended to tell me that, or was I just going to come home to find your truck gone?"

"I'm telling you now."

"So you are. See you tomorrow then." He grabbed his briefcase and thermos of coffee and walked out the front door.

CELESTE ARRIVED in Traverse City just after five p.m. She checked into her room at the Park Place Hotel, then took a quick shower.

She texted Harris, who she'd spoken to on her drive up. He planned to meet her at the brewery to see River play.

Celeste walked two blocks to the brewery and entered to find many of the tables full. She spotted an empty one and hurried over to set her bag on the table.

Arnie walked in a side door carrying a guitar case. Celeste waved. "Arnie. How are you?"

"Too blessed to be stressed." He grinned, adjusting a loop of cords over his shoulder. "How's the furball? Settling in?"

"He's good. Putting on some weight."

"Celeste," River exclaimed, standing from a long table where the server was clearing the plates. "Owen said you might be coming. It's so good to see you."

Celeste hugged River. The young mother seemed thinner, her eyes red-rimmed, her skin ghostly in the dim light. "Is everything okay?" Celeste didn't want to tell River that Owen had mentioned she'd been struggling on the tour.

River smiled and brushed her hair away from her face. "Sure. Yeah. Taking it a day at a time and all that."

"River, there's a couple of girls over here who'd like you to sign their t-shirts," Shay told her.

"If you have some time, maybe we could grab coffee in the morning and talk," Celeste said. "I'm staying at the Park Place, room 319. The hotel with the glass bar on top. There's a restaurant in the lobby."

River rubbed the skin beneath her eyes and nodded. "That'd be good. I better go sign these. Thanks again for coming, Celeste."

"How has the tour been going?" Celeste asked Shay when River hurried to the table of t-shirts.

"Amazing!" Shay gushed. "We've never seen a turnout like this."

"And River is enjoying the tour as well?"

Shay's eyes drifted to River where she leaned over a table signing the t-shirts of the two girls. "I think so. I'm sure she misses Hope and Owen, but she's killing it up there."

From a side door, Morgan walked in with a large cardboard box.

"That's my cue," Shay said. "I'm selling merch for the band tonight. Better go get the rest of it out. Nice to see you, Celeste."

Celeste ordered a Scotch and water and sipped it. River seemed far away, her eyes often veering toward the windows as if she'd rather be out there.

The door to the brewery opened and Harris walked through. Celeste called out his name and waved. He moved through the crowded restaurant and slid into the booth opposite her.

"Good grief, it's packed in here. This town gets busier every year. Sorry for my dirty shirt. I came straight from the nursery. I popped in to check on things, not at all intending to get dirty, but they were transplanting some saplings, and as you can see..." He gestured at his shirt.

"You own the nursery?"

He nodded. "It was something I came away with after my near-death experience, this sense that trees were sacred. It stayed with me. I had no intention whatsoever of buying the nursery. I didn't even know it existed back then. But as I'm sure you're starting to realize, everything lines up a certain way. I received an inheritance literally the day I met the woman who owned the nursery, and she'd decided to sell. Guess what her asking price was?"

"The amount of your inheritance."

"Bingo." He spread out his palms and grimaced. The grooves of his hands were dark with black soil. "Apparently, I need to excuse myself to wash my hands. I'll be right back."

Celeste watched him hurry away. She wondered about his new girlfriend, Robin. She'd prepared herself to see them walk in together, but he'd arrived alone.

River stripped off her sweatshirt. She wore a gray tank top and her chest appeared splotchy. She slipped a Grace not Grit t-shirt over her head and picked up her guitar.

When Harris moved back toward the table, Tex bumped against him. "Sorry, man," Tex said, hefting up a large amp.

Celeste watched Harris stare after him, a crease between his eyebrows. "What is it?" she asked when he slid into the booth.

Harris rubbed his hands together, brushed off both his shoulders and shook his hands off as if flinging off water. "Is he in the band?" Harris asked.

"No. He's a groupie. That's what they call themselves. Helps carry equipment, load and unload. Did you feel something just now?"

Harris continued watching Tex, who'd joined the band and was helping Arnie connect the amp. "Yeah. A little jolt of... something. Unease, wariness. It happens sometimes. I'd steer clear of him."

"Really? You think he has bad intentions?"

"Hard to say." He sighed and returned his eyes to Celeste. "I've learned to trust my instincts. Something feels off about him. That being said, he may just be one of those guys who tailgates you in traffic and tips badly."

"I could see that," Celeste said.

The waiter arrived and Harris ordered a beer. "We found Kris," Harris said after the waiter left.

"Who?"

"Kris Monroe. The missing boy."

"Oh. Gosh, yeah, of course." Celeste thought again of the young man, the whisper of him that she'd seen, the sudden jolt to her heart.

"You were right. He overdosed in his uncle's barn up in Munising. The uncle's been traveling for work, just got home and found him."

Celeste frowned, imagined the eighteen-year-old's mother, the new reality of life without her son. "I'm sorry," she murmured.

"The sign you saw, the eight-pointed star—there's one painted on the face of the barn. It's a symbol meant to bring good luck and abundance. Apparently a lot of farmers paint them on their barns or hang the signs on their houses. Now that I've heard about them, I'm seeing them everywhere. Also, I went ahead and forwarded that list of car rentals to the detective working your hit-and-run case."

"Detective Bowman?"

"Yep. Turns out he was at the meeting I went to in Grand Rapids, didn't even realize it until I called the station later to speak with the detective on the case. He and I had spent half an hour chatting over coffee about how to get Japanese beetles away from his cherry trees."

"Bowman is a tree guy as well?"

"He has a mini-orchard. Mostly it's his wife's baby, but he's taken the beetle problem on himself. Anyway, I sent the list, and he's having a look."

"Did he say anything about leads or suspects?"

Harris took a long drink of his beer, then shook his head slowly. "Nothing concrete, but they're working it."

Celeste noted something in Harris's face, an expression

there and gone so quickly she might have imagined it. She suspected he was holding something back.

"I have the next week off," he said, as if wanting to change the subject. "I put in the request last summer and forgot all about it." He laughed.

"Do you and Robin have plans?"

"Nope. She's in Boston for a work thing. She asked if I wanted to fly out for a couple of days, but..." He shook his head. "I don't think I'm ready for that."

"But things are good with the two of you?"

"Yeah. It's new and we're taking it very slow, but... we mesh pretty well."

"That's good."

"How are things with Jonathan?"

Celeste remembered his expression that morning when she'd told him she was going to Traverse City. "Not amazing. He wasn't happy I came up here, but more fodder for our therapy sessions." She laughed dryly. "Want to go to Drummond Island tomorrow?"

He raised an eyebrow. "You're kidding, right?"

She pursed her lips. "Maybe, maybe not. The ferry runs all day and starts at five a.m. It's a three-hour drive from here."

"Celeste, why did you even look that up? You can't seriously want to track that Frank guy down. It's one thing to look him up, to trace River's birth line, to talk to her family, but you suspect this guy of being a murderer."

"No. I know. It's crazy."

Harris took another drink and looked at her again. "You're going to go, aren't you?"

Celeste nodded. "Yeah. I think I am. What does it hurt to talk to him?"

"I'm not even going to answer that." He shook his head. "Fine. I'll go."

She looked up abruptly. "You're not serious?"

"Why not? I've got the week off, plus I…" He closed his eyes, smiled. "I'm seeing a green light. That's a 'do it' signal for me. I try to follow that."

Beyond them, River began to sing, and a hush fell over the bar.

Celeste woke in her hotel room to pounding on her door. She stood, searched the darkness along the wall for her cane, and hurried across the room. Blinking, she pressed her eye to the peephole and stared out.

River stood in the hall, face frantic, wet hair plastered against her cheeks.

Celeste unlocked the dead bolt and opened the door. "River? What's wrong?"

River cast a fearful glance down the hall. "Can I come in?"

Celeste nodded, the fog of sleep blurring the edges. She peered quickly down the hall, feared she'd see someone there, but the hall was empty.

"Oh, God, I'm sorry to show up like this, and I know I shouldn't have come here because maybe I led them here or… maybe…"

"Led who here? Was someone following you? Tell me what happened."

34

River stripped off her sweatshirt to reveal her soaked tank top.

"After the gig tonight, we got invited to an after-party at the brewery owner's loft. We all went, the whole band, and, umm... I had a drink, but I wasn't really in the mood. I decided to walk back to the hotel. About a block from the loft, I heard someone behind me. I kept walking slower, waiting for them to catch up and pass, but they'd start walking slower, so I walked faster and again, they matched my pace. Every time I turned, they were gone, like they ducked behind something.

"I tried telling myself I was imagining things, but one time I turned and caught sight of someone, just for a moment. A man all dressed in black, a hood over his head. He was too far away to catch any features, but when I saw him, he ducked behind a big tree. I ran and turned a few times to lose him and I got completely lost. If it wasn't for the rooftop bar at your hotel, I wouldn't have made it here. It's lit up, and I ran toward that."

She paced to the door and stared through the peephole. After a moment, she returned and sat on the edge of the chair near the window, then, noticing the cracked curtains, pulled them tight.

Celeste, still dazed from sleep, tried to focus on River's story. "Could he have just been some random guy who saw you play tonight and decided to follow you, or—"

River shook her head. "There's been someone, I think... someone following me."

"For how long?"

"A few weeks. I'm not sure exactly." River fidgeted, then stood and walked back to the door and peered into the hall.

"Would you like a drink?" Celeste asked. "I have Scotch."

"Yeah, okay, yeah. Maybe that will help." River picked up the bottle from the bureau, twisting the cap off. Her hands trembled as she shook two plastic cups from their cellophane covers. She didn't ask if Celeste wanted one, simply poured them each a cup and carried one to Celeste.

"When did you first start to suspect someone was following you?"

River bit her lip. "It's hard to pinpoint because... I haven't been myself. A few times I wrote it off, figured I was being paranoid."

Celeste remembered her time at River and Owen's cabin and her disturbing experience of waking in the night, her body paralyzed, the dark spirit in the corner, and a man outside the window. "I saw someone when I stayed at your place."

River, who'd been staring into her cup, looked up sharply.

"When I mentioned it to Owen, he said you had a stalker last year."

River's face paled. She swallowed the entire contents of her cup.

"Are you afraid it's him?" Celeste asked.

"Before we left for the tour, I found a note under my windshield, the same notes he sent last year."

"With the love poems?"

River nodded.

"What did the note say?"

"'Good luck.'"

"That's it? 'Good luck?' What do you think it meant?"

"Good luck on the tour, I guess. At the time, I... I don't know. I found myself shoving the thought of it away."

"Was there a poem?"

"Yes. 'She Walks in Beauty' by Lord Byron."

"I'm not familiar with it, or with much poetry at all. Anything disturbing in it?"

"No. It's quite innocent."

"Did you tell Owen?"

"Yes. He wanted to call the police, but we were literally leaving for the tour that day. I didn't want to screw this up for everyone and maybe..." She tugged on a strand of her damp hair. "Maybe I'm imagining things. You know? This guy tonight. I've been struggling for a while now. All this emotion and fear and stuff. It's gurgling up out of this sewer of my past. I can feel it, like a geyser getting ready to explode, and when I try to think about this guy following me, there's no face, there's nothing distinct. It's like he's a phantom, a figment of my imagination."

"Do you really believe that?"

"I honestly don't know." River's eyes slid shut for a moment and she popped them back open. "I should go," she whispered. "We have to be on the road by nine in the morning. I have to try to sleep."

"Stay here tonight. Take that bed. I'll drive you back to your hotel in the morning."

"I don't want to invade your space, Celeste. You already drove all the way up here."

"It's not an invasion. It's good for me too. Please. Stay."

CELESTE'S NIGHT was a garble of fragmented dreams.

She was in a dark field, woods in the distance, the sky black, starless. A man chased her, the tall grass crunching beneath heavy boots, his breath like a raging bull violently searching.

She ran forward, arms outstretched, and the earth opened beneath her. She fell and fell, eyes clenched tight, and when she opened them, she stood on the sidewalk in front of the little blue bungalow. Candles lit inside, flames flickering against the blood-splattered windows.

The ring of a cellphone jerked her from sleep. She sat up and turned to see River, face sleepy, groping for her phone.

"Hello?" River answered, her voice thick. "Mm-hmmm. Okay. Yes. I'll be ready. Bye." River looked at Celeste. "I'm sorry that woke you. It was Arnie. We're leaving in an hour."

Celeste got two cups of coffee from the lobby and drove River back to her hotel.

"How are you feeling?" Celeste asked before River climbed out.

River tilted the mirror down and grimaced. "About how I look, like crap."

"I think you could go a year without sleep and still look great."

River didn't smile. "I miss home. I just want to go home."

"Maybe you should."

River opened the door. "I can't. A few more days and it's over. I can do this." She seemed to be convincing herself more than Celeste.

"You can," Celeste agreed. "You have my number. Don't hesitate to call. I'm closer than Owen and I'm happy to meet you anytime."

"Thanks, Celeste."

35

Harris arrived to pick Celeste up at the hotel just after ten in the morning.

"Are you sure you don't mind driving?" she asked.

"Not at all. Hop in. How are you feeling about this?"

Celeste plopped her backpack on the floor of Harris's passenger footwell. She unzipped a front pocket and took out a bottle of water. "I'm trying not to let myself feel much of anything."

"Why is that?"

"Because Jonathan would be furious I'm going."

"You didn't tell Jonathan?"

"No. I texted him I was staying another night up north, but didn't give specifics."

"Why?"

"To avoid a fight."

"You've opted for the 'easier to ask forgiveness than permission' route?"

Celeste uncapped her water and took a drink. "I'm not this person. This person who hides stuff."

"Is it because he's resisted hearing about your experience?"

"Yeah. The tension in our house is so thick you can taste it."

"Is that why you keep choosing to help people far from home? It gives you an excuse to leave?"

Celeste frowned. "It doesn't feel like a choice. I mean, I know it is, but Joanna, River—I feel called to help them."

"That I can understand."

"River showed up at my hotel room last night afraid someone was following her."

"Did she call the police?"

"No. She lost him and came to my room."

Harris glanced at her. "That's not very safe."

"She's worried it's in her head."

"What do you think?"

Again, Celeste shifted back in time to her night in River's cabin. She too had questioned if the man hovering outside was real. "No. I think he's real."

THE FERRY ACROSS THE ST. Mary's River to Drummond Island took only fifteen minutes. Despite the serenity of the boat ride, Celeste's mind churned with thoughts of Frank Fulton. Were they about to come face to face with River's dad? Would he be the nightmare she'd been imagining for the previous weeks?

The ferry's horn blared and seagulls hovering on the boat took flight.

When the ferry docked, Harris and Celeste drove through the heavily forested island to the address she'd found at the nursing home.

"Pretty remote," Harris said, turning down the dirt driveway.

The driveway was long and winding, flanked by trees. When they pulled into view of the house, Celeste was surprised to see the yard was recently cut. Pine trees flanked the stone walkway to the front door.

Celeste followed Harris up to the house.

"Mind if I take the lead on this?" he asked.

"No." She didn't want to tell him that she felt suddenly afraid, convinced Frank somehow knew they were coming, had been warned by his insane mother and hunched behind the door, shotgun in hand. No one would hear them scream out here, be alarmed by the shots, if they heard them at all.

Harris knocked. No one answered.

From the corner of her eye, Celeste caught the flick of a window shade. Someone was watching them.

"Do you have your gun?" Celeste whispered.

Before he could answer, the door cracked open. A woman with frizzy brown hair tucked beneath a red bandana stared out. "Yeah?"

"We're looking for Frank Fulton."

The woman eyed them. "I don't know no Frank. Must have the wrong house."

"Are you sure?"

"Positive." She closed the door in their faces.

Celeste and Harris walked back to the car. "That was weird. Maybe he doesn't live here anymore."

"She's lying," Harris said.

"How do you know?"

"I just do."

"Well, crap. What do we do then? Bang on the door and demand she talk to us? Flash her your badge?"

He smiled. "My badge doesn't mean much in these parts, plus that's why she's lying. She sensed I was a cop. Let's drive back up the road a bit and wait it out."

"Wait for Frank, you mean?"

"Sure. Maybe he's out."

"Or maybe he was hiding in there."

Harris shook his head. "I don't think so. Come on."

For nearly an hour, they sat halfway down the driveway, watching and waiting. Celeste told Harris about the dreams she'd been having for the previous couple of weeks—the blue bungalow, running in a dark field.

"Did you dream much before the accident?" he asked.

"Rarely, and never like this. It's vivid now. Scary."

He nodded. "I get it. I dream a lot now too. Sometimes it's exhausting."

From the road, they heard the sound of an engine and then tires bumping over stones. A beat-up green Jeep drove into view.

Harris, who'd been sitting on the back bumper, hopped off and waved at the man behind the wheel.

Celeste studied him as he rolled down his window. His face was long and thin, his brown hair curly with flecks of gray at his temples. He was tan, blue-eyed, and his smile appeared genuine.

"Are y'all broken down out here? This ain't a dirt road. It's private property," the man said.

"Are you Frank Fulton?" Harris asked.

"That I am. Fresh out of dry firewood though, if the campground sent ya. I believe Billy Rauch has some a mile or so down the road."

"Actually, we saw one of your paintings," Celeste jumped in. "We thought you might have some for sale."

Frank's eyes slid to Celeste. He bobbed his head. "Sure, I got some. Mostly sell 'em in the shops in town. Is that where you saw one?"

"Yes," Celeste lied.

"We're looking for a couple pictures for our cottage," Harris added, reaching for Celeste's hand. It was warm and large and the contact sent a jolt up her spine.

"I've got some new stuff in my studio. Come back to the house and I'll show you."

"We talked to the woman at your house," Harris said. "She acted like she'd never heard of you."

Frank chuckled and scratched his chin. "Oh, yeah. That's Tilly for ya. Suspicious of her own shadow. Don't need a guard dog when you've got a Tilly."

They followed Frank in the car back to his house. "Good call on the paintings," Harris said as he parked behind Frank's Jeep.

"Are you getting anything from him? A feeling or vibe or whatever?"

He stared at the man as he climbed from his Jeep. "Nothing yet. No alarms are going off, though."

"For me either. He isn't what I expected."

"Come on in," Frank told them, walking through the front door. "I need a big glass of ice water. Been chopping wood all day. Tilly?" he called. "Where you at, girl?" He bent down and picked up a fluffy white dog and scratched its head.

Celeste stared at Frank, tried again to align this wiry man with the image of Ted, the hulking father figure who'd abused and abandoned a five-year-old River. As he stood rubbing his cheek against the dog's upturned snout, it was a hard image to reconcile.

Tilly emerged from a back bedroom and eyed Harris and Celeste. "I'm walkin' up the road to Pattie's," she mumbled.

"These folks just wanta check out some paintings. No reason to be throwin' 'em the evil eye." Frank returned the dog to the floor and walked into the kitchen.

Tilly said nothing, but gave them a wide berth as she moved to the front door, quickening her pace when she reached the front steps.

"Are you from Drummond Island?" Harris asked when Frank reappeared.

"I was born in Wisconsin, but Drummond Island is my home. Been here more than twenty years."

"What brought you here?" Celeste asked.

Frank scratched at the stubble on his chin. "Needed a change of scenery and I had a buddy with a cabin up here. Came up for a summer and celebrated my twenty-fifth birthday with two shots of tequila at Al's Pub about a week after I arrived. I never left and made those two shots an annual tradition. I'm not big on that kinda thing—celebratin' birthdays, makin' a fuss over all that—but that's somethin' I've kept on doin'. Almost superstitious about it now, like if I miss those two drinks, I might not see the end of the next year. These far-flung places do that to you, get you thinkin' funny things like that."

They followed him into a back room, nearly as large as the front of the cabin.

"Knocked a wall out back here years ago and turned this into a studio. Got a real nice view off the back." He pointed at the large picture window.

Behind the house, the property sloped down, the forest fading toward a pond.

"How long have you been painting?" Harris asked, walking along the perimeter of the room and looking at the paintings, which nearly all depicted some nature scene—a sun-dappled lake, the branches of a willow brushing a stream, birds in flight.

"Started a couple years after I moved up here. Helped me clear my head and after I finished a few, I realized I wasn't half bad."

"Much better than that," Harris said, picking up a painting of a rocky beach with a golden sun rising over the lake.

"You said you're from Wisconsin?" Celeste asked, feigning interest in a painting of a dragonfly perched on a piece of bone-colored driftwood. She realized as she looked at it that Frank Fulton was talented. A tiny spot of blue reflected the lake in the dragonfly's eye. "I recently visited Wisconsin. A town called Wild Rose. Ever been there?"

Frank took sheets off a couple of paintings propped on easels. He showed no sign of recognition at the mention of the name. "Wild Rose," he murmured. "I'm aware of it, but I've never been. I come from Milwaukee."

"Are you and Tilly married?" Harris asked. "Have any kids?"

"I never had any kids. Tilly's got a couple. I could sell that painting to ya for a hundred fifty. They usually go for two hundred at the shops downtown, but seein' as I won't be givin' a cut to the store owner, I'll make ya a deal."

"That seems like a good price," Harris agreed. "Can we sleep on it? Call you tomorrow?"

"Sure. I'll walk you out. I have some business cards in my Jeep."

As Celeste moved toward the door, heavy with a sense of defeat, her eye caught on a photograph propped on the long wooden mantel above the fireplace. It was a young man holding a little girl on his lap. The toddler girl, dark hair in curly loops sticking from her head, had one blue eye and one brown.

Celeste moved closer to the picture, started to reach for it, then saw Frank from the corner of her eye. He'd stopped and stood watching her. She dropped her hand to her side and hurried out the door.

"IT WAS HIM. It had to be him," Celeste said, as they drove away from Frank's house.

"Why?"

"There was a picture of River on his mantel. She looked to be maybe two or three. One blue eye, one brown. It's her."

When they arrived at their hotel, Celeste called Jonathan

and breathed a sigh of relief when she got his voicemail. She left him a message that she'd be home the following day and she hoped work had gone well.

Celeste and Harris ate dinner in the hotel restaurant. She ordered fish and chips, too greasy, and she struggled to force it down.

"Not hungry?" Harris asked as she picked at her food.

"What do I do now? He denied having children. Obviously, he's not going to admit River was his daughter if he abused her and murdered her mother. Where do we go from here?"

Harris took out his phone and pushed it across the table to her. She looked down to see a picture of Frank taken that day.

"When did you take this?"

"When he was getting his business card out of the Jeep. I'll text it to you. Send it to the woman he left River with, Dottie."

CELESTE COULDN'T SLEEP. A headache had been brewing, her hip ached and, after two hours of tossing and turning, she slipped on her jacket and left the hotel. Outside, the stars dazzled. Unlike the sky in Grand Rapids, light from the city obscuring the brilliance of the cosmos, here in Drummond Island they pierced the black veil with astonishing clarity.

She walked away from the hotel, across the parking lot to the trailhead that led, according to the woman who'd checked them in, to a twenty-mile loop of scenic hiking trails. She wouldn't walk far, but the bones and ligaments in her leg whined and at times movement offered the only reprieve from the dull throb.

As she walked, movement at the opposite edge of the parking lot caught her eye. Celeste squinted towards it, trying to see into the shadows.

Frank Fulton stepped from between two trucks.

36

River struggled through the set. As she sang, she scanned the faces in the crowd, thought of the person who'd followed her in Traverse City. Once she nearly lost the words to the song, distracted by a man off to one side of the stage watching her too closely. When she turned to look directly at him, she realized his head was tilted down and he was gazing at his phone.

After they finished their last set, the groupies took down their equipment and started to carry it out. The bar remained bustling, with several more hours of operation, and the band gathered at a lengthy table.

"That was a killer show," the bar owner said. "I haven't seen customers dancing like that in ages."

"Thanks for having us," Arnie said. "We're hoping to do a tour like this every year. Maybe even a couple of times a year. Right, guys?"

Everyone murmured their agreement, passing bottles of beer around the table.

"None for me," River said, trying to hold her head up, keep her eyes open. The tiredness was all-pervasive, fleeing only when she performed, otherwise pursuing her relentlessly. The beer smelled strong—the bitter yeasty odor of IPAs. "I'm going to catch an Uber back to the hotel. I have a headache."

"Do you want me to drive you in the van?" Arnie asked.

"No. I'm good. You guys enjoy your time."

As River opened the app and requested a driver, a gaunt man in an army fatigue jacket hovered near the bar and stared at her. She quickly looked away, imagined him stalking her through the streets of Traverse City. Had he followed the band to this new venue, perhaps following their movements on social media?

She used the restroom, splashed cold water on her face and stared hard at her eyes in the mirror. They appeared red and stranger than usual.

Mutant Eyes. That was what a boy had called her on her first day in third grade at a new school, only two weeks into life with a new foster family. His cruel nickname had stuck and for the following three years at Riverside Elementary she'd carried the moniker, often wearing sunglasses even on gray winter days until the teachers demanded she remove them.

That girl was gone. At least River wanted to believe that she was gone, that the woman who'd replaced her was strong and brave and resilient, but, looking at her reflection, she saw the person she'd been—scared, broken, hopeless.

River walked out to the curb and waited for the Uber driver. She jumped at footsteps behind her and spun to see a couple leaving the bar. Their arms were linked, their faces split with smiles. River caught a scent of vanilla perfume, heard the man let out a bellowing laugh.

Her heart ached for Owen and Hope, for their little house, for Luna's and Garth's warm bodies at the end of the bed and the rooster crying at dawn.

A minute later, a small blue car pulled to the curb.

"Hey, River. I can give you a ride," Morgan said.

She stared at him, surprised. "You rented a car?"

"Yeah. I have an old friend here in town I wanted to visit. Didn't seem fair to run off with the van."

"Okay. Sure." She opened the app, canceled her Uber ride, and climbed into the passenger seat. "Thanks, Morgan."

"Glad to help out."

"How's Lisa? I haven't seen her at any shows lately."

Morgan shook his head. "We broke up. She doesn't like the late nights, the girls at gigs. Not everyone is comfortable dating a musician."

"Dang. I'm sorry."

"Nah, it's fine. I don't think we really clicked." He drove away from the bar, turned south.

"The hotel is that way," she murmured, pointing the opposite direction.

Morgan had locked the doors when she climbed in, a mindless gesture, something she'd given little consideration, which now seemed heavy with significance. A pit formed in her stomach.

"Gotta fuel up," he said, gesturing at the neon Shell sign up ahead.

"Oh. Sure." She let out a little breath, relaxed against the seat, feeling foolish for her alarm.

Morgan parked at a gas pump, filled the car. He opened his door. "Gonna run in to pee. Can I get you anything? Bottle of pop? Or a lemonade? I know you like those."

"No. I'm good. I've got a water in here somewhere," she said.

River searched around in her bag for her bottle of water, but couldn't find it. She leaned forward and groped beneath the seat. Her fingertips brushed the corner of a book and she pulled it out, stared at the title in big red letters against a gold foil cover: *Classic Love Poems*. Pages had been torn out, leaving the book fat and misshapen. River's mouth went dry. The sounds beyond the car faded to a distance and rushing began in her ears.

Morgan emerged from the gas station and moved across the lot. River forced herself out of her stupor, shoved open the passenger door, and nearly fell scrambling from the car.

"River?" Morgan called, his face lined with worry. "Are you okay?"

She didn't respond, but turned and sprinted toward the woods, her sandals slapping the pavement. She risked a glance back, and her stomach plunged when she saw Morgan break into a run.

37

"Who are you really?" Frank demanded.

Celeste stared at the gap between herself and the hotel door. She couldn't sprint to the door without getting intercepted by Frank Fulton. If she fled into the woods, he'd catch her. He lived here, thrived in this remote place. She didn't have a chance.

"Harris is a cop, a detective. If anything happens to me..." She trailed off.

Frank stared at her, face unreadable.

"We're looking into... a child abandonment case."

He looked puzzled. "Tilly didn't abandon her kids. Her ex stole them. She tried to fight for custody and the court severed her rights. It wasn't abandonment."

"I'm not talking about Tilly. I'm talking about Agnes."

No reaction. None. The name meant nothing to him.

"The little girl with one blue eye and one brown eye."

Now that landed. He took a step back, his brow creasing. "Spring?"

"Is that her name?"

"How do you know her? Where is she?"

"How do *you* know her?"

"Celeste?" Harris stood outside the front door of the hotel, his eyes moving between her and Frank Fulton, his hand near his hip, where Celeste suspected he'd tucked his gun.

"Spring is my niece. My half-brother's daughter," Frank said.

THE THREE OF THEM, Celeste, Harris and Frank, returned to the hotel and sat in the empty lobby. Despite the warmth of the day, the nights were cold and someone had built a fire in the massive stone fireplace.

Harris filled little paper cups with hot water and carried a handful of tea bags to the table. "Chamomile, black and green tea. Those are the choices."

Frank peeled the wrapper off a chamomile tea and plunked it in the water.

"Spring," Celeste said, "now known as River, reached out to me several weeks ago. She was abandoned as a young child and she wanted help tracking her birth parents, specifically her mother."

"Fawn's not still with her? She gave her up?" He looked surprised and angry.

"Her mother's name was Fawn?"

"Yes."

"Where's your half-brother? Her dad?"

"Jared's dead. He died over twenty years ago. Spring was three years old."

"He's dead..." she murmured. He'd died when Spring was three, which meant he couldn't have been the man who'd abandoned her with Dottie Smith. "Are you sure?"

He glared at her. "I went to his funeral. I'm pretty goddamned sure."

"Okay. I'm sorry."

"How did Jared die?" Harris asked, exchanging a look with Celeste. He too had made the connection that Jared had not been the man who'd abused River and possibly murdered her mom.

Frank rubbed his face. "The medical examiner called it undetermined. Some hunters found him in the woods, too decomposed to identify his cause of death, but... we all pretty much agreed it was suicide. When we put two and two together, it made sense."

"How so?"

"Fawn broke up with him. They'd been having some trouble. She moved out and took Spring with her."

"How does Jared fit into your family tree?" Celeste asked. "I spoke with your Aunt Birdie. She didn't mention him."

"She doesn't know he exists."

"Okay... and why is that?"

"Because my mom kept him secret. She got pregnant at sixteen, had a baby in a home and gave him up."

"And no one in her family knew?"

"Oh, her parents knew. They set it all up, for her to go to the mother's home, have the baby. My grandfather made it very clear she was never to speak of it, that she'd be bringing terrible shame to her family if anyone ever found out, so she hid it."

"But she told you?"

"She confided in me. At eighteen, she had me. By then, she'd married Amos, my dad, who treated her like garbage. She longed for her firstborn, the baby she gave up. She found him. We did. I mean..." He shrugged. "I was seven when she started looking for Jared. Eight when we started to visit him, her and I. We'd go to his school and hide in the woods by the playground. Then she'd send me out to get him and bring him to the forest."

He pulled out his tea bag and dropped it on a napkin. "Pretty brazen. I didn't think of it that way at the time, but now when I look back, I can't even imagine how the school would have reacted if they found her lurking out there. I was closer to Jared than to any of my own brothers or sisters. My house was a nightmare. My dad was an alcoholic who beat my mom and me until we were bloody or he passed out. Usually both, in that order. I started running away to Jared's house. I'd ride my bike over there and hide in a woodshed on his adopted parents' property."

"And no one in your family ever found out about him? Even after he died?" Harris asked.

Frank shook his head. "My mom insisted we not tell. My dad would have gone mad if he found out. He had a lot of opinions about what he called 'bastard children.'"

"Did Jared's adopted family know you and your mom visited him?"

Frank shook his head. "He kept it secret. We all did, and it became a pact among the three of us, something special that only we knew. His adopted parents had problems of their own. They got divorced when Jared was fourteen. His mom got remarried, ended up having biological children and not really wanting anything to do with Jared. His adopted dad worked a lot."

"And how about Fawn? What was she like?" Celeste asked.

A small smile curved Frank's lips, but his eyes looked sad. "I was with him when he met her. Somehow, he talked me into camping outside this record store in downtown Milwaukee for U2 concert tickets." He chuckled. "He loved music. Played the guitar, had been in a couple of bands in high school. I never had much time for music. Life at home was too insane. Not that Jared had it much better. For him, music was an escape. Anyway, we had sleeping bags and we were sitting with our backs against the brick wall of this record store. There were fifty of us out there at least, and all night the line kept growing. Around midnight, a girl walked along the line handing out lollipops. She was singing that U2 song *With or Without You*. Know that one? She had a really beautiful voice. Shut the crowd right up. She got to us and handed Jared a lollipop and it was like"—Frank pressed his hands together—"this instant connection. They stared at each other for a solid minute. It was pretty uncomfortable being the kid next to them trying not to crack a joke."

"Fawn was a singer?"

Frank bobbed his head up and down. "Aspirations of going big. Typical teen dreams. Jared had similar ones. They formed a band, played gigs around Milwaukee, then she got pregnant and shit hit the fan. Fawn got kicked out. She lived with her mom and stepdad in some shoddy apartment in Bay View. So her and Jared scraped together what they could and rented an apartment in this old house. They were upstairs, hot as Hades in the summer, colder than Antarctica in the winter. They had to give up the band. Jared started working construction. Fawn worked at a convenience store.

"I used to take the bus to see them a lot. By then, I'd dropped out of school and I couldn't get my head screwed on straight. I was furious at the world. Sometimes my mom would go with me, but she was weird about Fawn, said she'd trapped Jared. She was always putting her down, saying she'd gotten too fat with the pregnancy, that her ankles looked swollen, that Jared shouldn't have to work so hard to take care of her." He scowled. "I love my mother, but I started to hate her as much as my dad in those days. She made Fawn cry a lot. So I stopped taking her with me. Fawn would never tell Jared how she felt about our mom because she knew he wanted that sort of fairy-tale mother bullshit. It's hard when you've been given up because you form this idea of the perfect parent who, by no fault of their own, had to let you go and someday they're going to swoop in and rescue you. The trouble is my mom couldn't rescue anyone, including herself."

Celeste thought of Esther in the senior home, the words she'd yelled. *Whore! She trapped him.*

"I got arrested a few times. For a couple of years I saw a lot less of Jared and Fawn. I'd crash at their place. Got into buying and selling dope. It was stupid, typical battered kid shit. I can say that now because I've read a lot of books about kids who act out. When I moved here, I started doing some soul-searching and came to terms with why I made a lot of the choices I did as a teenager."

"When did you last see Fawn and Spring?"

"A few months before Jared died. They had a birthday party for Fawn at this little park downtown. They'd hung all these pink streamers, balloons on everything. Spring loved the Muppets, so they had a Muppet cake and Muppet birthday banner. I bought her a rainbow bear Beanie Baby, which was all the rage at the time. She loved it—wouldn't let it out of her sight. I noticed Fawn and Jared bickering about money. I think they had a late electric bill, some medical bills. There was tension."

"And you never saw them again?" Celeste asked.

Frank nodded.

"What about Jared?" Harris asked. "When did you last see him?"

"A few weeks after the birthday. He called me pretty upset, wanted to talk. I stopped by his place and he looked rough. He'd been crying, said Fawn moved out and took Spring. The next week he disappeared, but I didn't know it. I was busy with my own stuff and then one day I ran into a guy he worked with who asked about him, said he'd stopped showing up to work, nobody could get in touch with him. I went by his apartment and found it locked. Two weeks later, they found him dead in the woods."

Celeste sagged back on the couch. Her heart hurt for River, for the family she'd had for a moment in time, two parents who'd loved her and each other even if things had begun to unravel.

"The coroner called the cause of death undetermined?" Harris asked.

"Yeah."

"Did they rule out foul play?"

"I don't think they really considered that. I mean... Jared had no enemies." The lines around Frank's mouth deepened as he appeared to consider the possibility Jared had not taken his own life.

"River was abandoned by a man at an apartment building in Madison when she was five. The man claimed to be her father. He said his name was Ted and her name was Agnes. He'd been sexually abusing her. There was no mother with them, but River started drawing some pictures that were very disturbing. Pictures of a stick figure woman she called Mommy who was lying on the floor with red crayon all around her. Blood, the woman who took River in assumed. The man she called Dad was standing over her with what looked like a knife dripping blood."

Frank stood abruptly and paced away. "No!"

"River entered foster care. The man named Ted never returned and has never been found."

"Jesus." Frank raked his hand back through his hair. "How could he just disappear?"

"People do it all the time," Harris said.

"He used a fake name and social security number at the apartment building. The police apparently tried to find him, tried to track River's identity, but he'd changed her name to Agnes."

"Fawn would never have left her. Never."

"Do you know anything about Fawn's family? Her friends? If we can track them down, we might be able to figure out where she took Spring after she left Jared."

Frank nodded and paced away. "Yeah, okay. Uh... She was from Milwaukee, like us. Her last name was Hearse. I remember it because Jared sort of poked fun at her for having a death car for a last name. After she married Jared, she took his last name, Shaw."

Celeste wrote the names down on a napkin she'd grabbed from the coffee bar.

"Jared never told you where they went? Who they left with?" Harris asked.

Frank looked troubled. "He just said they moved out. She had a close girlfriend." Frank scratched his face. "What was her name? She'd been in the band with them, played the drums. Had this crazy punk-rock pink hair and a bunch of piercings. She was part of the Milwaukee grunge scene. Damn." He chewed his bottom lip, eyes focused on the carpet. "It was like... a rockstar name. I don't even know if it was her real name. Bowie!" He clapped his hands together. "Her name was Bowie."

"Bowie?" Harris raised an eyebrow.

"It might not have been her legal name, but that's what she went by. Like David Bowie."

Celeste added the name to her napkin. "How about Fawn's parents? Any idea what their names are?"

He shook his head. "Not a clue. She lived with her mom and stepdad when she met Jared, but they didn't get along. That's all I know."

"Last name Hearse," Harris said. "That's probably enough to find them."

"Well... her mom's last name might not have been Hearse because she was remarried to someone other than Fawn's dad," Frank said.

"True. Hopefully we can find a birth record and that will give us her parents' names."

Frank returned to his seat and fixed his eyes on Celeste. "What's she like? River? I'd like to meet her."

"She's a singer, a very talented one. A mother. She has a little girl named Hope. She's created a really lovely life, but it's been hard for her. Very hard. She spent most of her young life in foster care, was abused by Ted. She's struggling right now because she wants to know her mom. You might be one of the few people who can offer that to her, especially if Fawn is dead, and I think she is."

38

River had listened to Morgan tromping through the forest for hours. She hadn't moved. After finding a fat oak tree low enough to the ground to climb, she'd crawled as high as she could and sat facing the trunk, legs and arms wrapped around the thick tree, praying that he didn't look up or look down and spot the sandal she'd lost during her ascent.

For a while he'd circled below her, calling her name and mumbling to himself, though she couldn't make out his words. "River!" he howled, his voice hoarse. He'd gotten further away, back in the direction of the gas station.

River's legs had gone numb. Her head throbbed, and she was so exhausted she feared she'd nod off and fall from her hiding spot. A part of her longed to climb down and just let him do what he wanted. Maybe it wouldn't hurt. Maybe she could exit the world and be done with the pain of living, find some lasting peace.

Each time she tried to justify giving up, she thought of Hope. Of never seeing Hope again, of Hope growing up as River had, without a mother. She clung tighter to the tree and fought her grief down with dreams of a moment not too far away when she'd be hugging Hope and Owen and the night would be fading like a terrible dream.

It was daybreak when River came to. She faltered and nearly fell sideways off the branch, realized almost too late she was tucked high in the oak tree and squeezed onto the trunk.

She listened, but heard no sounds beneath her. It didn't mean Morgan had left, but in daylight, she doubted he'd attack her. Soon they'd be looking for her, Arnie and the others. Now was the time to move.

Biting her lip against the needling pins streaking through her stiff limbs, she struggled from the tree, jumped and landed on her feet with a gasp, the prickling ache so intense she nearly fell.

River didn't spring to her feet and run. She held her breath and waited. If Morgan was still in the forest, he'd have heard her climb out of the tree. He'd be coming.

No sounds. No footsteps. No labored breath.

She shoved on her sandal, still lying at the base of the oak, and moved away quickly in the opposite direction of the gas station. She didn't know how large the wooded area was, but they weren't far from town.

After walking several minutes, she heard the sound of a car door slam and then another. She picked up her pace, grunted against the continued pain in her feet and legs. The trees thinned and River broke into a limping run, bursting from the forest into the parking lot of the Rise and Shine Diner.

"I can't believe it was Morgan," Arnie murmured. "I just... fuck. I don't even know what to say."

River turned and stared out the window. She'd showered and put on sweats, and Owen had wrapped her in a blanket. They sat in a large room at a Comfort Suites hotel. "I want to see Hope now," she told Owen.

After she'd reached the diner, River had managed to keep her composure while an elderly waitress with kind eyes called the police. River had then taken the phone and called Owen, burst into tears the instant she heard his voice. Now, hours later, he'd arrived with Hope. Her day had been a blur of police interviews, followed by explaining the long terrible night to Arnie and Owen. Exhaustion had settled over her like a weighted blanket. Her eyelids were sandpaper, her thoughts an incoherent sludge.

"Are you sure you're up for it?" Owen asked.

"Yes, please. I need to see her."

"I'll text Shay to bring her up."

A few minutes later, someone knocked on the door, and Owen returned carrying a sleeping Hope, Shay following.

"Two minutes into *The Lion King* and she was out cold," Shay told River. She squeezed River's shoulder.

River took Hope and cradled her, staring at her little pink mouth, a bubble of spit clinging to her lower lip. There were tears buried deep behind her ribs and she wanted to cry them, needed to, but the eyes of everyone in the room were focused on her.

"I'd like to take her in the room and lie down for a bit," she told Owen.

"Of course." He leaned over and kissed her temple. "You must be exhausted. Arnie and I are going to go back to the police station. Shay, do you mind staying here with River?"

"Not at all. This is what I'm here for. River, anything you need, say the word."

"Thanks, Shay," River murmured.

It was evening when River woke. Everyone was gone except Owen, who sat in the adjacent room.

"Where's Hope?" River asked.

"Everyone went downstairs to have dinner. Shay took her so you could sleep. I ordered room service."

"Thanks."

Owen stood and walked to her; he pushed her hair from her face. "I'm so sorry, River. I can't even imagine what last night was like for you."

River rested her head on his shoulder and stared out the window at the lights of the city. "What happened at the police station?" she asked.

"Morgan was there. Turned himself in today about an hour after you filed your report. I talked to him."

She pulled away. "What did he say?"

Owen took out his phone. "I recorded our conversation. I can play it if you want, or if not, that's okay, too."

River walked to the couch and sat down. "I want to hear it."

Owen sat beside her, set his phone on the table, and hit play.

Morgan's voice emerged from the phone, and River shuddered. "I wasn't going to hurt her."

"But it's been you all this time?" Owen demanded. "You're the one who's been stalking her? Who left all the notes?" River heard the rage in his voice, but also the hurt.

"I left the notes, sure, but I wasn't stalking her. I was playing at those gigs too. God, you're making me sound like some kind of psycho."

"Have you been at our house? Been outside at night?"

"No. I swear. It's not like that, Owen. I love River, appreciate her. I wanted her to know, that's all, not in a sick way. I didn't have dreams of chaining her up in my barn or anything."

"Instead, you've been mentally torturing her. Did you put the sunshine drops in her purse at the supermarket?"

"The what? I have no idea what you're talking about. I'm telling you the truth, Owen, I care about River. I never meant to hurt her."

"Morgan, you're not stupid. You expect me to believe you weren't aware you were hurting her, scaring her?"

Another sound came, a door opening and a man's voice—less clear. "Time's up. The detective needs to come back in."

A few seconds later, the recording ended.

"Do you believe him?" River asked.

Owen rubbed his face. "What's there to believe? It's been him all this time. Whatever his intentions, or his claims about his intentions, he's been following you. He's... he's sick."

River rubbed her arms. She thought of all those nights playing gigs, sitting feet away from him, safe in the comfort of her band, of the guys she'd known for years. Morgan had been like a brother—one of the good guys.

Someone knocked on the door. It opened before Owen reached it.

"Dinner delivery," Arnie called. He walked into the room with a paper bag.

"Thanks," Owen said. "I'm starved. How's Hope doing?"

"In seventh heaven downstairs at the pool with Shay and Wayne. Shay bought her a floatie in the gift shop and, as you can see," he gestured at his shirt, "she managed to drench me before I could make my escape."

River smiled and tucked her legs beneath her.

"Did you get some sleep, River?" Arnie asked.

"Yeah. I feel a lot better."

"I hate to do this now," Arnie said, leaning against the back of a chair while Owen unpacked boxed sandwiches and French fries, "but we have a gig tomorrow night. I'm okay with canceling. So is Wayne. But if we're going to cancel, now is the time. Our big show at the Velvet Theater is on Saturday and if we need to cancel that, say the word."

River's chest felt heavy, her lungs tight. She stared at the grease on the parchment paper beneath Owen's fries. The smell of the food made her stomach gurgle.

"What do we do? What's the best way forward?" Arnie asked.

River warred with the idea of giving up their night at the Velvet Theater, but they'd just lost Morgan, their bass and violin guy. How could she possibly go on stage and sing and play guitar and act as if nothing had changed?

"It's up to you, River," Arnie said. "If you're not up for it, we cancel."

"We don't have anyone for bass or violin. We can live without the violin, but—"

"Elijah, one of the groupies, he plays bass. Kills it. He's already offered to step in. He knows the songs inside and out."

Owen wrapped his arm around her shoulders. "It's all right to let this one go, Riv. There'll be more shows."

She wanted to cancel, feared she didn't have it in her, and yet this was their big dream, too. Arnie had been working tirelessly for years to bring them to this point, the pinnacle of their success, and the show would open doors. He'd already been contacted by a music producer who was attending the show at the Velvet Theater.

Arnie stared at her, then quickly looked away. She saw the hope there and the fear. He wouldn't pressure her, but he desperately wanted to finish the tour.

"We're not canceling," she said, sitting up straighter. "We've got two more shows. The Velvet Theater is what we've all worked so hard for. We're playing."

Arnie hooted and pumped his fist in the air. "We've got this."

Owen didn't share the enthusiasm. He looked worried.

"All right," Arnie said. "I'm going to let Wayne and Shay know and then call Elijah. The groupies are staying at a motel down the street and they've been in limbo, waiting to see if they should pack up for the trip to Chicago or just head back to Baraboo."

After Arnie left, Owen handed River a box with a sandwich. "Are you sure about this?"

She took the sandwich, but didn't take it out of the container. "I am."

"You need to eat," he told her.

She eyed the food, her stomach knotted. "I don't think I can. I'd like to go down to the pool and swim with Hope. We've never done this, taken her swimming at a hotel pool. I don't want to miss it."

He sighed and closed the lid on the sandwich. "Okay, but promise me you'll eat when we come back up."

"I promise."

39

The ferry left Drummond Island at nine a.m. As Harris and Celeste sat in his car waiting to drive aboard, Frank's Jeep screeched into the parking lot. Frank, looking harried, jumped out and ran toward them.

Celeste rolled down her window. The cool morning air off the lake rushed in.

"There's something else," Frank said. He looked like he hadn't slept the night before.

In front of them, a man waved Harris forward.

"I'll meet you on the boat," she told Harris, stepping from the car. "What is it?" she asked Frank.

"I introduced Fawn and Jared to someone, a guy I met in jail. Roscoe. I took him to their apartment a few weeks before Fawn left. I could tell right away he was into Fawn. He had this very charismatic personality and he talked like... like he lived this really big life. He drove a BMW, said he had a boat and a house in Texas and... I don't know. Back then I was so young and dumb I believed him too. But then... Fawn started to pull away and Jared showed up at my house crying. He'd seen her out with Roscoe. He confronted her and they had a big nasty fight. That's when she moved out."

"Do you think she went with Roscoe?"

Frank rubbed his face. "Maybe. Yeah. The truth is after Jared went missing and then was found dead, I felt so guilty. Like it was all my fault. I'd brought the guy in who stole her away. I blamed her too. I was pissed she'd left. She didn't even come back for his funeral. I was fuming."

"But you never saw her again. Do you know if she even realized Jared had died?"

Frank shook his head. "At the time I assumed she had, couldn't show her face, but now… I don't know."

"Roscoe," Celeste repeated the name. "Not Ted?"

"No. But Roscoe wasn't his real name either. I remember the guards called him Peters. They referred to all of us by our last names, so… his last name must have been Peters."

"Could his name have been Roscoe Peters?" she asked.

"I doubt it. I think he used aliases."

Which lined up with Ted and Agnes. If Roscoe was Ted, he was likely proficient at using false names.

"Can we find this guy?" Frank asked. "Maybe Harris could track him down? Wouldn't a detective be able to call the jail we were at and get his real name?"

"Possibly. I'll see what he can do. Do you remember anything else about him?"

Frank scratched his jaw, his forehead creasing. "One thing, totally random and weird, but he had a thing for dolls."

"Dolls?" The dreams that had plagued Celeste instantly flooded her thoughts.

"Yeah. Two or three times when we were out together going to the bars or just bumming around, he made a point of going into thrift stores. He'd make a beeline to the toys and stand there for ten, fifteen minutes picking up the dolls. I made fun of him for it once and he looked at me with the most blank, black eyes. I stopped hanging out with him after that. Course, by then, I'd already introduced him to Fawn and Jared and the damage was done."

Celeste stared at Harris's car creeping onto the ferry. "I better go," she murmured, disturbed by Frank's admission.

"I have a picture of him somewhere," Frank added. "I'll try and find it. Maybe the woman who took in River can confirm if it was him."

"That'd be good. Send it to me as soon as you find it. You have my cell and my email."

CELESTE FILLED Harris in on what Frank had told her as they drove back to Traverse City. When he dropped her at her car, he assured her he'd see if he could find a Roscoe Peters in the system.

It was nearly six in the evening when she made it back to Grand Rapids. Jonathan's car sat in the driveway. She found him inside at the kitchen table, a glass of wine in front of him. He'd never been much for alcohol, loved to lecture others on the many studies pointing to its hazardous effects on the body, but like Celeste, he seemed to be consuming more and more of it.

"You missed our appointment with Joyce yesterday," Jonathan said.

"Shoot. I forgot all about it."

"Having too much fun in Traverse City?"

"Actually, I went up to Drummond Island yesterday."

"Huh. Felt like some sightseeing?" he asked, white-lipped.

"I was trying to track down River's birth father."

Jonathan flashed a brittle smile. "That's just great. This is the birth father who molested and abandoned her? How'd that go?"

"It's not her father, but I found out who was. He's dead."

"Not to be crass, but I can't say I'm disappointed. Maybe you'll finally put a stop to all this nonsense."

Celeste refused to rise to his comments. He wanted a fight, wanted to argue with her. She wasn't going to do it. "What's been happening at the lab?"

He stared at her, said nothing.

"Jonathan, I'm not doing all this to get under your skin. I wish you could try to understand that this is important to me."

"Funny. That used to be me, us, our life. Maybe you could try and understand what it feels like to get displaced from that position, to suddenly barely register in your wife's mind at all."

"That's not true."

"Isn't it?" He didn't wait for a response. He finished his wine and loaded his glass in the dishwasher. "I'm going to meet Dean for another drink."

Celeste found Romeo and Cash both asleep on the bay window in the living room, curled together. She ran her fingers along each of their backs before she retreated to her office.

She searched online for Roscoe Peters, but didn't find anyone who seemed to fit. She then searched for Spring Shaw. A birth notice had been printed in a Milwaukee newspaper. It was less than a paragraph, but stated Spring Grace Shaw had been born on June twenty-fifth to parents Jared and Fawn Shaw. She'd weighed six pounds and three ounces.

The next month, River would be turning twenty-five years old. Celeste now knew River's birth date as well as the names of her parents.

"Spring Grace Shaw," she murmured.

Her phone rang and River's name appeared on the screen. She hesitated before answering. She didn't want to tell River over the phone what she'd found. It would be better to tell her in person and the truth was it wasn't enough that she had their names. She wanted to give River proof of what had become of her mother. "River, hi. I was just thinking about you."

"You were?"

"Yeah. How's the tour going?"

"It's... um... not great. I found out who's been stalking me."

"You did? Oh, my God. Who?"

"Morgan."

"Morgan, your bandmate?"

"Yes."

"Oh, no. I'm so sorry. Did something happen?"

"Yeah, but I can't get into it all right now. We have a show tonight and... I'm trying to clear my head. I just wanted you to know since I showed up at your hotel and... I just thought you should know."

"Are you still playing at the Velvet Theater Saturday?"

"Yes."

"That's really brave of you. I'm going to come to the show, okay? Maybe we can find some time to talk Sunday."

"Did you find something out? Something about my mom?"

"I'm still working on it, but we'll go through everything Sunday. Does that work?"

"Sure. Yeah. I'll see you then."

After she ended the call, Celeste searched online for the name Bowie. She had no last name, but found an Instagram profile for a person with the username Andrea 'Bowie' Ketchum. The account looked promising. Photos of musicians, instruments and concerts populated the account. Celeste sent a direct message to Andrea asking her if she used to know someone named Fawn Hearse or Fawn Shaw and to please reply if so.

IN THE MORNING, Jonathan was gone. He'd left his coffee cup and bowl on the counter. His clothes from the previous night, stinking of the bar, lay in a heap in the laundry room.

Celeste took out a notepad, bit her lip and started to write. She told Jonathan in the letter that she had left for Baraboo, would be back in a few days. She was sorry she'd hurt him, continued to hurt him. They could visit Joyce when she returned and talk through it. She thought about the words that had been rolling in her mind for days—*a separation, some time apart*—but as her pen hovered over the page, she couldn't bring herself to write it. It was wrong to blindside him on a sheet of notebook paper. If she wanted that, and she still wasn't sure she did, it had to be a conversation they had in person.

She signed the note *Love, Celeste* and propped it against the vase in the center of the kitchen table.

40

After driving off of the ferry in Milwaukee, Celeste typed 'Wild Rose, Wisconsin,' into her GPS. As she traveled north, she thought about the note she'd left for Jonathan. Her stomach squirmed at the thought of him finding it, how he'd react. Things had been set in motion she couldn't change, didn't want to change, and yet the momentum scared her.

Celeste walked into the Wild Rose Grill just after one o'clock. The diner smelled of cheeseburgers and coffee and for a moment she was back in the Sidewinder in Graves watching Joanna bustle between tables.

"Sit where ya like. Be with ya in a sec," a middle-aged woman wearing a t-shirt and jeans told her.

Celeste walked to the counter and sat on a black cracked-pleather stool. Through the serving window she could see another woman, this one older than the waitress, gray hair trapped beneath a hair net.

When the waitress returned, she handed Celeste a plastic menu. "Get you a cup of coffee? A sodie pop?"

"Coffee, please. But also..." Celeste fished the photograph of a child River wearing the Wild Rose Grill t-shirt from her purse. "I'm trying to track down a family. The daughter was in here once a long time ago. She has a t-shirt. I hoped you might recognize her."

The waitress grabbed a mug, filled it with coffee, then slid a bowl of creamers and a canister of sugar toward Celeste. She leaned down and studied the picture. "Nope. I'm guessing this was before my time here. I've never seen those t-shirts. Tootsie, the owner, might be able to help. She's cookin', but I'll walk this back to her."

"Thanks. That'd be great." Celeste added milk and sugar to her coffee and tried not to stare when the waitress offered the woman in the back the photograph. The woman looked at it, brow creasing.

A minute later, the waitress returned and handed the photo back. "Tootsie remembers her. She'll come talk to you in a few minutes when her prep cook gets here and can take over the grill."

TOOTSIE WALKED out fifteen minutes later and leaned on the counter in front of Celeste. "I remember that little cutie. A lot of people have come through the Wild Rose over the years and a few stick with me. This girl and her mama came in almost every single day one summer. I gave that little girl the t-shirt when she spilled chocolate milk all down the front of herself."

"Can you tell me anything about them?"

"They walked here, and it was quite a trek. They were renting Morris Granger's place out on Rayner Road. They barely had two quarters to rub together, but her ma would buy a cup of coffee and order a lemonade or chocolate milk for her girl. She'd sit and read the papers that got left behind and her girl would ride the penny pony we used to have by the front door. Big Ed, we called him. He died a decade or so ago, but I still have him in my barn. Figured I'd hire somebody to get him up and running again, but..." She chuckled. "With the iPads and the phones, the kids who come in nowadays aren't interested in taking a ride on Big Ed. She had a Polaroid camera, the mom did, wore it on a strap around her neck. She'd take pictures of her girl mostly."

"Was there ever a man with them?"

Tootsie tucked a loose hair back under her net, forehead scrunched. "Yeah. A man came once. I assumed he was the dad. I remember him because he had a mean look about him. Pulled the mom up out of the booth by her arm when he thought no one was lookin'.

"That whole morning had been an odd one. Had an accident that happened right here in front of the diner, which created a bit of madness. Then the mother asked me for a quarter to use the payphone and I saw her standin' outside cryin' and then she came back in and I noticed the bruises. I'd seen some before, but that morning her neck had a red burn around it. Her one eye was black and blue when she took off her sunglasses. I meant to talk to her, ask her if she needed help, but I got busy and next thing I knew, I was looking through the serving window as the husband jerked her up by the arm and marched her and the girl out the door. I never saw them again."

"They just disappeared?"

Tootsie nodded. "I went out to the house once, knocked on the door, but nobody came out and that was that. I never saw them again. I did see him once. I think it was him anyhow drivin' through town, but had a different woman in the car, couple of kids. Might not have been him at all. What happened to this girl and her mama? Do you know them?" Tootsie asked.

"I know the girl. River's her name. She's a musician now."

"Huh. That's real sweet. Her mama used to sing along to the radio. I remember that. She had a real pretty voice."

"Does Morris still live in the area?"

"Oh, sure. Already has a plot at the Wild Rose Cemetery. His whole family is buried out there."

"Can you give me his address? I'd like to speak with him."

"Morris Granger?" Celeste asked when the man opened the door.

He was bald and thin, his face mottled by age spots, his eyes dark and squinty. "Yeah?" He held the door tight as if afraid she might try to force her way in.

"I'm hoping to ask you some questions about a family who rented your house on Rayner Road nearly twenty years ago. This is the little girl who lived there." Celeste held up the photo of River.

"Don't remember her," he grumbled.

"Are you sure? Can you take a closer look? She had one blue eye and one brown. I'm actually trying to locate the mother."

"I said I don't remember," he snapped. "Go on. Leave an old man be." He shooed her away and started to close the door, but as he did, a figure appeared behind him. She wasn't clear, a shadow, a trembling of the air, but she felt motherly.

Lies have short legs.

The words streamed into her mind, clearly sent by the spirit of who Celeste suspected was the man's mother.

"Lies have short legs," Celeste told Morris.

He reacted immediately. His eyes went wide and darted around. "What'd you say?" he demanded.

The presence remained behind the man, and another message arose in Celeste's mind.

Remember Otto.

"Your mother is here. She wants you to remember Otto."

He slammed the door so hard in Celeste's face the glass window rattled in its frame.

Celeste sighed, started to walk back to her truck, but the spirit spoke again.

Wait.

And so she did. Celeste stood and gazed out over the barren yard. An old camper on blocks sat to one side, weeds grown nearly to the windows.

After several minutes, the door opened and Morris walked out, slumped into one of two rusted aluminum chairs on his front porch.

"Who sent you here?" he asked. "Who are you?"

"I'm a friend of the child who lived in that house on Rayner Road. That's it. Sometimes I see people who have passed. Your mother is here."

"You some kind of witch? Or a fraud? If it's the latter, look around. You ain't gettin' rich off of me."

"I'm not looking for money," Celeste said, keeping her voice measured. "I told you why I'm here."

"And how is it you know about Otto? Huh?"

"I don't. I can... sense spirits, hear them. After you told me to go away, your mother appeared. Everything I told you came from her. I don't know what it means, and I don't know Otto."

The man scratched at the white stubble on his chin, tapped his foot. He looked at her and then back at the ground several times, clearly disturbed by the mention of Otto, whoever he was.

For a minute he said nothing, looked hard at her a few times then grumbled, "Otto was my baby brother."

Another silence lapsed. Morris had fixed his gaze on his hands that looked knobby and curled. He massaged his knuckles. "When I was thirteen, we was messing about. Otto was eight. We got in an old car my pa was fixin' and went drivin'. The brakes didn't work. I didn't know and drove us right into a lake. I got out, couldn't get to Otto. I panicked. I lied. I told my ma I hadn't seen him when he didn't come home for dinner. Wasn't 'til the next day I finally fessed up. By then he'd drowned, but if I'd have run home and told the truth, he probably would have lived. There's an air bubble in the car. He was in the backseat. The back of the car goes under last and he probably got himself back to the air and who knows…mighta been alive for an hour, longer. Nobody knew. My ma left the story at Otto drowned, didn't give no details because she knew how horrible I felt. She still here right now? My ma?"

An image came into Celeste's mind—a small golden swan on a gold chain. "She's showing me a necklace, I think, with a golden swan charm. Does that mean anything?"

His foot tapped faster. He rubbed his eyes, his hands twitchy. He glanced at her again, looked away quickly as if afraid if he stared too long, she might turn him to stone. "You couldn't know about the swan. I didn't tell no one about that."

"Like I said, I don't have any context for what I'm seeing," Celeste explained. "She's showing me the necklace, but I have no idea what it means."

"It was a gift. My pa got it for her a long time ago. She cherished it. He never bought her nothin'. Then one year she lost it and we tore the house apart looking, never found it. She was convinced somebody stole it and that bothered her. All the way to the end of her life, she talked about that golden swan."

Across the street, a dog chained to a stake began to bark. Morris stared at it, licked his chapped lips.

"About a month ago, I was diggin' up this broken planter in the backyard—that's where she always had a garden—and up came that damn necklace. The clasp musta broke when she was gardening. I about cried. I couldn't believe it. I took it to the graveyard and buried it at her headstone." He shot her another uneasy look. "I don't know what to make of all this. Why's she coming to you? Why now?"

"Because she wants you to help me. What I'm doing matters and she thinks you can help me." Celeste didn't know if Morris's mother truly wanted Morris to help, but she suspected that was why she'd appeared. Celeste held out the Polaroid again. River with her mismatched eyes staring at the camera, her smile hesitant. "Do you remember her? Or the parents? Fawn and Ted."

"His name wasn't Ted. It was Roscoe." Morris's face twisted in a scowl.

"Roscoe," she breathed.

"Roscoe the Wanker. That was my nickname for him after he bailed and screwed me on the rent."

"Did they move out together? Him, Fawn, and the little girl?"

"Beats me. I didn't know they was gone for a month, maybe longer. I'd been in and out of the hospital with some gall bladder problems. Finally got out and realized he hadn't sent a rent check in two months. I kept stoppin' by, pounding on the door. Finally, I jimmied the lock. I'd given him the only key I had for the place."

"What did you find?"

Morris blinked at the ground. "Buncha their stuff, furniture and clothes and whatnot, but enough was gone for me to think they'd skipped town."

"What happened to their belongings? Did you get rid of them?"

"God's honest truth? I tried to go in there a couple of times and clean everything out, get it ready for new renters, and I always had some kind of issue."

"Like what?"

"Lightbulbs bursting, plumbing going haywire. It was the fall that did it for me, fell head first, right down the stairs. Got a bit paranoid and left it to rot after that. Doc said I nearly broke my back. If I had, I'da been laid up for months, maybe been paralyzed."

"What caused you to fall?"

An expression crossed his face, a tremor of fear, and she thought he'd not tell her or he'd lie. "A push. I was just startin' down and suddenly got shoved from behind so hard I landed about three feet beyond the bottom of the stairs. Ain't never set foot back inside again."

"Why didn't you sell it?"

"Tried to once. Picked up the phone to make a call to a real estate guy I know and got the strangest feeling, like if I listed that house something bad was gonna happen to me. I put the phone down and that was that. I quit that place. Already a hard place to rent, seein' as how isolated it is, then that dead girl showed up and that pretty well ruined any rental potential. Didn't matter no more. I was drawin' the social security, have my fourplex in town."

"Wait. Did you say dead girl?"

41

"I sure did," Morris continued. "About ten years ago, some kids messing in the old orchard found them. Two boys from town were playing hiding and seek. One of 'em jumped down inside a sinkhole There's three or four of those holes in that orchard. He hunkered down in there and felt something poking him in the back. Started digging at the grass and dirt wall and what was left of a girl came tumbling out."

"And this was on your property? At the house on Rayner Road?"

"Nah. The Rayner house butts up to the woods. I own all that, but on the back side of the woods is the orchard. Used to be an apple orchard when my pa was a kid. Joe Norman owned it. To hear my pa tell it, Joe was too busy chasin' women to make a go of the place. The orchard went to rot ages ago. When I was a boy, we'd go out there and pick apples, but not much grows these days."

"Was the girl they found a young woman?" Had they found River's mother and never identified her?

"Nope. A kid. They reckon she was between five and eight."

Celeste frowned. "Who was she?"

"That's the big mystery around these parts. Nobody knows. Police couldn't find a report of a missing little girl. They figure whoever took her nabbed 'em from another city, maybe even state. Could even have come down from Canada. No telling who she is or where she came from. Buried in Wild Rose Cemetery at the back side in a section for people too poor to buy a gravestone or pay for a burial. The town raised money to have a little funeral for her. They called her the Apple Girl."

"Do they have any idea when she was killed? Or how she died?"

"They figured she'd been dead fifteen, twenty years. Murder, most definitely. She had damage to her skull. They found some weird stuff with the body too, glass eyes, like dolls' eyes." Morris shuddered. "Ain't a homeowner in a five-mile radius around that orchard who didn't suffer from the discovery of the Apple Girl. Ain't nobody wanted to buy or rent anywhere near that place. They even tore old Joe Norman's place right to the ground. He'd been dead for decades and left the house to his kids, but they didn't do nothin' with it. It was one of them old modular things, walls warping and mold growing from the floor."

"Did anyone live in the house during the time the girl was killed?"

"Nope. It's been vacant since Norman died in the fifties. I think kids broke in and vandalized it." He grinned. "Well, shit, I know they did. I was one of 'em back in the days before I had to start actin' like a man. We'd sneak in and drink beers, smash the bottles. Probably there's been teenagers doin' that all this time, but I find it real hard to believe they could have had a hand in the death of that girl. If she'd been local, that'd be different, but like I said, ain't a whiff of her in Wild Rose, probably not in all of Wisconsin. I'm sure the local police did some lookin', but"—Morris shook his head—"nada."

"Can I go to the house, Morris? I'd like to go inside."

Morris's eye twitched. "Didn't ya hear nothing I said? Ain't safe in there."

"It's something I need to do."

THERE WAS no mailbox at the end of the weed-choked driveway. The grass stood waist high, the forest crowded and bushy. Had she not been given directions by Morris, Celeste wouldn't have suspected a house lay down the overgrown path at all.

She turned the pickup truck and bumped along the uneven ground. The path narrowed and branches scraped against the windows and doors of the truck. She jerked the wheel seconds before sending one tire into a massive rut at least two feet deep and a foot wide next to the driveway.

When the house slid into view, she let off the gas and drifted to a stop. This was the place River had lived, the last known place she'd been with her mother.

Celeste parked and climbed from her truck. The wood of the house looked worn. The roof was absent several shingles. The grass grew above her knees as she waded through it to the front door, pulled out the key on a rabbit's foot keychain Morris had given her, and inserted it into the rusted lock. It didn't budge. She wiggled it and the key stuck. She pulled it free and tried a second time, managing to loosen the lock. When the dead bolt slid aside, the door opened instantly, though she hadn't turned the knob. The hinges screeched, and Celeste winced and blinked into the darkness.

A wave of dizziness enveloped her. She planted her cane hard and pressed her other hand to the doorframe. When the faintness passed, she moved into the house. Her eyes fell first on a little hallway table. A lamp with a broken shade beside it was still plugged into the wall. Beneath the table lay several pairs of shoes. Two were women's—weathered leather boots, a pair of scuffed white sneakers—and then a child's shoes, small, a size that might fit a three- or four-year-old, pink with rainbow stripes. A gossamer thread of cobwebs lay inside one of the little shoes.

Disturbed, Celeste took out her phone and snapped a picture of the shoes. She touched nothing, sensed with certainty she'd walked into a crime scene. It was covered in dust and perhaps the evidence had long since been erased by the passage of time in the same way years take a toll on the human body, stripping cells and adding new ones. All things in constant flux.

Except this place felt like a tomb, a relic, and she suspected if a forensic team descended on the house, they would find trace evidence of that long-ago little family—a woman and her daughter and the man who'd stolen them from their lives.

The living room lay off the front hall, sparsely furnished with a single sagging plaid sofa. In the corner of the room stood a playpen, a wadded-up purple blanket inside. An old-looking TV sat on the floor, the screen smashed out. There were no photographs and there was little to reveal details about the family who'd sat on the sofa, the child who'd napped in the playpen.

Celeste walked upstairs and froze. The hallway from her dream returned. This was the place she'd encountered, and the vision of the woman, the ghost, returned.

Behind you.

The woman had been sitting in the room behind the last door and Celeste avoided it, now turning into the first room, a large bedroom. A grimy mattress lay on the floor, a pile of magazines beside it.

It was a depressing room. The entire house struck her that way. A hidden place where the worst things could happen—did happen.

A bare bulb dangled from an electrical cord in the open

closet and, as Celeste watched, it began a slow pendulum swing. Clothes hung in the closet. Celeste touched nothing, but she studied the clothes. T-shirts, sweatshirts and a jean jacket covered in patches—music notes, the names of bands. On the floor, covered in dust, lay a guitar.

Celeste stared at the guitar for a long time. It was Fawn's guitar. This had been her room, likely the last place she'd ever been with her daughter.

In another bedroom, Celeste discovered a child's bed, faded pink bedding still neatly tucked in place. This room, unlike every other, had a bit of personality. Several pictures hung on the walls. They appeared to be pages cut from a *Corduroy the Bear* children's book and pressed into frames. A tattered pink and blue polka dot rug lay on the floor. A rocking chair, the cushion worn flat, was angled near a window. The window trim had been painted with tiny white clouds and rainbows against a pale blue backdrop.

River's memory had been real. Her mother had rocked her in this chair, sung her to sleep.

Celeste stared at the chair and willed Fawn to appear. She wanted to feel her, wanted her to somehow lead Celeste to her remains. Nothing moved in the house.

Reluctantly, Celeste walked to the last bedroom. As she'd seen in her dream, a single wooden chair sat in the center beneath a bare lightbulb. The rest of the room was empty, but she noticed the space in front of the chair was free of dust as if someone had placed their feet there. Celeste eased open the closet door. In the corner lay a jumble of porcelain dolls, their faces smashed, their legs and arms askew. Celeste shuddered and pulled the door quickly closed.

One door remained in the upstairs. It was closed and when Celeste turned the knob it stuck. She twisted hard several times and finally, with a pop, the latch gave and the door creaked open. A gust of foul wind rushed out and a long echoey scream rose and then faded as if down a tunnel somewhere in the room.

Celeste gasped and stepped back, but no one emerged from the room and no one occupied it. The scream had come from nowhere, from the past, she thought, locked in the room for decades.

A small tiled bathroom lay before her. Immediately, Celeste's eye was drawn to the tiles, each stamped with a black star. She imagined River's drawings, the stick figure inside an oval shape, stars surrounding her.

"She was in the bathtub," Celeste murmured.

Somewhere in the house a door slammed and she spun around, heart racing. Quietly, she returned to the hall and listened. A sound came from the room at the end of the hall, music, and it had been that door, open moments before, that had slammed.

Celeste moved toward it slowly. Could someone have slipped down the hall behind her, snuck into the room? It was possible, but she didn't think so. She opened the door. The music drifted from the closet and when Celeste walked over, she realized it emerged from one of the dolls. It was facedown and she saw the small metal key on its back slowly revolving. The song, a tinny melody, was the sound that had come from the spirit's mouth when she'd stayed at River's cabin.

The corner of an envelope stuck from beneath the dolls. Celeste pushed them aside and discovered a small bundle of letters rubber-banded together. They were addressed to Jared Fulton in Milwaukee, no return address. She pulled one from the stack, opened it and took out the piece of lined notebook paper, so crammed with writing she could barely read it.

Dear Jared,

Have you gotten my letters? I'm scared. Please come get us. I'm sorry I left. I never meant to hurt you, to hurt us. That last night when you said I was being selfish, that I didn't know what love is, you were right. I was being selfish. I wish I had never met Ted. Looking back, I don't know how he convinced me to leave, tricked me into believing you were holding me back, holding us back. All of it was lies. I've never loved anyone but you and Spring.

I'm afraid all the time. He hurts me, but I can't tell anyone. He has the car and the money. He watches us, keeps us locked out here in this isolated house, cut off from the world. I've tried to call you from the payphone at the Wild Rose diner, but the number says it's disconnected. Did you move? I'm so afraid you've moved and forgotten about us, or maybe you don't even realize I've been writing, that I'm desperate to come home, that Spring cries every night for you. Please come get us. Please. I'm begging you. I'll spend the rest of my life making it up to you.

You know what I dreamed the other night? That I was back in Milwaukee and you and I had a gig at Billy Gee's and you walked out the door and down that alley that always smelled like Chinese food and I was running after you, but you kept getting further and further away. I woke up crying because even though the dream was sad and scary it also took me back there to all those night eating buckets of popcorn because it was free and singing until I was hoarse and you playing for so long your fingers cramped and afterwards we'd go back to our shitty little apartment and snuggle together on that giant beanbag Frank gave us. God, I miss you.

Please come get us soon.

Love so much it hurts,

Fawn

Clearly the letters had never been sent. Celeste imagined Fawn sneaking them out to the mailbox only to have Ted intercept them, allowing her to believe Jared might show up any day and rescue her and Spring.

Slowly, Celeste climbed back to her feet. Her hip gnawed at her and it took a few steps for the tingling to leave her leg.

"Where are you, Fawn?" she murmured.

Across the room, the lightbulb began to sway.

42

River sat at a bar, half a block from the brewhouse where Grace not Grit played in a half hour. Owen and Hope had left that morning. Owen needed to return to work. She'd see them tomorrow when the band returned to Baraboo. She had to get through tonight.

She drank her second vodka tonic and ordered another. She'd never been a big drinker, had had a few too many close calls in her teen years when she'd drunk to excess and behaved recklessly, ended up in cars with guys she didn't know, or passed out in the fields behind Be Free. Clay and Cordelia hadn't punished her for those errors in judgment. They seemed to understand that every teenager needed to explore that side of themselves.

The bar was mostly empty. Near a dark hall that led to the bathrooms, she glimpsed a man in the shadows, tall and broad with a blond beard, and she thought it was Morgan, but when she blinked, she saw he wore a grease-splattered apron and he didn't actually resemble Morgan at all.

"There you are."

River looked toward the door to see Shay making her way across the room.

"Everything okay, hon?" Shay slid into the seat across from her.

"Yeah. Just needed to calm the nerves." River held up her glass.

"You know they serve alcohol at the brewery and your drinks would have been paid for."

River gazed out at the dingy bar with sticky linoleum floors and foggy amber lights. "I didn't want to make a bad impression for the band."

Shay squeezed River's hand. "I'm here for you. We all are. Look." She leaned back so River could see her t-shirt. 'We're Ravenous for River,' it said in curly black writing against the yellow fabric.

"Oh, gosh," River murmured, pressing her fingers against her warm cheeks. She didn't know if it was the shirt or the alcohol causing the heat in her face.

Arnie appeared a minute later. River downed the last of her drink.

"Are you sure you're up for this?" Arnie asked.

"The show must go on." River heard the slur in her words and saw the alarm in Arnie's face, but refused to acknowledge it as she pushed past him and left the bar. She felt them behind her—Arnie and Shay, likely watching her walk down the sidewalk, not quite steady.

As she wove through the busy brewery, Tex appeared, glass in hand. "I ordered you a Moscow mule, sweetheart. Figured you might need a boost tonight."

"Thanks," she mumbled, taking the drink and slurping it down. She spilled some down the front of her shirt.

River set the glass on the bar, nearly stumbling over a pile of cords when she reached the corner where Shay and the others had arranged their equipment. Wayne grabbed her arm and steadied her. "River? What's wrong?"

"Nothing. I'm good."

He frowned, clearly not comfortable with her answer. She saw his eyes slide past her and when she craned to look behind her, she saw Arnie, his expression equally troubled.

"River." Arnie took her hand. "You don't have to sing tonight if you don't want to. Wayne and I can play some of the non-lyric stuff."

"I'm fine." She shook him off and sat heavily on her stool. She picked up her guitar, looped the worn strap over her shoulder and looked out at the crowd, blinking away the dizziness. The hollow ache spread from her stomach beneath her ribs. It threatened to swallow her whole.

Arnie introduced the band and the song, but River trained her eyes on her fingers on the chords, forced them to focus. When she began to sing her voice was thick, raspy, but the lyrics, her lyrics, were there and the memory of the chords was there.

Somehow River made it through the night. When Arnie walked her to her hotel room, she crawled beneath the covers, not bothering to remove her shoes, and fell asleep.

RIVER WOKE to knocking on her door. It was soft, but persistent. Her head throbbed dully. She hadn't eaten anything after the show, hadn't drunk more than a single glass of water.

The knocking continued and she forced herself up and across the room. When she peered through the peephole, she saw only black. She rubbed her eyes and looked again. Still darkness. Was it broken? When she stepped back and gazed at the crack of light beneath the door, she saw two strips of shadow. Someone's feet.

On tiptoes, River returned to her bed and grabbed her cell phone off the bureau. She clicked Owen's name, but didn't hit send. After returning to Baraboo, he'd likely played catch-up at work and would be sound asleep, him and Hope both. If she called the landline, not only would it wake them, it'd send the dogs barking too.

Celeste had said call anytime. All of them had—her bandmates, Shay, her family at Be Free—and yet, as she'd so often felt, she struggled to call anyone, to disturb anyone's peace.

She curled on her side on the bed and eventually fell back asleep.

IN THE MORNING, River woke with the memory of the knock from the night before.

It might have been anyone. A person confused about their room number, even Arnie or Wayne or Shay.

River returned to the door and looked through the peephole. It had been black the night before, as if someone had pressed their finger over the eyehole. Now she could see the hall, empty, though something sat on the ground. She twisted the knob and eased the door open.

On the floor across the hall, resting against a blank wall, sat a porcelain doll. It wasn't the doll from her property. This one had blonde hair and blue eyes, wore a purple and white checkered dress that reminded River eerily of a dress she'd made for Hope. Its face was cracked, a jagged fissure splitting its painted red lips.

43

Celeste checked into a small hotel outside of Wild Rose. She called Harris and told him about discovering the last house Fawn had lived in with River and Ted, aka Roscoe. "I'm sure Fawn's there—her body, I mean. Either in the house or somewhere close."

"And another body was found nearby? Are you sure it's not Fawn?"

"No. It was a child. They estimated her age between five and eight years old."

"That's disturbing."

"Yeah. But what do I do? How do we get police to search the house?"

"It sounds like the guy who owns it will likely give them permission to search. The issue will be to get the police on board with the idea a crime occurred there."

"I have proof Fawn lived there. She signed her letters, she mentioned Roscoe in them, and he committed a crime by abusing and abandoning River, so…"

"You're right, except the statute of limitations may have run out on any crimes he committed against River. The other issue is A, proving the crimes, and B, tracking the guy down to prosecute him."

Celeste sighed.

"Don't lose heart. You've got the go-ahead to be in the house, right?"

"Yeah. I still have the key. Morris said to mail it to him or drop it off when I'm through. I could probably move in and he wouldn't care. Not that I'd want to."

"First step, contact the Wild Rose police and tell them what you know. They have the unsolved murder of a child on their books. If you can convince them Roscoe killed that little girl—and in all likelihood, he did—they'll get a lot more motivated. How long are you staying in Wisconsin?"

"River plays at the Velvet Theater tomorrow. I'm going to that and have a room booked at the Nightshade Inn."

"The Nightshade Inn? Sounds ominous."

Celeste laughed. "Yeah. Apparently in addition to River's show there's some big classic car event downtown, so it was the only hotel with any vacancies. I figured I'll head to River's on Sunday and fill her in on everything. I wish I had something more concrete, but..."

"You've got Frank. He'll be important for her, a link to her past, a way to know her mom and dad even though they're gone. Or likely gone. I guess we still don't know about her mom."

"Yeah. I'm dreading the conversation, but also so grateful to have something."

"And then home after you talk to River?"

"That's the plan."

"How's Jonathan feel about you being gone again?"

"I don't know. I haven't talked to him. I left him a note."

"Ouch."

Celeste closed her eyes and imagined Jonathan at home. He

had not contacted her since she left the note. No calls, not texts, nothing. "I'm sure he's not happy."

THE FOLLOWING MORNING, Celeste woke to discover a message from Bowie. Celeste had time before River's evening performance and agreed to meet the woman at a coffee shop in Milwaukee.

Celeste parked downtown. As she walked toward the coffee shop entrance, a woman at an outdoor table shielded her eyes and spoke. "Celeste Cleary?"

Celeste stopped. "Hi. Yes. Are you Bowie?"

The woman stood and extended her hand, her fingers thick with silver rings. "Andrea now. I mostly dropped Bowie when I hit my forties." She laughed. "The name seemed a tad too young and cool for a fortysomething mom, even if I am still spending every Friday and Saturday night at the clubs in Milwaukee. Not in a band anymore myself, but I managed a few. It's been a good life. Helps that my husband is a teacher, keeps us in a steady income and insurance."

"You were friends with Fawn Shaw?" Celeste took a seat opposite from Andrea.

"Best friends." Andrea's mouth turned down. "She's dead, isn't she?"

"Why do you think that?"

"Because she left and never came home. Because that guy Roscoe was bad news. I knew it the second I laid eyes on him, but he'd somehow pulled the wool over her eyes. Her and Jared had been having problems and suddenly here was this older guy buying her stuff, taking her out to fancy dinners. I remember he showed up at their apartment when Jared wasn't home with this fancy gold and ruby necklace for Fawn.

Honestly, it looked like something he'd stolen from his grandmother, or off of a corpse like those grave robbers do.

"I told Fawn, 'Get your head out of the clouds. Jared's brother met that guy in jail. He's a creep.' Not to mention he was older than us by a decade at least. She wouldn't listen and then one day I called the apartment and Jared said she'd left, packed a bunch of her and Spring's stuff and just left."

"And you never heard from her again?"

Andrea looked skyward. "No. And God, I was mad at her. Especially when Jared died, but even then, I started..." She picked at her fingernail. "I started thinkin', *Something's gone wrong.* She'd have come back if she knew he was dead. It would have broken her. She loved Jared, crazy loved him. They were in a rough patch, struggling with money, but they would have eventually gotten through all that. Spring had been sick a lot the winter before and they didn't have health insurance. It turned into a whole thing. Jared was young too, proud, and neither of them had any decent coping skills. Music had been their outlet and suddenly neither of them had much time to play. Who has the money or energy to run all over town to gigs when you've got a baby to feed, rent to pay?"

"Did you try to find her?"

"Hell yeah. I called her mom a lot, but she was so self-absorbed, couldn't be bothered. She'd get mad and say Fawn ran off and she'd hang up on me. I called every one of our friends, hoping by some crazy chance one of them would have heard from her, but no one had. When I was twenty-five, I met my husband and he worked for the DMV then. I got him to run a check on her driver's license. Her ID had expired a year after she left with Roscoe. She'd never renewed it. I swear, not a month ago, I got online and tried to find her. I do a search every few years, look up her name, look up Spring's name, sure one of them would show up on social media. Nothing. You're the first person who's mentioned her name to me in almost twenty years. So, let me ask again, is that why you're here? Because they finally found her and she's dead?"

"No one has found her that I'm aware. The last person I've spoken to who saw her alive is a woman named Tootsie who owns a diner in Wild Rose. Did you ever hear Fawn mention Wild Rose?"

Andrea shook her head. "That's, what, a little town a couple hours up north?"

"Yeah. At some point she lived there with Roscoe, her and Spring. The next information I have is over a year later. Spring was abandoned at an apartment building in Madison by a man who called himself Ted, though I'm pretty sure he was Roscoe."

"He had Spring on his own? No Fawn?"

"No. There was no mother with them. And he told people he was Spring's dad and that her name was Agnes."

"That sick fuck."

"Is Fawn's mom still in Milwaukee?"

"She died. I don't know how many years ago, five or six. I saw her obituary in the paper or I wouldn't even have known."

Celeste sighed. "Is there anyone else who Fawn might have contacted over the years on the chance she's still alive?"

"She's not alive." Bowie said, tears shimmering in her eyes. "She would never have left Spring with that dirtbag. She would have died first."

CELESTE DROVE to the Velvet Theater. She'd done what she'd agreed to—she'd found River's mom and dad—but it disturbed her that she'd be leaving the young woman with even more mysteries.

As Celeste turned onto the road that led to the theater, she slammed the brakes before her brain fully registered the urgency to stop. On the corner sat the little blue bungalow from her dream, red door and shutters and flower boxes bursting with color. Behind her another car turned onto the street, and Celeste twisted the wheel and coasted to the curb. She sat and stared at the house.

Celeste rolled down the window. She could smell the recently cut grass. A part of her wanted to sit and watch the house or walk up to the door and knock, meet the person inside. But River's show started in a half hour and she didn't want to arrive late.

THE THEATER WAS BUSY, the parking lot and lobby crowded. Celeste spotted Shay and walked over.

"Hi, Shay. Looks like a full house tonight."

Shay grinned. "This is it! What they've worked so hard for. I feel like it's my own kids getting up there, even though Wayne's older than me." She laughed. "Makes me sick about Morgan though. I still haven't come to terms with it."

Another woman approached Shay and hugged her from behind. Shay turned and squealed then pulled the woman in front of Celeste. "Celeste, this is Dee Simmons, another River fan who can't usually do the groupie events because of her work schedule. She's a nurse."

Celeste gazed at the woman and the fine hairs on the back of her neck prickled. An uncanny feeling, like déjà vu, settled over her, and she searched her memory for a time when she'd encountered Dee. Long wavy brown hair fell over her shoulders. She wore high-waisted flowy black pants paired with a paisley shirt that revealed her pale midriff. She was very pretty, beautiful even with bright honey-colored eyes and golden eyelashes.

"You're stunning," Celeste said.

Dee blushed and looked at Shay, who nodded. "That's what I tell her every time I see her."

Dee smiled. "Thank you. I was so pumped I could come tonight. I work overnights, so it's always a struggle making the concerts work. I still have a shift tonight, but I get to catch the first half of the show, so I'm grateful. A shame I can't make it to more shows too because I live right down the street and can walk here."

A trickle of unease slid down Celeste's spine. "Where do you live?"

"In the little blue bungalow three blocks north of here. It's right on the corner."

"The one with the red shutters?"

"That's the one. My pride and joy. I even named her Joy, my house. My boyfriend thinks that's odd, but then again, I am odd." Dee laughed.

The sounds of the room grew muffled and the dreams—so many of them, dreams Celeste hadn't even remembered having—crowded in, all focused on that little blue bungalow, her stilted movements as she travelled the sidewalk, stepped onto the stoop, turned the handle on the door, walked into that front hallway.

"Celeste!" Celeste looked up as Cordelia reached for her. "We're so glad you made it. Wonderful to see you."

Tex, who'd been walking toward the stage, suddenly collided with a young man carrying two large cups of beer. Tex swore as the beer poured down the front of his shirt.

"Oh, shit. Sorry, man," the guy said.

Tex looked annoyed, but he glanced toward them and caught Celeste's eye. He turned back to the man and fanned out his shirt. "No big deal." He shrugged and disappeared into the crowd.

"So great to see you too," Celeste told Cordelia. "I'm so excited for River."

"As are we. And by the way, I don't know if you saw it, but I found a couple more notes that had been in River's file that must have slipped out. Nothing major, mostly health stuff, but I emailed them to you."

"Did you?" Celeste reached into her bag for her phone, but couldn't find it. "Oh, shoot. I left my phone in the truck. I'll be right back."

Celeste slipped out the front door, ensuring she had her ticket so she'd be let back in. She unlocked her car and grabbed her cell phone from the console where it sat plugged into the charger. As she started back to the theater, she spotted Tex next to a brown truck. He'd stripped off his shirt. On one side of his chest, he had a large, disturbing tattoo—a vintage doll face with cracks running through it and lifeless black eyes. As she stared, Tex looked up and saw her. He didn't immediately smile and the cold expression in his eyes caused her to falter for a moment.

Someone in the parking lot honked and Celeste broke the stare and hurried back to the theater. As she walked inside, she nearly collided with a man in a gray hooded sweatshirt.

He mumbled an apology and Celeste looked up sharply. His voice had sounded like Morgan's, but the man had already turned and hurried into the crowded theater.

44

River stood backstage, her body coated in icy sweat. From behind the heavy red velvet curtains, she heard the murmur of voices, imagined the seats filling. It was almost show time and she wasn't sure she could will her legs to walk onto the stage.

She'd arrived home to Baraboo the day before and hadn't told anyone about the porcelain doll, the late-night knock on her door. She'd forced it from her mind. It could all be dealt with after the night's show.

Owen, Hope, and Cordelia had already been backstage and left to find their seats. River looked up to Clay approaching her. He pressed a guitar pick into her palm.

"A little good luck token," he told her, kissing her cheek. "It's your first one."

"What? You saved it?" She stared at the pick, the edges worn and faded.

"Of course I saved it. For tonight. I always knew you'd be here." He pulled back, the skin around his eyes crinkled. "What is it, River? Why so heavy?"

River closed her eyes against the tears struggling to break

through. "I dreamed of this." She gestured at the curtain. Beyond it, hundreds of people had filled the auditorium. Voices, laughter, the buzz of excitement. "And now I'm here and I'm..." She rested a hand on her chest, hollow, the rapid tap of her heart an odd disembodied sensation. "Empty. Numb."

Clay reached into his jeans pocket and pulled out his wallet. From an inner compartment he drew out a wrinkled photograph. He smoothed it flat and held it out to her.

River stared at herself at thirteen, awkwardly clutching the guitar Clay had restrung just for her. She'd been at Be Free for mere months, was still getting the hang of commune life, of believing she belonged there. *That* River looked scared and hopeful and a little sad too.

"This girl fought hard to be standing where you are now," Clay said. "Sometimes when we fight for so long, a piece of us has to retreat, has to go have a nap on the cot in the back. Not feeling the enormity of this moment isn't a tragedy. It's this exhausted girl saying, 'I'm grateful for all this, but I'm worn out. I'm keeping a piece of myself back.' You're still here for it, River. So what if you're not bouncing off the walls with joy? Some of that joy might come later. It's going to come pouring out when you get up there and sing. That joy trapped inside you will reach out and lift that crowd. You're going to see it all. You're going to absorb it. Don't force yourself to carry it all the time. Let this girl rest. You're here. You made it. And for all this fanfare, tomorrow you get to wake up snuggled under the blankets with Owen and Hope, rooster crowing in the backyard, sun creeping up over the vegetable garden. Just be here for it. Expect nothing else of yourself."

River swallowed the grief thickening her throat. She hugged Clay, inhaled the smell of him—sawdust and soil. For a moment her ribs filled to bursting with love for this man who'd given her the gift of music, this man who was not linked to her by blood, but loved her far more than she'd ever loved herself.

"It's just another show, darlin'. I'll see you right here after."

As she stepped onto the stage, the hornets' nest of nerves suddenly quieted and grew still. The crowd subsided. Arnie grinned at her and Wayne gave her a thumbs-up. Her lungs, resisting breath seconds before, opened and oxygen flowed in. She walked—more like floated—to her stool and sat down, adjusted her guitar and looked into the sea of faces.

Arnie introduced Grace not Grit, and River searched the crowd and found Owen, Hope standing on his lap waving pudgy hands at her mama. In the row beside him sat his family and then Clay and Cordelia and several others from Be Free. Behind them she saw Celeste, Shay and the other groupies.

"This is *Old Oak Tree*," Arnie said.

River took a breath, cast her eyes down and started to strum the guitar. For a moment, she heard a woman's voice singing into her ear, *Angels Walk Among Us,* and then the voice was gone and her own voice began.

"What if I quieted the voice in my head and listened to this old oak tree instead..."

45

Celeste had scanned the crowd for Morgan for the previous half hour, but couldn't find him.

As the night wore on, some of Celeste's unease about Dee and the blue bungalow abated. She allowed the good energy of the night to carry her. River had the room buoyant. People were dancing, singing along, clapping and stomping their feet.

When Celeste slipped away to the bathroom, she encountered Dee alone washing her hands in the sink. If the dream of the house were a premonition of something to come, she had to warn Dee and yet she dreaded the prospect. Instant alienation was what she imagined would be the response to telling a complete stranger she'd been having nightmares about her house for weeks.

It was now or never.

"Can we talk for a minute?" Celeste asked.

"Sure. In here?" Dee asked.

For the moment the bathroom was unoccupied, though Celeste doubted it'd stay that way long.

"Yeah..." Celeste searched for the right words. "This is going to sound strange, but I need to warn you to be careful."

"To be careful? Of what?" Dee took a step back, eyes narrowing on Celeste's.

Celeste's face burned. "Sometimes I get premonitions. I've had one about you. I've been thinking all evening about how to say this to you without coming off as nuts, but there isn't any other way except to come out and say it."

Dee wrapped her arms across her chest. "What do you mean, premonitions?"

Celeste fiddled with the strap on her bag. "Dreams mostly, but when I saw you tonight, I had a feeling like I'd met you before, but it wasn't a good feeling. It was a 'you need to warn her' feeling. I just think you need to take extra precautions. Lock your doors, umm... be alert, more vigilant."

Behind Celeste, the door banged open and three young women walked in, all talking loudly.

"Thanks for listening," Celeste said. She turned and hurried out, her face burning. She imagined Dee telling the rest of the group, River's friends and the groupies and God knew who else. 'There's that crazy lady,' she'd whisper when Celeste walked by.

Celeste wove through the crowd to the concession stand and ordered a beer.

Despite the awkward conversation in the bathroom, the evening continued smoothly. Celeste listened to River sing. She swayed with the surrounding people, closed her eyes and let the magic of the music obliterate everything else.

Celeste's phone vibrated in her pocket. She pulled it out and saw a message from Frank Fulton.

Frank: *Check your email. I found an old photo of Roscoe. Not the best shot, but it's him all right.*

She opened her phone, scrolled to her email, and waited for the photo to load. The image came through blurry and pixelated. She could see three individuals in the photo, but no distinct features. Her reception in the theater was poor.

"I'm going to step outside," she told Cordelia, who gave her a thumbs-up.

Celeste navigated the crowd, slow moving in the mass, and wriggled between people out the door.

She reloaded the image and, when it came into focus, she recognized Frank first, a much younger Frank wearing a cut-off flannel and standing with two other men, both shirtless, in front of an enormous mound of dirt. All three man held shovels. As her eyes moved to the man in the middle, a lazy smile on his face, Celeste's breath caught.

The man had a tattoo on his chest—a tattoo she'd seen hours before in the parking lot. A porcelain doll's head with a cracked face. Her eyes flickered between the tattoo and the man's face. It was Tex. He looked younger, his hair long over his shoulders, his body chiseled. On his jeans was an enormous cobra-head belt buckle.

Her body grew cold.

Frank had written on the scanned picture with permanent marker. An arrow pointed toward the man with the doll's head tattoo. Above the arrow were the words: *This is Roscoe.*

"Have you seen Tex?" Celeste asked Shay.

She didn't want to sound the alarm in the middle of River's big show, but she wanted eyes on the man she now suspected of being the person who'd abused and abandoned River twenty years before.

"He drove Dee home," Shay said. "I guess someone spooked her. She normally walks. It's only a couple blocks, but for some reason she seemed scared to walk tonight, so Tex offered to drive her."

Celeste didn't think. She turned and strode up the aisle, ran smack into a woman carrying a tray of food. The tray tipped sideways and several containers of nachos splattered against Celeste's chest, the cheese hot and oozing.

"I'm sorry," Celeste blurted, but she didn't pause to help the woman clean the scattered food. She broke into a run, shoved her way through the crowded lobby and into the parking lot.

Her hip whined as she ran across the parking lot. She climbed into her truck, shoved the key in and started the ignition. The drive to the blue bungalow took less than a minute. She screeched to a stop, front tire on the curb, and climbed out.

Celeste moved trancelike up the walkway to the red front door, already aware it was slightly ajar. Her blood pulsed in her ears. The dream played on repeat in her head, becoming more and more real with every step.

Music poured from the open doorway, cranked too loud, as if to drown something out. Screams, she thought, her body slick with cold sweat. He'd turned the music up to drown out Dee's screams.

Celeste shouldn't have walked through the door, should have picked up her phone and called the police, but all logic had fled. She stepped into the house to the smell and sight of candles. They burned along the long narrow front table. Another scent overpowered them, metallic and bitter.

Something crunched beneath her feet and she looked down to see bits of porcelain, as if someone had shattered a dish, but as she moved forward, she saw it was not a dish, but a porcelain doll, its face smashed, its ragged body lifeless in the open doorway at the end of the hall.

Before she reached the bedroom, she saw the blood. It

splattered the white wall above the headboard, left streaks on the tasseled purple lamp. It saturated the gray carpet. Dee lay diagonally across the white butterfly bedspread, her battered face and head unrecognizable. Celeste didn't move forward to check her pulse, to offer aid.

The woman was dead.

Something moved behind her and Celeste screamed and spun as a hollow glass ball, a trinket filled with shells and beach sand, rolled off a dresser and landed at her feet.

46

River's body vibrated as the curtain closed before them. Her smile was so wide her face ached. Arnie squeezed her shoulder and held his banjo high. "That was insane! Holy awesome!"

Beyond the curtain, the crowd roared.

"They want an encore," a stagehand yelled. "Can I lift the curtain?"

"River?" Arnie asked.

River gave the guy a thumbs-up and the curtain rose again.

The cheers and claps were deafening, but she tuned it out, closed her eyes and strummed her guitar.

When the song ended, the audience again went wild. For a moment, River caught sight of someone near the back and her breath caught. It looked like Morgan, but he'd already slipped away, ducked out the exit door, and she suddenly wasn't sure if it had been him or someone who looked like him.

The scream that ripped through the auditorium was sudden and intense. The clapping and cheers continued, but people began to turn and look toward the group gathering in the back near the door. A spectacle was unfolding. Had someone fallen? Been hurt during the show? Had Morgan walked into the lobby and attacked someone?

"River, come on." Arnie took her arm and led her backstage.

"Did you guys hear that?" she asked. "A lady screamed."

"Yeah. That was weird," Wayne agreed.

"I'll go find out what's happening," Arnie offered.

River didn't want to wait, but Owen appeared with Hope and his parents and then Cordelia and Clay and others from Be Free. Owen handed her a bouquet of yellow roses and kissed her hard on the mouth. "That was amazing." He beamed.

They were all talking to her, praising her, but beyond them she saw Arnie return, his face pale. River broke away and strode toward him.

"What is it? What's happened?" She realized Celeste had not come backstage after the concert and she couldn't remember seeing her in the crowd at the end. "Did something happen to Celeste? Is she hurt?"

"Not Celeste." Arnie dropped his voice. "Dee. Someone attacked her at her house. There are police everywhere."

"I think I saw Morgan tonight," River blurted.

Arnie's face fell and Owen looked enraged.

"Do you think he hurt Dee?" Owen asked, fists at his sides. "If he did, let's go get him."

Clay put a hand on Owen's arm. "Let's not jump to conclusions. Is Morgan out of jail? I thought they arrested him."

"They released him on bail the next day," Arnie admitted.

THE CROWD HUDDLED inside the theater. Police had poured in and begun to question people. They took down names, phone numbers and license plates before they allowed anyone to leave.

River sat on the edge of the stage. Hope nestled between her and Owen.

When Celeste appeared in the theater, walking with a man who looked like a plainclothes detective, River stood and hurried to her. "Are you okay? Someone said Dee was hurt?"

Celeste's eyes cast down. She looked like she might be sick.

"Is this the person you were talking about?" the detective asked.

Celeste nodded. "This is River. River, this is, umm... umm..."

"Detective Lopez," the man said. "We're looking for information about a man named Tex. Celeste said he helps the band?"

"Tex?" River looked at Celeste, who struggled to meet her gaze.

"He gave Dee a ride home tonight," Celeste murmured. "That's what Shay told me."

River spotted Shay and waved her over. "Shay?" she called.

Shay wove between groups of people standing in the aisle, her face drawn. "Any news? Is Dee okay?"

River stared at Celeste, who seemed to be drawing further into herself with each passing moment. "Is she okay, Celeste?" River asked.

Celeste shook her head. The movement was small, but the detective spoke over her. "We need details on this Tex person."

"And I'm happy to tell you everything when you tell us if our friend is okay."

"We're not releasing details right now—"

"She's dead," Celeste blurted.

The detective shot her a warning look, but she didn't appear to notice.

River saw the horror on Shay's face, felt her stomach clench and her bladder suddenly grow heavy. She shook her head, stared hard at Celeste, whose eyes looked glassy.

Owen put his arm around River's waist and was talking to the detective, though she couldn't hear him. A raging river of blood rushed between her ears.

"And you think Tex did it?" Shay's words registered from far away and then Owen's.

"That's a pretty horrific accusation."

"It was him," Celeste said. She still sat in the folding theater chair, eyes fixed on the ground, littered with bits of popcorn and food.

"How do you know?" Shay demanded. "Did you see him?"

"The priority right now is to find Tex," the detective said, looking at Shay. "What's his address, his phone number?"

"I have no idea."

The detective raised an eyebrow. "This guy worked with you and you don't even know his phone number?"

"He's a groupie. You just show up. It's not like we had a background screening," Shay snapped.

"So you know nothing about this guy?"

"Only what he told us. He said he worked out at that factory on Brighton Road. They make plastics or whatever."

"What did he drive?" the detective asked.

"A Ford pickup," Owen said. "Brown."

"Any identifying characteristics?"

"Yeah," Owen said. "A bumper sticker, 'God Bless Texas.' He said he was from Texas, hence the name."

The detective wrote in his notebook. "Was he married? Have a girlfriend?"

Shay spread her hands. "He wasn't a big talker. He'd show up, help unload equipment, watch the show, help tear everything down and be on his way."

"And you didn't find that unusual?"

Shay blew out a breath. "No. He isn't the first man I met who wasn't keen on talkin' and I'm not keen on nosin' into anybody's business. The groupies are here for the music and to support the musicians. That's it. I don't remember a wedding ring."

"Did he ever threaten anyone? Get in fights at any of the shows?"

"No. Never," Shay said. "But hold on, you know, Dee told me something strange tonight. She said someone warned her—told her to lock her doors and keep her eyes open or somethin'. It freaked her out. That's why she left early and why she accepted the ride from Tex. She was scared to walk home alone."

"Who told her that? Does anyone know?" the detective asked.

River noticed Celeste had shifted her gaze. She stared at them now, her expression filled with shame.

"I did," she whispered.

47

Celeste sat in the theater, hands clammy, her stomach twisted.
She'd explained to the detective and the others the dream she'd been having for weeks, the blue bungalow, and how, when she'd met Dee that evening, a terrible foreboding had come over her. She'd warned her in the bathroom.

The detective's expression remained impassive, but his eyes revealed his disbelief. Shay, too, wore an expression of suspicion. Only River and Owen didn't look at her as if she'd sprouted a horn from the center of her forehead.

"I understand it sounds crazy," Celeste said, pushing her hands between her knees. "But last year I... I was hit by a car. I had a near-death experience and ever since I've seen things, known things."

"But if what you're saying is true, she only asked Tex for a ride because of what you told her. You literally put her in the truck of her murderer," Shay said, staring down at her.

River put a hand on Celeste's back. "No. That's not true. Celeste didn't know Tex would hurt her. She was trying to help."

Celeste tried to imagine how to tell the detective what she'd discovered without simultaneously dumping all the disturbing revelations on River at once. She turned to River. "I've found some things out the last few days. It might be hard for you to hear all this right now. Maybe I should talk to the detectives alone first and then—"

"I, for one, would like to know," Shay said.

"It's up to you, River," Celeste said.

"Go ahead, Celeste," River murmured.

Celeste reached into her pocket and pulled out her phone. She opened the picture Frank had sent her and showed her phone to River. River recoiled from the photo and stood quickly, stepped away and then came back, leaning in for a second look.

"That tattoo," she muttered. "I've seen it before."

"This is Tex," Celeste said. "A much younger Tex. When this photo was taken, he went by the name Roscoe."

The detective reached out his hand. "May I?"

Celeste offered him the phone, and he studied the image. "I'm pretty sure," Celeste said haltingly, "that Tex is the man who abandoned you when you were a little girl."

River shook her head. "Wait. No. You're saying Tex is my dad?"

Owen stared at Celeste, confused. "Wait. What? That can't be. Tex is a groupie. He's been helping us with almost every gig for the last year. How could he—why would he?"

"He's not your dad," Celeste continued. "He befriended your uncle in jail a long time ago, and that's how he met your mom and dad. Your mom... she took you and went with this man, Tex. She regretted it, but I don't think she could escape him, and your dad... he was already dead by then."

River stared around the room, eyes wild. She looked like she wanted to run away, to cover her ears and scream, 'Stop!'

"How did you find all this out?" Owen asked.

"It started with a cousin who was linked on your genealogy account. From there, I tracked down an uncle, Frank Fulton, in the UP. He told me about your parents, Jared and Fawn Shaw, and then he told me about that guy." Celeste pointed toward her phone, which the detective still held.

The detective handed the phone back to her. "I'm going to need you to come down to the station."

THAT NIGHT and following day were a blur of detectives and questions and endless explaining about how River had first contacted her, how Celeste had used the genealogy database to track down River's uncle, the eventual image of Roscoe that had arrived only moments after Celeste saw his tattoo. Had she not seen it, she wouldn't have recognized Roscoe, wouldn't even have made the connection that Roscoe and Tex were the same person.

Owen and River had also been at the police station, and she'd filled them in on everything she'd discovered. River had been stoic through the conversation, though Celeste feared how she would feel after a night of coming to terms with the knowledge that both her parents had likely been murdered by Tex.

When the police finally released Celeste from the questioning, she drove to the liquor store, bought a bottle of Scotch and returned to her room at the Nightshade Inn.

She hadn't told Jonathan what had happened, had only texted she'd been delayed, would be home the following day. She'd called Taylor several hours before and, drunk, had unloaded the entire story, blurting it all in a rush of shame and despair. To her credit, Taylor had allowed her to vent for fifteen before cutting in to tell Celeste she was at a comedy show in Ann Arbor. She'd promised to check in the next day. Taylor had told her to dump out the Scotch, go outside in nature, quiet her mind. She'd done none of those things.

The dark thoughts were winning.

Shay's words echoed through her mind: *You literally put her in the truck of her murderer.*

The bottle of Scotch stood nearly empty, lamp light flickering off the remaining golden-amber liquid. Celeste twisted off the top and finished it. In the corner sat her angry ghost. The woman did not move or speak. Her eyes remained fixed with cold fury on Celeste as if she, too, blamed her for Dee's murder.

At some point, Celeste passed out and woke to banging on the door. It grew louder and Celeste's head throbbed. The room swam when she stood up and she pressed both hands against the wall and willed the floor to steady.

Finally, she made her way to the door and pulled it open. Harris stood in the hallway.

"How'd you find me?" Celeste asked, struggling not to slur her words.

"Taylor called and told me what happened and you told me you were staying at this hotel. Can I come in?"

Celeste shrugged and walked back into the hotel room, legs wobbling beneath her.

"I see you opted for the tranquilizer tonight," Harris said, attempting to pour the remaining Scotch in the sink, but not even a drop emerged. He dropped the bottle in the wastebasket and filled a glass of water. "Here. Drink this."

"Mmm..." she grumbled. "Not thirsty."

"Satiated on liquor, huh? Last time I checked it does the opposite of hydration. Humor me. Take a sip."

Eyes drooping, Celeste sat heavily on the edge of the bed. She spilled most of the water down the front of her t-shirt, drained the last of it into her mouth.

"It's not your fault, Celeste."

"It is."

"You were trying to help."

"Doesn't matter. She asked him for a ride because of me, because of what I said."

"Blaming yourself won't bring her back."

Celeste lay on her side and closed her eyes.

"I know this feels terrible. I've had my own experiences with this kind of thing and it's... it's not easy to deal with, but hiding out, getting wasted, is only going to make it worse. You know that we're so much more than this. The girl from Wisconsin—she's free now. She's free."

Celeste imagined the place she'd gone to after her hit-and-run, the love and beauty and peace. In the hotel room, the comforter scratchy beneath her cheek, her head rolling from the booze, it felt like a dream, like it had never existed at all.

"Don't give up because of this," he murmured.

48

When Celeste woke in the morning, the light through the open drapes caused her head to throb. She sat up slowly, felt the bed tilting beneath her. She bunched the comforter in her hands and waited to see if she might vomit. The nausea passed.

In the corner of the room, Harris slept in the single chair, chin on his chest, hands in his lap. She had a vague memory of him arriving the night before, but hadn't realized he'd stayed.

Quietly, she stood and went into the bathroom, closing the door behind her. She turned the shower on hot and stepped inside, grimacing as the scalding water pummeled her aching head. She sat on the floor, pulled her knees into her chest and cried.

CELESTE EMERGED from the bathroom and a wave of steam followed her out. Harris no longer slept in the chair. She toweled dry, put on clean clothes and drank a cup of lukewarm water from the sink.

A knock came on the door and she opened it to find Harris holding a cardboard drink carrier with two cups of coffee and a paper bag.

"Breakfast," he said.

"Thanks." She held the door open for him.

"There's a couple chairs and a table in the breezeway that look out on the pool. Why don't we go sit down there?" Harris asked.

"Sure." Celeste pulled the towel off her head and hung it on a bathroom hook. She followed Harris down the hall and sat beside him. Wind whipped the handful of faded red umbrellas near the deserted pool. A sullen gray sky threatened rain.

"The water looks cold," she mumbled, taking a sip of coffee.

"I'm sure it is. How are you feeling this morning?"

"About how you'd expect."

"Here." He withdrew a bottle of aspirin from the paper bag. "And I have breakfast sandwiches in here. Bacon or sausage?"

"None just yet. I'll start with a couple of these and some coffee." Celeste shook two pills into her hand.

"Do you want to talk about what happened? With the girl."

Celeste had never wanted to talk about anything less. At some point in the night, before Harris had arrived, she'd lain on the floor and prayed to have her old life back, for the near-death to never have happened, for the visitors and premonitions to fade back to the place they'd come from. She'd return to Old Celeste, as Jonathan called her, whose idea of peak frustration was when a rat had an adverse reaction to a drug they were testing.

"Then we won't," Harris said. "But let me say one thing."

She sighed and stared harder at the window, imagined walking out, setting loose one of those enormous red umbrellas and letting the wind carry her away.

"He had his sights on her long before last night. That's how predators work. Especially a guy like this one. He stalked her, and I'd bet money he intended for weeks now to do it last night to rile River, to ruin her night. I was thinking about that on my trip to Wisconsin. Why? Why would he be pushing into River's inner circle? It's simple. Because it nearly always boils down to power and control. What could make him feel more powerful than being in the same room as his victim, buying her drinks, making friends with her husband, her bandmates, all the while knowing she'd suffered terribly from his abuse, been orphaned by him? He likes to hurt her. That's why he murdered that girl during her big show. You think if you hadn't warned the girl, she wouldn't have accepted a ride home? Maybe, or maybe she would have. It wouldn't have changed her fate. He'd already set his sights on her. She was dead the instant he decided she was the one."

Celeste massaged her temples. His theory made sense and yet the voice in her mind refused to accept it. It let her off too easy.

"Where's River now?" Harris asked.

Celeste shook her head. "They weren't going home. I think maybe with Owen's family."

"I might know Roscoe's real name," Harris said.

"Really?"

"Yeah." Harris turned on his phone and scrolled to his email. "I called PD at the jail where Frank was locked up at the same time as Roscoe. They've only digitized records for the last ten years, but I got the desk sergeant to dig around in the filing room. He found three guys with the last name Peters during that time frame. Lawrence Dwayne Peters, date of birth 08/04/57."

"Too old," she said.

He nodded. "Yeah, but the other two are in the range. Bernie Allen Peters, date of birth 04/17/1971, and Kurtis Theodore Peters, date of birth 12/13/1968."

"Anything else for either of them?"

"No. I didn't get a chance to do much looking. The desk sergeant just sent these over to me this morning, but I'll see if I can look them both up in the system, see if they had additional arrests."

"Can you forward those names and birth dates to me?"

"Yep." Harris typed on his phone. "Sent." He set his phone face down on the arm of his chair and glanced at her before focusing back on the window. "I have something else I need to tell you. I've been sitting on the information for about a week. The detective working your hit-and-run asked me not to say anything, but I don't feel comfortable holding it back."

She stared at him. "Do you know who hit me?"

"I think so. Yes."

Celeste shifted in her seat, the ache in her hip suddenly buzzing. "Who?"

"Darlene Stiles."

She let the name run through her mind, imagined her relationship with Darlene. They'd worked together for more than five years. They'd been friendly, though not friends—had never had any disputes, any issues at all. Darlene had been one of the few colleagues she and Jonathan occasionally had dinners with. "Are you sure?"

"Pretty sure, yes."

"Why?"

"That I don't know. Bowman will be pulling her in for questioning in the next forty-eight hours. He's finalizing some search warrants."

"It doesn't make sense."

"It might after he talks to her. Hopefully she'll confess, save everyone the frustration of trying to figure out the why of it all."

"Is that likely?"

"I think so. A lot of people confess when they're confronted with irrefutable evidence of their guilt."

"And Bowman has that?"

"He's spoken at length with the rental agency in Ohio where the Cherokee was rented. Percy Stiles is Darlene's brother. He rented the car for his sister because she went camping that weekend, apparently told him a story about needing four-wheel drive and she couldn't rent a vehicle herself because she'd lost her purse, didn't have her credit card and ID. None of which is true. She never reported any credit cards missing or stolen, never cancelled anything. Darlene called Percy the Sunday after he rented her the car.

"She was stranded at a primitive campsite. She told him she woke up to find the vehicle gone. She said she'd left it unlocked with the keys inside because she was in such a remote location she couldn't imagine anyone stealing it. Percy called the rental agency, who reported it stolen to the police. He pretended he'd been camping with Darlene, that he'd been driving the car, since otherwise he'd be in trouble from an insurance perspective. Once he found out it was possibly used in a crime, he came clean to Bowman, admitted he rented it, dropped it off to her, and never saw it again."

"Does her brother know she hit me with the car?" Celeste's voice sounded far away. Some piece of her was back on that stretch of road, the spring morning chill and the dampness in the air, the sound of the engine behind her and the surety Celeste had had that the vehicle would simply drive around her. She tried to imagine Darlene behind the wheel and couldn't.

"No. He's aware the vehicle is suspected to have been used during a crime. He believes whoever stole it committed the crime. He's unaware it was Darlene and she likely disposed of the vehicle afterwards."

"But how do you dispose of a vehicle? I mean, what could she have done with it?"

"The area she was camping had two lakes within a five-mile

radius and a deep reservoir only about a half mile away. The most likely scenario is she dumped it in one of those."

Celeste sagged back against her chair. Her head ached despite the aspirin, and the bomb Harris had just dropped continued to explode in the recesses of her mind. She thought of her encounter with Darlene at dinner weeks before. Quiet, soft-spoken Darlene. "I don't know what to do with this information. Do I call Jonathan?"

"No. Not just yet. Bowman will reach out soon. Wait for his call."

49

River hadn't returned home after the show. They'd all agreed it wasn't safe there. Instead, Owen and his brothers had gone to the property and packed some of River's and Hope's things, and they'd moved into a spare bedroom in Owen's parents' house. Now River had begun to grow antsy, desperate to not be surrounded by people.

She sat on the bed, listening to the thrum of voices below. Owen's parents and his three brothers and their wives and children crowded the house, Owen and Hope somewhere in the hubbub. They'd all been at River's show two nights before, all witnessed the terrifying aftermath, and now seemed to be avoiding the topic, discussing instead how Owen's brother would soon be deployed for six months.

Celeste's discovery about Tex's true identity continued to poison River's every thought. All the gigs where he'd picked up Hope and swung her through the air, where she'd looked out from the stage to see him twirling Shay or some other woman around the floor, the times when he and Owen shared a beer and discussed farm life or politics. How had he so seamlessly entered her life? How had she not recognized him, had some sixth sense that this was the guy? It reinforced some long-held belief that her mind was not to be trusted, that she lacked some basic instinct that recognized danger.

She'd had little time alone with Celeste. They'd been surrounded or separated at the theater, then the police station, and later when they said goodbye in the parking lot. Still, Celeste had given her the overview of what she'd discovered, each new revelation like a wrecking ball against the fragile structure of her River's life. All that she'd believed lay in a heap around her.

The last known place River had lived with her mother and Roscoe—or Tex, or whatever the hell his name was—had been an old house in Wild Rose, Wisconsin. That house sat somewhere in the depths of her memories. If she concentrated hard enough, she thought she could smell it—damp earth and old wood and a sour-sweet smell of rotted fruit. She could hear it, wind whispering through the cracks in the walls, through unsealed windows and a dark, empty chimney. She knew that the memory of her mother singing *She Talks to Angels* and rocking a toddler River had occurred there, and so had something else, something much worse, but that memory stayed away. Maybe her brain in its quest to protect her had erased it —sent a signal to that bit of gray matter to shrivel up and die, laid something new and fresh over the top, something less traumatizing, something she could live with.

She forced herself downstairs for dinner. Butternut squash soup, her favorite, with a slab of sourdough bread thick with butter.

"I made it special just for you, River." Owen's mom, Sue, slid a glass of water in front of her seat at the table. "We all just loved watching your band at the Velvet Theater. All the other stuff aside, we're so very proud of you."

Sue kissed River on top of the head and Owen, sitting beside her, squeezed her hand beneath the table.

"Thank you," River whispered, staring at the soup, the torrent of emotion rumbling. She couldn't let it out, wasn't sure if she'd scream or sob.

From the living room, she heard Hope squeal as she played with her cousins.

"I NEED TO TAKE A DRIVE," she told Owen after dinner, resting her forehead against his chest in the backyard.

"I can drive you anywhere you want to go." He took his keys from his pocket and jingled them. "Your wish is my command."

River shook her head. "I need to go alone. I need some time to process everything."

He tilted his head and stared at the sky, then nodded slowly. "I want to argue with you, but that's not fair, is it? Promise me you'll be safe. Don't stop anywhere, just drive and keep an eye on your rearview mirrors. You see anything suspicious, you call me. Where's your cell phone?"

"It's in my bag. I'll take it with me."

FOR A HALF HOUR, River drove aimlessly. She cranked her music loud, a playlist of Joni Mitchell, Sarah McLachlan and Bob Dylan. Her eyes were gritty, not enough sleep in the previous days. Whenever she lay in bed at night and closed them, Dee's face rose in her mind. Dee, who'd loved River's music, who'd once told her listening to River sing was the closest she'd ever felt to God. And now Dee was gone—with God perhaps, but that didn't change the end. River hadn't seen the bedroom where they'd found Dee's body, but she'd overheard an officer at the Velvet Theater and the word he'd used was 'slaughter.'

River slowed and pulled into her driveway. She hadn't

intended to go there, had stopped paying attention to the turns some time before, lost in her thoughts, her grief. Owen would be furious if he knew, but she urged the truck forward just the same. Luna and Garth were at Owen's brother's house, but she wanted to see Simon and Garfunkel and the chickens. She needed to sit in a rocking chair and stare at the garden and remember that even in the most unimaginable chaos, their sweet little world remained.

River touched everything as she moved through the house and out the back door, the walls and instruments and soft quilt Cordelia had made, the rocking chairs on the back porch, the spear thistle and creeping Charlie that grew on the side of the house. The sky had turned gray and heaviness filled the air. When River reached the pasture where the goats grazed, she sank into the high grass and gathered them both in her arms and finally cried. Tears she'd held for days spilled out into their coarse fur. They pawed at her with their hooves and nuzzled her face.

Some time had passed when River heard the truck in the driveway. She knew the sounds of Owen's vehicle, and this was not his. Slowly, as the goats continued to herd around her, she stood and walked to the side of the house, where Morgan climbed from behind the driver's seat of his truck.

As she stared at Morgan, an odd calm fell over her.

He held up both his hands. "Please. Please don't run away. I swear I'm not going to hurt you."

She watched him. The wind had picked up, blew her hair in her face. "I know that."

He slowly lowered his arms. "You do?"

"I think so. I hope so."

"I am sorry. I..." He shook his head. "I never meant to scare you. I had this idea in my mind that the poems and notes were uplifting. I've always admired you, loved you, really, since the first time Arnie brought you to Revival. I just... wow. I could hardly believe it. Your talent and your resilience. Which I understand in my own way. My mom died when I was twelve. It was so hard. I've never gotten over it and for you... what you've been through and to come out on top... I noticed last year you were struggling. That's when I started leaving the notes. I didn't know they upset you until Owen showed up at the gig one night and said he and the groupies would patrol the parking lot. I stopped then. Just done." He shook his hands out.

"Why did you start leaving them again?"

"I didn't. I swear it. I don't know why I still had that damn book in my car. Idiot." He slapped himself on the forehead. "The truth is my mom gave me that poetry book. She loved poetry and music. She taught me to play. And I'd always left it in my car. I felt like when I pulled pages out of that book—poems—I felt like I was sharing her with you."

"You weren't the one who left the note on my truck when we were practicing at Arnie's right before the tour?" In the distance, thunder rumbled and dark clouds had begun to move swiftly across the sky.

"No. Gosh, no. We were together the whole night. I never left. Right? I mean, you would have noticed if I left."

River thought about that evening. She'd met the band at Paulie's Diner for dinner and together the four of them had walked to Arnie's house to play. Not once had Morgan left the room for more than a couple of minutes to use the bathroom or grab a drink.

It had been Tex, Roscoe, the man who'd hurt her, who'd probably killed her mother, maybe her father too. All her life, he'd been stalking her, toying with her. This had been another of his games, a way to throw her off kilter before she left on her tour.

"Were you at the Velvet Theater?"

Color flushed his face, and he nodded. "Only for a few minutes. I had to... I couldn't miss you up there." He fidgeted.

"You were so good." His eyes welled with tears. "Best you've ever sung."

"Do you know about..." River swallowed the lump in her throat, didn't think she could say her name without crying.

"Arnie called me and he said it was Tex. I'm still reeling." He opened his mouth to say more, never got the chance.

The bullet came from nowhere.

The seconds after stretched into infinity. The world froze, blood flying from Morgan's face, and then there was no face and he was slumping sideways and thunder cracked overhead, closer now, or was it another gunshot? River needed to move, to run, to scream.

She did nothing at all, stared, feet stuck to the ground, as Tex ran at her from the woods. He didn't slow, but barreled into her at full speed, sent her sprawling to the soft earth. He thrust the gun under her chin, sank his hand into her hair, and leaned close to her ear.

"Don't make a fucking sound."

He pushed her to the ground and tied her hands and ankles. When he shoved her into the backseat of his truck, and she watched her house fade in the rear window, her stomach plunged.

"Where are you taking me?"

His eyes, empty, flickered up to the rearview mirror. He flashed her a ghoulish smile. "Home."

River's instincts kicked in. She screamed and thrashed, bucked against the door.

Tex slammed on the brakes, and River rolled forward, got wedged behind the front seats. She watched him twist around. His hand lifted, and she clenched her eyes shut as he slammed something into the side of her head.

The world went dark.

50

Celeste had found the true identity of Tex. She'd spent the previous day after Harris left searching online, holed up in her hotel room. She'd talked to Jonathan, assured him she was okay and would return home soon.

Eventually she'd ruled out the second name Harris had given her, Bernie Allen Peters, when she discovered he'd died in 2003.

Which left one name, Kurtis Theodore Peters, and after a couple hours of sleuthing, she hit the newspaper archive that seemed to confirm Kurtis was Tex.

Son of Local Dollmaker Arrested for Murder

The quiet town of Roscoe, Texas, was shaken this morning by the arrest of seventeen-year-old Kurtis Peters, son of local dollmaker Agnes Peters, in connection with the abduction and murder of eight-year-old Jenny Robinson. The news has sent shockwaves through the small community.

The investigation began last week when Jenny was reported missing by her parents. She was last seen walking to school.

A massive search effort, involving local law enforcement, volunteers, and search dogs, was immediately launched. Despite these efforts, it wasn't until two days ago that Jenny's body was discovered in a shallow grave on Cole Samson's cattle farm just outside of Roscoe.

Jenny's tragic death has left the community heartbroken and in search of answers. The discovery of her body marked the beginning of a complex investigation, which soon led authorities to Kurtis Peters.

Kurtis, a senior at Roscoe High, has been described by fellow classmates as 'friendly, but troubled' since the death of his mother last year. Agnes perished after a fall down the stairs in her home, a house familiar to many Roscoe residents, as she sold her handcrafted porcelain dolls in the parlor.

Yesterday morning, Roscoe police executed a search warrant at the Peters residence. While authorities have not released specific details about the evidence, sources close to the investigation suggest that items found in the Peters home played a significant role in his arrest.

Chief of Police Dwight Locklin spoke briefly at a press conference earlier today. "This is a tragic and heartbreaking case," he said. "We are doing everything in our power to ensure that justice is served for Jenny and her family. Our thoughts are with them during this incredibly difficult time."

Kurtis is currently being held at the Roscoe Juvenile Detention Center. He is expected to be charged as an adult due to the severity of the crime.

Celeste imagined the heap of dolls in the eerie house on Rayner Road, their faces smashed. A grainy photo of a young Kurtis accompanied the article. At the time of his arrest, Kurtis had shaggy dark hair, and he smiled strangely at the camera as police led him, handcuffed, into the jail.

Celeste continued searching, finding multiple other articles related to the murder of Jenny Robinson. Her stomach plunged when she discovered an article with the headline: **Son of Dollmaker Acquitted of All Charges.**

Kurtis Peters left the Wise County Courthouse today as a free man. When asked for comment, he told reporters, 'I never hurt anybody, especially not that little girl. I hope they find who did it.'

The trial lasted for just under a month and involved more than twenty witnesses. Peters' defense attorney dealt a fatal blow to the prosecution before the trial began by having the witness who claimed to have seen Jenny climb into Kurtis Peters' car blocked from testifying after he told multiple friends and family he hated Peters, whom he suspected of having poisoned his dog.

Celeste clicked the next article.

Suspicion Still Follows Dollmaker's Son

One year after Kurtis Peters was acquitted for the murder of local third-grader Jenny Robinson, he sold his mother's house in Roscoe, where she famously crafted and sold porcelain dolls. The three-story Victorian house built in 1922 by Peters' grandfather is considered something of a landmark. The family who bought it said they're not concerned about living in the home of a suspected murderer.

When asked for a comment on the status of the Jenny Robinson case, Chief of Police Dwight Locklin said, "The man who did it was acquitted. When I heard he was moving out of Roscoe, I dropped to my knees and thanked the Lord. My advice to people in his next town? Put a curfew on your daughters and tell them to steer clear of Kurtis Peters."

The article included a photograph taken inside the house. Kurtis's mother, Agnes, sat in a large room full of porcelain dolls. She was beautiful, with pale skin and piercing dark eyes. Her son, Kurtis, stood behind her, unsmiling, a hand on her wingback chair.

At eighteen, Kurtis had left Roscoe, Texas, and gone where? Over a decade later, he'd abandoned River in Madison, Wisconsin, but what had happened in the intervening years?

As she searched for any more records using her newspaper archive subscription, she found an obscure little wedding announcement in a Winterset, Iowa, newspaper.

James and Evelyn Dodd, owners of the Hayfield Inn, are overjoyed to announce the marriage of their only daughter Brandy Elizabeth Dodd to Theodore Peters in a small ceremony at the River's Edge Methodist Church on Sunday. The happy couple, along with Brandy's six-year-old daughter Caroline, plan to relocate to Cedar Rapids in the summer. If you see them around town, congratulations are in order.

A color photo accompanied the announcement. A chill skittered up Celeste's spine as she stared at Brandy Dodd, the spirit who'd been haunting her for weeks. Brandy had wide-set blue eyes, long lank straw-colored hair, and a smile with a slight gap between her front teeth. And beside her, eyes dark and shining, was Tex/Roscoe/Ted. Again, he looked different, his hair slicked back and combed to one side, a dark mustache above his full lips, but he had that same strange, wolfish smile.

Celeste opened another browser window and searched for Brandy Dodd in Iowa. Instantly a stream of results populated about the mother who'd moved away as a young bride with her daughter twenty years before and her family had never seen her again.

On a Facebook page titled 'Have You Seen Brandy,' Celeste found a phone number for the admin listed on the page, Brandy's mother, Julie.

A woman answered after several rings.

"Hi, is this Brandy Dodd's mother, Julie?"

"Brandy's my daughter. Yes." The woman's voice had an odd quality—a reluctance to engage, a tinge of suspicion.

"I found your Facebook page about Brandy. Is she still gone?"

"Who am I speaking with, please?"

"My name is Celeste Cleary. How I've come to make this phone call is a long story, but it mostly centers around Kurtis Peters. Or maybe you knew him as Theodore Peters."

"Where is he?" The woman's voice rose a pitch.

"I think he... killed someone in Baraboo, Wisconsin, Saturday night."

The woman sucked in a breath. "I knew it. I knew it. James! James, come to the phone. Hurry." Celeste heard the woman, nearly hysterical now. "This lady knows Theodore! And he murdered someone in Wisconsin. Here, I'm putting it on speaker phone."

Her call waiting beeped and Celeste saw Owen's name appear on the screen. She ignored the call.

"What is this about?" a man barked into the phone. "Is this a scam? If it is, we're sick of you people calling here and harassing us."

"No," Celeste insisted. "I swear to you. I've been helping a woman track down her birth family and, in the process, I discovered the man who abandoned her as a child is Kurtis Theodore Peters."

"Wait. He abandoned a child? Is it our Caroline?" The hope in his voice caused her shoulders to sag.

Before he could go on, get more excited, Celeste interrupted him. "No. I'm sorry. I've found her birth family. Their names are Jared and Fawn."

The man said nothing, but he sounded as if he were trying to calm down his wife, who was still talking and had begun crying.

When he came back on the line, he was more measured. "Where is he then?"

"I don't know. He—" Celeste's call waiting beeped again— Owen. "Shoot, umm... I'm sorry to do this, but can I have you hold on for one second? I have a person trying to call me and I need to take the call."

"Yes, but please don't hang up."

"I won't." Celeste clicked to answer the other line.

"Celeste?" Owen's voice sounded strained.

"Yes. Is everything okay?"

"Is River with you? Have you talked to her?"

"No. Not since the police station. Isn't she at your mom's? You can't find her?"

"I'm driving to our house now. She left about an hour and a half ago to take a drive, clear her head, but she's not home and she's not answering her cell."

"Okay, call me as soon as you find her." Celeste switched back to James and Julie. "I'm sorry, I—"

The television switched on. In the scene, a man walked up a long driveway toward a rundown farmhouse. It grew louder. Celeste fumbled the remote from the bedside table and clicked it off.

"The police are looking for Peters," Celeste explained, "but I wanted to find out when you last had contact with your daughter and Caroline."

"Twenty years ago. After Brandy and Theodore got married, they moved to Cedar Rapids, spent about a year there. Then he left her, told her some cockamamie story about a job in Wisconsin and how he'd send for her and Caroline. He'd come back, stay for a few weeks, then off he'd go again. Then out of the blue he called her up, said he was coming to get her. He had another kid with him when he showed up in Cedar Rapids, a little girl," James said.

"He drove to Iowa to get Brandy and Caroline and he had another child with him?" Celeste asked.

"Yep. Sold Brandy some story about how the girl's ma was a drug addict and abandoned the kid." James sounded bitter. "Then off they went, Caroline, Brandy and this little girl, back to Wisconsin, where he claimed to have bought some kind of farmhouse."

"We never heard from her again," Julie said.

"Do you remember anything about the little girl he had with him?"

"We didn't see her," James said. "Brandy and Caroline were

still living in Cedar Rapids, but she had a few friends she'd made. One of them saw the kid, said she was strange, almost mute, had one blue eye and one brown, and looked like she hadn't had a bath in days."

The alarm clock radio suddenly sputtered on and for a moment the song *Brandy* burst from the little speakers and then the song cut out and, for an instant, barely enough time to register the voice, Celeste heard River.

"Where are we??" River asked, her voice muffled, scared.

"Don't remember this place? Guess I don't blame ya for trying to forget," a man responded, and Celeste recognized that voice too.

It belonged to Kurtis Theodore Peters.

The voices vanished and the song *Brandy* returned, the volume ratcheting up. Celeste stood and slammed her fingers on the buttons on top of the alarm clock. When the volume only continued to rise, she yanked the cord from the wall.

"I have to go," she said, already moving across the room and grabbing her bag.

"Wait," James said.

"I promise to call you back."

"Please don't hang up!" Julie wailed, but Celeste ended the call and dialed Owen. His cell rang and rang with no answer.

51

Celeste climbed into her truck and sped toward Wild Rose. She tried repeatedly to get Owen, but he wasn't picking up.

She fumbled to her web browser and searched for the phone number for the police department in Wild Rose. It took her several minutes and, when she finally found it, she dropped her phone and it wedged between her seat and the console.

"Shitshitshit!" She thrust her hand in and wiggled it out, screamed when the person in front of her braked suddenly and she nearly rear-ended him. She jerked the wheel and narrowly missed the car, but lost her phone back into the crevice.

"Slow down," she commanded herself. "Slow down and breathe." Eyes trained on the wheel, she reached back into the crack and pulled out her phone.

As Celeste bounced down the rutted driveway, a lump of dread formed in her stomach. There were no police cars, no flashing lights. It had taken her twenty minutes to get through a deputy at the Wild Rose sheriff's office and, though he'd agreed to send someone to check out the house, only one vehicle sat in front of the decrepit old house, a brown pickup truck. Though she couldn't see it clearly through the rain, she knew a bumper sticker clung to the back fender, 'God Bless Texas.'

She picked up her phone, dialed the number for the police, got only the repeating dots as it attempted to make the connection. She had no cell service.

THOUGH THERE WAS no power in the house, as Celeste moved up the dark stairs, she saw a trickle of light from the bedroom at the end of the hall. She crept slowly, her cane clutched in her hand. She didn't use it for fear of its clack against the wood floor. Steadying her breath, wishing her heart would quiet its raging, she strained to hear anything within the house.

There wasn't a sound, no rustling, no voices, no footsteps.

She stood outside the door for a minute, then two, peered through the crack where candlelight flickered. Finally, gritting her teeth, Celeste pushed the door open.

A porcelain doll hung from its neck by a length of black rope. It swung like a pendulum, casting a strange shadow back and forth on the wood floor. A wood chair positioned beneath the doll created the uncanny image the doll herself had climbed up and slipped the noose around her fragile neck. More dolls spilled from a black trash bag on the floor. A dozen or more lit candles lined the floor along the baseboards. Candlelight flickered in the doll's glassy eyes.

Celeste eased into the room, moved toward the closed closet door fearing she'd find River's crumpled body within.

Behind you. A woman's voice rasped in her ear and for a moment the air filled with the stench of rotted apples.

Celeste spun around as Kurtis, a hammer in one meaty

hand, stepped into the room. She moved to the side and considered trying to dart around him. He countered her, blocking the path.

"Wanna dance, sweetheart?"

Outside rain drummed against the roof. The front of Kurtis's Grace not Grit t-shirt was splattered with blood. Celeste held her cane tight, aware of the slickness of her hand on the raven. Even if she yanked the dagger free, she'd probably drop it. The scent of the candles and the flickering light made her feel woozy and she braced the cane hard against the floor and forced her mind to steady.

"Where's River?" Celeste asked, forcing her voice to steady.

He stepped closer, and she shrank further back, nearly knocked over a candle.

"River's taking a nap. She's had a long day." He grinned.

Celeste searched for what to say, how to buy herself some time. She remembered the photograph of Agnes Peters with her piercing dark eyes.

"Your mother is here, Kurtis. She's with us right now," Celeste lied.

He stared at her, unmoved. "My mother's a bag of bones. She wasn't worth the Mahogany casket she got buried in. Course, every chinwagger in Roscoe would have been talking if I'd have tossed her in the lake for the fish to eat." He released an insane-sounding laugh. His free hand snaked out and grabbed the hanging doll. He stared at it. "She wanted a porcelain child with an empty head she could dress up and sit on a shelf. 'Don't touch that!'" he screamed. "'Don't do that! Don't say that. You're dirty, a dirty disgusting little boy.'" Kurtis released the doll and swung the hammer, smashing the doll's face as it dangled. A piece of porcelain cracked off and clattered across the floor.

Dizzy with fear, Celeste stood very still, strained to hear any sound from River, but heard nothing. "It's wrong she treated you that way. It wasn't your fault."

"Wasn't it? She used to tell people nurture was a lie, it's all nature. We're either born good or evil." He rested the hammer against his chest in the place Celeste knew the cracked doll's face tattoo was inked onto his skin.

"Did you kill your mother?"

"I watch a lot of crime shows," he said. "And in the made-up ones, the Big Bad Wolf always spills his guts in the end, doesn't he? Watching those as a kid, I thought, *I'll never do that. I'll take my secrets into the ground,* but then something happened with Lolly. She was laying there breathing her last, bloody spit sputtering up from somewhere deep, and I started talkin'. God! What a high to see the look in her eyes as I told her all the ways I'd imagined the moment we were in—her chokin' on her own blood. It felt good, like the ministers say confess!" His eyes lit up. "Now I tell every one of 'em—I tell 'em about every girl or woman or man I've taken and how none of them will ever share my secrets. Just me and them, like it's just me and you now, Celeste. You're going to thank me in the end, you're gonna beg me to finish you."

Celeste tried to follow his rambling. His mother's name had been Agnes, not Lolly. "Who's Lolly?"

"Lollipop." He stuck his finger in his cheek and popped it out releasing a sharp, hollow sound. "Was my mom's best friend. Used to take me out to the woods to hike, swim. She liked me, really liked me, if you catch my drift." He winked at her.

Celeste frowned, shuddered. "She abused you."

"I was a doll. She could do what she wanted and she did until she couldn't anymore."

"What happened to her?"

"Strangest thing, on one of those trips, she just vanished. They never did find her."

"You killed her?"

"Me?" He cast a shocked expression at her. "I was twelve. What could I have done to her?" He watched the doll swing back and forth, gruesome-looking with its single eye and half smile, the black cavity revealing the clumps of hair glued inside. "She loved to swim, Lolly. Naked, of course." He picked up the hammer and smashed it again against the doll. The rest of its face cracked and fell away. The hunk of porcelain landed at Celeste's feet, the single blue eye staring up at her.

The door to the room creaked open. Kurtis glanced at it then quickly returned his eyes to Celeste. "After Lolly got gone, my ma started being a little nicer to me. Is that the right word? Nicer? She'd lock herself up in her room and work on her dolls, shove some money under the door for me to go to the movies or get candy. After that I was free. I'd walk the neighborhoods all night, peek in windows. Sometimes I'd go in and watch the girls sleep. You can stand right over someone's bed and they won't know you're there. You can lean down and smell 'em, the shampoo in their hair, the sour smell of their breath, their sweat." He ripped the doll from the rafter and flung it on the floor.

Celeste thought back to the night in the cabin on River's property, the man outside her window. It had been Kurtis watching her sleep. "Why did you keep River as a child? Why didn't you kill her like..." She almost said 'everyone else,' but bit back the words.

"River... I like that name. Agnes never suited her." He chuckled. "Didn't suit my ma either, not in the way she looked anyhow—beautiful woman—but her personality, oh, it suited that just fine. Had the personality of one of them old nuns who beats kids with a ruler, who makes 'em take scalding baths if they wet the bed." He had that strange smile again, but his eyes had turned hard and black. "Why didn't I kill River? That's an interesting question..." Kurtis reached into the black trash bag and yanked out another doll. He sat the hammer on the chair, eyes locked on Celeste. "Don't get any ideas." He quickly tied the noose around the doll's neck and hung it before snatching the hammer back up.

"My mother made one boy doll. One." He held up a finger. "Ugly as sin, that's what she called it. You know what she told me once? She said, 'I made this doll because it holds your soul. What happens to this doll happens to you.' And I believed her. Sometimes when she'd get mad, she'd hurt the doll. That was later, after I got too big for her to hurt me. After she was scared of me, I'd see that doll hanging from its neck outside her bedroom window. She'd tie it to a tree branch out there. You know what that doll had?" He tapped beneath one eye. The skin beside it twitched. "One brown eye and one blue. Weirdest thing, when I first met Spring, I knew she and I were linked. Fate brought her to me."

"That's why you didn't kill her? Because it would have been like killing yourself?"

He glared at Celeste. "You think I'm stupid to believe some nonsense like that?" He picked up his hammer and smashed the face of the newest doll. "Spare me your psychobabble bullshit, Dear Celeste. That's who you are, right? Some nutter advice columnist who tells people they're sad because their parents spanked 'em?"

"What did you do to River's mother, Fawn?"

"Faaawn." He stretched the name long. "My little deer. You know what she tried to do? Sneak out of here in the middle of the night. Told me some line about giving Spring a bath to cover the sound of her packing their stuff and trying to creep out. But you know what we do to deer, don't you, Celeste?" He dragged the hammer across his stomach. "We gut 'em."

He lifted the doll with its cracked face and studied it. "This one kinda looks like her. Don't ya think?" He turned the doll toward Celeste, its cracked face missing its nose, part of its chin.

"Probably thought she'd run home to Jared." He made a face. "Poor Fawn hadn't heard Jared was feeding the worms by then."

Celeste's hip and leg ached. She struggled to bypass the zings of pain and focus on his words. If she could keep him talking, the police would come. She wasn't sure there was any other hope. "Did you kill Jared?"

52

River woke to voices. The side of her head throbbed. Pain pulsed from her bound wrists and ankles. Tex had hog-tied her. She lay on her stomach, cheek pressed against the cool, sticky floor—the room too dark to distinguish where he'd left her. River had no memory beyond the moment in Tex's truck when he'd struck her in the head.

Had Owen gone to their house yet? Discovered the carnage. She tried not to think of Morgan, of his blood splattering the high grass, but the vision held her like iron chains, metallic teeth puncturing her heart. Where was Owen now and Hope? Would she ever see them again?

River concentrated on the voices and tried to make out their words. It was Tex and a woman and as she strained, she felt sure it was Celeste's voice she heard.

She had dragged Celeste into her terrible past and now they both would pay with their lives. For years, River had tried to convince herself the horrors she'd endured in childhood had been distorted by time. But now, as she lay there, powerless, she realized that the truth was far worse. The monster was real. He had always been real.

Beneath the voices, she heard another sound as if someone were plucking the strings of a guitar. River closed her eyes and listened, oddly comforted by the notes. The music made no sense, but it didn't matter now. It was only a matter of time before it would all be over.

Tears stung River's eyes, dripped into the stickiness beneath her face, which she suspected was her own blood.

The music faded and disappeared.

River pulled in a shaky breath and another. Her heart thundered against the floor beneath her and she thought of the mother she'd barely known, the snatches of memory or dream. The woman rocking her, singing, *She Talks to Angels*.

"Mom," she whispered. "I need you."

The music came again, the strumming of a guitar so faint it might have existed only in River's mind.

Gritting her teeth against the pounding in her head, she rocked from side to side, willing the ropes binding her wrists and ankles to loosen.

"Did I kill Jared?" Kurtis yanked the doll from the string and dropped it on the floor, stomped its face beneath his boot. "Jared was a sad little boy who needed to be put out of his misery."

"So you murdered him?" Celeste asked.

Kurtis kicked the crushed doll towards her. Celeste flinched when it struck her leg. "You know what the police said? Suicide." He laughed and slapped a hand on his leg. "If brains were leather, the cops couldn't saddle a flea. Course, the bozos on his case were probably more lazy than stupid, but I reckon it was a bit of both. And that's what you need to know, girlie, I've been flying under the radar my whole life. Ain't nobody got their thumb on me. This here"—he gestured toward her—"will be just another mystery. Whatever happened to them two girls went missin' in Wisconsin? Maybe someday they'll dig you up, maybe they won't. You know they never did find Lolly? Never have, probably never will.

"You know why I didn't kill River? So I could keep her. Not literally. I was no good at that. The eating and the crying and trippin' over toys. And it was only a matter of time before she told someone about what we did together, our special relationship." He winked at Celeste and a fiery rage burned into her chest. She'd never wanted so much to claw someone's eyes out, to snatch the hammer from his hand and beat his face in with it. She clutched her cane tighter, needed to time the perfect moment to rip the dagger free and attack.

He grinned, eyes gleaming, and glanced at her cane. "I see. That's your trigger, huh? Your button? It's easy to find. Throw out a few twisted scenarios and see what makes someone's eyes get real narrow, laser beams. You don't like kids gettin' abused. Not many people do." He shrugged. "I let River go because she was already mine, would always be mine. And someday I'd take her back. I wanted to see what she'd do. I was curious."

"And you've followed her all these years?"

"I came in and out. Saw what she was up to, went on my way. Waited until the right time to take her, waited until she peaked. My God, she's somethin', isn't she? That body. Voice ain't bad either, but up top, she's all screwed up. Ever listen to those songs she sings? You can thank me for that. Her band should be called No Grace without Grit, that's the truth. All those songs come from the ugly place. Without me, she'd be singin' about some boy who broke her heart, how her parents grounded her."

"Where are Brandy and Caroline?"

He didn't seem startled by the question. An eerie smile crept over his lips. "Been slaving over that keyboard at night, huh? Looking for me? Digging into my travels? You're scratching the surface, I'll give you that."

"Even if you kill me tonight, everything I've found out about you is in my laptop, my phone. I've told friends. You're done, Kurtis."

He leered at her, face gleeful. "Is that what you think? You've smeared my good name? I haven't used my legal name in years—shit, decades. I don't use my social security number. I'm a ghost." He whooshed his hand low. "New names, cash only, move every few months. You wouldn't believe how easy it is to be a phantom in this world. Grow a beard, shave my head, get a spray tan. Do you know how many times River has met me?" He widened his eyes. "People see what they want to see. Who do you want me to be, Celeste? Hmm... How do you make sense of a man like me? I've read your columns. You're a bleeding heart. Other people look at you and see the sensitivity—'ahh, she's so compassionate.' But guess what? I look at you and see a victim. You're the kind of person who walks up to the van when some guy stops and asks for directions. Do you know how many times I could have made you disappear? I wanted you to find out about this place. This is exhilarating to me. This is what I live for."

RIVER HAD FOUND a weak spot in the ropes—just a slight give in the knot near her wrists. She pulled at it. Her hips ground into the hard floor. The throb in her head shot occasional bolts of light behind her eyes, and she struggled not to vomit.

She still heard the voices and once there'd been another sound, a crack that had caused her to freeze, terrified he was coming. But he hadn't come, and she'd resumed her wriggling. River's body was bathed in sweat and her face felt feverish.

Almost there.

She twisted sideways and put more weight on the ropes. Suddenly, her right wrist had space to move. Gasping, she pulled it free. The flesh around her skin burned in the open air. With her free hand she tugged the rope from her other wrist and unwound it from her ankles.

Her legs were numb, and when she sat up, her head spun. She steadied her palms against the cool floor. River needed time to gather herself, to steady her breath, to encourage blood flow back into her legs.

But she didn't have time.

On hands and knees, she crawled the room, a bathroom, she realized. Tile floor, the edge of a large bathtub, a toilet, grimy beneath her searching fingers. Nothing to use as a weapon. The only chance she and Celeste had was for River to run.

She gathered an image of Hope and Owen in her mind, sent a prayer to the God Box at Be Free, and surged to her feet.

After a disorienting moment of flailing through the dark, she found the doorknob and twisted it. The door opened.

Candlelight flickered from an open doorway at the end of the hall. The voices were clear now. Tex was speaking. She didn't wait to hear what he said. She turned the opposite direction and ran.

A DOOR SLAMMED open somewhere in the hall and Celeste heard footsteps pounding down the hall and then the stairs.

Kurtis rushed Celeste. She screamed and tried to pull the raven dagger from her cane. He shoved her hard. Celeste stumbled back, hit the wall. Her breath rushed from her lungs.

and managed not to go down. She righted herself as Kurtis ran from the room. Her leg and hip were stiff. She heard River's scream and then the sound of a door opening downstairs and then the sound was drowned by the wind and the rain.

Celeste held the banister as she fled down the stairs and out the front door. She saw River running hard, slipping in the grass, watched as Kurtis overtook her. He dragged her thrashing to the puddle beside the driveway Celeste had nearly bottomed out in during her previous visit. It was filled with water. He thrust her head beneath the surface.

Panicked, Celeste lunged toward his truck. Her cane sank deep into the mud and stuck. She tried to jerk it free, but it refused to budge. Swearing, she left it and hurried to the truck, yanked open the driver's door, and searched for a weapon, some way to stop him. She saw nothing. She climbed in. She'd run him over or at least get close. Hopefully, he'd release River.

The keys weren't in the ignition.

"No..." Her hands trembled as she opened the glove box, yanked down the visor. Nothing. No weapon, no keys, no cell phone.

Behind you.

That whisper again and the putrid stink of decayed fruit.

Celeste twisted around. Brandy, hair lank, a fissure in her once-pretty face, hovered in the backseat, hand resting on a wooden box. Brandy's glittering, furious eyes flickered down to the box. Celeste grabbed it and opened the lid, expected to find a revolver. Instead, a doll sat inside. It rested on a satin bed, had one eye brown and one blue. Celeste snatched the doll and jumped from the truck. She ran toward Kurtis, but stopped short, out of arm's reach.

"Kurtis!" Celeste held the doll out toward him.

She turned and ran back to the house, forcing her legs to pump, her hip and leg to cooperate. She could not afford to slow down, feared he'd already stood and begun to chase her. Through the front door, up the stairs and into the back bedroom. She slammed the door and locked it.

53

Spring laughed as the swing went higher, legs outstretched toward the unmarred blue sky. Her stomach dropped as the pendulum of her body swooped down. Her dad, hair messy, waving a multicolored toy bear, smiled and hooted.

"Higher, Mommy!" she yelled.

Spring felt her mother's hands on her back, the push warm and soft. Spring squealed and twisted around to gaze at her mom behind her, long dark hair floating around her, her eyes shining like the sun.

And then River opened her mouth and choked. Water spewed from her lips. Cold, wet mud pressed against River's nose and lips. She sputtered, blinked at the murky ground, watched droplets of rain hit the mud puddle and ripple out. The dream of her parents faded, the warmth gone, and she was back in that muddy driveway, the abandoned house looming before her.

River pushed herself, body quivering, onto her hands and knees. Her hair, rain-soaked, swung out, heavy. Tex was gone, and she fixed her eyes on the house, sure he was back inside with Celeste and it was up to River now to stop him.

Shaky, her throat raw, River stood. Goosebumps covered her clammy skin. She shivered as she limped toward the house.

CELESTE DUMPED the bag of porcelain dolls in the center of the room. She gathered candles and held the flames to the pyre of glassy-eyed dolls.

Kurtis bashed into the door a second time. On the third he broke through, wood splintering into the room.

Celeste held his doll above the growing flames. "I'll burn it," she said.

He stared at her, the firelight in his black eyes. Without a word, he lunged at her. Celeste dropped the doll onto the mini-inferno and scrambled sideways, narrowly avoided him as she darted past him into the hall.

He'd stop to pull out his doll. She'd have time to escape, but she didn't. His huge hand snatched her by her hair and jerked her off her feet. She screamed and tried to twist away.

Dizzy from the pain, she dug her fingernails into his hands. He laughed and looped an arm around her waist, lifted her kicking, and carried her into the bathroom. He shoved her into the bathtub and climbed in on top of her, pinned her arms with his knees at her sides.

Kurtis traced a finger along the line of her face, beneath her jaw. "Very pretty. Not quite delicate, though. Delicate enough, I think." He pressed both thumbs into her cheekbones. The pressure was instant and horrific. Light burst behind Celeste's eyes.

He released the pressure and leaned close, whispered in her ear. "I'm going to crush your face."

River smelled smoke. It rolled from the upstairs hallway. She heard the struggle as Celeste tried to break free and Tex caught her. Wincing, her brain screaming at her to turn around, go the other way, River forced herself up the stairs. Smoke billowed from a back room. She saw the flames within, growing larger.

She had no weapon, no way to stop him. Beside her, the first door in the hall creaked open. Uneasy, she peered in. A sound drifted in the air for a moment, the strumming of a guitar, and then it was gone. River eyed the room, scanned the old mattress, the pile of magazines.

She hobbled to the open closet. On the floor sat a guitar covered in a fine layer of dust. It had belonged to her mother. River had no evidence for the belief, but she knew it was true. She picked it up and returned to the hall.

Celeste and Tex were in the bathroom she'd escaped from minutes before. River heard his voice, the harsh puffs of Celeste's breath, a pained moan.

When she walked in, her head swam and a memory broke through—her mother in a tub of pink water, the man above her, a knife rising and falling, the little star tiles splashed with dark red globs.

And the man was there now, in the bathtub, Celeste whimpering beneath him.

River lifted the guitar above her head.

Celeste groaned as Kurtis began to dig his fingers into the soft hollow beneath her eyes.

Over his shoulder, she saw River, haggard, her face as white as the tiled floor, bloodshot eyes fixed on Kurtis. She lifted a guitar above her head. It was light, would bounce right off him, but then Celeste saw Brandy there, that rage-filled stare, and the guitar fell fast. It cracked Kurtis on the back of the head—

harder than seemed possible. The guitar broke into pieces. He grunted and twisted around.

Celeste winced. One punch and he'd knock River out.

River still held the splintered guitar, the handle little more than a sharpened stake. She drove it into Kurtis's eye.

54

It wasn't the police who finally came roaring down the overgrown driveway at the house on Rayner Road, but a firetruck summoned by a motorist who saw smoke billowing into the gray sky.

By the time they arrived, Celeste and River, supporting each other, had stumbled from the house. They sat in Celeste's truck with the heat blasting and watched the house burn. They should have driven away—Celeste had suggested as much when they first climbed in—but River had put a hand on her arm and said, "No. I want to make sure he doesn't come out," and in staying it was as if they'd made a silent pact that if he did, Celeste would put the truck in drive and run him down. Kurtis Theodore Peters would not be leaving that land alive.

When the firetruck pulled in, it hit the deep rut with its front tire and stopped. Men jumped off the back, unspooled the hose and ran toward the flames. By then, it was too late to save anyone inside.

River, teeth chattering, tears pouring over her face, stared through the windshield. Celeste took her hand. "I'm going to get out and talk to these guys. It's okay if you need to stay here a bit longer."

River said nothing, just continued to watch the burning house.

CELESTE SAT in the hospital next to River's bed. Her face was sore and bruised, but Kurtis had been stopped before he could inflict any real damage. When River had climbed from Celeste's truck, she'd passed out. Paramedics had treated her for a head wound caused when Kurtis had knocked her unconscious with the hammer when he'd first taken her to the house on Rayner Road. River had needed eight stitches, and they'd cut away a clump of her hair.

Owen had been in and out of the room several times already, pacing the halls like an agitated Doberman Pinscher, alert to anyone who dared come near River. Now he appeared in the doorway, his eyes oddly bright. "He's dead."

Celeste looked at River, who stared at Owen. "Are they sure it's him?"

"They're sure. The bathtub kept him from getting completely burned. Arnie identified him. It's him."

Celeste leaned her head back. River cried, putting her hands up to her face.

AS CELESTE DROVE BACK toward the ferry to Michigan, her cell phone rang. Harris.

"Please tell me you're not part of the homicide arson case I'm hearing about in Wild Rose, Wisconsin."

"I am. I was. He's dead. Kurtis is dead."

Harris released a loud breath. "Wow. Okay. Are you all right?"

"A little bruised, but otherwise intact."

"I'm glad to hear that. Up for filling me in on what happened?"

Celeste slipped her sunglasses on. "Soon. I'm driving to the ferry now. I'll be back in Grand Rapids tonight."

"Did you tell Jonathan?"

"Yeah. I called him from the hospital this morning."

"How did that go?"

Celeste sighed, remembered the painfully drawn-out silence after she described the previous seventy-two hours in Wisconsin. "He didn't say much."

"At a loss for words, I'm sure. Listen, Celeste, be careful at home, okay? They questioned Darlene today. She hired a lawyer immediately and refused to talk. It's hard to say what her next move is going to be, but don't take any chances."

"I won't. Thanks for caring, Harris."

"I do. A lot. Call me when you can."

River accompanied Owen to the police station, where they'd assembled a table covered in the items they'd found in the back of Tex's truck. Plastic bags filled with porcelain dolls, half a dozen driver's licenses he'd stolen, nearly ten thousand dollars in cash. A mangled book of poetry.

She moved toward a shoebox filled with Polaroid photos. They were mostly of her and she knew now her mother had taken them.

Kurtis had been planting the photos where River would find them, some twisted mind game where he urged her toward remembering the despicable things he'd done. He'd told Celeste she belonged to him and it was time for her to know it.

But the photos had not been Kurtis's, they'd been Fawn's. It had been her mother who'd lovingly captured images of her little girl twirling in pretty dresses, picking flowers, chasing a kitten. River reached a trembling hand into the box and drew out a picture.

She saw herself on the swings, legs stretched toward the blue sky, her dad in front of her beaming. And though she couldn't see her, River knew her mother stood behind her.

CELESTE ARRIVED BACK to Grand Rapids just after five p.m. She limped into the house. Her cane had burned in the room with the dolls. She felt oddly naked without it.

She found Jonathan sitting on the back deck, his face drawn, a glass of wine on the table beside him. He jumped up when she slid open the door and stepped toward her as if unsure what to do or say. After a moment, he wrapped his arms around her and kissed the top of her head. She hugged him back though the embrace felt stiff and awkward.

Celeste sat in the chair beside him and gathered her courage for her next words. "Jonathan, I've decided... to move out for a while."

He swiveled toward her. "You're not serious. After everything you've put me through now, you're leaving me?"

"I'm not leaving you. I need some space, some time."

He crossed his arms over his chest, his jaw set. "Where will you go?"

Celeste watched a raven drift down and land on the smooth gray branch of a beech tree. "To West Virginia. I need to find out what happened to my mom."

"West Virginia?" He stared at her, incredulous. "Do you even know anyone at all in West Virginia?"

Celeste shook her head. "Not yet, but I was born there.

Someone is going to remember us, and I want to talk to them, whoever they are."

EPILOGUE

"That was hard," Owen murmured, hands on the wheel as he drove toward Wild Rose.

River sat in the passenger seat, Hope asleep in her car seat between them. She brushed her fingers over Hope's soft curls, eyes welling with tears.

Owen and River had attended Morgan's memorial service that morning. Morgan's mother had stood stoic beside her son's closed casket, but Morgan's little sister had cried openly in the front row of seats.

River, too, had cried. In the days since Kurtis had murdered Morgan and nearly killed her and Celeste, she'd cried more than she had in years. On the casket, she'd placed a copy of the song she'd written feverishly in the previous days, *Deep River*. It was a tribute to her fallen friend and bandmate—an amalgamation of songs she'd been writing for months with lyrics that had come to her since Morgan's death. And though her feelings about Morgan remained complicated, in her heart, she knew the man had loved her.

The following weekend, Grace not Grit would play a show in Morgan's honor. A show that would be attended by her uncle, Frank Fulton and her mother's former best friend, Andrea Bowie Ketchum, who Celeste had connected her with online in the previous days. The phone calls River had shared with both Frank and Andrea had offered her the first real glimpse of who her mother and father had been.

Owen flicked on his blinker, though the country road was empty, and turned down the two-track to the old farmhouse on Rayner Road. The driveway was no longer overgrown. The weeds had been mashed by dozens of police and emergency vehicles in the previous weeks.

The search for River's mother, Fawn, had taken only days. Police had found her skeletal remains in the basement of the old house. She'd been buried beneath a slab of concrete. Dozens of broken dolls littered the grave around her.

Brandy had been discovered four days later, not far from where the boys had found Caroline, the Apple Girl, who'd been buried in a nameless grave a decade before. When River had looked at their photos, a memory had swum up, brief and watery like so much of her past—her and Caroline each clinging to one of Brandy's hands as they fled through the apple orchard at night. The sound of boots falling heavy behind them. And then nothing.

Was the memory real? She thought so. Brandy, like River's mother, had tried to escape, had tried to save Caroline and River. She'd paid with her life.

"Are you sure you don't want me to come with you?" Owen asked as River eased open her door, quietly so as not to wake Hope.

"No. I won't be long."

River stood for a long time at the burned shell of the house. The faint smell of smoke remained. Yellow caution tape surrounded the foundation. She stared at the hole in the cellar where'd they'd unearthed her mother's bones. Bits of broken doll faces were all that remained in the ashy hollow.

After a while, she walked away from the blackened ruin, moved through the forest and into the forgotten orchard. She gazed out at the twisted branches of the apple trees.

Thick white fog rose from the dewy ground, the land at last giving up her ghosts.

In the mist stood a fawn, golden fur and white spots and two obsidian eyes locked on hers for a moment, and then she was gone.

CELESTE READ the headline of the article about Kurtis Theodore Peters: *The Worst Kind of Predator.*

The journalist who'd written it had meticulously researched the history of the man who went by Kurtis, Tex, Ted and Roscoe, among other names. He'd managed to track Kurtis across the country, everywhere he'd targeted young single mothers and their daughters. There were more bodies to be found. The journalist had described his many personas as masks he put on, no more real than the porcelain faces of the dolls his mother had created.

Celeste exited the screen, closed her laptop, and added it to her bag. She'd booked a room for that night outside of Cleveland, Ohio, a halfway point on her drive to West Virginia, and had put off packing for the previous several days.

She pulled her small black suitcase from the closet and sat it on the bed. She unzipped it and folded it open. In one zippered pocket, she found a crumpled receipt. She walked it to the plastic trash can next to her bed and started to drop it, then paused and opened it instead.

She pressed the receipt flat in her palm and squinted at the words, frowning.

The hotel listed was a Marriott in St. Pete Beach, Florida. Four nights in January, months before her hit-and-run.

Jonathan had attended a conference alone. Celeste, busy at the lab, hadn't wanted to slow her momentum.

But the conference had taken place in Tampa, not St. Pete, and had been held at a Hilton. They were always at Hiltons and the company paid for the accommodation. Why would he have stayed at a different hotel, nearly thirty miles away?

Celeste sat on the bed and stared at the receipt for several more seconds.

He might have decided to blow off the conference and spend a few days at the beach. They'd done it together a few times over the years, but she struggled to imagine him doing it alone. He wasn't a beach guy, burned easily, found the crowds and the party atmosphere irritating.

It didn't matter now. She dropped the receipt in the trash can and returned to the closet in search of her large rolling duffel bag. It wasn't in there. She moved to Jonathan's closet and pushed his clothes aside. Tucked in the far back corner, she spotted a small metal box, a lockbox. She'd never seen it before.

The contents were an odd mishmash, nothing valuable, and yet Jonathan was not a collector. He hated clutter, rarely saved anything, and yet here he'd compiled stubs from concert tickets, movie tickets, and other receipts. She picked up a single memo he'd printed from an email at Dynamic Laboratories that stated the cameras would be out of operation during the time when his tires had been slashed. Also in the box, she found a vial of pills. PX962 was written on the label, the drug Liz had mentioned at dinner weeks before. It made no sense. Jonathan could get fired for taking pills out of the lab. Why would he do such a thing?

She leafed through a second time and read several of the ticket stubs, a jazz concert from the previous January. It was during the time she'd been in Graves. Another pair of stubs was from a movie. Celeste stared at the date. It was the night she and Adam had joined her dad for dinner weeks before.

Unnerved, she closed the box and shoved it back into the corner.

As she descended the stairs, Celeste paused. Jonathan must have come home for lunch. She heard his voice, sharp and urgent, on the phone. He likely hadn't realized she was home—she'd parked her truck in the garage to load her bags, something she rarely did.

"Listen to me," Jonathan's voice was sharp, clipped, a tone she barely recognized. "You need to stay quiet. Do you understand? Not one word unless your lawyer is asking."

Celeste's pulse pounded in her ears. She gripped the banister.

A second voice came through the phone, soft, pleading, but unmistakable.

"Jonathan, please—"

Celeste's heart stopped.

The woman on the other end was Darlene Stiles.

ALSO BY J.R. ERICKSON

Dear Celeste Novels

Troubled Spirits:
Where paranormal fiction and true crime meet.

The Northern Michigan Asylum Series:
Ghost stories inspired by a real former asylum.

You can find all my novels and join my reader team to find out about new releases, book giveaways, and more at www.jrericksonauthor.com

ACKNOWLEDGMENTS

Many thanks to the people who made this book possible. Thank you to Team Miblart for the beautiful cover. Thank you to RJ Locksley for copy editing *The Worst Kind*. Many thanks to Emily H., Saundra W., and Rhonda R. for finding those final pesky typos that slip in. Thank you to Dee Simmons for offering up her name as a character in this novel. Thank you to my amazing Advanced Reader Team. Lastly, and most of all, thank you to my family and friends for always supporting and encouraging me on this journey.

ABOUT THE AUTHOR

J.R. Erickson, also known as Jacki Riegle, is an indie author who writes ghost stories. She is the author of the Troubled Spirits Series, which blends true crime with paranormal murder mysteries. Her Northern Michigan Asylum Series are stand-alone paranormal novels inspired by a real former asylum in Traverse City.

These days, Jacki passes the time in the Traverse City area with her excavator husband, her wild little boy, and her three kitties.

To find out more about J.R. Erickson, visit her website at www.jrericksonauthor.com.

www.ingramcontent.com/pod-product-compliance
Lightning Source LLC
LaVergne TN
LVHW091505230325
806641LV00007B/176